**W9-BCP-637**

# What happens to a country out of control—and to people on the brink?

**CLAIRE BEATON**—A beautiful and ambitious economist, she knew how to end the global panic—but no one believed her . . .

**PETER HANRAHAN**—A millionaire in government service, his private life reached a torrid climax in the midst of the nation's greatest crisis . . .

**GEORGE McCONGER**—The President's closest advisor, whose fanatical policies split the administration—and the country—in two . . .

**CATHY GRAHAM**—Hanrahan's 17-year-old mistress, not even her father's millions could save her from the inferno . . .

**GOVERNOR WHITELAW**—With his powerful charisma and violent rabble-rousing, he pushed the country even closer to the brink . . .

---

# ON THE BRINK

Benjamin Stein
with Herbert Stein

BALLANTINE BOOKS • NEW YORK

Library of Congress Catalog Card Number: 76-30823

ISBN 0-345-27650-7

This edition published by arrangement with
Simon and Schuster, a Division of Gulf & Western Corporation

Manufactured in the United States of America

First Ballantine Books Edition: October 1978

*For my mother.*

IT was going to be another of those killing August days in Washington, D.C. The sky was completely blue and by 7:30 A.M. the temperature was already 80 degrees. It would surely reach 90 by noon. By late afternoon the sky would turn dark and there would be a brief cloudburst. This would turn the city into a large steam room.

But at 7:30 A.M. Washington was still bearable. At the south end of West Executive Avenue—the narrow, closed-off street that ran adjacent to the West Wing of the White House—the White House police had not yet turned on the air-conditioning in their small glass guardhouses.

A few minutes before eight, like elephants in a procession, the gleaming new black Chrysler New Yorkers with their special White House license plates started pulling into West Executive Avenue. Each car slowed down or stopped completely so that a guard could verify that the car and its occupants were allowed entry. Then the Chryslers glided noiselessly through the iron gate to park at a 45-degree angle to the curb on either side. The passengers went either right, into the West Wing of the White House, or left, into the Executive Office Building. With economic conditions the way they were, even Saturday was a working day.

One of the first cars to arrive discharged a worried middle-aged man with thick curly hair. He turned left and walked briskly. Harry Ratner, Chairman of the Council of Economic Advisers, knew that he had only a few minutes to get up to his office, Room 315, in the building that looked like a Victorian airplane hangar. Harry Ratner had a lot on his mind. He did not pause to admire the elegant stonework and masonry that made the Executive Office Building the most beautiful office building in America.

Ratner was thinking about the 8:10 meeting of the Emergency Inflation Stabilization Group and what he was going to have to tell them. He wanted to make sure he had the information that had reached him the night before neatly typed. It was important and it had to be just right.

"Good morning, Joyce," Ratner said as he walked into his outer office. "Have you got that stuff?"

"Yes, Mr. Ratner. Here it is." She handed him several sheets of paper. Ratner didn't bother to proofread them. Joyce was one of the highest-paid secretaries in the government, but she was worth it. She never made mistakes.

"Any calls?" Ratner asked.

"Nothing important," Joyce said, which meant nothing from either the President or Ratner's wife.

"Call the mess and find out what they're having for lunch." Harry Ratner did not object to good food.

Ratner rifled through the notes as he sat down at his desk. Most of his calls were from newsmen, which meant that he didn't have to return them, at least not right away.

Outside, on the aveune, an elegant woman with dark auburn hair was getting out of her car. Claire Beaton was determined not to be late for this meeting. Director of the newly revitalized Cost of Living Council, which was headquartered at 20th and M, she had done something today she rarely did—she had overslept.

Under this President, the director of the COLC was a Cabinet appointment, and Claire Beaton did not want to become known as the woman Cabinet member who was always arriving late. She didn't think jokes like that were funny, and she didn't want to give them a chance to get started. Even when the jokes about women came from the President, Claire Beaton didn't like them, and she didn't laugh. She didn't even smile.

She was trying this morning to arrive before Eugene Donnelly, the free-wheeling Texan who had somehow, incredibly, become Secretary of the Treasury and Vice-Chairman, below the President, of the EISG.

Today the President was at Camp David.

Claire Beaton did not care for these Saturday meetings. She considered them largely make-work projects designed to show the White House press corps that the honchos put in their hours. She had been drafted from her professorship at Yale, and she could not recall any Saturday meetings there.

But Claire Beaton had played by the rules to become the first woman chairman of the Economics Department at Yale, and she would play by the rules at the White House. She saw Ratner and Colonel Lionel Edwards, Staff Director of the National Security Council, hurrying into the West Wing and followed them out of the glaring sunlight. The guard at the desk inside the double doors stood up as they entered. When he recognized their faces, he said a respectful "Good morning," sat down and returned to his *Sports Illustrated*. As they waited for the small elevator adjacent to the guard's desk to ascend, Tom Ebersole, Special Trade Representative, stepped in.

"Good morning, Claire," Ebersole said. "Hot enough for you?"

Claire Beaton had decided that if Ebersole ever said anything that was not a cliché, she would pass out on the spot.

"Yes, Tom," she sighed.

When the elevator got to the second floor, they all turned left down the narrow corridor into the room that had served so many functions under different Presidents. Low-ceilinged, with one small window looking out on Pennsylvania Avenue, it was furnished with easy chairs, all from Ethan Allen, and small Colonial-style tables and bookcases. On the walls hung pictures of Revolutionary War-era fighting ships, the staple of White House art.

Claire Beaton noticed with annoyance that Donnelly was already there. She braced herself for his wisecrack, but he was engrossed in a conversation. She hoped it would be a long one.

A Filipino steward poured coffee for those who wanted it.

Peter Hanrahan gave her a friendly smile, flashing his big Irish teeth, and took the empty chair beside her. She was always a bit unsettled by Hanrahan. Good-looking, suave and dapper, he looked completely out of place at these meetings, but when he spoke, he was right on target. A long-time friend of the President, he had been appointed Director of International Economic Policy. He was extremely rich, scion of a steelmaking fortune said to be larger than old Joe Kennedy's. And unlike most rich people in government, he was not the slightest bit defensive about it. He must have the robber-baron genes of his grandfather, Claire thought. Hanrahan had been a fighter pilot during the Korean War, and he had a kind of toughness about him which showed through his polish. That was unusual in this group too.

Eugene Donnelly, Secretary of the Treasury, looked them over with his shrewd blue eyes to see if everyone was there. Everyone was present but Flynn. Then he remembered that Flynn was sitting next to him. Flynn was so quiet and neat and buttoned-down—he wore a three-piece suit even on this August Saturday morning—that it was possible for long periods to forget that he was there. That was how these intellectuals were—quiet and careful. But they could also be deadly, and Donnelly had to use all his down-home country charm on the President to keep his status as the "big enchilada" of economic policy. True, his training was in politics, not in economics, but that didn't mean a thing—economics and politics were both basically about people, and Donnelly knew people.

Frank Trout, head of the Federal Energy Commission, sat next to Flynn.

"I guess we'll start this week's session of Ding-Dong School," Donnelly said with a smile. Trout and Flynn smiled back. "Sometimes these meetings are like school. They're not much fun, but they're good for you. Now, Milt's been filling me in on the President's view of the ball game and I think we ought to get that before we go on to other things."

Milt Greenberg, tall, thin, stoop-shouldered, looked up from his yellow pad. He had spoken to the President just before the meeting, and the President, even at Camp David, his favorite resting spot, was in a foul mood. If all his economic advisers were so goddamned smart, he had complained, why was he running into so much trouble with inflation and unemployment? "Get them off their asses, Milt," he said. "We've got to come up with a program—something to show the people we're not just sitting in the Oval Office playing with ourselves."

Milt had been with the President a large part of his life, and he knew that the President wouldn't want such a blunt message to go out. It would be in *Time* the next week and it would offend people. So Milt Greenberg didn't tell the EISG to get off their asses. Instead he turned his bald head slowly from left to right to include them all, cleared his throat and spoke. "The old man wants you all to know how much he appreciates the kind of hours you've been putting in. He realizes it's August and that most of you have families." Claire Beaton, who lived alone, felt the familiar twinge. "But he's working too, up at Camp David, and he wants a full report after this meeting. He wants ideas. He wants initiatives."

Nobody responded. Greenberg had expected a quip of some kind from Harry Ratner, but it didn't come. Greenberg, Ratner thought, was using kid gloves.

Greenberg went on. "I know that we can't work miracles. The President knows that too. But we all know that this is a political issue and the Republicans are using it to murder us."

"Maybe," said Ebersole, "but we're still not dead. They haven't come up with a program either."

"The truth is, the President isn't as worried about the Republicans as he is about Governor Whitelaw. Whitelaw does have a message, and while it may seem crazy to us, it makes sense to a lot of people out there."

Claire felt herself getting angry again. What was

Greenberg trying to say? That Whitelaw plays in Peoria, as Ehrlichman used to put it? How could sensible people take Whitelaw seriously? Rednecks and hillbillies and Jesus freaks, maybe, and a few dropouts from the new left of the sixties, but how could they actually be discussing Whitelaw seriously in the West Wing of the White House? However popular the polls showed him to be, the American people would never turn to someone like Whitelaw for a leader.

His denim-coveralled, scrubbed, smiling young disciples, perpetually handing out leaflets and preaching to passersby on sidewalks, were a nuisance, but more of a bad joke than something to be taken seriously.

Whitelaw had come from a mediocre record of governing a Midwestern state to national prominence with a mishmash of half-baked ideas. Even those were stolen from all over the lot. He got his ideas about sharing the wealth from a million different people—including Huey Long. He got his ideas about law and order from George Wallace, and Wallace had faded dismally. Whitelaw's ideas about going back to God and making America safe for Christians sounded like something from a fundamentalist anti-Communist crusade, but his thoughts on destroying the wealthy were too similar to Karl Marx's for the comfort of traditional Christian anti-Communists.

Milt Greenberg was back on the subject of a program that either the President or the Congress would buy. Ratner reassured Greenberg that the President was still alive and well in the minds of the people.

"Maybe so, Harry, but his programs are dying a little each day. Whitelaw doesn't have to have a program that would get him a Ph.D. from Yale. It just has to be vague and sound good. He's not in the White House. He can snipe away all day, and that's what he's doing."

"Harry knows good and well what we need," interrupted Donnelly. "We need some new ideas to stop this inflation and curb unemployment at the same time. We need a brainstorm."

Claire couldn't contain herself. "This may come as a surprise to you, Gene, but we are facing a major economic problem of the kind that has never before had to be solved within the political constraints we have today. No one wants to go through what it takes to stop inflation. To ask us to suddenly come up with a brainstorm is like asking the people who built the atomic bomb to do it in one day."

Christ, how Donnelly hated her. She thought she was so fucking smart. She loved to make him feel like a yokel. But if he knew anything, he knew how to charm women, even brainy ones. He smiled and focused his eyes on the picture of a frigate hanging right behind and above her head. "He doesn't expect the impossible. He just wants everybody here to try a little harder."

Greenberg spoke up. "We're not looking for miracles, Claire. We want some ideas that'll help the President's image."

Claire Beaton hated that word "image." No one gave a damn any more about what was real. All anyone cared about was "image."

Donnelly grinned. "Exactly," he said. "Now I think we'll have Show and Tell." That was the term that he used for the reports that some of the group made every Saturday morning.

Harry Ratner began: "Last night I got the preliminary reports on the next Consumer Price Index figures. They're not good, but they're nowhere near as bad as they could have been."

"How bad?" asked Hanrahan.

"The July figure is up two point one percent. That's less than June, but higher than May or April. It would have been a lot higher if we hadn't gotten that good crop. Agricultural commodities really saved the day. A lot of the savings were passed on."

Donnelly lifted his stately face and rubbed his chin. "Let's see. That comes out to an annual rate of about twenty-five percent, right, Harry?"

"Right," said Ratner.

"That's about what the rate has been for the last two years, right?" Donnelly asked.

"Right again. I'm not happy with the figure, and

I don't know anyone, besides maybe Whitelaw, who is."

"Of course, we're still way below the rate for Western Europe and Japan." This was Ebersole, ever the optimist.

"Yes, but we're still too high. The President knows that and we all know it." Ratner had said it a hundred, maybe a thousand, times.

Greenberg spoke again. "The President does know that. What he wants to learn is a feasible way of stopping it."

Ratner sighed. "I got some more news last night that worries me more than the CPI figures. It came from George McConger."

Peter Hanrahan swore under his breath.

When he and Ratner had first heard the news about McConger, neither of them could believe their ears.

"Did the President talk to you about it?" Ratner had asked.

"Not one goddamn word," Hanrahan said. "I swear to Christ it's like putting a whore in charge of a nunnery."

"McConger wasn't so bad when he was just the bigmouth populist from North Dakota telling people that he was going to give the little man a break by printing more money. It was OK as long as he couldn't get his hands on the printing press," Ratner had said. "Jesus, I don't know what the hell's going to happen now."

"The thing that's so scary," Hanrahan said, "is that I think he really believes all that crap. I think the President has named a Federal Reserve Chairman who believes it is God's will that he flood the country with greenbacks. I can see why McConger took the job. He'd only been in Congress for thirty years. He wasn't going anywhere there. But why in the hell did the President appoint him?"

Ratner had shaken his head. "McConger's got a hell of a lot of friends. You can't go around the country for most of your lifetime talking to influential people about something you believe in without convincing at least a few of them that you're right. He can turn out more Midwestern votes in Congress than the President can. And he can bring out the voters too. That's why he got the job. I mean, you tell people you're going to give them more money, so why should they be suspicious? Especially the dopes."

"It's not just the dopes, Harry," Hanrahan had said. "Look at Ponds and Murphyson. McConger's got them in the bank." Ed Ponds owned the largest chain of newspapers and TV stations in the Midwest, and Sidney Murphyson had so much oil and land in Texas and Louisiana that he made Eugene Donnelly look like small change.

"Hell, I don't know how he does it," Ratner had said.

"He looks at them with eyes like doomsday and whispers that he has been told the secret of eternal salvation, and that it's easy, and that it's printing more money. It's the biggest pile of shit in the world, but people believe it. That is the sad truth. He just says it over and over again, with enough conviction, and people believe him."

Peter Hanrahan had often wondered if McConger had some secret hold over the President. It was no secret that McConger had pushed him like hell when the President was just a second-termer in Congress no one had heard of.

At least McConger was not present today. They could thank the good Lord for that.

"I had quite a long talk with George McConger last night," Ratner continued. "He won't budge an inch. He says that what we need is more money creation plus controls. He says he's sure the people are with him, and that the President will be too."

Claire Beaton could not restrain herself. "Why does the President put up with him? We tried controls. Even Nixon tried controls. They didn't work. They don't work. Doesn't McConger remember his friends in the Midwest shooting their calves to keep from sending them to market at the controlled price?" Claire sometimes wished that she was back in New Haven, where people did what was smart, not what got them applause or TV coverage.

"I think George is just convinced that only he knows the answer," said Ratner. "He won't listen to anyone else. I think if somebody, maybe the President, could get him to slow down his printing press for a while, we could get a handle on things."

Even Donnelly looked dour. "Fat fucking chance," he said, then looked across the table. "Ooops, sorry, Claire."

Claire smiled. "I'm used to it, Gene. My students at Yale use the same language."

"Well, nobody can accuse me of going to Yale," Donnelly said, and led the laughter that followed.

Even Claire laughed. A moment of humor that didn't hurt anyone was welcome at these sessions.

Colonel Edwards did not laugh for long, though. He straightened his face and cleared his throat. "Mr. Secretary, I have some news that I think we'd better get to right away. The Secretary of State already has the news, but he only got it a few minutes ago. I'm giving this group first priority."

Like hell, thought Donnelly. Ever since Kissinger, the NSC has served the Secretary of State before the President even gets a bite. Some day he would change that. That's what the President had him around for. But all Donnelly said, in a calm voice, was, "By all means, Colonel."

"We have cable traffic from the CIA station chief in Riyadh about the meetings between the Iranians and the Saudis. It doesn't look good. A mutual friendship-and-non-aggression pact is only a matter of days away. Khashoggi has been there for four days now, and we think he's worked something out with Stanfi."

Aram Khashoggi, the Iranian Interior Minister, in charge of oil production, tall and floridly good-looking, had nevertheless always reminded Claire of a self-important, overgrown Turkish rug merchant. She pictured him flanked by Ismail Stanfi, the squat and ungainly Saudi Oil Minister: It must be something to watch them negotiate.

Hanrahan frowned at Colonel Edwards. "I think the President might have been notified before the Secretary of State. This is extremely serious. Too serious to go around in back alleys."

"With all due respect, sir, the Secretary of State is not a back alley. I'm sure he has told the President." Colonel Edwards' face was flushed.

Sure, thought Donnelly. He hasn't told him a damn thing until he's figured out how to make himself a hero in the process.

Donnelly turned to Ratner. "Harry, could you explain to me just why we're so worried about the Saudis and the Iranians becoming friends?"

"Because I'm the only Arab in the room?" It was an old Ratner joke. "I'll explain what I know, but no one has all the pieces."

"We don't expect perfection," said Greenberg.

"Good," said Ratner. "Ever since OPEC quadrupled the price of oil after the 1973 war, different members have wanted oil sold at different prices. Generally countries like Algeria and Nigeria, which have a lot of people, want to sell their oil at the highest possible price. Good for them, bad for us. Even with the Alaskan pipeline going, we're still importing about twenty million barrels a day, close to two thirds of what we're using.

"To keep the price up, Saudi Arabia, which has the most oil, has to keep a lot of its capacity shut down. If the Saudis produced at capacity, there would be a world oil glut, and the price would come down. The other OPEC countries wouldn't like that. Iran especially wouldn't like that, since Iran is spending every cent it gets right now.

"Now the Saudis are producing enough to keep the price down closer to what we'd like than what the Iranians would like," said Ratner. "We're not sure why, but we think it's politics. The Iranians use a lot of their oil revenues to buy arms—our arms. If the Iranians got enough oil money, they could build a military force strong enough to dominate the entire Persian Gulf. The Saudis don't want that, so they've been keeping the cartel price down. To put it bluntly, the

Saudis are hurting themselves a little to keep the Iranians from hurting them a lot."

"So," said Donnelly, "if the Saudis and the Iranians get together . . ."

"The Saudis have no reason to keep the price down," Ratner finished.

Donnelly looked at Trout. "Frank, does the FEC have anything to say about this?"

"We've done projections of where the price of oil would go if the Saudis weren't holding it down." Trout paused. "It's twenty dollars a barrel now for light Arabian crude. We wouldn't be surprised to see it go to thirty-two dollars."

"Thirty-two dollars a barrel!" Donnelly shouted. "I thought they couldn't sell it all at twenty."

Ratner explained. "They may not sell quite as much, but they won't sell much less. People will pay almost anything to drive a car and heat their homes."

Donnelly smiled. "But we can live with it, can't we? Hell, we've got to live with it, somehow."

Jim Flynn, who had been silent, coughed and said, "Gene, we've had our computers working on this problem. There's a big difference between this time and the other times OPEC raised the prices. The other times, we were able to keep the effects to a minimum —with the help of the Federal Reserve. They held down the money supply so that there just wasn't enough cash around to chase prices up too much."

"But this time it's different," Claire said. Now she was on her own ground, explaining economics to people who didn't know much about it—specifically Gene Donnelly. "With the way McConger's grinding out money, any OPEC price rise wouldn't be offset this time. It would be magnified." She paused a moment, for effect, just as she did when she was conducting her seminars at Yale. "It would be magnified a lot. A great deal."

Milt Greenberg began to sweat. Claire Beaton was the straightest female shooter he knew. "How much are we talking about, Claire?"

Harry Ratner was ready. "If OPEC goes to thirty-two dollars, we're looking at a one-shot increase of ten percentage points. That means we'll be over thirty-five percent inflation for the next twelve months—if McConger doesn't get any strange ideas."

"That's about what we see over at the Office of Management and Budget, too," Flynn added.

Donnelly whistled softly. "Jesus H. Christ. Thirty-five percent. Has anybody told the President?"

No one spoke.

Donnelly looked at Claire Beaton. "Claire, do you go along with this?"

"Absolutely. If anything, I'd say the thirty-five percent figure is conservative."

Donnelly turned to Ratner. "You said this would be a one-shot increase. Could the inflation settle down after that, in a year or so?"

"It could. If we did everything we should do. If we cut spending. If we raised taxes. Most of all, if McConger could be persuaded not to print so goddamn much money. There are a lot of ifs. But it could be done. Definitely. It's not really an economics question. It's a question of political willpower."

Donnelly put on a grin and said, "You let us politicians worry about that. I think maybe we're all a little pessimistic because we're spending our Saturday working instead of playing golf."

Peter Hanrahan looked straight at Donnelly and said, "Gene, if what Colonel Edwards says is true, it's damn serious. It can't be swept under the rug. It can't be laughed off. If people are paying two dollars a gallon for gasoline, we're in bad trouble. If McConger makes it worse, they'll be paying two-fifty."

He turned to Greenberg. "I hope the President is getting the message, Milt."

"Peter, you know that I don't pass the buck and neither does the President. Of course he'll get the message. And he'll do what he has to do."

"We're looking at major dislocations unless we handle this right," said Ratner.

"And if the President wants to know the first thing to do, tell him to fire McConger." This outburst from Claire Beaton startled Donnelly. He was used to more subtlety, more discretion.

"I'll be frank with you, Claire. I can't see that happening. But I think the President can make the Fed do what's right." Donnelly gave them his best Texas smile and said, "Let's just keep this under our hats for a while. This whole thing is speculative and we may just be worrying ourselves to death. You economists are always gloomy. Life isn't so bad. We'll figure out what to do. It'll be all right."

"Wouldn't it be nice to think so?" Peter Hanrahan muttered under his breath to Claire.

Ten minutes later, at his office two doors down from the Oval Office, Milt Greenberg was telling the White House operator to put him through to Camp David. When the Marine operator there picked up, he told Greenberg that the President was on the phone at the skeet-shooting range. Greenberg asked the Marine to ring the President the moment he was free. Yes, Greenberg would be in his office. Yes, it was important.

The President had stopped skeet shooting five minutes earlier when he had gotten a call from Gene Donnelly, who was talking to him from the anteroom of the EISG conference room before most of the group were out of the White House. Gene Donnelly had not gotten where he was by wasting time.

And in the small cabin where the President had picked up the phone, George McConger watched the color drain from the President's cheeks as he said into the phone, "Are you kidding? Thirty-five percent? Good God." The President was going to need a lot of calming down. But George McConger was the man to do it. He had always been able to make the President see the right thing to do, and he would be able to do it this time too. Whatever it was, George McConger and the President could handle it. They always had.

The President walked out of the shack with his arm around McConger's shoulders. As they reached the range, the President turned to his dog, Freda, a champion Weimaraner named for an old aunt. "Come on, Freda," he called. The trim gray dog came running. The chief magistrate of the land bent over and patted his dog on the hip. "Fuck 'em, Freda. Right?" The harsh features of McConger's face softened.

Larry Hyde was mad. He swiveled the tan vinyl chair away from his desk and looked at the clock on the beige wall of his office. Fifteen minutes after five o'clock. It was the Friday before Labor Day and out his window he could already see the traffic backing up on the East River Drive. By now his friends would have decided he wasn't coming and would have left for West Hampton without him. They would beat the worst of the traffic on the Long Island Expressway. They would get out to the house early, in time to rest, shave, and put on exactly the right clothes for the Friday-night round of parties.

That was where you met the girls—the junior editors and assistant account executives with names like Tiffany and Caryn and Alida, the girls you could expect big things from if you came on just right at those Friday-night parties.

But Larry Hyde was stuck in New York. His boss had told him at about three that the messenger from Lissitzyn Brothers might be late, but that Larry should wait for him. Now, even if the messenger came within the next few minutes, Larry would arrive in West Hampton late and bedraggled, without time to change out of his dark gray suit. He would not cut much of a figure at those parties that counted for everything in the Hamptons. Worse, he would have to drive his own car, a 1975 Cougar, six years old already and constantly breaking down. What a bitch that would be, to get stuck on the Long Island Expressway on an August afternoon with ten thousand cars honking at you personally. No, waiting for the messenger from Lissitzyn Brothers did not make Larry Hyde happy.

He knew he had to wait, though, both for himself and for his employers. Melloan's was a good place to be, and Larry Hyde wanted to go straight up. All the companies that traded in gold bullion were good places to be these days, Larry thought, and Melloan and Company was one of the most prestigious.

Ensconced on the twenty-sixth floor of a ten-year-

old building at 100 Wall Street, Melloan and Company
displayed no sign in the lobby to indicate what it did.
It was, in fact, a kind of store, selling one thing only
—gold. Ever since the 1978 law which had allowed
unrestricted trading in gold bullion, subject only to the
rules of the Commodity Futures Trading Commission,
New York had steadily been eating into London's and
Zurich's leads as the world's gold-trading centers. In-
creasingly, people who believed that gold was the
best possible hedge against inflation had been placing
their orders at firms like Melloan's. Computers and
satellite communications had made New York the
place where a buyer could get the smoothest possible
transactions at the best possible price. The differential
on an ounce of gold might be only a fraction of a percent, but if the orders were large enough, that mounted
up.

And the orders had been large, especially in the last
six months. Melloan and Company was doing especially well lately, and that was largely because of the
large, steady purchases by Lissitzyn Brothers. Larry
Hyde was only one of five junior executives working
on the account, but he meant to show his boss that he
was the best of the five. He had been given three raises
in the last six months. It was true that two of them
were simply to cover cost-of-living increases, but the
third was surely for merit.

Sitting at his maple desk, Larry Hyde decided that
for the sake of his future he had better wait patiently.
The whole problem of the Hamptons and the girls and
a new car would have to take a back seat. He did
some mental arithmetic as he waited, figuring the commission on one hundred troy ounces of gold. Of
course he didn't get commissions yet, but some day he
would, and that would be a momentous day. That
would be the day he would show up at those parties
in a Mercedes convertible, instead of his miserable
Cougar.

Even if Lissitzyn Brothers was only partly his account, he would be making big money when he went
on a commission basis. Every day for the past six
months the messenger from that very old and very

white-shoe private bank had arrived at just about closing time with an order for gold. It was always for the maximum amount, at the market price. And if the Commodity Futures Trading Commission raised the limit about one thousand ounces per day, the commissions would be even bigger. Larry Hyde didn't know how much longer gold could keep going up like this, and people could keep buying, but whoever was buying now would eventually sell, so there would always be commissions to be made. He would have his Mercedes. He was twenty-seven years old and he could wait.

Just as he was imagining how it would feel to pull up to a house party in East Hampton, the best Hampton, in his blue Mercedes, his phone rang. Mike, the ancient receptionist who came on at five, was calling.

"There's a, uh, gentleman out here to see you, Mr. Hyde." Mike coughed before he said "gentleman" when the messenger from Lissitzyn Brothers was a Puerto Rican.

"Thanks, Mike. I'll come right out." Larry took another look at his clock, which now showed 5:25, looked at the East River Drive again, and walked out of his office and down the hall to the sparsely furnished green-carpeted reception room. He recognized the messenger as Ricky. He never knew their last names. The thought struck him that he should know their last names, that it was racist of him not to. But he was in a hurry. He would ask Ricky his last name next time.

He greeted the slightly built messenger and thought how ironic it was that this little man was carrying around orders for more dollars' worth of gold than many millionaires would ever see.

"Hi, Ricky. Got something for me?"

"Yes, Mr. Hyde." Ricky unzipped his vinyl pouch and took an envelope from it. "Here it is. I'm sorry to be late."

"That's OK, Ricky. Have a nice weekend."

"You too, Mr. Hyde." Ricky waved and disappeared into the elevator. He left without telling Larry Hyde that the reason he was late was because he had just come from delivering an identical envelope to another bullion dealer uptown, and the traffic was a mess. He had been told not to tell anyone where he went on his rounds, so he also didn't tell Larry Hyde that Melloan's was the tenth bullion dealer he had visited that day, as it was on every business day.

Ricky couldn't have told Larry, because he didn't know, that the envelopes he had dropped off at each stop had identical purchase orders and checks inside, each one for the maximum allowable purchase of gold per dealer per day. And Ricky Jimenez did not know, and probably would not have cared, that there were other messengers traveling around the financial districts of the City of London and Zurich making similar rounds for the same client, and had been doing so for the past six months.

Larry Hyde put the purchase order into the computer terminal next to his desk so that the trade would be executed first thing on Monday. He put the certified check in his office safe, which was a drawer of a wood filing cabinet. He felt proud of himself. Even at a serious inconvenience to his social life, he had stayed late to do his job. He chalked it up to his good training at Bernard M. Baruch College and to his ambition. On Monday his boss would see what time the order had come in and would thank him for having waited. An order for a thousand ounces of gold at $482 an ounce was worth waiting for.

Larry Hyde could already see himself in that Mercedes.

He gave one more look at the now completely stalled traffic on the Drive and walked out of his office. He was on his way.

Aram Khashoggi looked out the window of the conference room of the Kuilima Hotel. As usual in September, the Hawaiian sky was a magnificent crystal blue. On the beach about twenty people lay stretched out in the afternoon sun. Only one woman was swimming in the azure waters of the small atoll that extended from the beach. Probably there would be more people swimming on the other side of the hotel, in the large, heated pool. Kuilima, on the northernmost point of Oahu, was like a small child's image of paradise.

Certainly it looked that way to Aram Khashoggi, even at fifty-two, and he was glad that he had been able to persuade his fellow members of OPEC to hold their quarterly session there. He believed that such a big step should be taken in a place with a special aura, and that was what he liked about Kuilima. It looked like a place where great things should happen, and now great things would. It would also be a slap in the American face.

Khashoggi, Interior Minister of Iran, returned his gaze to the room, into which his fellow OPEC delegates were now filing after their luncheon recess. He waited especially for Sheik Ismail Stanfi, the Saudi Arabian Oil Minister, who was his co-host in announcing the major news that would come from this meeting. In a moment the short and pudgy Saudi walked in and smiled at him. Khashoggi, a tall, imposing man, got out of his chair and started over to the corner of the room where Stanfi was getting papers out of his brief-case.

The room was circular. The enormous windows were tinted so that the people in the conference room could see out, but the people outside could not see in. The center of the room was covered with Oriental rugs that Khashoggi had specially flown in for the meeting. On top of the rugs was an unusual table which had a large oak central portion, and a series of form-fitted tables abutting it, so that each delegate could have his own table. This gave the delegates a sense of privacy and dignity which they had missed in the cramped meeting hall at Texacohaus in Vienna.

Khashoggi was stopped by several of the delegates and staff members who wanted to mention this or that small detail, or simply pay court to the man whom they now considered the most powerful voice in OPEC. The delegates came in all colors and sizes, though there were no Europeans. It would be hard for him to talk about the exploitation of the oil states by the industrialized states if there were any Europeans there, or any Americans, for that matter.

At one time, in the late 1970s, it looked as if the United Kingdom and Norway might become members of OPEC, but Britain's production had been hampered by a political struggle over nationalization and Norway had held down its potentially huge production because of environmental fears. So, as Khashoggi walked up to Sheik Stanfi, he saw no blue eyes.

"What did they have for lunch?" Khashoggi asked his co-host.

"Lamb, as usual. Whenever we go anywhere, they always serve us lamb. It's becoming a joke."

"To many people we are a joke," Khashoggi said. "They need us and they kiss our asses, but behind our backs we are a joke to them."

"I think that will stop today," Stanfi said. "Unless the Americans have a perverse sense of humor."

"Let's walk outside for a moment, my friend," Khashoggi said, taking Stanfi's arm and leading him out to the flagstone veranda overlooking the beach. On the way they passed the somewhat sinister-looking security men. Since the raid of December 1975, there had been much better protection at OPEC meetings.

"I want us to be well prepared if our fellow members ask us how we finally got together," Khashoggi said.

"Since we are all involved, I think we might as well tell the truth," Stanfi said.

"My thinking exactly. Shall we begin with the Carlos incident, or do you not want to go that far back?"

"Let's start with Carlos. Or whatever his name is."

"Fine, we'll start with Carlos."

A few minutes later, again inside the air-conditioned conference room, which had been built especially for this meeting, with special places for security men, stenographers and translators, Aram Khashoggi told the fourteen member states of OPEC a story.

"I hope my fellow members will pardon me if I begin our afternoon session with a story that has important bearing on today's meeting. I promise it will be brief, and I promise you will be interested in it."

Pierre Bateaux, Petroleum Minister of Gabon, took it upon himself to make a sweeping gesture of sycophancy from a state that had barely made it into OPEC. He said to the Iranian official, "All of your stories are interesting, and all of them are a privilege to hear."

Aram Khashoggi smiled at the nattily dressed African and said, "Thank you, messieurs, for your indulgence." He then looked out the window as though the room were too small for the scope of his vision. "As you all know, six years ago a terrible thing happened at our former headquarters. Some of you were there. I was, and so was my former friend, Sheik Ahmed Zaki Yamani." There were general nods of approval at the name of the man who for several years had existed as the symbol of the power and wealth of OPEC. Khashoggi noted that no one seemed surprised when he claimed Yamani as a friend, though Yamani and he had not been on speaking terms for many years. Khashoggi also noted that most of the oil delegates now affected the same sober three-piece suits of dark wool that Yamani had liked so well. They bespoke oil and power, and the delegates liked them.

"Also at the fateful meeting was my former superior, Jamshid Amouzegar, whom my countrymen miss so dearly."

Right on cue, Bateaux spoke up. "I can speak for the people of Gabon when I say that he is missed as well by our country."

Khashoggi paused only long enough to marvel at the pliability of human nature, and resumed his speech. "That was a terrible meeting. Three people lost their lives. Others were kidnapped and flown through the skies without rest or sleep, held hostage by a demented man, the terrorist who was called Carlos."

The delegates nodded their heads. They knew that some day it could happen to them.

"As it happened, Carlos seated Minister Amouzegar and Sheik Yamani next to each other. Everyone here knows that our two great countries, Iran and Saudi Arabia, were not always in agreement on many things. One of those things was the price of oil.

"But as the hours of the terrorist kidnapping dragged on, the talk became fatalistic and turned to religion.

And of course, our two great leaders shared the same belief in Allah. What is more, that faith, for both men, was more than lip service. For them, as for many of us, the Koran is real and living, not only a great classic, but a prescription for what to do in the world.

"What Minister Amouzegar and Sheik Yamani saw, as they flew through the night, never knowing if any moment might be their last, was that the forces that bound them together were far more powerful than the petty rivalries and fears that kept them apart," Khashoggi said solemnly. "They saw, in fact, that oil had been given to our countries at this time in history to enable us to spread the true faith around the world. Of course," he said with a nod toward Minister Velasquez of Venezuela and General Porto of Ecuador, "we will not force Islam upon anyone. But our leaders saw truly that we need not fear to trust one another so long as we all believe in the words of the Prophet."

Khashoggi looked around the room to see what effect his words were having on the delegates. They all looked extremely sincere. If he and Stanfi took off their clothes and stood on their heads, Khashoggi thought, the other OPEC delegates would probably do exactly the same thing.

Khashoggi continued. "Now the great King of Saudi Arabia has cooperated with the rest of us in helping to set prices. And we have been working very hard to reach an agreement to fix the absolute maximum price for our oil, with complete Saudi Arabian cooperation.

"Life is complicated, and many details had to be worked out. But we have reached an agreement. It will be announced this afternoon in Riyadh and Teheran. It is a treaty of friendship and nonaggression. I wish it long life."

There was murmuring among the OPEC delegates. Had most of them not been Moslems, it would have been an occasion for breaking out champagne.

Only Pierre Bateaux looked bewildered. "Does this mean that the Zionist racist swine are going to be thrown into the sea?" he asked.

Khashoggi looked at him patiently. "No, M'sieur

Bateaux. This treaty has very little to do with Israel. It is between the countries of Iran and Saudi Arabia. It will make us all stronger, but it is a treaty not specifically against anyone."

The Gabonese delegate sat back into his chair, happy to have been answered at all by the powerful Iranian. If he did not understand the answer, that was all right. He was flattered to have been acknowledged so courteously.

"Our friend raises an important point," Khashoggi continued. "Although we in Iran are not at war with Israel and never have been, this treaty will make those states of the Middle East which have oil steadily more powerful. The condition of 'no war-no peace' which has gone on in the Mideast for so long will not continue forever, and when it ends, we feel that the power of OPEC must bear upon how it ends."

"Let me make this all clear," Sheik Stanfi said with a small bow toward Pierre Bateaux, who was now overjoyed at being the center of attention. "What this treaty means is that my king has now instructed me to help find a price which will reflect oil's real value in the world economy. The days when the West could count on us to adjust our prices to suit their comfort are over."

Once again Bateaux took the floor. "Revered friend," he said, "I do not understand. How does the friendship of your two countries, which I welcome, affect the price of oil?"

With a smile masking his contempt for the chubby African, Sheik Stanfi said, "That need not be fully answered here. Let me just say that we in Saudi Arabia will keep the supply down low enough to force the price high."

"Do you mean. . . . ?" Bateaux began.

"We mean," Khashoggi interrupted, "that we have the industrialized countries' testicles in our pocket. We have them by the balls. We can charge any price we want for oil!"

The delegates were astounded. They had expected something big, but not this big.

Stanfi resumed his role as co-host. "We cannot forever charge the moon, because at some point the Americans will start converting coal into oil. But so far they have shown so little interest in doing so that we believe the sky is the limit right now."

Once more M. Bateaux looked puzzled. General Porto tried to be helpful. "Our friends are saying that we can charge a great deal, although not a million dollars a barrel."

"Not yet," Khashoggi said with a laugh that spread around the room.

"What, may I ask, are you proposing as the new price?" General Porto asked. There was an undercurrent of tension in his voice.

Sheik Stanfi answered, "We have had studies commissioned at the Brookings Institution, an American group famous for using computers to solve economic problems, to determine how high we could go without forcing the Americans to use synthetics."

Sheik Stanfi seemed to be stalling, as if he were about to propose something almost embarrassingly outrageous.

"And what will the new price be?" General Porto asked.

Before Stanfi answered, he had an image of his childhood spent at an English boarding school and his later training at Harvard Business School. The hundreds of hurts and humiliations that had nicked and cut him, the general air of superiority that the English and Americans had felt toward this short, dark, clumsy, rich stranger flashed before his eyes, followed by the delicious feeling of a man who is about to get the sweetest of sweet revenges. But Sheik Stanfi did not talk about revenge or past hurts. Instead, he looked straight at the olive-skinned Ecuadorian and said in an even tone, "For light Arabian crude, at the well head, thirty-eight dollars a barrel."

Everyone in the room except Khashoggi and Stanfi gasped. Even Pierre Bateaux had speculated on a rise to $30, at most, but he had thought that optimistic. There was general pandemonium in the room as the delegates asked the interpreters over and over again if they had heard correctly.

"Yes, I said thirty-eight dollars a barrel," Stanfi repeated. "And if we have to shut down eight percent of our capacity to do it, we will."

Then there was wild back-slapping, hand-wringing and congratulations, as if everyone present had won the Irish Sweepstakes at the same time. Everyone except General Porto. He waited until the room quieted down, holding himself aloof from the self-congratulations. Then he spoke.

"I am no academic or bureaucrat," he said, choosing his words carefully, "so I ask your pardon if I speak bluntly."

Khashoggi looked straight at Porto. He had expected some opposition to the price rise, but he had not known who it would come from. Now, though, it seemed logical that General Sylvio Porto, the tough little head of the Army-Navy-Air Force junta that ran Ecuador should be the one.

"I too, like everyone else here, welcome the new friendship between Saudi Arabia and Iran. I welcome it for its own sake and for the sake of world peace. I also welcome the spirit of cooperation and self-sacrifice which has been shown by Saudi Arabia."

Pierre Bateaux, thinking that he was about to be one-upped in praising Saudi Arabia, interrupted General Porto. "Pardon me, General, but I would like to say that my country yields to none in its gratitude for the actions of the Saudi Arabian people and their great king."

General Porto frowned, paused for a moment, and went on. "I too think that we should get a fair price for our oil. But I must say candidly that charging thirty-eight dollars a barrel is a suicidal gesture."

A shock wave rippled across the room, but Khashoggi and Stanfi kept their eyes steadily on General Porto, who looked straight at them.

"The industrialized countries did not get that way because they are fools. They will not lower their standards of living to allow us to become richer. They will continue to do what they have done in the past. They will raise the price of the goods they sell to us by more than enough to offset the raise. Speaking for my own country, I have no doubt that we will wind up losing money because we import so much more American and European goods than we export oil."

Khashoggi looked at him with half-lidded, unruffled eyes. "We appreciate what you are saying, General, and we especially appreciate your frankness. But it is the opinion of our economic experts that an increase of this magnitude will lead to a lowering of the standards of living in the industrialized countries and a transfer of wealth to our countries. I include even a modest producer such as Ecuador."

"Minister Khashoggi, I respectfully tell you that your experts are mistaken. We in South America have seen far better than you what inflation can do when it gets started. It will hurt us all. It will even hurt the countries like Saudi Arabia, because no one will be able to buy your oil. This increase is too large. It will lead to economic repercussions which will have harmful effects on all of us. Yes, we deserve an increase. But let it be a responsible increase, one that does not play Russian roulette with the economy of the whole world."

General Porto wished he knew more about economics so that he could have made a more eloquent speech. He should have had charts and slides and computer printouts to show what he was talking about. But he didn't have those things. All he had was a feeling in his gut—that same gut that had told him so many times just which way to jump when things reached the coup point in Ecuador—that this $38-a-barrel business was nonsense, and dangerous nonsense at that. It was grandiose and preposterous.

But the delegates were clearly with Stanfi and Khashoggi. When the meeting adjourned two hours later, thirteen states voted for the new price of $38 a barrel, and only Ecuador voted against.

"Fellow delegates, I think I speak for us all when I say that this afternoon we have taken a major step toward altering the entire balance of power in the world. The world will remember September fifteenth, 1981, as a date when a new system of the distribution of this world's wealth began in earnest." Khashoggi expected applause when he finished, and he got it.

Only General Porto held back. "Before we leave," he said, "before we announce to the world what we have done, I want to sound only this warning. You have thrown down the gauntlet to the industrialized world. They may not respond to it by military force. They may not even respond to it in any organized way. But we will not get away with it, and we will be sorry for our actions. We are poisoning our own well." General Porto sighed and lowered his eyes.

The delegates were ill at ease for a moment, but then General Porto's remarks were forgotten as Sheik Stanfi, official moderator of this meeting, which had made such a monumental decision, closed the meeting and went out to meet the throng of reporters who had been hanging around all afternoon in the hotel lobby, oblivious to the beautiful sunshine outside. It had been decided that Stanfi and Khashoggi would make the announcement. Khashoggi in particular relished the idea of dealing this body blow to the Americans while standing on U.S. soil.

Khashoggi and Stanfi, tall and short, dressed like any two businessmen, walked to the center of the circle of reporters and stopped. Khashoggi smiled at them and said, "Thank you, gentlemen, for your patience. I have an announcement to make which will be of some interest to you. . . ."

# 2

AS Johnny Carson introduced his *Tonight Show* guests on the Sony television in Peter Hanrahan's bedroom, Hanrahan stood next to the window looking out at the Potomac.

He was waiting for two things, both of which made him uneasy. The first was a call from Hawaii telling him the results of the OPEC meeting. The second was the arrival of Cathy Graham. He knew that both events could shatter the neat facade he presented to the world, and sometimes to himself.

Hanrahan lived on the sixth floor of Watergate South, a luxurious cooperative on the Potomac whose name had become famous in the seventies. His apartment faced the river. The view looked across to Virginia. He lived alone there except for the sometime presence of an elderly part-time housekeeper and cook, and the visits of Cathy Graham.

If anyone could be addicted to a person, Peter Hanrahan was addicted to Cathy Graham. A year ago, Richard Graham, an old college friend and business associate before his White House days, had asked Hanrahan to do him a favor. Cathy, Richard Graham's daughter, had been attending a public school in Connecticut, but her parents had decided to put her instead into Madeira, the exclusive boarding school near Maclean, Virginia, just a few miles outside Washington.

But a problem had come up. Richard and Ellen Graham had to go to Brussels on a trip of great importance at just the time that Cathy was to begin classes. Graham had called Hanrahan and had asked if, as a favor to an old friend, he could pick up Cathy at the airport and get her settled in at Madeira —maybe show her a few sights and generally hold her hand until she started classes.

Hanrahan cheerfully agreed to his friend's request. He had not seen Cathy for years; he was not deeply involved in the campaign at that time, and he would be glad to show the kid a good time. When Cathy's shuttle arrived, Hanrahan saw no one who looked like the girl he remembered. He did see a very young version of Catherine Deneuve, and he wondered what lucky boy had her for the weekend. When Hanrahan finally had Cathy Graham paged, the Deneuve lookalike picked up the courtesy telephone. After that it was all a blur.

He barely remembered introducing himself, kissing her on the cheek, and feeling more excited than he had been since he was a teen-ager. He drove her all around the city, held her slender arm at every opportunity, took her to dinner at the Jockey Club, drank wine to her Coke into the early morning, and then tentatively kissed her. He had been amazed at her hungry, experienced response.

They had been secret lovers all that school year, and then she had gone with her parents to Geneva for the summer. And tonight, as he was waiting for the call announcing a decision that would rock the industrial world, Hanrahan was far more excited waiting for Cathy to ring from downstairs to say that she was back in Washington than he was for the call from Hawaii.

Peter Hanrahan had sometimes felt guilty about Cathy. She seemed so young. But Cathy had told him right away that he was not her first lover. And he knew that he was better to her than anyone else would have been. Their affair had a clandestine aspect, since, for good reasons, both Cathy and Hanrahan did not want it to become common knowledge. Cathy probably talked about him with her friends back at school, but Peter Hanrahan was beyond caring. He was a cautious person, but not so cautious as to walk away from the most exciting sex he had ever had.

At 12:16 Hanrahan heard the phone ring from the lobby. A moment later he opened the door. She stood there, breathless, in the Madeira uniform, her pale-blue eyes lighting up the whole room. Hanrahan hugged her as if he could squeeze her whole body into himself. She knew he dug her uniform.

"God, I've missed you!" He pushed her away from him to look at her face. "You look great. More beautiful than ever."

"Oh, Peter, I couldn't wait to get here. What a drag it was in Europe without you," Cathy said. "I wanted to come back here after two days, but my parents wouldn't let me. But I missed you each and every night." She didn't mention that some of those nights she had spent with a young Italian student named Paolo, but then, he wasn't important to her and Peter Hanrahan was. "I used to read about you in the Paris *Herald Tribune*. It made me feel very important."

"Are you hungry? Do you want to go out for dinner? Let me make you a drink."

"No, no. I ate on the plane. I just want to be here with you."

"When does your school start?"

"In two days. But this year, if I keep my grades up, I get unlimited overnights, which means that it won't just be weekends and afternoons any more."

"You can't imagine what it's like working without having you near me, even if it's just for a few hours. It's been fucking miserable."

"Well," she said, in her best Deneuve imitation, as she sat back against his couch and crossed her legs, "I'm here now." She had decided to major in French.

Later, she did her strip. First she took off her saddle shoes and blue socks and put them on a chair. Then she took off her blazer, and her long blond hair fell onto her blouse. She put that on a chair. She smiled at Hanrahan. She took off her skirt and put it on the chair. Then she took off her blouse and put it on a chair. She was not wearing a bra.

Hanrahan couldn't take it any more. He reached out and pulled her into bed.

Afterwards Peter looked at Cathy, then at the ceiling, and laughed. Cathy nudged him in the ribs and asked, "What's the joke?"

"The joke is that I'm sitting here waiting for a call about something that could be very bad and I'm the happiest man in the world. That shithead Donnelly said that the world wasn't such a bad place, and he was right."

Cathy got out of bed and shook her silky hair. "I think I'll make a drink. Do you want one too?"

"Served by a topless waitress named Cathy? Sure."

As Cathy started to walk toward the kitchen, the telephone rang. Peter picked it up. It was the White House operator. "Mr. Hanrahan? I have Harry Ratner and Claire Beaton on a conference call."

Hanrahan was glad that video telephones were not yet in wide use to catch the scene in his apartment. "Harry? Claire? What's happened?"

"It's unbelievable, Peter," said Claire. "OPEC has posted thirty-eight dollars a barrel."

"Jesus Christ! Can that be accurate?"

Ratner answered. "It's definitely accurate. We were working late at the White House. We got patched in directly to the press conference."

"Has the President responded?" Hanrahan asked cautiously.

"Not yet. We've given him a statement that even McConger can agree with. He 'deplores the action' and says we'll take the 'appropriate measures' to insulate ourselves from the effects. What the hell that's going to mean, I'm damned if I know," Ratner said.

"We're having a meeting tomorrow morning at seven," said Claire. "We'll see you there."

Hanrahan said goodbye just as Cathy appeared in the bedroom, naked except for two Scotch-and-waters.

"What's the matter?" she asked.

"The fucking Arab sons of bitches have nailed us. Again."

"Are they having another war?" Cathy asked as she sat on the bed.

"They've almost doubled the price of oil." He took the drink from her hand and drank. "It's going to hurt like hell."

"Is that all?" Cathy asked. "Isn't that what they did back in 1973?"

In 1973, Cathy Graham had been nine years old. He didn't know whether to laugh or to shudder. "It's really worse now than it was in 1973, Cathy, although it's similar."

Cathy crossed her legs Indian-fashion on the bed and said, "Explain it to me." She loved it when Peter explained things.

"Well, back in 1973, we weren't anywhere near as dependent on foreign oil as we are now. So the price rise back then was much smaller for gasoline because we had so much domestic oil at low prices. But now all the oil is decontrolled, and we're importing most of what we use."

Cathy looked confused. Peter picked up the look and smiled at her. "The main thing is that the OPEC price increase is going to be passed along to consumers right away. It'll mean two dollars a gallon for gasoline."

"Wow," Cathy said. "I'm glad I've got a Datsun."

"But things are worse than that. McConger has already got inflation going so strong that every little thing just pushes it up farther and faster, and this oil deal is a big thing. If McConger starts printing even more money to pay for it, we're going to see an inflation that will be like the whole country is tripping."

"Well, you've got plenty of money, Peter," she said brightly.

"That's true," he said, "I do. But it's not just a question of money, and I'm not the typical American. The typical American won't be able to cope with runaway inflation if it gets started. People start acting crazy when their money isn't worth anything. It happened in Germany during the twenties. They were paying billions of marks to buy a loaf of bread. It drove people fucking crazy."

Cathy Graham shook her head. "I just can't see that happening here, Peter. I mean, surely it's not going to cost us a million dollars to buy a loaf of bread, is it?"

Peter Hanrahan closed his eyes for a moment and imagined a loaf of bread costing a million dollars. He opened them again and looked at Cathy Graham's blue eyes and white, smooth flesh. "If it does, it won't be pretty," he said. "We can count on that and we can't count on much else."

Alexandra Hanrahan, Peter's niece, sat by the banks of the Choptank River some eighty miles farther east. The Choptank, which runs diagonally across the Eastern shore of Chesapeake Bay, the Delmarva peninsula, was called "the last unpolluted river on the East Coast" by local real-estate men. Alexandra wasn't thinking about real estate as she sat on the veranda of the Caroline County Country Club, just south of Denton, Maryland, and looked across the table at Shelby Kelsey. They made a handsome couple.

She was tall and thin, with light-auburn hair cut short on her neck. Her large and shining eyes were almost the same color as her hair. She wore a sleeveless dark-blue dress, and her fair skin, slightly freckled, made a lovely contrast with the dress.

The man across from her had not been cut from so delicate a mold. Large, raw-boned, he had a hardness in his features that no one would have called mean but that looked as though it came from a grueling, relentless life on the land—which it did. His eyes at first looked almost black, but when a person got close the eyes were not black at all, but rather an incredibly dark blue, like the sky before a rainstorm in that part of the world. He looked slightly out of place in a country club, with his obviously new and not very well tailored sport coat and slacks.

It was that incongruity Alexandra was considering as the Choptank River flowed by. Shelby Kelsey was a twenty-nine-year-old farm boy and a dreamer of big dreams.

"You know, Shelby," Alexandra said, "I didn't always like this river. When I used to come down here to visit Daddy, the river just made me think of how boring this place was compared to New York. I don't think that any more."

"I know you don't," Kelsey said. "I can tell by the way you look at it."

"I've changed my mind about the whole place. I don't like to even think about New York any more. The first time I came down here I had just gotten out of Vassar. I was working at *Town and Country;* I couldn't wait to get back to New York."

"Well," Shelby said, "a lot of people like New York."

"When I was a kid, and we had that apartment on East Fifty-sixth Street, it seemed like the center of the universe. I mean, Chapin was a terrible bore, but Mother used to have the most wonderful parties."

"Chapin?" Shelby asked.

"Oh, it's a girls' school in New York. Chapin was a drag, but I used to meet the most interesting people at Mother's parties. I used to remember that on a certain tile in the living room I had talked to Truman Capote, and on another to Lauren Hutton, and on another to Lillian Hellman. It all went to my head."

Shelby Kelsey watched her wistfully. She had everything he wanted.

"I mean, these people made such a big deal over me. It was great," Alexandra said. "But maybe it wasn't really that good in the long run. It was a pretty superficial way of life, especially compared to yours."

It had been superficial, but she hadn't thought so then. She would go to Bergdorf's after school. And the same night at dinner she talked to people who did important things. In her last year at Chapin she was going regularly to the Café Carlyle and the St. Regis Maisonette, and she thought it was the greatest life a person could lead.

Shelby Kelsey looked down at the table and tried to explain. "It wasn't such a great life for me, Alex. It may sound romantic and earthy as all hell to be the son of a sharecropper and get up at sunrise to feed the cattle, but it isn't that way. It's a miserable, grinding life that wears out your soul, and you've got to believe that you're going to get out of it somehow or you start to go crazy."

There was silence for a moment. Then Shelby Kelsey continued, "I remember shoveling out the stalls and thinking that it would be great to lie in bed all morning and read the newspaper and give out orders to people on the phone. I guess that's not such a great dream, but I had to think of something besides shoveling cowshit. I *had* to. A lot of people around here say I'm too ambitious, but the people who come from where I came from don't say that. They know what I'm talking about."

"So do I, Shelby, I know how it feels when you have to get out," Alexandra said, taking his hand.

As the waiter served them each a Tom Collins, Alexandra remembered how she had felt a few months ago when she had decided she had to get out.

She hadn't had many friends at Chapin. But she didn't need them. By the time she was fifteen, she was attracting the attention of much older men, and she was more comfortable in their presence anyway. She hated to leave New York to go to Vassar, but Poughkeepsie would only be ninety miles away. Just before she left for college, her mother died. She had been suffering from cancer for over a year, but had not told anyone.

Her death hardly slowed Alexandra down at all. She thought that the best way to get over her sorrow was to do the same thing her mother had done: to live it up. So, although Alexandra was only a fair student, her social life was brilliant. She hardly deigned to go to the mixers and dances at Vassar or the nearby colleges, but instead took the train down the Hudson Valley to New York City for the parties that counted, the ones that were in Eugenia Sheppard's column and on the society page of *The New York Times*.

Shelby Kelsey continued to reminisce. "Working my way through college was about the easiest thing I had ever done. I did all kinds of work, like bussing tables at a fraternity. People would say 'Christ, Shelby, how can you stand to wait on those slobs?' and I'd say that it was a damn sight better than serving food to hogs, which I'd done plenty of. That was great, over there in College Park at the University. I didn't like to come home for vacations." Shelby Kelsey looked ashamed for a moment and then squared his shoulders. "I was embarrassed about my folks. But by the time I was a senior, I had saved enough working at odd jobs to buy them their own place, and then things were a lot better."

"When I hear stories like that it really makes me feel like a twerp. I just used college as an excuse to pass time. Oh, I did a little work—modeling."

Alexandra was being modest. Two months before the end of her freshman year she had been approached to model, and before the summer was over, she had her first *Vogue* cover. By the time her sophomore year started, she was going at such a dizzying speed that the days at Vassar just blended into a blur of textbooks and professors with dandruff on their clothes and grubby-looking boys and girls who didn't know how to dress. The times she remembered best were the nights at El Morocco, the nights of gossip with friends late into the night at penthouses overlooking the East River. By then she was a rising star of the "millionettes" as Andy Warhol called them. There were rumors linking her with various European men with titles, and a few of the rumors were even true. In her circle, people made love out of ritual more than out of feeling.

Shelby Kelsey was talking again. "I was in college when I first started playing with commodities futures." Alexandra knew they were a hazardous form of speculation on what the price of a certain thing might be in the future. "Yeah, I got some of those rich kids from Chevy Chase to back me, and by the time I graduated, we'd done right well. I had a nice little place of my own too, and I didn't have to get it by kissing anybody's ass."

"It's really amazing to think of what you were doing while I was just lying around and going to parties," Alexandra said. She was genuinely impressed at the scope of his activities—at his intensity, his sense of purpose. That was what she had never had—a purpose.

"The thing is," Kelsey said with a laugh, "if I had been brought up with your kind of money, I wouldn't have done any of those things. You have to be standing in the field on a hot day watching the Cadillacs go by when you don't even have a bicycle to know what I mean. If I had been born with everything, I wouldn't have given a damn. However lazy you say you were, and I bet you really weren't, I would have been ten times as lazy."

"I doubt it, Shelby," Alexandra said.

That last year, the year she had graduated from Vassar, she was going with Wolfgang Shafer, a thirty-year-old German playboy, heir to a coal fortune that predated the first Kaiser. With his blond, straight hair and his regal bearing, he seemed to be the most suave man she had ever met. Every day during her final semester a half-dozen roses would arrive for her at Main Hall, where the seniors lived. Always there would be a note saying, in German, "The world is dumb, the world is blind, except for you."

Once she graduated, she and Wolfgang were inseparable. Then, about six months after graduation, she had discovered that she was pregnant with Wolfgang's child. In a way she was glad, because she wanted to to marry Wolfgang and now it was being thrust upon them. She could already see herself in the society pages as a bride, and in Central Park with the baby, while photographers from *Interview* watched her every move. She would certainly be in *Town and Country,* for which she was working.

But the day after she told Wolfgang the happy news, she received by messenger a check for five thousand dollars and a note saying that he had to go out of town on business for several months. In a word, he had bolted. Alexandra never told a soul about the abortion, just as she never told a soul that a lot of her had died in that operation.

Kelsey was talking about her father, William Hanrahan. "He never had to worry about money, and he takes as good care of that place of his as if he had to do it to pay for his food."

"Well, Ridgeley is more than just an estate to Daddy. When Mother died he was in pretty rocky shape. It wasn't until he sold the place in New York and moved down here that he started to recover. He loves the way it faces the river and the way the mist comes in all winter long. Daddy just loves that place."

"Down here you've got to love the land," Shelby said with a force that awed Alexandra. "Alex, I don't mean to brag, but I've got about two thousand acres now, and options on twenty thousand more. I just can't get enough. There's something in land that makes you want to go out and get more. I've always felt it."

"You know something?" Alexandra asked. "I think I'm starting to feel it too." She had moved down to Maryland two weeks after the abortion, and she had immediately felt the sense of relaxation and peace the whole countryside created.

"I'll tell you something. I think your father ought to sell some of those bonds and buy more land. Land just keeps getting more valuable, and they're not making any more of it." Shelby Kelsey paused. "I mean, with this inflation, bonds are really taking a pasting, and land just keeps going up."

"That's something you'll have to take up with Daddy," Alexandra said. "Meanwhile I think we'd better go home. He still waits up for me sometimes."

As they walked to Shelby's Buick (a new replacement for his old Ford pickup), Alexandra was thoughtful. It was strange to be going to her father's home and not to Shelby's. Even though she had been going out with Shelby for six weeks, ever since he had asked her to come with him to look at a farm he was thinking of buying, they were not yet lovers.

There was a kind of fierce pride about Shelby Kelsey, as though he were determined to do things the right way. It went beyond shyness. It was a kind of aloneness, the same indomitable quality that had taken him from slopping hogs to playing with $100,-000 option deals within a few years.

As they pulled into the long driveway for Ridgeley, while they were still far from the big house, Shelby Kelsey stopped the car and turned off the motor and the lights. He turned to Alexandra. "Alex," he said, "in all my life, I have never known a woman like you. When I think of where I came from, I wonder how much longer you'll put up with me." Alex tried to interrupt him, but he kept on talking. "I'm not a gigolo, Alex. I'm not going to come to you like that. I just hope you'll wait a little while before you decide I'm not worth spending any time with." Alex could see his eyes in the moonlight moving slowly from side to side, as though to memorize her face.

"Nobody thinks you're a gigolo, Shelby. You've done a lot more with your life than I have with mine. I know that and Daddy knows that. You're just as good as any person I know and a hell of a lot better than most."

"I just want you to wait a little longer, Alex. That's all." He pulled her to him. He always kissed her on the driveway, before they got to the house, as if he were afraid that it would be disrespectful to kiss her in front of the house. She pushed her body against his on the car seat, but he drew away.

"You don't have to wait," she whispered.

"I do, Alex. You're still too precious for someone like me. But please have patience. Give me just a little while."

"I will, Shelby. You know that," Alex said, feeling tears come to her eyes.

She was still deeply touched when she entered the house. She walked through the living room, through the dining room, and through the hallway to the den, where her father was sitting in his robe, watching television. "Hi, Dad. Why are you up so late?"

"Oh, hi, Alex. I didn't hear you come in. They have this special show on about the OPEC decision."

"Oh?"

"OPEC is going to try to get thirty-eight dollars a barrel, and I think they're going to swing it."

"Is that bad?"

"It's very, very bad. I mean, you and I won't

starve—" it sounded funny, coming from her father—
"but it's damn bad for the country," William Hanrahan continued. "I'll have to talk to Peter tomorrow morning."

"All right, Daddy. I'm going to sleep."

She gave him a little peck and went up to her room. William Hanrahan continued to watch television. Martin Agronsky and a group of experts had been hurriedly gathered for the late-night talk show. The only person Hanrahan recognized was Claire Beaton, the well-dressed Cabinet member.

"Ms. Beaton, in the overall scheme of things, will this seriously affect the American way of life?" Agronsky asked in his sonorous voice.

Claire Beaton frowned and answered firmly. "Absolutely, Mr. Agronsky. We're already running at the highest inflation level of this century. Everything that pushes up the rate of inflation hurts."

"But really, Miss Beaton, won't it just mean using the car less frequently?" Agronsky asked. "Things like that?"

"That is only one aspect of it," Claire said. "Almost everything we eat, drink, wear or use requires some oil in its preparation. All these will get more expensive. Food especially—and the price of food is already high. The worst thing will be if we don't fight inflation here at home by keeping a tighter rein on how much money is in circulation."

"Doesn't that place you somewhat at odds with George McConger, the Chairman of the Federal Reserve? Isn't it his policy to create as much money as possible?" Agronsky asked with a smile.

"It might," Claire said firmly. "But this is an open administration. If we have an opinion, we're allowed to express it. And I am saying that this whole thing, with McConger printing money like an express train and the OPEC countries raising the price of oil— well, it could just get out of hand. It's like starting to roll a snowball down a mountain covered with snow. You don't know how big it's going to be when it hits the bottom. It could be as big as the mountain."

William Hanrahan dozed off into a dream. In the

dream, there was a snowball of dollars rolling down from Washington and crushing his Ridgeley estate, killing both him and Alexandra. He awoke from his dream as the station was signing off. He was covered with sweat and trembling.

In Park Ridge, a residential suburb of Chicago, Jim Adams and his wife, Laurie, were getting up as the morning news was beginning on the *Today Show*. The announcer was saying, as a graph rose steeply on a chart behind him, "Last night brought more bad news to Americans already rolling with the punches of inflation. The OPEC countries announced that they were raising the price of oil by almost one hundred percent, from twenty dollars a barrel to thirty-eight. Government and private economists agree that the move will have widespread ramifications in the American economy."

Jim Adams jumped out of bed and snapped off the TV. His bare, heavily muscled chest was running to fat.

He looked over at his wife, still lying in bed. "See? I knew it was a good idea for us to get that Chevette instead of the Impala. Gas is gonna cost a fortune." After five years of marriage, he was still in love with her baby-doll face.

"I guess you're right," Laurie said with a yawn. "Do you have time for breakfast?"

"Just some coffee and bacon, honey."

"I wish you'd stop eating bacon, Jim. You know it's nothing but fat and grease." Besides, Laurie said to herself, it's so damn expensive.

"I know, honey, but I'm not like a man with a desk job. I burn up those calories. I can still keep up with most of the kids on my varsity team."

"How're those kids treating you these days?"

"The boys I coach on the football team are still good kids. They try hard and they really care. But the kids in my regular gym classes are so damn insolent, I can't hardly stand it," Jim said.

"Well, I guess that's just how kids are these days," Laurie said, as she headed for the kitchen.

"Maybe so," Jim said, "but our baby's not gonna be like that, she's gonna have some respect."

"She's only six months old," Laurie said. 'She's got a while yet before she has to learn about respect."

A few minutes later they were sitting face to face in the breakfast nook.

"I think it's the inflation that's got those kids acting like this. They don't think about anything but money," Jim said, pushing a slice of bacon into his mouth.

"Could be," Laurie said. "The folks at the lab talk about money all the time too." Laurie worked as a lab technician in downtown Chicago.

"I think about it all the time too," Jim said as he picked up another slice of bacon. "It used to be sex. Now it's money."

"I know you do," Laurie said. "I wish you wouldn't worry so much." In fact, Laurie herself worried about it constantly.

"Well, if someone had told me ten years ago, when we graduated from college, that I would be making thirty thousand dollars a year teaching school, I would have expected to be in Fat City. Instead, we're just barely keeping our heads above water."

"Oh, come on, Jim," Laurie said. "It's not as bad as that."

"Maybe you're right," Jim agreed, drinking his Max-Pax coffee. "But it's damn lucky we bought this house two years ago for a hundred thousand. Because a house just like it down the block sold for a hundred and forty thousand last month."

"Wow, that's really something. I guess that was a lucky move."

"It really was," Jim said. "That's gonna save us in this inflation. This house keeps getting more and more valuable. That's why our taxes went up."

"We've got to pay the doctor's bills for Marie's flu," Laurie said.

"Christ, those doctors! They really know how to get money out of you," Jim said bitterly. "They sure look after number one."

He looked so angry that Laurie didn't ask him for more grocery money as she had planned. Prices at the

Safeway were getting out of sight. She would ask him tomorrow.

"I guess this oil increase means it's gonna cost more to heat the house this winter," Laurie said. "I'm glad you put in that insulation."

"It's people like us, the little people, who are getting screwed. Poor people get welfare and rich people just keep getting richer," Jim said, as if he hadn't heard Laurie. "It really makes me mad. Sometimes I think the only one who's talking sense is Whitelaw."

"He scares me, Jim. He gets people so worked up."

"Well, maybe they should get worked up," Jim said. "I mean it's the people like you and me, who go out and work their tails off, who're getting it in the neck. And with this new oil thing, I don't know if we'll be able to go on a vacation this Christmas."

"You know I don't care about that," Laurie said. "I'm just as happy here at home with you and the baby. I like Christmases in our own house." She was trying to calm Jim down. He got so jacked up about the inflation.

"Well, I care," Jim said, eating the last of his breakfast. "I want to be able to take you somewhere nice."

"Don't you worry about it," Laurie said. "Being here with you is nice." She put her hand on his arm.

"I know how hard you work and scrimp and save," Jim said. "You don't think I know, but I do. And I do without a lot of stuff too. It doesn't seem right that we should have to do without when I make thirty thousand and you're bringing home money too."

Laurie sighed. "I guess money's just not the same as it was when we were growing up."

"I guess not," Jim said. He pushed himself away from the table. "I better be running along. You be good, sweetie." Jim gave Laurie a swift kiss on her lips.

"I will be. You try not to worry so much," Laurie said.

She watched Jim drive down the street, where all the houses looked the same. The whole money thing was starting to get her down. She had been scrimping all her life, and she was still scrimping.

Laurie tried to look on the brighter side. She and Jim and the baby were healthy. All of them looked fit. She might still have passed as the college cheerleader she was when Jim, who had been varsity football center at West Virginia Wesleyan, had met her. She guessed that was what middle-class life was like these days—a lot of scrimping. But Laurie had been born to poverty and she meant to stay middle class for the rest of her life, even if it took a life of scrimping and saving. She had sworn that her baby would never go hungry—nor her husband, come to that.

Hal Burton sat in clear, warm sunshine in the Loggia of the Beverly Hills Hotel waiting for the woman across from him to order her lunch. She was a nervous, somewhat aggressive redhead, with hazel eyes that were quick and intelligent. Hal Burton, who at fifty-eight was short and overweight, knew that his guest, Joan Bellamy, was the most attractive writer he had ever known. Not that he had known that many female writers.

"The spinach salad," Joan Bellamy said.

The waiter wrote it down. "And you, Mr. Burton?"

"The steak with Béarnaise sauce, very rare," Burton said. "Good for my hangover. And we'd like a carafe of red wine, if that's all right with you, Joan," he added as he handed his menu to the waiter.

"I've been a fan of yours for a long time, Joan," Burton continued. *"Beyond the Pass Line* is my favorite book."

"That's very kind of you," Joan said. Her fair skin flushed slightly. "I've followed your movies for a long time. I have a theory that what really counts in a movie is more the producer than the director, and I've seen your signature in a lot of movies."

"Thank you. I didn't know you were a movie fan."

"I'm not really, but I watch TV. And a lot of your movies are showing up on TV now," Joan said.

The Loggia was just outside the Polo Lounge, and Hal Burton could see at least two studio executives who owed him big favors. He also saw Shecky Greene having a solitary lunch. "Did you know I got my start in TV?"

"No. I didn't."

"I won't bore you with the story," Hal said.

"That's silly. We're here to talk about my writing the screenplay for a movie based on your life, so I certainly ought to know how you got your start."

Hal picked up a salt stick from the bread tray and toyed with it. "I came to Hollywood right after I got out of the army in 1946. I had done some aerial photography and I wanted to get into pictures, like everybody else. I played around a lot. But I was ambitious too. So I went around from one studio to another and finally at one place I got to be an assistant producer, which is very much like a delivery boy."

Joan Bellamy looked at him intently. Her gaze was unusually penetrating. Burton felt slightly self-conscious, but he went on. "The movie wasn't that big a deal, as pictures go, and it never made much money. But I was so friendly to everybody on the lot, I felt like a goddamn politician. And it looked like my politics didn't work, at first, because I lost the job when the picture was finished and I didn't get another one right away. But that was wrong. I had made some good friends."

"You have a lot of friends now," Joan said.

Hal Burton laughed like a steam engine letting out excess pressure. "Now, sure. After I've done forty-five pictures I can have any friend I want. But then it was a helluva lot different." The waiter brought the wine. Burton poured and lifted his glass. "Well, here's to a great screenplay," he said with a smile.

Joan Bellamy lifted her glass and drank. "Tell me about the friends."

An elderly man was being led in by two young blondes in jean suits. Burton remembered when that man had been the western star to beat all western stars. "Friends who'll do something to help you are damn rare when you're getting started. But after that first picture, I had one friend who got me a job with the first TV station in L.A."

Burton looked around the room. It was a habit he had gotten into and couldn't break. He had to see if there was anyone around worth being nice to.

"There wasn't much good television on in the afternoons. And I used to see all these kids riding around in cars with nice clothes. And I figured they had money to spend and somebody could get to them with the right kind of show. Something simple—just dancing and music. So I went to the guy who owned the station with an idea. I came out of there with a deal to write, produce, direct and generally create *Sock Hop*."

Joan Bellamy looked genuinely surprised. "You invented *Sock Hop?*"

Burton nodded and laughed. "That show made more money for the station than any other show they had. In six months I was doing five shows just like it for different stations in Southern California. I was doing it all by myself. Then I turned it over to a company."

The waiter appeared with Joan's spinach salad and Burton's steak. He cut into it and saw that it was suitably rare before he put Béarnaise sauce on it. Then he took a big bite and made a satisfied face.

"People thought I knew the way to reach the teen market. The studio I had been a flunky for offered me just about anything on earth to make a movie to reach the teen market for them. So I said I'd do it, but I didn't know how."

Burton paused to chew. "Then one day I was driving along the Pacific Coast Highway thinking what a crazy town this is. People give you money to do something you don't even know how to do. Behind me there were all these guys on fancy motorcycles, and off on the beach there were all these girls in bikinis. That was how I thought up the beach-and-cycle movies. The first one I did was *Chrome on the Beach*. It came in at under a million and grossed fourteen million. After that, I took off like a rocket."

Joan Bellamy was hardly eating. All her attention was focused on Hal Burton.

"Well, I made a bunch of those moneymakers. Then for a while, I didn't do anything. Sally and I traveled quite a lot, and that's when we had our children, all three of them pretty close together."

"When did you get the idea for *The Guru?*" Joan asked.

"That was right after our daughter was born. It was the early sixties, and I could see that there was a new kind of kid growing up. They had long hair and they smoked dope. They hated the establishment, but they went to the movies a lot."

A woman Burton knew slightly came by and kissed him on the cheek. She was a friend of his wife's and she was wearing a diamond as big as a postage stamp.

"So I got this idea for a picture about a college kid who dropped out of school, joined the army, then deserted in Indochina to follow a Buddhist holy man. Then he goes back to his small home town and beats the hell out of the racist sheriff and all the other bad guys with the Kung-Fu crap he learned in the Orient. That was my biggest picture until *Seven Soft Sonatas*. You know, *Sonatas* is still playing at a theater in Madison, Wisconsin. It's been playing off and on there for over fifteen years."

"Was that when they put your picture on the cover of *Newsweek?*" Joan asked.

"Right," Burton said. "But I haven't done much since then, truth to tell. I spent a lot of time with my kids, and I think it paid off, because now they're all good students in college and grad school, not bums like a lot of other people's kids. Sally and I didn't spoil them."

"And now you want to tell another story," Joan prompted.

"Right," Burton answered. "I've been wanting to for a long time. When I read *Beyond the Pass Line,* I knew you were the woman to write it. You can see the same crap going on that I see. It'll be a story about this town, about this crazy business, about how there's so little going on underneath all the mink coats and Rolls-Royces. I know you see that. I could tell."

"That doesn't sound like your usual moneymaking kind of picture. I mean, it isn't that upbeat."

"These days, a picture doesn't have to be happy to

make a lot of money. I want it to be something like that—about the emptiness of life here, how there aren't any real values, how everything's just shadow. Like *Taxi Driver* and *Day of the Locust*. I know there've been lots of movies debunking Hollywood, but they all wind up making it look even more glamorous. I want this one to show the studio people wanting to kill each other."

Burton finished off the last of his steak and started on his french fries. "And I'll tell you something, Joan. It doesn't have to make money. I don't care. I've got enough money. I want it to tell a story. I've got plenty of pictures still showing that make money. I've got land, stocks, money in the bank. I want to tell my story now. I'm entitled. You did it in a book, and now I want you to help me do it in a movie."

Joan abruptly changed the subject. "Have you been following the economic news?" she asked.

"Not closely. Of course, I have to see how the films are doing." Burton was surprised at Joan's question. "I didn't know you were interested in that sort of thing."

"What sort of thing?" Joan asked.

"Statistics. Stocks and bonds," Burton said.

Joan Bellamy laughed. "It's not just statistics and stocks and bonds, Hal. What's going on now is going to change people's lives. We're about to see an incredible national upheaval, and it's going to be terrible here."

"What are you talking about?" Burton said. He was genuinely puzzled.

"People are going to think that the whole damn country is falling apart. They're going to lose their whole grip on reality because one aspect of reality will be changing so fast. When people find out that money doesn't mean what it used to mean, they're going to be frantic. And here, where people are always living on sort of loose terms with reality, people are going to be the most desperate of all. I mean, the whole place is going to come apart. Hollywood is never that tightly stuck together, and with the value of money declining, it's going to come unglued."

"What's the basic problem?" asked Burton.

"Inflation," said Joan.

"I hadn't realized that inflation was so bad."

"It isn't yet. But look. What holds this place together is money. People come here and live this crazy life to get money. When they find out that money doesn't mean the same thing any more, there's gonna be lots of trouble."

"Well, maybe," Burton said. "But I don't see what that has to do with the movie project directly, although I appreciate the sociology lesson."

The old man with the two young blondes had risen to leave. "There goes a fellow who'll die happy," Burton said. He turned back to Joan. "I mean, maybe I'm dumb, but I don't see what you're getting at."

"Well, you've read my book, so you know something about my life, right?"

"Right," Burton said.

"Well, I've seen your movies. I didn't know they were all yours when I saw them, but I know that now. And your story is already out there."

"I still don't get it," Burton said. He was becoming annoyed. Was Joan Bellamy putting him on?

"It's all there, your whole life, Hal. The frustrated kid envying the motorcyclists; the desire to escape; then wanting to come back and destroy the people who've been mean to you. And it's great stuff. You're the American Everyman. It's the national success story. Hal Burton's story is the national story."

Burton sat there dumbfounded. Joan Bellamy was right. He had been telling his own story all along. "Maybe that's what it means to produce in this business. Maybe you're always talking about yourself." Jesus, he thought to himself, this was one hell of a smart woman sitting across the table.

"But the story isn't finished," Joan said. "Your story isn't finished, and the national story isn't finished."

"What's next?" Burton asked.

"That's why I was talking about inflation," Joan said. "That will be the next phase. That's the phase when we realize that the values we've built our whole civilization on are falling apart."

"What happens then?" Burton asked. He felt like a student at the feet of a great teacher.

"I don't know, Hal. But it'll be worse than the Depression, because life now is lived so much faster, and people have come to expect so much. They won't sit still for it like they did during the Depression. They won't accept it."

Burton suddenly felt uneasy. First he felt faint and then he had a chill. Sweat broke out on his forehead. What Joan Bellamy was saying had struck a nerve. There was a great emptiness in his life, too, that he had filled with money and material things. What would happen to him if what Joan Bellamy was talking about came true? What would happen to Sally and to their children?

"What are we supposed to do?" asked Burton.

"I don't know. I think maybe we kill ourselves. This may be the last chapter coming up."

# 3

CLAIRE Beaton was prepared to put on the performance of her life at the EISG meeting. She came through the double glass doors to her office like a tigress.

"Hello, Myrna," she said to her secretary. "Any messages?"

Myrna looked uncomfortable as she handed Claire a sheaf of yellow notes. "You'd better read the top one. It's from Donnelly. The EISG meeting has been canceled for today."

"Canceled?" Claire asked in astonishment. "Are you sure?" This was exactly the time the EISG should be meeting—a crucial time for the important decisions that had to be made.

"Yes. Donnelly said the President was going to meet with Greenberg, Ratner, McConger and Hanrahan this morning, and that you'd be briefed on their meeting this afternoon."

Claire flushed a deep red. She slammed down her fist on her secretary's desk. "I'm not going to take this crap. Damn it to hell! I'm just not going to take it." Myrna looked terrified. "Stop looking scared, Myrna. It's not your fault. I'm supposed to be part of this great battle against inflation. That's what they brought me down here for. But when the honchos get together, I'm out on the street with the secretaries. I'm not all that goddamn necessary."

She looked out the window onto 18th Street, where a stream of secretaries was heading into the steel-and-glass office buildings on M Street and the denim-covered minions of William Whitelaw were handing out flyers.

"I'm sure it's nothing personal," Myrna Lewis said.

"I'm sure it isn't too," Claire said. "No. I'm not sure. Maybe it is something personal. I don't know what goes through their heads. But it's crazy. I have good advice for them. They're ignoring it. They're just turning down a helping hand."

"Well, maybe they'll figure it out," Myrna Lewis said.

"I doubt it," Claire said. "I mean they must all know that I'm the one who built the model on runaway inflation. I thought that was why they brought me down here. Now that runaway inflation has started, why aren't they listening to me?"

Claire was furious. She wondered, not for the first time, if maybe she had been recruited because of her father. He was considered one of the world's greatest scientists, a physicist in a class with John von Neumann. But Claire had done plenty on her own.

"I wonder if the President even remembers that work I did," Claire mused. She had worked for two years in New Haven on an economic model of what would happen if, after a sudden shock to the Western economy, the industrialized countries responded by printing more money. It was a model made to order for what was happening now.

That work had taken a lot of Claire's time. There were a million things—literally, a million—to feed into the computer. But the results had been worth the effort. Claire had found that if the government tried to compensate for inflation by printing more money, absolutely nothing could stop inflation from rising geometrically to a level that approached infinity. There were simply no barriers in the economic system to prevent it.

The report had created a mild sensation for a while. It had even been translated into Chinese. Then it had been overshadowed by more qualified views. It was, after all, a "worst case" scenario—the worst that could possibly happen. Surely we lived in a country too healthy to let it take place.

But that was before McConger became Chairman of the Federal Reserve Board. Now Claire was watching her worst predictions begin to unfold before her eyes.

The "worst case" was coming true.

The meeting to which Claire had not been invited began promptly, as usual with the President.

Harry Ratner was sitting in an oval room, on a couch next to a big gray dog who was licking his hand. If the dog had not been the President's weimaraner, Freda, and if the President had not been sitting on the other side of Freda, Harry Ratner would not have let the dog lick his hand.

The President said, "See, Harry, you're not such a bad guy. Freda likes you and she's a great judge of character." So Harry let the dog continue to lick his hand.

It was the only way he was scoring points.

George McConger, his gnarled, sinewy neck joining his body to a head that looked like an Old Testament prophet's, had his bony hand on the President's knee, one finger outstretched. His glowing eyes were locked with the President's as though to set them ablaze with fervor.

"This must not be viewed as a disaster, Mr. President," McConger said. "It's a historic opportunity, perhaps the greatest challenge of your career in public life. The country is angry and upset about what the Arabs have done. They're looking for a brave new policy."

The President's eyes were steady on McConger's. "The people are always looking for something new, George. But for Christ's sweet sake, I need something new that'll work. I've been doing what you wanted me to do, and I've been getting my ass handed to me in a sling."

Peter Hanrahan cleared his throat. "That's exactly right. I wish we had brought Claire into this meeting. She's done the definitive study of what happens when we react to a big oil price increase by creating more money. And I'll tell you this: It doesn't look good."

The door to the Oval Office opened. Freda leaped across the room, and jumped up on Milt Greenberg, knocking him against the door.

"Come here, Freda," the President said, pointing. "Get up on the couch." The dog made a few attempts to lick Greenberg's face, then jumped back on the couch between the President and Ratner, her tail wagging furiously.

"I don't know why Freda likes you and Ratner so much," the President said to Greenberg. "You must be part dog."

"Well, I'm sure I don't know which part," Greenberg said, straightening his clothes. "I've arranged for you to appear in the press office in fifteen minutes to make a statement."

"That's just great, Milton," the President said. "Thanks a lot. What the hell am I supposed to say?"

"Mr. President," Greenberg said drily, "you were the one who told me to ask for the time."

"I know, I know," the President said. "Don't remind me. It's such a fucking mess."

"There is only one thing you can do, Mr. President," Ratner said. "You've got to fight this inflation tooth

and nail. You've got to cut down on the money supply
and cut the deficit. You've got to raise the taxes on
gasoline. There's no other way to go except the inflation route, and this time it could really be bad. I've
seen Claire's study too. It's frightening and it's true."
He turned to McConger. "George, I know you have the
good of the country at heart, but we've got to stop
throwing so much money around. We've *got* to. Otherwise, inflation is going to kill us."

McConger replied like a zealot. "It may kill *your*
friends, Harry, but it won't kill mine. If we create more
money, the little people will have more money to buy
gasoline with. Interest rates will come down so people
can buy new houses. It may be true that banks and the
rich won't make as much money. But there are a lot of
people who think that we've made policies aimed at
protecting the rich too long as it is." His eyes were on
fire.

"I'll tell you something else, Mr. President,"
McConger continued, "you need the voice of the little
people on your side. In the White House *and* in Congress."

"Very subtle, George," the President said sar-
castically. "I already know how popular you are in the
Midwest. But for Christ's sake, George, we're talking
about a potential horror show if we don't start cutting
back on this money creation. That is the crux of the
matter. At some point I've got to stop doing things just
to get the votes of your friends."

"Mr. President," McConger said, "my plans work.
That's why, in their hearts, people trust me and my
ideas. They know that it can't be wrong for people to
have more money. They know I'm being hamstrung
by the banks and the big multinational companies.
They know that."

The President felt the full power of McConger's
eyes. It was no wonder he had such a following. He
was probably one of the few men in politics who believed what he was saying. And the message came out
clean and pure, cutting through the objections of those
who said it was wrong. It came out clean and pure because it was being said by a man who believed it with

every fiber of his being. Maybe, the President thought, maybe he'd better stick with George McConger for a little while longer and see how things came out. Surely a man of such burning conviction couldn't be wrong.

"George, I know you believe in what you're saying," Hanrahan argued, "but it just doesn't work that way. If we create more money, there'll be higher interest rates, then a recession, if not something worse, and the little people will suffer more than anyone. You're dead wrong if you think the rich are going to suffer. Believe me, George, the rich can take care of themselves."

McConger's smile was tolerant. "Peter, I'm not trying to hurt rich people. I'm trying to help people of all kinds. If we can get more money into the right people's pockets, we'll be all set. It may take some regulation of interest rates and prices, but the money will reach the right hands eventually."

"We're not going to have controls, George, that's for damn sure. Controls don't work," the President said.

"Look at it from this standpoint, Mr. President," McConger said. "If we keep doing what we've been doing, people will complain. But think how many more people are going to complain if we cut back on government spending and raise taxes at the same time that they'll be paying a helluva lot more for heating oil and gasoline."

Ratner and Hanrahan had looks of utter resignation on their faces. It was like struggling with a messiah. Donnelly, who hadn't spoken for a while, though he had listened carefully, chimed in. "There's something to that, Mr. President. I think George has got something there. It's better to deal with a snake you know than a snake who's a stranger. I guess that's the sad truth." He shot a look at McConger. "Not that I'm calling anyone a snake, George," he said evenly.

"That's OK, Gene," McConger said. "We've got homilies in North Dakota, like you've got 'em in Texas. We're just folks like anyone else. I guess we've got a few snakes in North Dakota, too."

The President had made up his mind. "Cancel that appearance before the press corps, Milt. I don't have anything new to tell them. Say we had a thorough review and all that crap. Hell, you know what to say. But don't let anyone think we're just sitting around jerking off, OK?"

"Mr. President, does this mean that we're just going to keep on doing the same thing?" Hanrahan asked. "We're looking at thirty-five percent inflation right now."

"It means," the President said, an edge in his voice, "that I haven't made up my mind." Then his tone softened. "There are obviously arguments on both sides, Peter. If what we're doing turns out to be wrong, we'll change it. This meeting is over."

Hanrahan and Ratner were the last to leave the room. "Jesus, Harry, what the hell are we gonna do?" Hanrahan was shaking his head.

"One day the President will know that McConger's giving him the worst advice since Haldeman told Nixon to put in a tape recorder. Then he'll do the right thing. But until then, it's gonna be a long ride, all downhill."

The two blue Chevrolets, both rented cars, swept up Route 1 from Monterey toward San Francisco. They observed the speed limit exactly. It would not have looked good to get a speeding ticket. Four men sat in each car. One of them was older than the others by several decades.

The road ran close to the ocean for a while, passing the giant power plant just north of Monterey, then went inland between banks of pine trees and rocks. Then the road swerved; suddenly on the left the light-gray mirror of the sea broke into a trillion pieces, rising and falling and crashing against the shore. It was a hot October day. The beaches were dotted with people.

Soon the two cars were coming into the suburbs of Santa Cruz, a coastal resort town about eighty miles south of San Francisco. The older man, who looked somewhat like a noble Douglas Fairbanks, Jr., said to the man next to him on the back seat, "It might be nice to stop in Santa Cruz. You know, see the ocean, see a few people. Does Santa Cruz have a nice beach, Jimmie?"

The younger man said, "There won't be any TV cameras there."

"That's all right," the older man said.

So, where Route 1 whipped through the Victorian houses and fast-food places of Santa Cruz, the two cars pulled off the highway and wandered down Pacific Street and then onto Front Street and down some more streets until they came to a parking area for one of the city's beaches. As soon as the first car stopped, the older man jumped out of the back seat of the car and started walking briskly toward a sign that said "Twin Lakes State Beach." Six younger men, two from the first car and four from the second, followed. The four men from the second car wore denim coveralls, clean faces and big smiles.

Before the distinguished-looking older man reached the steps leading down to the beach, he was recognized. In the parking area and on the steps, faces turned to look at him. He stopped and bent over, removed his shoes and socks, and turned up the bottoms of his trousers. A small crowd had started to gather around him, and his two young assistants, their shoes still on, stayed close to him.

William Whitelaw walked straight down to the beach. The group of people followed him, growing steadily larger. When he was almost at the tideline, a young woman yelled out, "Give it to 'em, Bill!"

Another woman shouted, "Welcome to Santa Cruz!"

Whitelaw walked into the surf up to his ankles. The water felt cold and refreshing.

"Give 'em hell up in San Francisco, Bill," a teen-age boy on the beach shouted.

Whitelaw lifted his gaze from the water to the crowd. He had the look of a visionary, a prophet. "I will," he said simply.

Two lifeguards came up to Whitelaw and stood there awkwardly. One of them said, "Let us know if there's anything we can do for you, Governor. Anything at all."

The other lifeguard said, "This is Whitelaw country, Governor. We'd like you to know."

Whitelaw took the boy's hand and squeezed it.

"Thank you, son. I haven't come to Santa Cruz to make a speech, just to get my feet wet."

A man at the fringe of the crowd picked up the cue. "Give us a speech, Bill!"

Another man said, "Tell us what you're gonna tell 'em in San Francisco."

Whitelaw's large, handsome head bent toward the sand. Then he lifted it back up and looked at the crowd. "You all know what I stand for. You're the kind of people I stand for—honest, decent Americans who still think that God isn't a dirty word, that work and principles mean something. But I didn't come here to give a speech."

"What're we gonna do about the price of gasoline?" someone shouted.

Whitelaw squinted. "Well, that's a good question. How much does gas cost in this part of California? Two dollars a gallon?"

"Pretty near."

"Well, I'd just like to know, so's I can carry it around in my head, how many of you people can afford to pay two dollars a gallon for gasoline?"

Nobody spoke.

"I can't either. Why does it cost that much? What do you think?"

"The Arabs did it."

"They did part of it," Whitelaw said, "but only because we let them get away with it. They know they can kick us the hell around because we won't do a thing to stop them. You and I know that if the President doesn't."

The crowd was quiet now. They could sense that they were going to hear Bill Whitelaw at his best—it was coming.

"It's not all the Arabs, though," Whitelaw said. "Everything's sky-high—even stuff we grow right here at home. Now the Arabs didn't do that. You can't walk down a street in a big city without feeling scared to death, and the Arabs didn't do that. And your kids don't get a decent education and can't find good jobs, and the Arabs didn't do that.

"And rich people drive around in Mercedes sports

cars while decent, hardworking people can't afford to sit down to meat more than twice a week, and the Arabs didn't do that."

"Damn right," a woman shouted.

"Tell it like it is, Bill," a young girl joined in.

"We've got a bunch in Washington who don't know how to do a damn thing except feather their nests and make their own lives more comfortable while the rest of us want to kill ourselves when we go to the grocery store." Whitelaw paused, looked at the crowd. "And the Arabs didn't do that."

The crowd shifted back and forth in the sun. Whitelaw stepped into the water again. He got his feet wet and then turned once more to the crowd. "Truth is, we did it all to ourselves. We did it by letting our country, our wonderful country, fall into the hands of people who don't have any faith in anything, who don't know a damn thing about principles, who've forgotten that this is a nation founded under God."

The crowd was murmuring its agreement. "So we got what we deserved—a bunch of hogs swilling at the public trough and not giving a damn about the people who worked to make this country great."

"That's the God's truth, Governor," one of the lifeguards said solemnly.

"That's what I'm gonna say to the folks in San Francisco." Whitelaw turned and started walking back to the car.

"You've got my vote, Governor," a middle-aged man said.

"Mine, too," said another.

Without breaking his stride, Whitelaw said, "I thank you, but I'm not running for a damned thing. I'm just trying to help people see what's going on around them, and what they've got to do. I'm no politician. I just tell the truth."

By now, Whitelaw was back at the steps. He climbed them, brushed the sand off his feet and looked down into the faces of the crowd that had followed him. "Lots of people don't want to hear the truth, but I tell 'em anyway. I'm not looking for votes. I'm looking for a new America, an America that's safe for Christians."

"God bless you, Governor," the voice of an old man quavered.

"Thank you, sir," Whitelaw said and shook his hand. Then he shook a few more hands. He got into the car, his two assistants got into the car, and the four denim-clad men from the second car got into their car, still smiling broadly. They drove away, back up to Route 1 and toward San Francisco.

In the back of the first car, Whitelaw turned to Jimmie and said, "That won't hurt us a damn bit, and how long did it take? Fifteen minutes."

"It was a smart move, Governor," Jimmie said.

"You noticed how they responded when I talked about rich people making out like bandits during this inflation?" Whitelaw asked the young man in the front seat, next to the driver. "You notice that, Marvin?"

"Yes sir," Marvin said.

"We've got to get more of that kind of thing into my speeches. We're giving people something to be for. We've been doing that all along. Now let's give 'em something to hate. People like to hate. There's nothing wrong with it. Gets rid of their meanness. Let's get some more of that into the speeches," Whitelaw said as the cars sped up the coastal highway.

"I want to work in something about the cuff links incident, Governor. Could you tell us that again?" Marvin asked.

"First time I was in Congress, when I got so disgusted with getting the runaround everywhere, I asked to see President Eisenhower. But I only got as far as a special assistant to the President, and all he did was listen a few minutes and then give me a set of cuff links with the Presidential seal. And I didn't have any shirts with French cuffs! But the special assistant, he didn't let that bother him none."

"That's a great story," Marvin said. "Give me the one about getting your picture on the cover of *Life* once again."

"I'll tell it, Marvin, but I don't want it repeated in a speech. It just looks like bragging. But here's what it was. In 1944 in Tarawa the press had been following me around all over the Pacific. So one day I walked up to a group of photographers and I said, 'Cut it out. I'm not the only one. Every man in this outfit is a hero,' and that's when they put my picture on the cover of *Life* magazine. But let's talk about tonight. How many people gonna be at the stadium in Berkeley?"

"We're looking for thirty-five thousand," Jimmie said.

The car was now passing by the sheer cliffs that made Northern California so beautiful. For a while no one spoke. Whitelaw looked out the window at the water and the cliffs.

"That's nice," he said at last. "That's real friendly. Tell you what. Let's give 'em something to love first. And then, while they're chewing on that, let's give 'em something to hate."


"It's so goddamn ironic," Harry Ratner said to Peter Hanrahan as they walked down the hall of the Executive Office Building toward the White House. "The garage gave me an estimate of two hundred and fifteen dollars for a tune-up on my Plymouth. That was bad enough. But while I was waiting for the mechanics to figure out how much the traffic would bear, I heard two other fellows, a lawyer and an accountant, talking about how they had to raise their fees because of inflation. One was driving a Mercedes and the other had a Cadillac. And the worst part came when they bitched about how their increased taxes were just paying for bureaucrats like us to live it up."

"Not funny," Peter Hanrahan said. "Don't they know that the President froze all White House salaries to set an example for the rest of the country?"

"Maybe, maybe not," said Ratner. "But I sure as hell know it. I'm damn lucky that most of my payments are fixed and I have this White House car. I'm just about breaking even."

"It's tough," Hanrahan said. Neither man mentioned that it was, of course, far tougher on Ratner, a man of modest means who had always had to earn his own living, than it was on Hanrahan, whose assets before the current inflation approached a billion dollars.

"It's painful first. Then it's ironic," said Ratner. "I mean, if it gets unbearable I'll quit and get a job that'll pay enough for me and Betty to live decently. Meanwhile, while I'm preaching about how bad this inflation is gonna hurt everyone, it's hurting me. Something like an astronomer colliding with a meteor."

"Those guys at the garage were probably talking about the rest of the Civil Service. They've got their asses pretty well covered," Hanrahan said. "What is it they're getting now, weekly cost-of-living reviews?"

"Not quite weekly," Ratner said. "Quarterly."

"Still, this situation is ridiculous. It's the middle of October; gasoline is giving people heart attacks after they fill the tank. And when commodity prices come through at the retail level, there's gonna be big, big trouble."

"That's why this Cabinet meeting is so important," Ratner said. "We've somehow got to get the President out from under McConger's thumb. We must do it, Peter. We've got to stop that printing press or the whole country is going up in smoke."

"We will, Harry. I'm optimistic," Hanrahan said.

"I don't know how you can be so damn cheerful," said Ratner as they walked across West Executive Avenue in the chilly breeze.

Hanrahan was on the verge of telling Ratner that he'd be cheerful too if he had spent the night with a beautiful seventeen-year-old girl who worshiped every part of his body and hung on his every word although it was, matter of fact, getting to be a little bit boring. She was sensational in bed, but sometimes she made him feel more like a daddy than a lover. That, he knew, was part of the game. Still, it would be nice not to have to explain everything to her.

"Harry," Hanrahan said, patting his friend on the back, "sometimes you've got to laugh to keep yourself from crying."

Ratner smiled and Hanrahan continued, "But if you really want me to be sad, we'll talk about trade. The Europeans are saying that if we don't stop inflating,

they're going to put up barriers to dollar-capital in-
flows. They don't want us buying up their countries
with our worthless dollars."

"Can't blame 'em," Ratner said. "I'm surprised they
haven't put up the barriers already."

"I think that Europe will start inflating like we are
soon. The whole world is so small now that when
we've got big inflation here, the Europeans and the
Japanese can't really protect themselves against it.
The U.S. is such a large and essential part of the world
economy that when we go through something like this,
everyone's affected."

As Ratner and Hanrahan entered the West Wing of
the White House, they nearly collided with Claire
Beaton.

"Hello, Claire," said Hanrahan. "It's always a pleasure to see you."

"Hi, Harry. Hi, Pete. Thanks for getting me invited
this time."

"You didn't miss a thing," said Ratner, "as it turned
out."

"Even so," said Claire.

"We won't let it happen again," said Hanrahan.

When they entered the Cabinet Room, there were
only a scattering of people there: Jim Flynn, Tom
Ebersole, Frank Trout and a few others. Claire, Hanrahan and Ratner walked over to a corner near the
Rose Garden and continued talking.

"Does the President know how bad the trade thing
is?" asked Claire in a low voice.

"Let me put it this way," Hanrahan whispered.
"I've told the President, but I'm not sure he gives a
damn."

"Pretty soon," Claire said, "people will be wondering why a new Datsun costs ten thousand, and why
the cheapest bottle of French wine costs ten dollars."

"It has to happen," Ratner said. "If the Europeans
and the Japanese don't jack up their prices, they'll
have to devalue or do something else. They can't let
us buy up everything they've got with worthless dollars."

The room had become extremely quiet. That meant

that the President had come in. Claire turned around, and sure enough, there he was, teeth and all, shaking hands with the Cabinet members and the EISG as if he were campaigning among them, seeking their votes. She never failed to respond to a certain aura about him. Some Presidents were like that. Once when she was a student on vacation in New York, she had seen John Kennedy walk out of a French restaurant. A friend who was with her said that Kennedy "had lights in him." She wasn't sure that this President had lights in him, but he had a Presidential look about him, that was for sure.

Deferentially the people in the Cabinet Room moved toward their seats to get to them before the President got to his, which was at the middle of the table facing the Rose Garden. They were fairly skilled at that kind of thing, so the President found himself sitting down just as everyone else in the room had reached their seats. Then, like dancers in the prologue of a classic ballet, they all sat down at the same moment.

The President smiled, turning his famous head from left to right. He's like a hound trying to pick up the scent of the meeting, Claire thought. This one's going to be tough for you, Mr. President, she said to herself, because this time you can't smile your troubles away.

With a small wave of his left hand, the President motioned to Melvin Forbes, Secretary of Agriculture, who had just come out of the hospital after a bad car accident and whose neck was still in an elastic brace. "Glad to see you up and about, Mel. How's the neck?"

"It's getting better, Mr. President, but I've still got a long way to go. The doctors are working on it."

"That's good. Tell Shirley that if your collar makes things too difficult at home, we'll get some of those Navy nurses to come over and take care of all your problems." The President laughed.

Claire flinched, trying not to let it show. That was just the kind of joke she hated. She was the only woman there; the President should have been more considerate of her feelings. She also knew that by now she was a fool to expect it.

The President stopped chuckling and became serious just as everyone in the room except Claire stopped their chuckling. His eyes swept the room again, this time without a smile. This time he looks like a radar antenna, thought Claire.

"I had a little talk with Milt here just before the meeting." The President nodded toward Greenberg, who kept his eyes lowered. "And what he told me didn't sound too good. Now we've got to be like Mel's doctors and get this situation in hand. The Bureau of Labor Statistics figures for September on inflation and unemployment are going to be horrendous. We're looking at a ten percent rise in the Consumer Price Index for one month. Jesus, for one fucking month. Unemployment figures are starting to head up too. There are problems, especially in automobiles and construction. Something's got to be done."

At last, thought Claire. Maybe the time has come. Then she noticed something strange. Usually every seat around the Cabinet table was taken, and the seats along the walls, where she sat, were usually taken too. But today there was a conspicuously empty seat—almost directly across from the President, wedged in between where the Vice President and Secretary Donnelly were sitting. Who was absent? She couldn't think of anyone. Someone new must be coming to this meeting, Claire thought. She had an idea who it might be.

The President resumed. "As all of you know, we don't usually have this big a meeting, but today we've got a mighty big problem. So we've got the folks from EISG here, and we're going to have George McConger here too. He had a meeting with some other central bankers over a worldwide telephone hookup just before we began, but he'll be here any minute."

Gene Donnelly was astounded. How could the President do such a thing? Especially, how could the President allow George McConger to saunter casually into a meeting like this whenever he found the time? Donnelly decided that he was losing his touch with the President. Certainly he knew that he, Gene Donnelly, couldn't get away with anything like that. He put on his most ingratiating smile.

The President was still speaking. "It's getting to be a bigger national problem than crime in the streets, bigger than anything in my administration. They're calling us the government that's fiddling while America burns. We've got to do something."

"Mr. President, I think you are exactly right," Harry Ratner said. "I know that when George McConger gets here, he's not going to agree with me, but I believe that what this government is doing now is not 'nothing'—it's worse than nothing. We're not neglecting the patient, we're killing him."

"Now just what are you talking about here, Harry?" the President asked.

"Mr. President, I'm talking about what we did after the last oil price increase, and what I hope we're going to stop doing." Harry Ratner paused for a moment. "You don't put out a fire by dousing it with gasoline. And that's what the Federal Reserve is doing: dousing the fire with gasoline. Remember the Vietnam War, when those monks would douse themselves with gasoline and then light up? That's what's starting to happen to this whole country."

"If I might interrupt for a moment, Mr. President—Harry—" It was Hanrahan speaking. "We're talking about something which is getting to be bigger than America. Our own inflation is spreading to the rest of the industrialized world."

"That's terrible news, of course, Peter," the President said, "but I'm much more concerned about what happens here."

"Mr. President, what I guess I didn't explain very well is that if this inflation starts spreading all over the world, it'll be that much harder to stop it at any given place, including here."

As the President was thoughtfully stroking his chin, the door to the Cabinet Room opened and George McConger, looking thin but happy—like Torquemada on his birthday, Claire Beaton thought—walked into the room. The President positively beamed. "Welcome to the intensive care unit, George," the President said. "We're talking about Topic A."

Harry Ratner felt a twinge of nostalgia. He had been an aide on the staff of the Council of Economic Advisers under Richard Nixon. In the last of those days, Watergate had been referred to as "Topic A." He hoped this President would handle his Topic A better.

"Don't everybody look so gloomy," McConger said as he sat down. "Having a lot of money floating around is a hell of a lot better than not having enough."

Claire Beaton picked up the challenge. "That's exactly wrong, Mr. McConger. There can be such a thing as too little money. There was too little money floating around in 1931. But we haven't had that problem for a long time, and we're not likely to have it again. We have too much money floating around, and we're drowning in it."

George McConger was not the slightest bit fazed by the likes of Claire Beaton. He took his pipe out of his brown tweed suit and held it up in front of him. "I'm not an economist, Miss Beaton," he said with a fatherly air, "but I know something about money. I know that there's such a thing as not having enough of it, even though you may not agree. When I was a young man during the Depression there were plenty of people in this country, there are plenty of people right now who don't have enough money. That's a fact. There's just not enough money around for a lot of the people in this country and that's the problem."

The President looked unimpressed. "That sounds good, George. But what about this inflation? What're we gonna do about it?"

For the President, McConger had a special beatific look of kindness, humility and authority all rolled up into one.

"Mr. President, the problem is not really inflation. The problem is that some people have too much money and some people don't have enough. Now I'm not one of those people who says soak the rich and give the money to the poor. I say spread the money around so that everybody has enough. That's the solution to inflation. It doesn't matter what things cost as long as people have enough money to pay for them. We can't go from house to house giving away money, but the Federal Reserve can spread money out over the system through the banks so that it's almost the same thing."

Harry Ratner was afraid he was going to have a coronary. That was the most dangerous economic nonsense he had ever heard. For a minute he was so stunned he couldn't speak. Peter Hanrahan didn't have that problem. "Mr. President, I could hardly disagree with Chairman McConger more. The problem is that there is too much money out there. It's true that we have too many poor people in this country, but we don't help them by inflating the price of everything out of sight."

"Well, it's hardly a problem that someone of your background would understand, any more than I would understand how to play polo." McConger gave Hanrahan a patronizing smile.

"Look, it hasn't a goddamn thing to do with Peter's background or with your memories of the Depression, Mr. McConger." Claire Beaton was livid. "Except for a few speculators, you aren't making people better off by this kind of thing. You're making them worse off." Claire turned imploringly to the President. "Mr. President, may I use an example from my economics class? I think it will illuminate what we're talking about.

"We started off with one hundred apples and one hundred dollars. The OPEC countries took away fifty of our apples but left us with the hundred dollars. That meant that the apples cost us two dollars each instead of one dollar each. But meanwhile, someone like Mr. McConger printed up another three hundred dollars. That means that now the same apples are going to cost eight dollars each. The apples are exactly the same, except that there are fewer of them. They aren't any better or any worse. They just cost more. And we don't have any more of them because we have more money. We just have to pay more money and each piece of that money is worth less."

The President looked slightly annoyed. He rubbed his eyes with his fists and said, "I think I get it, Claire. Just don't make it so complicated next time."

Everyone in the room laughed except Claire.

"Seriously, Claire, I really do understand the things you and Harry and Pete have been telling me. And they make sense. But what George is telling me makes sense too. I don't know if you can understand that, because you're so wedded to your ideas, but sometimes there are a few other good ideas around. That's the hardest goddamned part of my job—sorting out ideas when there are a few good options. If it were a clearcut choice of right or wrong, I think I could manage it OK."

Hanrahan said, "I think it is a clearcut choice of right or wrong. Whatever the political merits of George's plan, it's wrong."

The President smiled his flashiest smile. "But, Peter, you don't have to worry about the political considerations. I do. It means something, it means a great deal, that there are a lot of people out there who believe with all their hearts that George's ideas make terrific sense. They may not be in Claire's economics class, but they mean something nevertheless. I couldn't be President, I can't be President, without taking into account the political considerations."

McConger's eyes lit up like the fire in a steam locomotive. He stared raptly at the President. "I don't want you to do what I'm suggesting because of the political considerations. I want you to do it because you think it is right," he said, enunciating every word carefully. "The people who don't agree with me are smart people. But I believe that if a person doesn't have enough money, the solution to the problem is to give the person more money. That holds good whether it has political merit or not."

The President looked over at McConger. "George, let's not kid ourselves. The fact that you can turn out a lot of important people for your ideas has some bearing on life. You know that and I know that. Everybody knows that. The trouble is that I've got to do something pretty soon to stop this inflation or else people are going to be after my ass no matter what you do to help me."

"I don't think so, Mr. President. I think people can adjust to a rising level of prices as long as they have a constantly rising level of income. If we don't give them more money, a lot of people will have incomes rising much less rapidly than prices. And after a while, everything starts falling apart. Taxes alone are going to be enormous."

The President looked at Ratner. "I don't know if we can ask people to pay taxes when they're already swamped by inflation."

"They're going to have to do it some time," Claire said. "It might as well be now. The longer you wait, the more it's going to hurt."

McConger slapped the table with the flat of his hand. "That's exactly it, Mr. President. Why does the government have to hurt people? Why can't we have a policy that says that we're going to help people? This country has been making the little people suffer to protect the bondholders far too long. Why don't we turn the whole proposition right side up?" McConger seemed to be projecting the entire force of his personality through his eyes to the President as he spoke.

The President looked at George McConger calmly. "It's always a pleasure to see a true believer," he said somewhat sardonically. But he knew that McConger could get people a lot more fired up than Claire Beaton could with her talk about fruit.

Across the table, Gene Donnelly's shrewd blue eyes were darting from person to person. He could sense the power ebbing and flowing in the room. He could see it shifting steadily toward McConger, through McConger's zeal and McConger's power with the voters. It was time for Donnelly to make his move. "Maybe," he said with a slow Texas drawl, "we should look on this as an image problem. Instead of making new statements about inflation, why don't we say we're going to get money to the people who need it?"

The President gave Donnelly a scathing look and

said, "That sounds like McGovern's idea of giving a thousand dollars to every family." He paused for a moment. "Let's go around the table and set out our views in an orderly way."

Briefly, one by one, they did so. Almost without qualification those present opposed McConger and supported Claire. Until Donnelly's turn came. Donnelly, as a teacher had once told him, had some sixth sense. McConger was obviously winning with the President, or certainly not losing. He did not want to be on the losing side. "Mr. President, I say that we listen to what Chairman McConger is saying. I think that after a while people will realize that they have more money in their pockets and they'll feel better about life in general—even if they can't buy more. And maybe some of it will go to people who didn't have it before."

Claire Beaton was stunned. She had never seen such a whore. But she repressed her anger, believing that the great weight of the other opinions would bring the President out on the right side. The President, she thought, just couldn't goof this time. It was too clearcut.

McConger did not choose to elaborate when his turn came. He said that the President already knew very well how he felt, and it would be pointless to review his position. "Of course the Federal Reserve is an independent instrumentality, but I will follow the dictates of the President on this as in all matters."

"This is going to hurt your feelings," the President said to the group, "but I'm not really happy with any of the alternatives I see in front of me. George, I'll tell you frankly, I'm very dubious about whether your ideas can work. I'm sorry, but that's the way it is. But I'm also not sure I can suddenly call for austerity while people are worried to death about prices."

The President paused. "I don't know what the hell to do except what we're doing. Sometimes I wish to Christ that my dog could talk. She might be able to give me some good advice." No one in the room said a thing. No one could remember seeing the President in such an insulting mood. "OK, it'll just be steady as she goes. And let's not have any of you people bleating to the press that I don't know anything about economics, folks, I'm getting a little sick of all the leaks. If you have something to tell me, say it to my face."

The President got up and walked out of the Cabinet Room. In a minute he was being greeted in the Oval Office by his dog, who jumped up on him and tried to lick his face. The President patted the dog and said, "Fuck 'em all, Freda. Not a goddamn one of them knows a way out of this that won't cost me my ass. Goddamn those assholes. I think I'll make you Secretary of the Treasury so at least you can't leak anything, except on the floor."

Back in the Cabinet Room, people were leaving in groups of two and three. Despondently, Claire Beaton turned to Harry Ratner and said, "It's steady as she goes right into the iceberg."

"It sure looks that way," Ratner said, shaking his head.

Gene Donnelly left the meeting with McConger. "Let's make that dinner real soon, George," the Texan said to the North Dakota populist. "We don't spend nearly enough time together."

Late that afternoon Hanrahan sat in his office with Harry Ratner. Both men were tired and discouraged. Ratner had just received startling news from two enconometricians at the office of the Council of Economic Advisers.

He stated it plainly. "If things continue on the present path, we're going to see more than a hundred percent inflation this year."

Hanrahan gave a low whistle. "Jesus H. Christ! I don't know what the hell the Europeans are going to do when they hear about this."

"The man from Bundesbank says they're going to have to start inflating too. I couldn't get him to believe that we're gonna fight this inflation."

"I can't blame him," Hanrahan said. "I find it hard to believe myself."

Ratner continued: "There's just no limit to how high it could go. We're looking at a situation like the 1923 German experience, when the mark went from four point three to the dollar to four point three trillion to the dollar."

"And we know where the German experience led," Hanrahan said. "It led to the Führer."

"Not immediately," Ratner corrected, "but certainly inflation paved the way. That's why the Germans' response now is so important. They hate inflation more than anyone else. If they're starting to inflate, they must think the situation is hopeless."

The telephone rang. Hanrahan picked it up. "Yes, Eliza," he said to his secretary.

"Miss Graham just called," the secretary said. "She said she's sorry, but she won't be able to make it for dinner tonight. She asked me to give you the message. She said she'd talk to you later."

Oh, great, Hanrahan thought, the end of a perfect day. Jesus! He was getting damn tired of Cathy's irresponsible behavior. This was the third dinner date she had canceled at the last minute in a month. She was behaving like a spoiled brat. That was, he knew, the price he paid for her youth.

"Thanks, Eliza," he said and hung up. Who could he find at this late hour?

"Anything wrong?" asked Ratner when he saw the annoyed look on Hanrahan's face.

"Nothing serious—a broken date."

The telephone rang again.

"Yes, Eliza?" Maybe it was Cathy saying dinner was on. If so, he was tempted to tell her he'd made other plans.

"Miss Beaton would like to see you."

"Good," said Hanrahan. "Send her in."

Claire looked fresh. Pretty.

He gave her the news at once. "Harry's been told to expect one hundred percent inflation this year. That's straight from the Council of Economic Advisers."

Claire looked stunned and sat down.

"Isn't there something we can do?" she said when she had recovered.

"Not today," said Ratner. "I've got to go home. My

wife will kill me if I'm late again. Besides, I'm too depressed."

When Ratner left, Hanrahan smiled at Claire. It was only the second time she had been in his office, and she had hesitated before coming.

"I'm desperate about this situation," she said. "I don't know what to do. There's usually something to do, but this time I'm stumped. Why is the President so blind?"

Hanrahan suddenly had an idea. "I know what we can do," he said. "Let's not even think about inflation any more today. Let's go to the Jockey Club and have some dinner?" This was where he liked to take women to dine.

Claire brightened. "That would be nice, Pete. That would be very nice indeed."

"Good. Send your car home. We'll go in mine."

Half an hour later they were sitting at a corner table at the Jockey Club, waiting for two steaks tartare.

"I feel much better already," said Claire. "What a day!"

"Let's not talk about it," Hanrahan said.

"Agreed."

"What was it like to have a genius for a father?" She had marvelous eyes—clear, responsive, candid. "I'm curious. What was he like?"

"He was strong." Her expression softened. "I've always felt lucky. So many of the girls I've known had fathers who weren't."

"How about your mother? Was she a scientist too?"

"Not only was, but is. Since Daddy died, she's been teaching math at the University of Chicago. They were a great couple, very much in love."

"They must have taught you a lot."

"Yes, they did. They taught me not to apologize for being bright."

"I envy you that," said Peter. "I had to learn by myself—my parents were no help at all."

"So many people do," said Claire. "They gave you a few advantages, though." She was smiling.

"Didn't they?" He was delighted. Most people were

self-conscious about his wealth, as though he might be too. "Though I wouldn't put their grades too high in other departments. Still, I shouldn't complain. I don't like self-pity, especially among the rich, and especially in myself." God, she was nice to talk to. He felt like celebrating.

"Let's have a good Burgundy," he said. "Do you like wine?"

"Love it."

When the sommelier brought the wine, he said it was the very last bottle.

"To the last of the wine," said Peter, lifting his glass and drinking. "And also the first. We must do this more often. Agreed?"

"Agreed," said Claire.

It was a delicious meal. Peter had never seen Claire so relaxed, so feminine. They talked about everything. There seemed no limit to her enthusiasm, her knowledge. And Peter found himself listening, for a change, to something a lot more interesting than Cathy's problems with her parents, her friends and her hairdresser.

He was talking to a woman! And maturity had never before seemed so desirable.

"What happened to your marriage?" he asked, as they drank their coffee.

"He wanted a sister," she said, "or a mother; I don't know which. He definitely didn't want an emancipated woman. If that's what I am."

"That's one of the things you are," said Peter. "Just one."

"I like to think so," said Claire, "so I hope you're right. It's sometimes a battle to be a woman these days."

"I've got a secret for you, then."

"What is it? I love secrets."

"You're winning the battle."

She felt herself blushing. Claire couldn't honestly remember the last time she had blushed.

Later they drove to Claire's apartment in Georgetown.

"How do you like Georgetown?" Hanrahan asked.

"It's going to hell, like the whole town," Claire said. "It's not safe to walk around at night any more."

"You ought to try the Watergate," Hanrahan said. "It's very safe there."

He walked her to her door, feeling both like a kid on his first date and like a man. Very much like a man.

"Claire," he said, when she apologized for not asking him in because a cousin on her way to Atlanta was staying over, "that was the best conversation I've had in years." He almost added "with a woman" but that instinct for the perfect strategy he had learned at so much cost stopped him. There had been enough of that kind of talk about the sexes already tonight.

"Me, too," said Claire. "It was very nice. I've never had such good wine in my life. Thank you."

On his way home, he felt very young again.

## 4

THREE hectic weeks later, Claire Beaton and Harry Ratner walked toward the White House. It was the coldest November fifteenth on record. Claire was wearing a black mink coat which she had bought several years earlier as a birthday present for herself. Harry Ratner was wearing a long black cape. To Claire's knowledge it was his only affectation—if it was one.

"We look like prophets of doom, Harry," said Claire.

"Doom is right," said Ratner, a scowl on his face. Then he brightened. "Elegant prophets, though."

Claire smiled. "The stores on Connecticut Avenue

have big signs announcing sales, and then you go inside and the prices are ridiculous."

"They may be ridiculous," Ratner said, "but they're real."

"And those Whitelaw kids, smiling and putting up posters everywhere, they're really getting to be creepy. There're too many of them," Claire said.

Ratner nodded. "They were canvassing in Spring Valley last weekend. They give me a bad feeling," he said.

"I had the driver pull up close to a record store. It was advertising LP's for twenty dollars as bargains. That's amazing."

"We've had over forty-five percent inflation since September fifteenth, and that's sixty days."

A new computerized system that gave a daily readout of consumer price changes had been installed.

"I went to the Jewel Box to have a brooch sent to Mother for Christmas, and they wouldn't take my American Express. They won't take any charge cards now. Cash or exchanges, but no charges."

Ratner's frown deepened. "Why should they? Why should they take a charge and not get paid for a couple of weeks? Or a couple of months? By that time the money will be worth much less. People are shifting back to a barter system." He hummed a few bars of "Whistle While You Work."

Claire looked at him. "Is that a gleam I see in your eye?"

"Yep," said Ratner with a sheepish smile. "The mess is serving Senegalese soup, and I just love it."

Claire had to admit that it was still a pleasure to eat in the White House Conference mess. She knew something about the pecking order at the White House in terms of eating. For high-grade civil servants and low-grade Presidential appointees, there was the executive dining room in the EOB. It had a good, rich paneled look to it and served a fine buffet.

But there was a big step between it and the next highest spot, the White House mess, which was a small dining room in the West Wing, where only special assistants to the President and a few others could eat.

It had about twelve tables covered with white table-cloths, each seating two or four people. At one end of the room was a large round table, seating perhaps eight, where staffers went to eat when they were alone. The food was ordered from a menu, and it was un-varyingly delicious and inexpensive, thanks to a large subsidy.

And there was still another step between that mess and the Conference mess, just to the right of the regular mess, adjacent to the National Security Council's Situation Room. Only Cabinet-rank officials could eat in that mess. It had subdued lighting, fewer tables farther apart, and, proportionately, more Filipino mess-boys. It was definitely the most exclusive eating place in Washington, and Claire Beaton was glad she was there. Her job might have its frustrations, but it also had its perks.

In the mess, the talk was all about inflation.

"The farmers are hoarding their grain." Ratner was waiting for his soup. "They say that the money they'd have to sell it for won't buy what they need for next year's planting."

"How's the Chicago market doing today?" Claire asked.

"Winter wheat opened at fifty-three dollars a bushel. That's the daily limit, and not much is being offered for sale at that price. I have the feeling the farmers are holding it off the market until things clear up."

"How long before that shows up in the CPI?"

"Well," said Ratner, "that's hard to say. Bread is about three dollars a pound, and will soon go to five. Not much of the cost of a loaf of bread is the wheat. But the unions in that industry are now getting weekly wage adjustments, and the teamsters and bakers are sending costs through the roof."

"You can't blame them. They want to keep ahead of inflation too," Claire Beaton said.

"And it's spreading to welfare and Social Security. Senator Clark's bill to key transfer payments to the CPI will probably get passed tomorrow, and the President's got to sign it." Ratner brightened as the mess-boy served his cold Senegalese soup.

"The national budget is going to be so unbalanced it'll be a joke. And that means that everyone on the government payroll is trapped."

"Trapped?" Harry Ratner looked up.

"Yes. Because now we've got to get McConger to keep printing money to cover the deficit. He's put us into a position where we can't tell him to stop printing money so fast or the Federal government will have to default. We're not raising nearly enough money through taxes to cover these new expenses, so we've got to sell bonds. And the only way to sell those bonds is if the Federal Reserve pumps out enough money to either buy the bonds itself or let banks have the money to buy them."

"McConger has really put himself in the catbird seat," said Ratner. "Listen, I don't want you to spread this around, but the President is having lunch today with Peter Hanrahan. I think maybe it's because he wants Peter to talk him out of what we're doing. Maybe he's ready to start fighting inflation instead of goosing it."

Claire felt a rush of different feelings. Peter, she knew, had been in London for two weeks. She was glad to know he was back. On the one hand, perhaps he could convince the President to stop acting like an ostrich. On the other hand, she knew as much, if not more, about inflation and how to stop it as anyone else. So why wasn't the President lunching with her? She resented the strength of the old school tie. The President was a Princeton man too.

Could she be jealous? She forced herself to admit it, then hoped such thoughts were unworthy.

Remembering the night at the Jockey Club, she could not repress a twinge of excitement that this man who obviously felt so warmly toward her had so much power that he could have lunch with the President alone. It made her want to get still closer to him.

He was overpoweringly attractive. But she had other things to worry about. "You know we're losing a tremendous amount of bullion? That trade is absolutely going crazy, and the same thing is happening in London and Zurich. Nobody seems to know where it's going."

"Yes, the gold flows. I've seen those figures too." Harry Ratner was staring at a painting next to them of a Revolutionary War frigate blowing the hell out of some poor British ship. It reminded him of the beating the dollar was taking. "I think it's going into the hands of private hoarders. I doubt that any of the big central banks in Europe or Japan are involved. I don't think any of them could afford to buy gold anyway."

"Have you noticed how Eurodollar borrowing is picking up too?"

"Truth to tell, I haven't," Ratner said. "Though that always happens during an inflationary period. People borrow dollars worth something and pay back the debt with dollars worth less."

Ratner seemed preoccupied.

"It's on a bigger scale than that, Harry." But Claire did not insist on elaborating. She was wondering what the President and Peter Hanrahan were saying upstairs in the Oval Office. She wished she were there.

The President wiped his mouth with his napkin. He had just finished eating. He sat, small table in front of him, on a white linen couch perpendicular to the fireplace, above which hung a portrait of John F. Kennedy. When the President had been in Congress, he had gotten into the habit of eating off a small table and watching television while he ate. He still liked to eat at a small table whenever he could.

Peter Hanrahan sat across from him on an identical white linen couch. He had ordered a small steak. "Mr. President, we cannot continue like this. It's just beginning, but the whole social fabric of the country is going to pieces."

"What am I supposed to do?" the President asked. He picked up his telephone and pressed a button. "You can send Freda in now."

The door opened and the President's dog bounded into the room. She jumped up on the President and sat there staring at the steak bone on Hanrahan's plate and panting.

"Do you mind giving your bone to Freda?" the President asked. "She loves warm steak bones."

Hanrahan was mildly amused. "Sure. She's welcome to it." He picked up the bone and Freda snatched it out of his hand in an instant. She took it over to a corner of the room and started gnawing loudly.

"What am I supposed to do?" the President repeated. He looked tired. "I know that all of your group wants me to put the economy through the wringer. But tell me, just for starters: How big a recession would we have to face?"

"A pretty bad one," Hanrahan said. "But soon, if we don't do something, we'll have a recession *and* inflation."

"That's a possibility," the President said. "But it's a certainty that if we shut off the spigot of money suddenly, the economy has to go through withdrawal pains. The whole country will go into convulsions."

"What do you think is happening now?" Hanrahan said. "Look, Mr. President, I can see what's going on around me. People consider themselves secure only if their money means something. That's what their faith is based on. If we take away that faith, we take away their belief in the whole society. People won't accept that kind of thing and go on like nothing happened. They get mad. They want somebody who'll give them a stable society."

"Are you talking about Whitelaw?" the President asked sharply.

"It could be Whitelaw. It could be someone else."

"Peter, I don't disagree with anything you've said. But if I put this country into another Great Depression, I'm gambling with the whole world's future. Maybe I'm doing that already. But at least now I've got some political support from McConger's people for the policies we've adopted. Christ, Pete, he's got a mortgage on my nuts. He knows I need his supporters."

"But, Mr. President, he isn't the only one who can give you supporters," Hanrahan said.

The President looked his friend in the eye and said, "If I gave you all week, how many Congressmen could you get to go out on a limb and support a tax raise?"

"A couple of dozen for sure. Maybe more."

"Well, McConger could get seventy-five in an hour. But that's not the whole reason I'm fighting you right now. I'm stuck, Pete. I can't plunge the country into a depression. We'll just have to wait and see how things go. It's tough on you and it's tough on everyone. But believe me, it's a helluva lot tougher on me."

Peter Hanrahan looked out at the trees on the South Lawn. These problems were putting a severe strain on their friendship. He wanted to plead. He wanted to get down on his knees and beg. But the President was utterly inflexible.

It was going to be a cold winter. People would forget what spring was like. Out of these peaceful and gracious rooms, out of this magnificent house with its antique furniture, its pictures of eighteenth-century warships, its black-jacketed Filipino messboys, its men and women who traveled in gleaming black cars, out of all that order and calm, a traumatic decision had been made, and blood in the streets of the nation would follow.

Freda was chewing happily on her bone near the windows. So much for Peter Hanrahan's lunch with the President.

Shelby Kelsey and William Hanrahan were standing in front of Ridgeley.

"I tell you, Mr. Hanrahan, you've got to buy it now."

"Shelby, if land is such a good idea, why hasn't the bank put me onto it?"

"They're too damn lazy. If you want something done, you've got to do it yourself. That's the truth, and you know it," Kelsey said.

"It's true that my bonds have been falling through the floor. But that can't go on forever," Hanrahan said.

"It can. It sure as hell can," Kelsey said. "At least long enough to ruin you. I'm telling you, Mr. Hanrahan, those bankers up in New York City are like rabbits in front of a spotlight. They're just paralyzed. You've got to do this on your own."

"Maybe you're right, Shelby. But I think I've got to at least ask the people at the bank why they haven't put me onto land," said Hanrahan.

"Agreed," said Kelsey. "Now don't forget, hear?"

"I won't forget," said William Hanrahan as Alex joined them.

"Hi," she said.

"How are you?" Kelsey asked.

"Fine."

"You ready?"

"Ready set to go," she said.

At the building next to the bank, three men waited for Kelsey. All three looked like middle-aged country lawyers, which is what they were.

"I have the certified checks here," said Kelsey.

"OK. I guess you're calling the shots."

The four men and Alexandra sat down at a small table. Papers were circulated and signed. Kelsey turned over several certified checks. No one spoke. The whole exchange took only a few minutes. Then the four men and Alexandra all shook hands and Shelby Kelsey, smiling like the cat that had swallowed the canary, took her by the hand and led her back to the car.

"What was that all about?" Alex asked.

"Well," Kelsey said, "I just exercised some options on some land."

"Did you make money?" Alex asked.

"You're goddamn right," said Kelsey. "That's exactly what I did. I bought two pieces of land, one for thirty-five thousand dollars and one for fifty thousand, and I could turn around right this minute and sell them for ten times that much. You know what that means?" Kelsey asked.

"It means you made a lot of money," said Alex.

"But why are you so excited? You've made money before."

"It means, Alex, that I'm now a millionaire." Kelsey looked positively aglow. He grabbed her in a bear hug.

Alex threw her arms around him. "That's terrific!" Alex said. "Oh, Shelby, that's absolutely terrific!" She knew how much he wanted it. "Why didn't you tell me?"

"I wanted to surprise you."

"Why did they sell you the land so cheap?" Alex asked.

"They had no choice. I had options on the property, forcing them to sell. I bought the options a few years ago, when no one dreamed they'd ever be worth so much. They're just small farms."

Alex frowned. "Well, what will happen to the people whose farms you bought?"

"I don't know. They can stay there and farm the land for me if they want. And if they don't want to do that, they can move."

"Are they poor now?" asked Alex.

"I don't know that either, Alex. But that isn't the point anyway. The point is, they needed my money when I bought the options. They needed my money *then*. It's not my fault that they couldn't pay it back. Business is tough, Alex. That's what you've got to learn."

"If you say so," said Alex. "Where are we going?" He was driving on an unfamiliar road.

Shelby wouldn't tell her.

"Are you going to give me a bigger surprise than becoming a millionaire?"

He still wouldn't tell her. She was patient. It was unusual for Shelby to tease, and she wanted to encourage him.

Finally he reached a marina, a new one, recently completed. He pulled his Buick into the parking lot and drove past the restaurant down several rows of piers until he came to a dock at which a forty-foot sailboat was tied up. The lights inside were on.

He was so happy and so proud. He was like a child

with a toy. And that's what he is, thought Alex. But he has to provide his own toys. He was so vulnerable to the pleasures that money can buy that Alexandra was moved, as she was by so many things about him. She had never known anyone like Shelby Kelsey before.

There was a teak floor. The cabin had a living room, in the middle of which a dining table was set for two. Behind the living room was the bedroom.

"This is fabulous, Shelby." Alexandra wanted him to know how proud of him she was. She put her arms around his waist, lifted her face up and kissed him on the cheek.

She often gave Shelby little signs of affection like that, and he usually responded by swallowing and looking intense. But on this late afternoon, he took her face in his hands and kissed her until Alex thought he would never stop—not that she wanted him to. This was a kiss that told her what she wanted to know: his body wanted hers. As he pulled her against him, his muscles tense, she could for the first time feel his full strength—a strength that he had acquired not from working out at the New York Athletic Club, but from hard work as a boy on the land. Alexandra lost all sense of time.

He broke the embrace and showed her how the cook from the marina restaurant had come aboard earlier and made Chesapeake Bay clams to put in the oven. And he took from the midget refrigerator a bottle of Dom Perignon champagne—Grand Cru. She knew it must have cost at least $150. But she wasn't supposed to think about money any more.

Kelsey turned the lights in the cabin down. Then he lit two candles on the table. The only sound was the sloshing of the Choptank River against the hull of the boat.

"It's hard for me to believe this is happening," Kelsey said to Alexandra.

"Well, I guess we're both very lucky," she said.

"It was blind luck that I met you," he said, his voice shaky. "The best luck I ever had in my life. That much I know."

She picked up his strong, bony right hand and pressed it to her cheek and kissed it.

"Let's have some brandy," Kelsey said. "Hennessy or Grand Marnier?"

It was an important question. He was offering her a choice, something she knew he hadn't always been able to do. "Hennessy would be great," she said.

Kelsey went to the galley and took out the bottle. He poured two drinks and handed one to Alex. "Here's to Alex and me," he said.

Then he took her by the hand to the love seat. As she sat down, he put his arm around her and pulled her toward him. For an instant she thought of how gentle and steady his movements were. Then they kissed again, and this time, for the first time, he touched her breasts, kissing her more urgently still. At last he stood up, took her hand and led her into the bedroom. But that was only an interruption. When they lay on the bed, he picked up the kiss where he had left off. Slowly, at the same time, he slid his right hand up her left leg, reaching under her dress. When Kelsey touched her thigh, she began to go crazy.

In a minute, they had their clothes off. Alex marveled that a man could be so hard. He tried to be gentle, but he had waited too long and it came out clumsy. And his roughness, the wild urgency he let her feel at last, was all she could desire.

"It had to be this way," Kelsey said afterward. "I had to come to you as an equal. I had to come to you with something to offer."

"Shelby, you've always been enough."

"It had to be more than the me who used to be. It's what a person has that makes him what he is." Even in the dimness, Alex could see the faraway look in his eyes. "It's not just money I'm talking about, it's achievement. When a man gets what he wants, he's more complete. Now I've got what I want."

"I think I understand, Shelby," Alex said. "I really think I do."

She put her head on Kelsey's shoulder. She could hear him breathing. She felt more fulfilled than she had ever felt before. But he was an enigma. The things in him she loved the most were the very things he hated.

Laurie Adams was watching Monte Hall on *Let's Make a Deal,* her eyes bright with wonder. The prizes had grown so big. A woman dressed as a piggy bank had just won $10,000 in municipal bonds.

"Goddamn, Laurie!" It was Jim.

"What's the matter, honey?" Laurie asked.

Jim was staring at the lighted digits on his pocket calculator. "It's just goddamn strange, that's all. At first it seems like I'm ahead and then it doesn't. I can't make it come out right and I'm really getting confused."

Jim looked next at a green card which showed his salary for the most recent two-week period, less deductions, and the net amount he was paid.

The card said that for the two-week period he had earned $1,000. That reflected the 25 percent pay increase that the Teachers Union had fought for and won. It had seemed like a miracle. But while his deductions for medical and life insurance were only a few cents higher now than before the raise, and his federal tax was only a few dollars higher, his state and county taxes were quite a lot more. So he hadn't exactly come out 25 percent ahead of the game.

As a matter of fact, he wasn't sure he was ahead of the game at all. "Here's the way it looks, Laurie," Jim said. "We can now make our car and house payments more easily because of the raise."

"Good," said Laurie.

"But the gas and electricity bills are up like gangbusters. And every time we take Marie to Doctor Malloy, it's an arm and a leg. I've never seen such doctor bills."

"Well, everything costs more now. We all know that. But I got a little raise too. And the President says it's only temporary—that prices are bound to go down."

"Yeah, I guess we're ahead for now. But we all need winter clothes, and if it's a real cold winter, our heating bills could wipe us out."

Laurie took her eyes off Monte Hall. She got up, walked over to Jim and put her arms around his shoulders as he hunched at the desk. "I know it's a squeeze, but we always get by. I mean, you're eating all right, aren't you?" She playfully patted his stomach.

"I sure am," Jim said. "Too well, if anything. We ought to have more plain old raw protein instead of so many casseroles and cakes."

"What's the matter, Jim? Don't you like my casseroles?" She knew he liked her cakes. He couldn't get enough.

"Of course I like them, but all those carbohydrates are slowing me down. What I need is more meat. Like you," he said playfully and pinched her on the bottom.

"I try to give you just what you want," Laurie said. She gave him a little kiss on his forehead and returned to her seat on the black Naugahyde sofa across from the color TV. With satisfaction, she looked around the room at the wall-to-wall carpeting, the drapes, the lamps, the Barcalounger and the rows of empty bookshelves. They had been built-ins; they came with the house.

If Jim only knew, she thought, what I have to go through to get the ingredients for those casseroles and cakes on the allowance he gives me. Recently her trips to the grocery store had become nightmares. She had begun shopping almost every day on her way home from work, in hopes of getting more bargains. The windows of the store would be covered with signs announcing great sales, but when she got inside, she found that the "bargains" were either long gone or no bargains at all.

Even the grocery store's own brand of bacon now cost more than $7 a pound. Chicken breasts—Jim didn't like dark meat—cost $8.50 a pound. And that was just the beginning of the week. God knows what it cost this weekend. One day there would be a shortage of something, say liver (another of Jim's favorites), and then the next day it would be back on the shelves at fifty cents more a pound. That was the way it seemed to work.

A lot of the time the big supermarket where she usually went was out of the things she wanted, period. She had recently tried an old, neighborhood grocery store which looked as though it dated back to the Depression. The food was even more expensive there, and it didn't offer the comfortable aisles of the supermarket in its crowded space, but Laurie wanted to feed Jim exactly the food he liked.

Besides, Bob Hartley, the owner, who was also the butcher at the store, had obviously taken a liking to her. She had noticed on more than one occasion that he would ask her how the baby was, or tell her how nice she looked, or something, and then she would see him slipping in a few extra chicken breasts without charging her for them. She guessed he must need the extra business, what with competition from the supermarkets and all, and that was why he was doing her a favor. And Laurie never resented compliments on her looks.

Since she had become a wife, mother and lab technician, it often seemed that nobody but Jim complimented her on her looks any more, and compliments were something she liked quite a lot. That was why she had been a cheerleader at West Virginia Wesleyan, working her way through college, and she still liked to be told that her blond hair and curvy figure attracted people to her. So she had been going to Bob Hartley's market more and more. But she didn't go if she knew for a fact that A&P or Safeway was having a special on something she really wanted—like bacon. And she would certainly stop going to Hartley's if he ever made any remarks that went beyond friendliness. She was a respectable, middle-class married woman, after all.

But still, Laurie thought, as she watched the winner of Monte Hall's big deal throw her arms around his neck, she would like to let Jim know how hard she worked at buying his food and staying within her budget. It was a great source of satisfaction to her. But she knew that if she told him, he would worry more than ever about inflation. And Laurie was sick of inflation. Bored, scared and sick.

She knew she had inflation to thank for their pay raises, but she hoped to God it would end soon. But if it didn't, she'd just have to keep struggling. This was America, after all, the most prosperous country in the world, and a resourceful woman like her could surely find a way to run a neat and efficient household, feeding her husband what he wanted to be fed, no matter what happened to the dollar.

Hal Burton turned the script over and over on his desk at 9255 Sunset Boulevard. He couldn't let it go. First he would put it face down, and then face up. Face down, he couldn't see the working title Joan Bellamy had put on the script. Face up, he could see it plainly: *The Wonderchildren*. Hal Burton thought it was an incredibly good script. He could not get over the fact that Joan Bellamy had written it in less than two months.

It was his story and it was everybody's story. It was poetic and it was exciting and it was real. He didn't need to ask anyone's permission to do it. He didn't even need to get studio financing. He would do it himself. It didn't need big-name actors or exotic sets. It just needed to be not only produced, but also directed, by Hal Burton.

He could see it now—not just how it took place in front of the camera, but how it would look on the screen. His life was the story, though not, of course, as he had actually lived it, and it was a great story. It reminded him of *Death of a Salesman*. Here was this man in a room interviewing people for a job. As each person passed through, the interviewer would ask this or that question about the person's past. The answers triggered a series of flashbacks in the interviewer's mind. It would become clear that life was a series of interviews, tryouts, if you will, and that even for the interviewer the outcome, the future, was still uncertain. The interviewer would, of course, be a powerful film personality and as each person passed through his office, though he would add to his stock of recollections, he would still come out feeling that he had missed something vitally important. He had become a bigger and bigger wheel, but it would mean nothing to him at the end. He would have learned nothing from it. All he would know at the end was that he had once had hopes and dreams. Now that they were realized, his life seemed empty, and he didn't even have the hopes and dreams any more. It was a film about memory. It was a film about waste. It was a film about life.

And Hal Burton had the feeling that if he read *The Wonderchildren* ten more times, he still wouldn't completely understand it.

He felt exactly like an interviewer today, by an odd coincidence, because he had just been talking to some production people about getting this film set up, putting the package together. God, he thought, the rules of the game were changing awfully fast with inflation. Les Levine, his production chief, had told him that he just couldn't count on anything being the way it used to be, in terms of the old costs.

"They've got this new thing called indexation," Levine had said. "It ties the wages to the cost of living according to some formula that's so complicated even I don't understand it."

"We can live with that," Burton said. "We're taking in plenty of money."

"Well," said Levine, "even if we could, the union guys want productivity raises to keep them ahead of inflation. I'm telling you, Hal, it's just a one-way street to disaster."

"Are you sure? I think we can handle it."

"OK, listen to this. Some of the on-camera people want to be paid bonuses in coke. Can you handle that? They say it's the only way they can keep ahead of inflation," said Levine.

Burton thought a moment and then said, "Yes, Les, I believe I can even handle that. This picture is really important to me. I'm willing to take a loss."

"OK, then. If you don't mind taking a loss, be my guest."

Burton looked out the window. On a clear day, he might have been able to see to Catalina, but today wasn't clear. To make the visibility worse, there were the fires. Burton glanced at his watch. It was almost 6 P.M. He turned on his TV to get the news.

He watched a commercial for a dog food which also claimed to kill worms, and then a commercial for a deodorant with Vitamin C. Then the news came on. The anchor man stood in front of a large map of Los Angeles.

"Good evening. In Los Angeles today the wave of arson that has been plaguing the city for the past two weeks continued. Fires burned in Watts, Compton and scattered areas of West L.A. all day, with hopelessly overworked fire and police services, already crippled by police and fire job actions, unable to stem the tide. For a live report from Compton, here's Joel Block."

The scene abruptly shifted to a black reporter standing in front of a smoldering block of former shops. In a deep, modulated voice, he announced: "Behind me, a fire has been raging all day. A few firemen, harassed by bottle-throwing youths, have been unable to control the flames. This block is only one of dozens throughout L.A. which have been set afire as mobs of angry shoppers seek to loot stores of all kinds. The sharply rising cost of food, placing it beyond the reach of many in this neighborhood, has been cited by local black leaders as the primary cause of the disorders. The problem is compounded, firefighters say, by the fact that the fires are often started by people in cars, who can outdistance the firemen and the police even as they start new fires." The camera panned to a collapsing brick wall. "For those of you who wonder why the smog is so bad lately, part of the answer is here, in these smoldering ashes."

The anchor man continued: "Mayor Farhood today appealed for private citizens to stop forming their own vigilante units and to trust the police. The Mayor spoke after a number of shootings on the West Side, as residents formed citizen-patrol groups to protect their homes after police effectiveness was curtailed due to their refusal to work at full-force levels until their cost-of-living demands are met."

The camera showed a hooded man with a shotgun in front of a house in Brentwood. "This man, who refused to be identified, expressed the feelings of many West Siders."

The man with the hood spoke into a microphone. "We are not going to hurt anyone who comes here on legitimate business. But this raiding of our neighborhood by people from other parts of the city has got to stop. We can't feed the whole city."

The anchor man continued: "Police say that six slayings are believed to have been caused by run-ins between vigilante groups and would-be trespassers."

Burton turned the TV off. He himself had been stopped last night by a roadblock in Coldwater Canyon. Luckily the guards knew him. They had been carrying enough shotguns to stop a whole county.

Burton had been thinking of buying new guns for himself and Sally. Now he decided he definitely would. A man had to protect himself. That was only fair.

His thoughts returned to the screenplay.

He had to make this movie. The money would be no problem, but the city was falling apart. That was a problem. He had always believed in a solution for every problem.

He reached into a drawer, took out a folder marked Emergencies. He opened it and took out a small packet filled with white powder. He removed from his desk a small spoon, similar to a salt spoon, and dipped it into the powder. Then he put the spoon first under his right nostril, then his left nostril, and inhaled. In thirty seconds he felt as if he could do any film he wanted. He felt invincible. He stood up and looked at the smoky city below.

L.A. was out there just waiting for his movie. The whole world was waiting for his story. Nothing would stop him now, not the fires, not the riots, not the vigilantes. Nothing.

The buzzer on Peter Hanrahan's desk interrupted his train of thought. He was trying to translate his copy of a speech by the French Minister of Finance about curbing American dollar inflow. The phone was a welcome interruption.

"Yes?" he said.

"Miss Graham calling," said Eliza.

"Put her through," said Hanrahan, frowning.

"Hi, Pete," said Cathy. "Guess where I'm calling from."

"The zoo," Hanrahan said. He was tired of her games.

"Silly. I'm in your apartment. How soon can you be here?"

For a moment he was tempted to say he had moved. Then the ache began in his loins and felt his pulse race. "Half an hour. Maybe less."

"Make it less," Cathy said. "I have a surprise for you. I came straight home from school." She hadn't called in a week. Her art class had made a field trip to New York last month and Cathy, he knew, had been seeing her latest crush—an artist who did second-rate imitations of Red Grooms—almost every day since. He knew because his brother William, for one, had seen them together at the National Gallery.

Hanrahan was almost fed up. She no longer amused him. He was weary to death of playing Daddy.

On top of that, Hanrahan had had a hard day. He had had briefings all morning and another disappointing meeting with the President after lunch. As he waited for his car, he looked out his window toward the Federal Triangle. The sky had a pinkish tinge from the sodium-vapor anticrime lights that made downtown Washington bright as daylight all night long. Hanrahan remembered that the last time he was at Dulles Airport he could make out the glow over Washington from the airport parking lot, a good thirty miles from the center of the city.

FARMERS VOW—NO MORE BEEF said a headline on the front page of the *Washington Star-News*. His driver always bought the paper for him. He picked it up. Beneath the headline, the story began, "Billings, Mont.—Ranchers here agreed at a meeting today that they would not sell beef cattle for anything but gold until the government assured them that ·it had an effective plan for controlling inflation."

That was McConger's own territory. Hoarding was inevitable; it always followed shortages in food.

Lower down there was another headline—ARIZONA WOMEN FORM BOYCOTT UNIT.

"Tucson, Ariz.—Housewives from the southern Arizona area met in the gymnasium of a local high school here yesterday to plan a boycott of supermarkets, in protest of rising food costs. Mrs. Norma Jean Denman, adviser to the housewives, proposed that the homemakers curtail shopping whenever possible to bring food prices 'down to a level where we can feed our families without having to rob a bank!' "

Hanrahan picked up the telephone in his car. The Signal Corps operator said, "Waca," which in some bizarre military acronym stood for White House Communications Agency.

"This is Peter Hanrahan. Patch me through to Harry Ratner."

"Yes, sir," the male voice said. After some static and a few clicks, Hanrahan heard the voice of Joyce Pitherington.

"This is Peter Hanrahan, Joyce. Would you please put Harry on?"

"One moment, Mr. Hanrahan," Joyce said.

"You must be calling from your car," Ratner said when the connection was made.

"I am," Hanrahan said. "Everyone loves gadgets. Why should I be different? Listen, have you seen the front page of the *Star?*"

"About the cattle and the housewives?"

"Yes. Say, I think we should shoot that over to the President, to show him that both sides are mad."

"It can't hurt, but I don't know what good it'll do," Ratner said. Even with the bad connection, Hanrahan could tell how weary Ratner was.

"It'll at least show him that inflation is screwing up food production and buying," Hanrahan said.

"OK. I'll send it over," Ratner said.

"Righto," said Hanrahan and hung up.

His car had reached the huge concrete area of the

Watergate. Just before Hanrahan got out of the car, he noticed a picture on page 2 of the handsome, distinguished-looking man, the man who looked like a gracefully aging movie actor. He was standing at a podium. Behind him on the stage were clean-cut smiling young men and women in denim coveralls. Over the picture a headline read: WHITELAW ADDRESSES 10,000 AT FRESNO RALLY. His eyes picked up two words the reporter used to describe the crowd: "savagely angry."

Wryly Hanrahan decided that those two words were a perfect description of the way he felt. He hastened up to his apartment.

When he opened the door, he saw Cathy curled up in a chair with her long legs folded under her, kitten-fashion.

"Hi, Pete," she purred as she got out of the chair. Hanrahan could see that she was wearing what he expected—her uniform. That was the surprise. She knew it turned him on. A plaid pleated wool skirt, blue knee socks, a white cotton blouse and a navy-blue blazer were the Madeira uniform for special occasions.

"I'm sorry I didn't have time to change out of my uniform," she said and laughed.

"Ho, ho," Hanrahan said. "I'll bet." It was when she laughed that she got to him most.

But he felt different tonight.

He bit lightly on her lower lip. Then, as his right hand reached down to stroke her small firm ass, she pressed to him hard and said, "Let's ball our brains out." She threw back her head, and her blond hair caught in his hands. In less than a minute he had stripped off her clothes. Usually he was more gentle, but tonight he was impatient. He picked her up and threw her on the bed.

He wanted to hurt her, not her usual play-acting kind of hurt, but something stronger. And he found that he had to restrain himself to keep from doing her bodily damage. He knew he was hurting her somewhat from the sound of her moans. He used his teeth to bite. He used his hands to grip her flesh wherever he could get a hold.

"Peter, oh, Peter, you're bruising me," she said, struggling briefly to make him stop, her protests not quite convincing. This is it, he thought as he fucked her, the last time, baby.

The first time she came, she screamed, and he worried about the thickness of the walls, before losing the use of his mind once more. He wanted to get it over with, he wanted to come one final time in this girl, and it was almost as though she sensed it. She was crying now, like a baby, struggling not to lose her breath, her skin wet from her tears and the sweat from his body. Why was it taking so long?

When she said "Peter" her voice was ragged, and she said it over and over, twisting her head from side to side.

Then she came again. Later, he could never remember the exact point in his head when her incredibly young body changed into that of a woman whose body he had never seen. One instant he was fucking a kid; the next he was making love to Claire Beaton. And it was when he felt her naked body waiting beneath him that he shuddered with wild excitement and hurtled through a long tunnel in the dark and suddenly emerged into dazzling sunlight. Cathy was clinging to him, exhausted.

It was a long time before they moved. "I don't think I would ever have known what life has to offer if I hadn't met you," Cathy said at last, disengaging herself.

"Uhhmm."

"Do you love me, Peter?"

He didn't answer. Somehow he had to try not to hurt her too much.

"Oh," she exclaimed, looking at the clock. "It's time for *Venceremos*."

"What's *Venceremos*?" asked Hanrahan.

"It's a new show with a Cuban refugee private detective as the hero. Last week the hero posed as a big cocaine smuggler from Colombia. He had just infiltrated a big drug ring, and then his cover was blown. The bad guys tied him up and they were just about to kill him with an overdose of coke when he was rescued by his buddy who was listening to the whole thing over a transmitter hidden in the hero's elbow."

"Uhhmm," said Hanrahan. She was a glutton for junk.

"Just once, I'd like to see the good guy not get rescued at the last minute," Cathy said, sitting up in the bed. "Look where you bruised me."

"Well, people like to see it happen on TV, because it doesn't happen much in real life," Hanrahan said.

After *Venceremos* he switched on the news.

Tom Harman, the perfectly groomed anchor man of the local CBS station, WTOP-TV, was saying, "Good evening on a day in which inflation and what, if anything, the government is going to do about it dominated the news. In Fresno, California, former Governor William Whitelaw spoke to a crowd of over ten thousand about the problem and got an enthusiastic response. For that story, we go to Lannie Hebb in Fresno."

On the screen there was the familiar screen-idol face of William Whitelaw, in front of a group of seated people. The first two rows were taken up with smiling, clean-faced girls and boys in denim coveralls. Around them were angry-looking listeners. Lannie Hebb began: "In his sharpest attacks to date on the administration for its failures in controlling inflation, Governor William Whitelaw told this California valley city that the inflation was their own fault." Then Whitelaw, in a close-up, was speaking:

"You didn't bring this crisis of inflation down on yourselves because you did anything wrong except for one thing: You let people govern you who don't know how to govern by either good sense or compassion. You let a lot of bureaucrats in Washington lead you to the slaughter like the Romans led Jesus Christ. Only we won't be raised up again unless we raise ourselves. And we can't do that until we're ready to cast the bureaucrats out of Washington like Jesus drove the money changers from the temple. Are you ready to do that?"

The cheering crowd filled the TV screen. Lannie

Hebb appeared in the foreground as the crowd rose to its feet shouting and raising its arms. Only for the first time did Hanrahan notice that the coverall kids looked fiercely angry when they shouted and waved. "What you see is the by now familiar 'One with God' salute that appears at Whitelaw rallies around the country. One woman in this crowd summed up the feelings of her fellow Whitelaw supporters."

A middle-aged woman wearing a scarf on her head said into the microphone that Lannie Hebb was holding, "Fact is, Governor Whitelaw is the only one tells us the truth. The people in Washington are just a gang of crooks."

"So," Lannie Hebb summed up, the dispersing crowd behind him and the kids in coveralls smiling again, passing among them, "in Fresno, California, feeling is running high over high prices, and Governor Whitelaw is obviously touching a very raw nerve. Lannie Hebb, CBS News, Fresno."

Behind Tom Harman appeared a map of Russia, a sheaf of wheat in the middle of it. "Rumors came out of the Soviet Union today through Berlin that because of the soaring cost of grain on the world food markets and the chronically poor harvests in the Communist state, Soviet citizens are facing drastically reduced food rations this winter. Bankers confirmed in Zurich, Switzerland, that the Soviet Union has been selling massive amounts of gold in recent months in order to buy grain abroad. Apparently it has not been enough, because today's reports spoke of large-scale rioting in Estonia and Latvia, with some deaths. The Russians appear to be angry."

"I can't take any more anger," said Peter and switched the television off.

## 5

L ARRY Hyde watched the moving men working in his new office with a great deal of satisfaction. They were taking out the old furniture and moving in the brand-new furniture that Larry had been allowed to order for himself. The old furniture had been conservative and old-fashioned, appropriate to the senior associate who had left Melloan and Company, Bullion Traders, to work for a rival. Larry's furniture reflected both his tastes and his new status. He had first gotten the idea for it from a late-night TV commercial.

The new furniture was completely "modular," and although Larry didn't know exactly what that meant, it sounded very modern and flashy. So he went to his boss and asked for new furniture. That was in late November, three weeks ago. His boss was agreeable, but suggested that if he was going to do it he should do it right away, since the price of furniture was going up so fast.

Larry thought that was a bit overanxious because, after all, the profits of Melloan and Company were going up fast every day too. But nonetheless he had gone right out and taken a taxi up to Bloomingdale's. The salesman in the furniture department on the fifth floor had not really understood at first what Larry meant by modular furniture—he had not seen the ads on TV. But he was happy to show Larry around until he saw what he liked. It was terrific: all chrome and smoked glass and molded plastic covered with Naugahyde and still more chrome. Very futuristic and suave and just right for a man who had just been made a senior associate at one of the hottest bullion dealers in town.

With that furniture to set off his sweeping new view of the East River, Larry could let people know, without saying a word, that he had arrived.

It was particularly felicitous that he was arriving at just the point in this crazy economic spiral when so many of his classmates from Baruch were taking it on the chin. He had found those movies of rich people during the Depression vastly instructive, and he felt it especially gratifying to be moving up while other people were moving down.

As of November fifteenth, one month before, Larry Hyde had been put on a commission basis on the sale of gold. His commission was an extremely small fraction of the price, but the prices were always going up. He laughed to himself as he thought of that phrase "doing well." It sounded so authoritative, so masterful, so understated, so accomplished—just the right words to describe the bright young man on the move who is really in command.

"Doing well" was an understatement. The price of gold was approaching $2,000 an ounce and probably would pass this figure before the new year. Larry wished he'd had enough money—and foresight—to have bought gold back in August when it was still under $500 an ounce. But that didn't really matter. He was doing all right. He had moved out of his one-bedroom apartment in Greenwich Village and taken a much larger flat with a den on the thirty-third floor of a modern building in the East 80s. There were a lot of good-looking chicks up there.

The apartment was $1,750 a month, but Larry could afford it. In fact, if things kept going well at the firm, Larry could start thinking about brownstones. But first he wanted to live it up, to enjoy some of the money that was coming his way. He had almost twenty winter suits now: Bill Blass, Pierre Cardin, Pierre Balmain—the works—so that when he went to parties, girls wouldn't think he was some creep.

But he wasn't quite there, not yet. His apartment had a curved driveway, and Larry wanted a lot of car to pull up to that driveway, where pretty girls always were hanging around. Larry wanted a Mercedes 750SE, the four-seater coupe. By now it should have been within his reach, but he hadn't figured on the D-mark going through the roof. Even with the Bundesbank inflating rapidly, the D-mark was holding well above the plummeting currencies of every other country, and the 750SE was now about $77,000, which was just a little too much. Still, it wouldn't be out of his reach forever.

The messenger from Lissitzyn Brothers was still coming every day. Every day, Ricky Jimenez or somebody else brought that envelope and that certified check. Whoever was buying had a damn good thing going, Larry thought. The purchase orders were for the maximum amount every single day. The guy must have made the biggest fucking bundle in the history of the world.

But that was all right. Larry Hyde had a piece of the action. And even if it wasn't a very large piece, it was large enough to matter.

When the moving men had finished, Larry signed the last receipt and looked around his office. It looked just perfect. It looked almost exactly like that ad on TV.

A cold and clear winter light was shining into Claire Beaton's eyes from the east as her Chrysler pulled into West Executive Avenue from behind the Executive Office Building. It was a few minutes before 10 A.M., and Claire had no cause to worry about being late to this extraordinary session of the Cabinet plus the Emergency Inflation Stabilization Group. But she had plenty of cause to worry about what she had seen coming over from her office this morning, and for the last few weeks before this meeting.

It was the Friday before Christmas Monday, and there were decorations up in all of the stores. But the stores looked strange indeed. In front of the grocery stores were police lines and sawhorses to keep the picketing housewives from smashing the big plate-glass windows.

"Hi, Harry," she said, when she reached his office. Harry Ratner opened the small refrigerator behind his desk. "I've got orange juice and tomato juice," he said. "Which would you like?"

Claire Beaton laughed. "Tomato juice. It has fewer calories. Do you do any Christmas shopping, Harry?" They had a few minutes to kill before the meeting. The meeting had been postponed for fifteen minutes because the President had tripped going down the stairs and was being treated for a bruise.

"A little, for my gentile friends. But it's painful to shop these days," Ratner said.

"It's hard to find a grocery store with windows any more. The rioters have smashed them, and the stores replace them with plywood."

Ratner sighed. "People are in an ugly mood, Claire."

"The 'specials' they advertise are incredible. A loaf of Wonder Bread is two dollars and ninety-nine cents. Sirloin steak is twenty-two dollars a pound—when they've got it. A quart of milk is six dollars, and a can of frozen orange juice is seven."

"Commodity prices are going crazy. The cost of living has risen over one hundred percent since the OPEC decision only three months ago."

"It's funny," Claire said, "but even though I see the printouts every day, it hits me hardest when I see something I want and can't afford it. I guess we get hardened to figures, to the tyranny of numbers."

"That's the way it is with everyone," Ratner said. "That's why inflation makes people so crazy. They feel as if things are being taken away from them and it makes them angry. They're earning more money, and they can't adjust to the fact that their dollars are worth less."

He looked pained. "I need a new suit," he said, "so I went to Brooks Brothers and found a suit I liked, just a plain, ordinary wool suit. It was fourteen hundred dollars. I couldn't believe it."

"I know," said Claire. "I wanted one of those Cartier tank watches, so I went to the Jewel Box. They didn't even have new ones in stock. They were selling slightly used ones for five thousand. I didn't know whether to laugh or to cry."

"Places like Lord and Taylor and Saks are jammed all the time," Ratner said. "That's the way it is in inflations. Those people who have money or valuable skills do well. They can raise their prices any time they want. Even people in strong unions can do very well. So can doctors, lawyers and farmers. But most people are in very bad shape."

"I guess that's where Whitelaw's people are coming from," said Claire.

"Exactly. He gets small businessmen, small farmers, retired people, young people who don't know what else to do, marginal people—and there are an awful lot of them out there."

Claire looked at her watch. "We'd better get over to the Cabinet Room," she said.

"Did you buy that watch for five thousand?" Ratner asked. "It looks like a Cartier tank watch to me."

"Yes, I did," Claire said, lifting her head. "If things get rough, I can always sell it for more." She laughed. "Besides, it's the best, and maybe I am, too." Then she laughed again—a wonderful girlish laugh that makes men's hearts ache and that is rarely heard.

Ratner took her arm. "I'll vouch for that," he said.

They ran into Colonel Edwards and Frank Trout as they reached the street.

"Merry Christmas," Claire called out.

"Merry Christmas," Trout answered.

"Merry Christmas, Claire," said Colonel Edwards. Neither man smiled when he said it. "Any news from Riyadh about the OPEC meeting there?" she asked.

"It's not official yet," Colonel Edwards said, "but it looks like another rise is coming."

"Does the FEC know how big it'll be?" Claire asked.

"About seventy-five dollars a barrel." Trout looked somber. They were walking up the steps to the hallway that led to the Cabinet Room.

"I think it'll be more like a hundred," Claire said, "or else it'll be indexed."

"You mean the price will be pegged to the CPI?" Edwards asked.

"Right," Claire said.

"I don't think that will happen, Claire. The OPEC people know we can phony up the statistics and screw them. Also, the deals become incredibly complicated when you have a price that isn't fixed, based on something that changes every day."

Frank Trout was probably right—at least Claire liked to think so. It gave her a sense of reassurance to find that he could occasionally be right about something.

As she walked into the Cabinet Room, Claire cursed under her breath. Sitting in the chair across the table from the President's seat was George McConger. Next to him was Gene Donnelly. This was going to be the key meeting, and McConger wasn't about to be late. Looking around the room, Claire saw Peter Hanrahan in a corner. She and Harry walked over to him. Hanrahan looked as tense as Ratner did.

Peter's eyes lighted up when he saw her. "You're looking especially lovely this morning, Claire."

"Thank you, Peter. Merry Christmas."

"Merry Christmas to you, too." Peter smiled, but the smile couldn't quite mask the concern in his eyes.

"What's supposed to happen at this meeting?" Claire asked.

"I don't know, Claire," Peter said. "But I do know this: There's no way on earth that we're going to come out of this without hurting like hell."

"I know. If he decides to fight the inflation, we're going to have to put the economy through the worst wringer since the Great Depression." Claire suddenly realized that this was not just an important meeting, but a crucial one—as vital as a meeting about whether or not a country should go to war. "But if we don't decide to fight the inflation, there's simply no telling what will happen."

"Have you heard about the OPEC meeting, Peter?" Ratner asked.

"Probably what you heard. Trout thinks oil is going to seventy-five dollars. I think it'll be more like a hundred," Peter said.

"Claire thinks so too," Ratner said. "Or else it'll be

tied to gold. Or it could be done on a strictly barter basis."

"That's a thought," Claire said. "Although the Arabs have so much infrastructure now, I don't know what we'd trade them."

Jim Flynn joined the group. He didn't look happy either. "I feel like going over to McConger and blowing his brains out. Do you know what's happening to the budget? Do you know what our inflation adjustments are like? We are going to have to spend more for food stamps this month than we had budgeted for the whole year."

If proper, buttoned-down Jim Flynn was feeling murderous, thought Claire, it must be happening to a lot of other people, too. But maybe, at this meeting, things would get turned around.

The room became quiet. Claire Beaton, Director of the Cost of Living Council, felt a hand on her shoulder. She turned around and found herself looking into the toothy face of the President of the United States.

"Merry Christmas, Claire," he said.

"Merry Christmas to you, Mr. President."

"We're going to need that big brain of yours today more than ever, Claire. I've got some new ideas about this inflation and I need to hear your best thoughts about them." The President turned to the others. "I need your help too. Jesus, I need everybody's help. We're caught between a rock and a hard place on this one."

Then the President abruptly turned and walked to his chair. The others scurried to their places and the meeting was under way.

"I think the first thing I should say is a personal thing for all of you who are on the White House staff. I've asked the Director of the Office of Management and Budget, Jim Flynn here, to remove the freeze on raises for White House staffers. I can't ask you to make that sacrifice any more. From now on, your wages will be adjusted to inflation like everyone else's in the Civil Service. I think that's only fair."

The President looked gravely at each face in turn. "We're in bad, bad trouble." He turned to Mc-

Conger. "I'm sorry, George, but things just aren't working out like you and I wanted them to. I've seen all the statistics. People are losing their buying power. Farmers are keeping their produce off the market. The November figures show unemployment going over twelve percent. That's terrible."

McConger kept perfect composure. He knew that his enemies had been working on the President. Milt Greenberg had been doing his best to keep McConger from even seeing the President. He knew how the Establishment worked. But he would get another chance at this meeting. He could still count on the President to be in his corner if he just kept his cool.

"Now, I have decided what I should do. The Congress is in a mess. They keep saying it's up to me, and it is. The question is, how do we put the economy into shock therapy and get a handle on this inflation? Harry, I'd like to hear from you first."

Ratner didn't hesitate: "Mr. President, we have to put the brakes on hard. Inflation is climbing so fast that we can't take gradual steps any more. Now, I'm against controls on economic grounds, but I do think they might have shock value now. If I were to choose the best possible program, I'd put on emergency price and wage controls. You already have the standby authority. Then I'd raise taxes. Then I'd change the management of the Federal Reserve System." Ratner did not look at McConger. "It's nothing personal, but the financial community needs a sign that things will be different."

McConger raised his hand. The President nodded, and McConger began: "You don't need to change the leadership at the Federal Reserve. If the President decides that what I'm doing is wrong, I'll do whatever he wants. I'm certain that the other governors of the Federal Reserve System will, too."

"Thank you for that, George," the President said. "I know you'll do what's right."

Claire Beaton was happy to detect the slightest trace of sarcasm in the President's voice.

Then the President turned to Donnelly. "Gene, I think we'll hear from you next, out of turn. What do you think we should do? What does your famous country wisdom tell you today?" Claire became concerned. The President was in an unusually sarcastic and ugly mood.

Donnelly was dressed like a Texas oil baron. He wore a tan cowboy-style suit with piping along the lapels and pockets. Claire knew without looking that he was wearing boots to go with it. It was as if he were trying to set himself off from the other males present.

Donnelly shifted uneasily in his chair and looked thoughtful. If he follows his usual pattern, thought Claire, he'll stall until he finds out what the President is going to do.

"I think that, uh, whatever you do, it's got to be done with a lot of, well, *fanfare*. If you decide we've got to bite the bullet, we've got to make it into a crusade. On the other hand, if you decide to keep on printing money, you've got to make that into a crusade too."

"What the hell does that mean?" the President asked sharply.

If Donnelly was shaken, his face didn't show it. "I mean you've got to act Presidential. Whatever you do, do it big."

The President looked him up and down, as if it was just dawning on him that Donnelly didn't have a single shred of integrity or an original thought in his head. "For Christ's sake, Gene," the President said, and shook his head. Everyone looked uncomfortable in the heavy silence that followed.

Then the President finally turned to Claire Beaton. "You're our resident genius. I ask you: Is there any way out of this mess without everybody taking a bath?"

"If there is, Mr. President, I don't see it. We've lost too much control. I think tough measures are all that's left. If we don't take them right away, the OPEC and others are going to make it that much harder. I'm afraid there's no quick fix, Mr. President." Claire Beaton regretted having used that last phrase. It sounded as if she thought that what the President wanted was something tricky, something shoddy, and today the President wasn't acting like that at all.

The President continued to look glum. "So we've all got to suffer to cure the patient?"

"Mr. President." It was George McConger. "May I say a word here?"

"Of course, George."

"I'm sure these people have the best intentions in the world. But if you do what they want you to do, you're going to be known as the man who made Herbert Hoover look like a beginner at depression-making. That's the image you're going to have. But what you look like isn't the important thing. Of course, it's important to me and to you, but what's best for the American people is what we're concerned about today. And what my opponents around this table are proposing is not what's best for the real American people."

The President already looked impressed, and Claire knew they were in for the same old crap. She braced herself for another large dose of the McConger prescription.

"What these good people are proposing is what economists have been proposing for centuries: Make the world safe for the rich. If I owe some rich man a big mortgage on my house, and then I get to pay off that mortgage a lot faster because inflation has given me a lot more dollars to pay it off with, then I'm not the one who's suffering. It's that rich man. It's all those rich people who own America that are getting hurt. Of course, the man on the street knows that everything costs more, but he also knows that he's got more money.

"Mr. President, my friends have told you that we've got to suffer to end this inflation. That is nonsense, dangerous nonsense. I'll tell you who'll suffer if you do what they suggest. The little guy will suffer. He's the one who always gets it in the neck. Do you think for one minute that the rich people in this country will suffer? Oh, maybe a little tiny bit. But not much. They figure, Why should we foot the bill? After all, we own the country.

"Now, Mr. President, this temporary period of inflation has presented you with a historic opportunity. You can turn the situation around from the way it's always been so that for once the rich people get it in the neck. You can completely reorganize the wealth in America, and make it an America which is really safe for democracy, which is just as equal for the little man as for the big man. That's an unqualified statement of fact. That's the God's truth."

The President's eyes were locked on McConger, who looked as if he were in touch with a celestial being. His large, deep-set eyes seemed to be not just staring at the President but seeing into the infinity beyond him. McConger had talked himself into a virtual trance.

Then the President broke the connection. "Christ, George, we're all family here. You don't have to give a speech like you were talking to a bunch of hicks. We're big boys, George. Your way isn't working. You know that and I know that. We all know that. So why the hell do you keep pushing it?"

Claire Beaton was taken aback. She had never before heard the President talk that way to McConger. Was there hope? Was it not yet too late?

But McConger was not through. He wasn't even slowed down. "Mr. President, my way isn't working because we haven't tried my way. Yes, I've been responsible for creating a lot of new money. And, yes, I've speeded up the inflation process so far. That's a fact. But that isn't my way. You've been misunderstanding me if you think that's my way."

McConger leaned forward in his chair as if he were about to anoint the President. His eyes glowed. "These people here are suggesting that you take a nasty fall just to make their calculations come out right, just to prove their theories. I've listened to them for a long time in the past, and all I know is that we've done what they said for hundreds and thousands of years, and people are still poor and people are still hungry and people still don't have enough money."

McConger's words came out with punishing force, like bullets fired from a rifle. He put his whole energy behind each one, Claire thought. And they were hitting the mark. The angry expression had left the President's face. He was listening raptly.

"Let me just say this to you, Mr. President. Even Harry and Claire admit, they *admit,* that their way is going to make people suffer like the living Jesus. Now my way is to create a lot more money, to get enough money into everyone's hands. Yes, some people will get hurt. But the little man won't get hurt, and the little man is most of the people in this country."

The President looked like a drowning man fished out of the sea in the nick of time.

There was silence for a moment, then an uproar in the Cabinet Room.

Peter Hanrahan exploded. "Mr. President, this is the most irresponsible, foolish demagoguery I have ever heard in my life. It is untrue. It is a formula for catastrophe. Chairman McConger is a damned fool if he believes even half of what he just said."

"Peter, I don't like that kind of talk in my Cabinet meetings. We're all on the same side here," the President said to Hanrahan.

"We are *not* all on the same side, Mr. President. At least one of us is on the side of irresponsibility and chaos. If this country is going to have a revolution, with violence and bloodshed, it should be over an issue of some moral value. It shouldn't be because someone with a twisted mind has gotten hold of a printing press, a money machine," Hanrahan said in a firm and angry voice.

Harry Ratner sought to intercede. "Mr. President," he said, "may I say something?"

The President smiled. "Of course, Harry. That's what we're here for."

In a weary voice, Harry Ratner said, "Mr. President, I have no doubt that Chairman McConger believes that what he is proposing is best for his country. I have no doubt that he is a patriot. But we don't have any more time now. What Mr. McConger proposes has been tried before. It was tried by the Germans in the Weimar Republic. It didn't work then. It was stopped eventually when people saw its dangerous effects, but it laid the foundations for National Socialism. Now, after months of testing his theories and seeing the inevitable disastrous results, it is time for a radical change.

"Mr. President, just please take it from me as your servant and your friend that what George McConger is saying, whatever his motivation, couldn't possibly be wronger." Ratner looked sadder when he finished the little speech than when he started, Claire Beaton thought.

Claire joined the protest. "Mr. President, I want to associate whatever authority I have with what has just been said. I believe I am the only one in this room who has worked out the practical world effects of continuing to follow the program Chairman McConger suggests. If we do, we will return to a barter economy within a few months. Our entire economic system will be totally wrecked. We will be setting the stage for a dictatorial repairman."

The President turned sharply to Donnelly. "What do you say, Gene? Does George's idea make sense to you?"

Donnelly hesitated only a moment before replying, "I don't want to question anyone's patriotism, Mr. President. And I must confess, I find George's idea daring. Can we lose by crusading against the rich? I say, let the word leak out that inflation isn't something we just let happen. Instead, let's call it a form of income redistribution that's bound to work in the end. Then, if it doesn't, we can always take another course. But we've got so much already invested in George."

Claire shot a look at McConger. He looked as though he'd just won the Irish Sweepstakes.

McConger pressed his advantage. "And since we're all family, as you said, Mr. President, let's put our cards on the table. I can call up Ed Ponds and a few people on the Hill, and pretty soon we'll have a tidal wave of support for the plan. But if you put the country through the wringer, you can be damn sure nobody's gonna stand up and be counted in favor of a depression. People will stand up and be counted for giving a new start to the little man."

The President looked thoughtful. "Maybe the solution is to call this goddamn inflation a crusade of some kind. It's only a question of words."

Hanrahan spoke again in a calm and self-assured voice. "If you continue to do what George McConger suggests, it will be the worst thing that ever happened to this country."

The President looked skeptically at Hanrahan. "I just can't believe inflation would be worse than another depression. I'm sorry, but I can't believe that. But I won't decide anything today. I'll think about what everyone has said."

Jesus Christ, thought Hanrahan, he's really going to do it. He's going to literally flood the country with bucks. It'll be like Noah and the flood. We'll all be drowned in megabucks.

"Before we continue," the President said, "I'd like this whole discussion to be confidential. If we start talking and the press picks up some things, well, it could defeat what we're trying to do. Let's try not to have any leaks, OK?"

Jesus, thought Claire, the President might just as well ask God to give him wings.

"One more thing," the President added. "I'm sure a lot of you are going to leave this meeting unhappy. I'm sorry. I like to keep my official family happy. But I'm running a country and not an economics laboratory. All of you who told me to put the economy through a wringer are sincere, I'm sure. But you people don't have to run for office. There's not one goddamn person here who has to run for anything but me. If my program ends badly, no one will blame you. No one nowadays remembers Hoover's advisers, but they know who Hoover was. So it's going to be my ass, not yours. And the next time your ass is on the line, and somebody comes along and offers you a way to save it without getting your cock chopped off along the way, let me know if you don't listen to what he's got to say."

He glared as he spoke and this time he did not apologize to Claire for his language. "I think we'll skip the rest of the meeting. Thank you all for coming."

With that, he got up and walked out of the room so

fast that he didn't have a chance to acknowledge it when they stood up in courtesy. In less than a minute he was in the living quarters on the second floor, where Freda lunged at him in greeting.

"Well, Freda," he said, "fuck 'em all. They got me into this goddamned mess and now they want to kill me getting out of it. Goddamn them all."

Freda tried to lick his face, but the President was walking too fast for that.

"I'm glad you kept after me," William Hanrahan told Shelby Kelsey, as they drove along Route 50 toward Baltimore's Friendship Airport.

"Well, Mr. Hanrahan, those people have a lot of your money. You ought to do something with it before they let it float away."

"I'll make sure they put it in something I can hold onto as long as this inflation lasts," Hanrahan said.

Hanrahan was on his way to talk to the people at the Trust Company of Manhattan about his bond portfolio. Kelsey had persuaded him that he should sell his bonds and buy land. William Hanrahan felt comfortable with the decision. Peter had told him there was a good chance that the President would bite the bullet, but that he, Peter, wasn't all that sure.

"Take care of Alex while I'm gone," Hanrahan told Kelsey as he got out at the terminal, "and thanks for the lift."

William Hanrahan went to the American Airlines counter and bought his ticket—$250 for a one-way coach flight to New York City. It was a bumpy flight.

He had not been to New York for over a year, and he was not looking forward to his visit. There were stories about how badly the city had disintegrated— even compared to the late Seventies, when people had thought it could not get worse. Even so, Hanrahan was not prepared for what he saw.

The airport was littered with trash and old newspapers. There were no porters, and the passenger lounges, once filled with neatly dressed businessmen, were in a state of almost total neglect. Lights were out and naked wires dangled from the ceiling.

Outside the terminal, a few battered Checker cabs were lined up. None responded when Hanrahan signaled. He walked over to the first one, where a black driver sat at the wheel asleep. Hanrahan cleared his throat. "I want to go to One Hundred Wall Street."

Groggily the driver turned his head around and said, with a heavy West Indian accent, "What'd you say, mon?"

"I'd like to go to One Hundred Wall Street. In Manhattan."

"I know where Wall Street is, mon," the driver said, annoyed. "OK. I'll take you for a hundred dollars."

"A hundred dollars? For a cab ride into town?"

"You don't want it, it's OK with me, mon."

"Is that about what the meter will say?" Hanrahan asked.

"Meters? Where you been, mon? No one uses meters any more," the driver said.

"I'll give you fifty," said Hanrahan.

"Ninety dollars, mon," the driver replied.

After haggling, they settled on $75, plus a $5 tip if they got there in an hour.

"You drive a hard bargain, mon," the driver said without smiling.

The cab pulled out onto the Long Island Expressway. Every few feet there were gaping potholes. Sometimes the cab hit them and sometimes the driver made a violent turn and missed them.

"It's that damn bitch Mayor Abzug," the driver said. "Her fault, mon."

Hanrahan didn't say anything, partly because he had nothing to say and partly because he was getting a headache from the bouncing around he was getting.

"No traffic, mon. You notice that?" the driver asked.

"Yes, I noticed that," Hanrahan said.

"Nobody wants to buy gasoline no more. Too expensive. People don't like to get their cars smashed up on these roads either. Me, I don' care. It's not my cab, you know?"

Hanrahan was glad when they got through the Queens Midtown tunnel and into Manhattan. Second Avenue, at least, didn't look too different from his last visit—until he saw the black women with platform shoes and blond wigs strolling back and forth. Against the walls of abandoned storefronts, smiling, clean-cut-looking boys and girls were putting up pictures of William Whitelaw with the words "One with God" under his handsome face. The boys and girls wore denim coveralls.

When the cab stopped at a red light at 21st Street, the driver laughed and turned to Hanrahan. "You want a piece, mon? It's all over. I get you some fine woman, huh?"

"No, thank you," Hanrahan said. "I'm here on business."

They were on the lower East Side. It had always looked like a disaster area to Hanrahan and it looked no better, no worse. At the bottom of the ladder there must be a permanently rotten state of life that didn't ever change much.

Soon they had driven past Chinatown and into the financial district. It was comforting to see that the office buildings still looked clean and well cared for.

When the taxi pulled up in front of 100 Wall Street, Hanrahan looked at his watch and saw that he owed the driver the full amount plus $5. He counted out four twenties and gave them to the driver, who looked at him expectantly for a further tip. When it didn't come, the taxi driver shouted at Hanrahan's back, "Fuck you, mon, you cheap bastud."

Edwin McDowell, his account manager at the Trust Company of Manhattan, was friendlier. "I hope you had a pleasant flight up, Mr. Hanrahan."

"The flight was all right, but I had a terrible ride into the city," Hanrahan said. "The roads are disgraceful."

"That's only too true," said McDowell. "But New York has been in receivership for over a year. There's just no money to repair them."

"How can you bear to live here?" Hanrahan asked.

"It's where my job is," said McDowell. "Let's go into my office."

When they sat down in a small office overlooking New York harbor, McDowell said, "I suppose you're unhappy about your portfolio."

"I'm unhappy as hell. I've lost about fifteen million this year on paper."

McDowell expressed sympathy.

"I think you should have gotten me out of bonds and into something else a long time ago," Hanrahan said. He was getting mad. "You've been pretty free and easy with my money."

McDowell flushed. "We never thought inflation would get this bad. Our economists kept saying it would stop and to expect a major rally in the bond market. But of course you're right. If you're unhappy, we're unhappy. We'll help you diversify your portfolio. We think that some of the railroad stocks look good."

"Hell no!" Hanrahan said. "I don't want railroad stocks. I want to buy land. It's going up like a rocket, and I want to get in."

McDowell recovered quickly. "That's fine. Of course, land is not a readily salable investment, but if that's what you want, I think we have the right thing for you. It's an agricultural land trust. We've bought several very large parcels of land in Wyoming and Colorado, about a billion dollars' worth. A trust owns the land, and individuals like you can have a piece of the trust. We just started it seven days ago," McDowell explained, twirling a pencil in his hand. "We're already selling two hundred and fifty thousand dollar units."

William Hanrahan had always been a cautious man. He liked to brood about things, turn them over in his mind. But today was different. He thought of how decayed the city had looked as he'd come in from the airport, and how urgently Shelby Kelsey had suggested he buy land. For once he decided to act on impulse.

"I'd like to buy forty units. Right now. Sell as many of the bonds as you have to. We'll sign the papers today."

"Right now?"

"Right now. Before lunch," Hanrahan said.

"Well. I guess we can do that. You're awfully quick on the trigger, Mr. Hanrahan." McDowell smiled and left the office. He returned in a few minutes with a few papers.

"This is just insurance," McDowell said. "I have a feeling that we've seen the worst of this inflation. There's a story on the Dow-Jones ticker today that the President is getting ready to announce a new program to fight it."

"Maybe," said Hanrahan. "But my brother works at the White House and he's awfully pessimistic. Let's take out the insurance."

"The land trust will be a good investment even when inflation recedes," said McDowell. "I think you're smart to diversify."

Hanrahan thought to himself that if land was so damn smart, why hadn't the Trust Company suggested it before? McDowell would probably agree with anything he said. Nevertheless, he went ahead and signed the papers. Then McDowell left the room again to check on the computerized printout of the results of Hanrahan's bond sales. He returned in a few minutes.

Both men looked at the clock and saw that it was almost noon. Hanrahan was hungry. McDowell seemed to sense it. "I'd be very happy if you would stay for lunch. We could eat here or go over to Eberlin's."

William Hanrahan remembered Eberlin's as a noisy, boisterous place with good steak. It was usually filled with brokers who kept one eye on the tickers spread around the restaurant and the large Dow-Jones projection ticker that played like a movie against one wall. "Let's go out to Eberlin's," Hanrahan said. "I haven't eaten out in weeks."

A few minutes later, both men walked in a chilling wind to Eberlin's on New Street, just behind the New York Stock Exchange. Hanrahan looked forward to a baked potato with sour cream and chives.

But he got a shock when he saw the prices on the menu. The New York cut steak lunch, including baked potato with sour cream and chives, was an even $100. Still, he thought, it's on the Trust Company of Manhattan, even if they do add it to their management fee. After he ordered, he watched the quotations on the ticker behind him and watched the Dow-Jones ticker announce various odds and ends of economic news, dividends, purchase orders and government contracts. He found it hard to talk to McDowell, who was too sycophantic for his tastes. He had gotten used to the straight-talking people of Caroline County. So he was happy when his steak came and he could eat rather than talk.

As he was putting the sour cream onto the potato, he heard a bell start ringing. Everyone in the room looked up at the Dow-Jones. "What the hell is that?" asked Hanrahan.

"It means something special is coming over the tape, like a stock split or a special dividend," McDowell said.

The bell rang for what seemed a very long time, and the restaurant became utterly silent except for the bell. Then the message appeared on the wall.

A FEDERAL RESERVE SOURCE REPORTED THIS AFTERNOON THAT THE FEDERAL RESERVE AND THE PRESIDENT ARE IN AGREEMENT IN A PROGRAM TO USE THE FEDERAL POWER TO CREATE MONEY TO CONTINUE INFLATION AS A MEANS OF HELPING DEBTORS PAY OFF DEBTS AND DISTRIBUTE INCOME MORE WIDELY. THE SOURCE SAID THAT A COMPLETE RESTRUCTURING OF THE CAPITAL MARKETS OF THE COUNTRY WAS CERTAIN TO FOLLOW. ASKED ABOUT WHAT THIS MEANT IN TERMS OF THE RATE OF INFLATION, THE SOURCE SAID THAT IT WOULD BE FAR HIGHER THAN THE CURRENT RATE, WHICH IS ABOVE 200 PERCENT.

Eberlin's suddenly exploded with noise. Men started to shout at each other. They leaped from their tables, throwing down hundred-dollar bills, running past the checkroom without their coats. "For Christ's sake, let's get moving," the man in the booth next to Hanrahan said. In his haste, he pulled the tablecloth off Hanrahan's table without stopping to apologize as dishes, glasses and silverware fell to the floor, crashing and shattering and tinkling.

McDowell grabbed Hanrahan's arm and said, "Jesus Christ, man, let's get the hell out of here." In seconds, Eberlin's was almost empty.

"What do we do now?" Hanrahan asked as they ran out the door toward McDowell's office.

McDowell's face was red, choked with confusion and fear. "The government is about to ruin the bond market. We've got to sell you out."

The two middle-aged men ran down Wall Street. Everybody they saw was running. It looked like a farce, except that no one was smiling.

The elevators were hopelessly crowded. One appeared to be stuck on the seventh floor.

"Can you walk?" asked McDowell.

"Fifteen floors?"

"It's your money," McDowell said, "and it's going up in smoke. We've got to get up there and sell."

"All right," Hanrahan wheezed.

By the time they got to the Trust Company offices, Hanrahan's heart was beating like a triphammer, his body rebelling. He felt lightheaded. McDowell dragged him down a hall toward a door marked ASSOCIATES ONLY. Beyond the door, two rows of men and women sat at long tables, watching the information on the three exchange tapes flash across the wall, talking into telephones and typing into computer terminals.

Every face in the room wore a frantic look of determination. Hanrahan felt sick, exhausted. He found an empty chair and slumped into it. Mesmerized, he watched the symbols flash across the boards. He didn't recognize most, but occasionally he saw one he remembered like an old friend—RJR for what used to be R.J. Reynolds Tobacco, LTV for what used to be Ling-Temco-Vought, TRW, ITT and a few others. The figures beside the names kept getting lower. A sign flashed the information that the Consolidated tape, which used to be the New York Stock Exchange tape, was ten minutes late. It had not been ten minutes since the news had flashed on the wall at Eberlin's. Soon the same sign flashed on the American Stock Exchange tape and the New York bond tape.

After a few minutes, Hanrahan felt better. He walked through the noisy, bustling room, where Mc-Dowell sat at a computer terminal.

"What's going on?" Hanrahan asked.

"We can't get a trade on your bonds," said Mc-Dowell. "Jesus Christ! Look at that bond tape. The market is getting wiped out."

Hanrahan looked at the bond tape. He could see that the numbers after the symbols were getting lower and lower; they would inch up to 7/8 and work down to 1/8, then 7/8 again and down. He saw it happen again and again.

Suddenly Hanrahan desperately wanted to leave that room full of fear and panic. He was in the middle of some kind of financial catastrophe, and he didn't want to face it in a windowless room full of angry, frightened people.

"I'm leaving now," he said.

"We'll keep on trying, Mr. Hanrahan. Jesus, I'm sorry," McDowell said. He looked as though he was about to cry.

Hanrahan went out of the trading room of the Trust Company of Manhattan, down the corridor, into the reception room, down the elevator and out into the empty street. It was as if he were the lone survivor of a terrible calamity which had depopulated the Wall Street area. Even as he thought it, he realized that he probably was a survivor after all. What an incredibly lucky break it had been that he had bought into that land trust. He felt as if a divine providence had watched over him.

He wandered down Broad Street and came to the members' entrance of the New York Stock Exchange. It was wide open, even on this cold December day. No clerks or messengers lounged around as they usually did. A muffled roar came from the inside. As if he were in a dream, Hanrahan walked in. He went down several corridors and through several sets of double doors, and suddenly he stood on the floor of the New York Stock Exchange.

He had been there before and it had always seemed disorganized, but today there was absolute, stark pandemonium. Men ran around shrieking at one another as if the world were coming to an end. Wild gestures of the arms and hands punctuated every communication. And the looks on the brokers' faces were worst of all—as if this moment had put a terror into them that would last the rest of their lives. It was a scene out of hell.

High on the wall at one end of the room the tape of transactions flashed the news with dizzying speed. Hanrahan was able to recognize a few of the symbols again. He noticed that the numbers after the symbols were moving down, and moving down fast. RJR 7/8, then RJR 1/2, then RJR 1/8, then RJR 7/8, then RJR 1/2, and down and down.

As he stood there, a man with a gray vest, a gray suit and a gray face walked up and sighed. "That's it. There just aren't any more buy orders in Xerox. I might just as well go home. I've used up every order in my book. And it just keeps flooding the market. I hope one of the other fellows can pick up some of these trades."

Hanrahan realized that the man must be a specialist, a broker whose function it was to make a market in a particular stock—in this case, Xerox. The gray man looked much older than Hanrahan had thought at first.

"You know," the man said, "I was just a messenger during the crash of twenty-nine. I never thought I'd see a day like that again. This is going to be much, much worse."

"How bad?" Hanrahan asked.

"So bad you shouldn't ask." The man studied Hanrahan. "You're probably new here. What a way to get started. This is a panic, man, a complete panic. Look at that." The tape was now twenty minutes late. "The Dow is off forty-seven points and the news from the Fed only came in a half hour ago when . . ."

His words were drowned out by shouts from the

floor. They were so loud and confused that at first Hanrahan couldn't make out what people were saying. Then he heard numbers. "A half, a half!" a gesticulating man in shirtsleeves hooted at a group of men near him, who nodded their heads until the man shouted, "A point! A point!"

The gray man walked slowly away shaking his head. "Good luck," Hanrahan called after him, but the man in gray did not turn around.

Hanrahan walked out the door he had come in, and down empty, paper-strewn corridors. He saw a sign for the New York Bond Exchange. In a moment he was standing on a far smaller and deserted trading floor. No tape flashed above. Only a janitor was present, slowly sweeping the floor. A single man in a suit walked in, as though in a trance.

"What's happened?" Hanrahan asked him without thinking. But the man simply turned and walked away, his eyes without expression.

Hanrahan walked up to the janitor. "What's happened here? Has the Bond Exchange moved?"

The janitor, a dejected Puerto Rican, said in a sad voice, "They've closed this place down for the day, man. There wasn't nothin' else they could do. The bottom fell out."

Hanrahan said, "Thanks," and walked out. He headed back to the Stock Exchange and went inside. Once again, the man in gray sought his ear.

"The Dow is off over one hundred points now. I don't see how the market can stay open much longer. The Chicago Board of Trade is going crazy."

Hanrahan didn't answer. He turned around, walked out of the building and flagged the only taxi in sight.

"I'll give you one hundred dollars for a smooth ride to La Guardia."

"You got a deal," the driver said.

The radio was playing Christmas carols.

"Can you get the news?" asked Hanrahan.

The driver turned the dial. ". . . denies that the report came from the White House. Moreover, the source reported that the President has not decided to attempt to restructure the nation's capital markets through inflation. The President is still considering all his options.

"There have been reports, however, from a high economic official that the administration plans to generate an even faster inflation in an attempt to fundamentally change the social system."

"Hey, man," the driver asked, "you want to hear any more of this garbage?"

"A few minutes longer," Hanrahan said, as the taxi lurched over the potholes. "Please."

". . . Meanwhile in Chicago, traders saw wheat pass the $100-per-bushel mark for the first time in the nation's history, and the price is still climbing. In Japan, prices on the bullion markets have reacted dramatically to the news out of Washington. In Tokyo, gold closed at over $4,000 an ounce, up more than $1,000 in the first half hour of trading, which is also a record.

"Here is a special CBS News Alert. The Board of Governors of the New York Stock Exchange closed the market at 2:10 P.M., almost two hours early. The Governors acted after a record-breaking plunge of 157 points on the Dow-Jones Industrial Average, when members were no longer able to find buyers for many stocks. This followed the report of a Federal Reserve plan to create a much higher rate of inflation for as yet undisclosed reasons. . . ."

## 6

CLAIRE Beaton watched the face of John Chancellor. It was unusually grave.

"Good evening on a day in which Americans learned what may be some of the worst economic news this country has every endured." Behind Chancellor's face was a picture of a jammed stock-market floor, and superimposed on it appeared a sharply fluctuating graph with a precipitous final plunge.

"The New York Stock Exchange dropped by over 125 points today following new reports from Washington, before the Board of Governors of the Exchange closed it nearly two hours early to stop what had become the worst selling panic in memory.

"The New York Stock Exchange Bond Market dropped so swiftly that trading came to a halt only fifteen minutes after the announcement which triggered both events and a lot more besides.

"For a report on that Washington leak and its impact on the nation's economy, we will bring you reports from Tom Brokaw in Washington, Cassie Mackin in New York and Tom Pettit in Chicago. First, here's Tom Brokaw."

The picture changed, and Claire saw Tom Brokaw standing in a glare of lights in front of a sign that read "The Federal Reserve Board," with the marble building of the Federal Reserve behind him.

In a rich and sonorous tone, Brokaw spoke. "The Federal Reserve Board was created nearly seventy years ago to prevent panics and economic instability. But today, a report from a high Federal Reserve source led to the most ominous behavior in American financial markets since the founding of the Republic. The announcement, which reportedly comes from extremely high sources inside this building, who refuse to be identified, said that the Federal Reserve, which controls the supply of money and credit in the United States and thus has one of the best handles on inflation, will use that power not to stop the inflation, but to make it grow faster than ever."

Brokaw slightly shifted his posture and looked very serious. "The rationale behind this seemingly suicidal behavior is that money will become so plentiful that the millions of Americans who are deeply in debt for mortgages or farms or whatever will be able to pay off those loans and start afresh.

"White House economic sources say, however, that this reasoning does not take into account the fact that most of these mortgages are really owned by other middle-income Americans through their banks and savings and loan associations and insurance companies. White House economic circles further say that the consequences of such irresponsible action by the Federal Reserve Board, which one senior White House trade official described as 'insane,' would be far worse than any good effects the action may have for debtors.

"Thus the split in economic policy making within the administration appears to have broken out into the open with a devastating effect on the nation's financial and commodity markets.

"The President's press secretary, Patti Matson, said that the President was extremely concerned about the situation. She also said that there was no concerted plan to make the nation's financial markets suffer during this inflation. Matson hinted that the President would make a statement later into the weekend. That may put to rest some of the anxieties generated by today's leak from the Federal Reserve. But for tonight, it looks like the United States won't be having a very Merry Christmas."

Claire Beaton's phone rang just as the picture was returning to John Chancellor to announce a commercial break. She picked up the phone next to the couch. Myrna Lewis, her secretary, said that Mr. Hanrahan was calling from the White House.

Claire told Myrna to put the call through and she listened for Peter's voice with a fair amount of puzzlement. Was Peter planning an economic countercoup of some kind?

"Hi, Claire, Merry Christmas. How are you?" Peter Hanrahan said.

"Oh, just great, Peter. I figure that people won't get around to executing me for a few weeks. Have they started setting up a gallows in Lafayette Square?"

"No, but the President has gone up to Camp David with Secretary Donnelly and the great George McConger."

"Are you kidding?"

"I wish I were. Unfortunately it's true."

"Jesus. What's happening in the international markets?"

"Well, the only important one that was still open when McConger opened his mouth was the Tokyo market. The dollar's falling like a stone, and the whole Tokyo stock exchange is in convulsions. The yen is going to take a beating too because of what's happening on the commodities markets," Peter said.

Claire noticed that at just that moment the screen showed Tom Pettit in front of a huge empty stockyard. He talked about the phenomenal day on the commodities markets. He said that farmers were worried, though, because while many had become millionaires and even potentially billionaires in a day, they were uncertain as to what would happen to their costs and to the value of the dollars they were receiving in such profusion today.

"Yes, I'm just watching it on the TV right now," Claire said.

"We've been getting the most amazing kinds of phone calls from Europe all day. And the OPEC representative in Washington wants to have lunch with me tomorrow. He thinks we're doing all this just to screw up OPEC. I wish he were right." Peter laughed.

Claire could just see Peter laughing. He laughed with great confidence. He did everything with great confidence, she thought.

"Anyway," Peter said, "I have had the most godawful kind of day, and I am hungry and dispirited, and I would love to take a pretty and charming lady to dinner. Are you free at this late notice?"

Claire suddenly had an image of Peter Hanrahan as Bing Crosby in *Going My Way*. He really was so wonderfully Irish and delightful.

"I'd love to, Peter," Claire said. "I haven't had the world's premier day myself. I don't suppose anyone has except for McConger."

"Well, mine will end well if you'll have dinner with me," Peter said. "I'll come over in an hour. How about eating at the Empress?"

"That would be fine," Claire answered. "Just call up from the desk. I'll be in my office."

Claire hung up the telephone and looked back at the television. The reporter, whom Claire did not recognize, was interviewing a welfare mother in Ohio. She was saying that it just seemed like the rich got richer. And she didn't see how she was going to feed her nine children unless the government gave her more welfare. "It just seems like there's no way for the little people any more," she said.

Next, the same reporter was interviewing a construction man from Lordstown, Ohio, who said he thought maybe McConger and the Federal Reserve had something there. "I don't really care that much how much things cost as long as I'm making good money," he said. "And it would be awfully good to get the house paid off. I just don't know how much the builders are going to be able to pay us though. But for now, I don't mind seeing the stock market go down. I ain't got no stock—never did."

Claire watched as two commercials, one for a denture adhesive and one for medication for hemorrhoids, came on. Then there was Barry Kalb interviewing William Whitelaw about the panic. "It did not surprise me one little bit," Whitelaw said. "The government has lived for so long with no sense of obligation to anyone but itself, and without any sense of obligation to the faith that made this country great or the discipline that made this country strong, that eventually something had to give." God, he was a good speaker, Claire thought. And handsome too. The camera angle shifted and the screen was filled with Whitelaw speaking to a rally that night in Orlando, Florida.

"How much longer," Whitelaw shouted to his audience, "are you going to let the bureaucrats and the self-promoters steal the soul of this country? You are being tested right this minute. You can only respond by demanding a new order—an order with decency, faith and discipline." The crowd of mostly young-looking people in sports shirts and cotton dresses clapped energetically and a few whooped. Claire could see the inevitable THIS IS WHITELAW COUNTRY banner in the background.

Barry Kalb fixed the camera with a sincere eye and

said, with the Whitelaw rally in the background, "A country in crisis often looks for a man who is speaking clearly and loudly. And the people here in Orlando seem to be hearing Bill Whitelaw loud and clear. This is Barry Kalb reporting from Orlando."

Claire turned off the television. Someone from NBC had wanted to talk to her, but she didn't want to talk. She was trying to decide something that day, something of great importance to her—whether to resign. She was glad she was going to be talking to Peter Hanrahan that night. She felt sure that he must be facing the same problem.

But the Empress was no place to talk. The tables were too close, and people recognized both her and Peter as soon as they came in. She liked being recognized, and she loved Peking duck, but they didn't discuss a word about their work during dinner.

When they got back into Peter's car, Claire asked, "How about taking me up on that nightcap I never offered you, Peter? I have something important I want to talk with you about."

Peter took her hand and squeezed it as they sat down, and he said, "Absolutely. I was hoping you'd ask."

Claire hoped that the day worker had done a good job on her apartment. She didn't want to seem like a slob in front of this man who exuded suaveness. But Peter wasn't worrying about whether her apartment would be neat. He was thinking that Cathy Graham had been away on vacation for two weeks and that he missed her, but that this slim, brilliant woman he was with was turning him on in a way he had never been turned on before.

When they got inside Claire's apartment—the second floor of a Federal-style townhouse—Claire turned on the lights and took Peter's coat. "It's not the White House," Claire said, "but I try to make it look presentable."

Peter Hanrahan looked around him. The long, narrow living room had heavy white curtains, which were drawn. There were two couches and two armchairs, both in a modern style, with an eggplant-colored burlap fabric covering them. There was a counter with a bar, and a number of small tables, on each of which books were neatly piled.

"What would you like to drink?" Claire asked.

"B and B, if you have it," Hanrahan said. "But don't go to any trouble."

She poured him a snifter of the liqueur and another for herself. Then she sat down next to him on a couch, and said, "I'm glad you could come over, Peter. I've been wanting to discuss something with you."

Hanrahan said nothing, but only looked intently at her lips.

"I wonder, I really wonder, what I'm doing here. I just can't decide whether or not I should resign. I mean, am I doing the right thing?" She was getting a powerful vibration from Hanrahan. "Am I doing any good here?"

"Yes," Peter Hanrahan said firmly, and pulled her toward him. He kissed her half-parted lips while her pulse raced. Then he pushed her slightly away from him and asked, "Are you crazy? You're doing everyone a lot of good by being here. Especially me."

He kissed her again and stroked her small breasts. She felt an excitement building within her. God, she thought, I can't believe this is happening. Peter Hanrahan wants me. They kissed and then Peter whispered in her ear, very distinctly, "Let's make love."

"I'd love to," she said, also in a whisper.

Five minutes later they were lying on her fourposter bed in the dim pinkness that the sodium-vapor lights cast through the lightly curtained bedroom windows. Claire Beaton marveled at Peter's sense of command. Never in her life had she been in bed with a man who was so sure of himself. His every touch generated a feeling that he was in charge, that the situation was both wildly exciting and perfectly under control. He hugged her to him as if she, and the whole world, belonged to him, she thought. He had no diffidence whatever about probing every part of her. And she, who was so used to the fumbling advances of her academic colleagues, was just lying back and letting it happen.

When they reached the climax of their lovemaking, Claire knew she had been mastered, and yet liberated. Peter Hanrahan's assurance had given her assurance. They thrust against each other with more abandon than Claire had ever dreamed of. She was aroused by the dominance of Hanrahan and she responded to it with her own strength. When the climax came she knew that Hanrahan was a man who had been worth waiting for.

For several minutes, she lay curled in his arms. Then she heard the chiming of the clock at 11 P.M., and, as if by instinct, she picked up the remote control for the TV in the bedroom and flicked it on. Peter Hanrahan did not object. He just softly stroked her back as she ran her hand over his chest.

On the TV screen, Eric Sevareid said, "Since 1776, there has been a feeling about America that the future would always be better than the past. That has been the faith that sustained America through a Civil War, through great social upheaval, through two World Wars, depressions and political convulsions. But that faith rested on a belief that there were some things in life that were secure. Today Americans may have lost that faith, because today, more intensely than ever before, people are feeling that the certainties are going out of life. From now on, we're in uncharted territory, and it looks threatening. Today, the future does not look better than the past or the present. Perhaps we as a nation have had it too easy for too long, or perhaps some long-sealed fate is catching up with us. But whatever it is, we are in for grim times, and we will need all our national strength to keep from coming apart. Our greatest testing is upon us, and the outcome is not bright."

But as Sevareid spoke those gloomy words, Claire Beaton was thinking that today had opened up new horizons for her. Her hand moved slowly down Hanrahan's waist as she moved her face up and kissed him.

The air was so cold and clear outside Harry Ratner's office that he could see past the leafless trees across the street, out past the Washington monument, even beyond to the Jefferson Memorial. It was a Sunday afternoon, and there was hardly any traffic around the Executive Office Building. The windows were double Thermopane glass, and Harry Ratner's thick oak doors were closed. He felt as if he were atop a peak, somewhere still and quiet and peaceful. He had to have that feeling sometimes or he would go crazy.

His days had turned into an unending stream of meetings, briefings, writing of statements—all about the inflation. Harry Ratner now had a computer terminal installed in his office. It was connected to the new computer that had been put in at the Labor Department, which gave daily readouts of the Consumer Price Index and twice-weekly readouts of the Wholesale Price Index.

Day after day, Harry Ratner would have to appear before some subcommittee or labor group or consumer group to explain why inflation of 100 percent per week was a sensible policy. It was giving him bad headaches.

The Saturday before Christmas, almost a month ago now, he had lunched with Claire Beaton and Peter Hanrahan, who seemed to Harry to be awfully thick with each other, and they had talked about the problem—Topic A. All three had agreed that it did not make sense to stay on at the White House, or in the government, when the President was not only pursuing a policy which they considered wrong, but was lying to them about it.

"Listen," Claire had said, so emphatically that people at nearby tables at Le Provençal had turned around, "here is one person who doesn't want to put up with these lies and this sickening policy any longer. I think we should all resign and try to set up some kind of lobbying group to get McConger out of the Federal Reserve." Hanrahan had agreed with her, and so had Ratner, although reluctantly. For Harry Ratner believed strongly in team playing. Once you were on the team, you stayed with the team. It made a lot of sense to him—it was a way to reconcile what he knew to be insane economic policy with his own personal sanity.

But Claire had convinced him that when the captain of the team either didn't know the signals or wasn't calling them straight, he was no longer on the team. And they were making the whole thing worse by giving it an air of respectability. Claire had put it bluntly: "Let's get the hell out and expose the fact that the economic policy of this country is in the hands of a crackpot."

So Harry Ratner called Milt Greenberg for an appointment with the President as soon as possible. To Harry Ratner's surprise, Greenberg said that the President wanted to see him. Greenberg said that the President knew that Claire, Hanrahan and Flynn were particularly unhappy with what had happened, and he wanted to meet with them right away as well. Flynn had gone to Antigua, but Peter and Claire were in Ratner's office while Greenberg was on the phone, so it was easy for Ratner and Greenberg to arrange a meeting for 4 P.M. that afternoon in the Oval Office.

Harry Ratner paused for a moment in his recollections and picked up the binoculars that he kept on top of his desk. He looked through them toward the Jefferson Memorial. The glasses were so good that he could make out the checks on a woman tourist's scarf, as she walked down the steps of the domed structure toward the Tidal Basin.

It was at that meeting a month ago in the Oval Office, Harry remembered, that he had first realized why some people get to be Presidents of the United States.

Milt Greenberg had been waiting for them when they came in through the West Wing door. "We have a few minutes, so let me fill you in on a few things. That leak yesterday was not authorized by the President. I know. I was with him when it came out, and he hit the roof. He was on the phone bawling out McConger for half an hour. He was up most of the night getting reports from Donnelly on what was happening in the financial markets. I just wanted you to know that before you go in." ￼

The President looked as if he had been up most of the night. He was always tanned, but under the tan he looked pallid and tense. His brown eyes were bloodshot and there were baggy circles under his eyes. He still had those white teeth, though, and that same winning smile. When the four economic aides entered the Oval Office, the President got up from his desk and walked over to them, greeting Claire Beaton first. He took both of her hands in his.

"Claire, you look particularly gorgeous on this particularly bleak day. Thank you for coming so quickly." He shook hands warmly with Ratner and Hanrahan. "Harry, Peter, thank you for coming too. Sit down."

They arranged themselves so that the President was sitting next to Claire on one couch, facing Hanrahan and Ratner on the other. Greenberg sat in the armchair adjacent to the President's couch.

Claire Beaton spoke first. "Mr. President, I must tell you that we have discussed the economic situation and the administration's response to it in private. I am grateful for the honor of being named to the Cabinet, but I can no longer usefully serve you. I'm sorry."

The President did not look the slightest bit surprised. He turned to the two men and said, "I suppose you are going to say the same thing."

Ratner said, "I don't know. I feel the same way as Claire. If the policy that we saw yesterday is your policy, I don't see how I can stay on. I don't think I can be useful to you any more."

Hanrahan followed: "Those are my feelings too, Mr. President. And I, too, add that I've been honored to have served in your Cabinet."

The President let out a long sigh. "Look," he said, "let's skip the horseshit about honor and service and so forth. I'm in a damned difficult spot. This administration is in a damned difficult spot. The whole fucking country is in a mess.

"My only consideration at this point is how to get the country out of this mess without making it worse. When I told you at the Cabinet meeting yesterday that I wasn't going to make any decision yet, I wasn't lying. But you know as well as I do that McConger has got me in a box.

"I know he sent out that story yesterday. And I know that even though George is a fine man, he's just a little bit bent out of shape about the whole notion that money is the solution to every problem. I know that, I assure you."

The President looked around the room again, with something approaching desperation in his face.

"I'm up a creek without a paddle if you people leave and start taking shots at me. McConger has a lot of friends on the Hill who will raise hell if I try to dump him. He's been making that same pitch about giving the little man another chance all over town. Why do you think we're not getting as much flak from the Hill as we used to get about the inflation? Because of McConger. He's spread the word that he's going to give us the chance to run on the most exciting platform since FDR—the platform of making every fucking man a king.

"All right. So here's where I am. The financial markets are going haywire over McConger's ideas. I know that you people know a lot about economics, and if you tell me that McConger's plans are completely off the wall, maybe that's right. I also know that your suggestions about austerity and that shit would make me look good in a hundred years, but would cost me my ass now.

"Maybe, eventually, we'll have to stop this inflation by doing the kinds of things you people suggested—raising taxes, all that kind of shit. But I just can't do that right now. The word is out that we're going to try a new kind of policy that's going to make the poor equal to the rich. If I turn around and say that we're not going to do that, it looks like I'm shooting Santa Claus. If I put the economy through the wringer to boot, Congress will be up in arms, my own party will be out to get me, and the country will just have to go through hell. I'll have to go through hell. Me. Not you."

The President paused. His toothy smile had gone.

It was replaced by a look of determination—weary, dogged determination. He looked as though he did not want any back talk, and at the same time the look evoked great sympathy, like that of a soldier who is shell-shocked but still fighting. For a moment, his eyes seemed far away. Then they snapped into focus. "But let me get to the point of why I desperately need you to stay, why I must insist for the sake of this country that you stay.

"With you here, people will think that there are still competent people around the White House. They'll think that eventually we'll change McConger's policy. If you three go, especially if you go out and raise the roof against the administration, the people will have no confidence that we are ever going to change Mc-Conger's way of doing things."

The President paused. "Look. I'm not going to lie to you. I need you around to make the people believe that this administration hasn't gone crazy. I need you to defend this administration, even this policy, so that people will think that there's some careful thought going into it."

Harry Ratner was confused. "Mr. President—I don't understand. You want us to convince people that the current policy will change and also to convince people that the exact same policy is right?"

"Exactly. I want you to go out there and say, 'Yes, it's a daring new policy, and yes, it is a gamble. And if it doesn't work, we'll change it.' I want you to go out and say that the policy of this administration is shaped not exclusively by McConger, and that even though we're trying his way for a while, we'll change it if it doesn't work."

Everyone in the room was silent for a moment. The President picked up the conversation with a new firmness in his voice. "If you leave, McConger and those people on the Hill will have people to replace you who will jump when McConger says to jump. There'll be people in your jobs who have no reputations. The public respects you. And if you leave, you're leaving McConger in the driver's seat. This way, at least, you'll be in a position to get your views to me."

The President turned to Claire Beaton. "This is the real world here, Claire. People don't give a shit what some economics professor at Yale says, and that's the truth. But down here you can get stuff done. You may have to go out and defend a policy you don't like, but that's part of the real world. In the long run, you'll have a chance to put your policy across if you stay, and you won't if you leave. That's the hard truth. I'm giving it to you straight. I'm asking you to stay for everybody's sake, including your own. If you stick it out here, you can do things that will change history."

He paused, took Claire's hand, and said, "This is a choice you have to make, Claire: whether you want to shape history or write about it."

Harry Ratner raised the binoculars to his eyes again. He could see the birds hovering over the Tidal Basin and occasionally skimming along its surface. He tried to remember what part of the President's arguments that afternoon had changed their minds. He decided it was the last part—when the President had told them that they had the chance either to be a part of history if they stayed, or to write about history if they left. Claire Beaton had been the first one to say she would stay.

That was why Harry Ratner was still at his post at the EOB on a Sunday in late January. He was writing a speech to give to the National Association of Manufacturers explaining why the policy of creating ever more inflation was good for them. He had the whole routine down pat now, and people were buying it. He said that corporations would benefit from the inflation, too, because they could wipe out their indebtedness just like individuals.

Apparently people believed that, and they were realizing profits, at least in inflated dollars, because even though the bond market had gone through the floor, the Dow-Jones Industrial Average had passed the 2,000 mark within a few weeks of its initial tumble. People were adjusting to inflation, at least on the stock market.

But in the commodities markets the situation was

still chaotic. Commodity prices had gone straight through the roof and were still climbing. Wheat was over $400 a bushel and still rising. Harry Ratner had addressed a meeting of the American Farm Bureau Federation and had gotten the most hostile reception ever. Farmers didn't want to sell anything, really, because no matter what price they got for it, in a few weeks their money was hardly worth anything. They wanted to be paid in something that would keep its value, they told Harry. He answered that they could demand to be paid in gold, but in that case no one would be buying, because gold was just over the rainbow.

The worst was when Harry Ratner left the cocoon of the White House and went out into the streets. The day before, he and his wife had gone to the Chevy Chase Lord and Taylor. It was mobbed. People were cheerfully forking over $2,000 for what appeared to Harry to be perfectly ordinary wool dresses. Men's neckties were in the $250 range if they looked at all decent. And people were buying everything in sight like devouring sharks.

If only McConger could have seen what was going on at Lord and Taylor. The rich weren't getting poorer and the poor, with a few exceptions, weren't getting richer—the rich were getting richer and the people in the middle were getting squeezed like hell. Ratner noticed that while the parking lots at Lord and Taylor and Saks Fifth Avenue on Wisconsin Avenue were filled, there were plenty of spaces at Woodward and Lothrop, which sold a much lower-priced line of goods.

As Harry Ratner resumed work on his speech, he looked at his calculator. These days everyone had them. Texas Instruments had come out with one with a function for multiplying a number by the cost of living over a period of days. Even maids used them to figure out how much they should get paid. The number for the day appeared in the newspaper every morning, and people just plugged it into their calculators to figure out everything.

Harry Ratner started to get another headache. The whole thing had to collapse. Prices were getting chaotic beyond belief. What was happening in the commodities markets would start happening everywhere. But Harry Ratner was there, in the cockpit of history, working on the team. He took two Tylenol with codeine out of his desk. He poured water into a paper cup from a pitcher bearing the Presidential Seal.

While Harry Ratner was staring out his window, Jim Adams was watching the Redskins play the Dolphins. He was enjoying the fine color of his Sony Super Trinitron III set, but he was troubled. Things just weren't working out right, in a lot of ways. He looked across the den to where Laurie was doing crewel work while keeping an eye on the baby. The baby was in the bassinet that said "Marie" on it in pink letters. Jim noticed that Marie slept like a charm when Laurie was watching her. She was so adorable that sometimes he felt like crying.

"I just don't know, Laurie," Jim said.

"What don't you know, honey?" Laurie said.

"About things at school. I mean the kids just don't seem the same. They're different from the way they've ever been. I'll give you an example. Every year since I've been at Wootton, about five times as many kids have tried out for the football team as could make it. I'm not kidding, five times as many. That's what happened this past summer too. So you've got to figure that the ones who make it really want to play.

"But now, this year, even the kids who made it are goofing off. They come to practice late, or they don't come at all, or something's wrong."

"Well, I don't know why that should be," Laurie said.

"I don't know either," Jim answered. "I swear, I just don't know. All they talk about is money—how much this costs, how much that costs. How much they got for doing this odd job or how much their fathers make."

"That's terrible, to be so preoccupied with money at their age," Laurie said.

"It is. We don't know what to do. The boys don't seem to give a damn about anything but the money.

I've talked to the other teachers about it, and they say the same thing. Kids missing classes. Kids not doing their homework."

"Things are sure different from when you and I grew up," Laurie said. "In those days, all the boys wanted to talk about was sex."

"And the girls," Jim continued. "Have you noticed what the girls are wearing? I mean, there ought to be some kind of dress code or something. Those girls look like Las Vegas hookers, wearing see-through blouses without bras. And that powdery metal-flake nail polish. They should all be sent home to get dressed and wash off their makeup."

"I don't think high-school girls should wear nail polish," Laurie said.

The Redskins had just scored a touchdown on a thirty-yard pass. What would he do about his team if he were George Allen? He would be mighty tough with the boys, that's for sure. But he didn't know what in hell could be done for the girls. That, he guessed, was up to the principal. But next summer, when the tryouts for the varsity came around again, he was going to read those kids the riot act. No more of this goddamn goofing off.

"You know," Jim said, "those Whitelaw kids are the only decent kids I ever see any more. They're always clean and polite. Maybe they know something I don't know."

He looked at Laurie. "What've we got to eat that's good?"

"Want me to fix you something?"

"I'll take a look in the refrigerator," said Jim.

That kind of question was beginning to worry Laurie. She was keeping less and less food on hand. It was nearly impossible to stock up on things any more. They were either too expensive or they just weren't there. Even the cheapest brand of bacon, which was almost all fat, cost $22.50 a pound the last time she went to the store. Sausage cost even more. A decent steak was selling for $40 a pound. But, they weren't starving. Jim's salary was close to $50,000. One week, when they had eaten at friends' houses every single night, they had saved enough money to pay off part of their mortgage.

But things were getting worse. At the supermarkets she couldn't find a lot of things. She went to Hartley's little market oftener than ever. Bob Hartley was still friendly and attentive, and he still put a little more meat into her bags than he charged for. And he always complimented her looks. Laurie got a little worried the day he had asked her if she lived nearby. ("Perhaps I could start delivering your food," he had suggested.) That was a little impertinent. She had a lot of self-respect, and while Bob Hartley had been very good to her, she didn't know quite what he had in mind. So she went to the store a little less frequently that week. But soon she was back on schedule. Hartley was just too nice.

As soon as Jim came back with his snack, she was going to talk to him about making up a new budget for the household. She wasn't getting enough money for groceries. Prices had gone up almost 100 percent this past week. Jim wouldn't give her a hard time, because he knew what was going on, but she hated so to ask. She didn't want to nag. More than that, she didn't want to admit that this terrible inflation couldn't be outfoxed by a really clever shopper like her, who knew the value of a dollar if she knew anything.

It was getting the best of her, though. That was the sad truth. And the only thing she could do was ask for more money.

Eating his sandwich, Jim looked out the kitchen window. He had to get a new fuel pump for the VW Rabbit. He had stopped in at the Volkswagen dealer near the high school, and they didn't have one in stock. They could order one, but Jim would have to leave a $200 deposit. Jim had nearly punched the dealer in the face. The damn fuel pump was going to cost $400, *unless* the price went up before the dealer received it. "What can I do?" he asked. "The prices on anything from Germany just keep going up and up."

That was the way things were. Jim brought home those enormous paychecks, but they were gone even faster than the old ones. It didn't seem fair.

Back in the living room, Jim watched a commercial for Armour Star Bacon. He was still hungry. "I hate to bother you, hon, but do you think you could fry me a few strips of bacon?"

As she headed for the kitchen, Laurie figured that six strips would be about ten dollars' worth. Jesus!

But Laurie was determined. She was not going to let the price of bacon, or anything else, get the better of her. She would manage. She would keep their heads above water. She hoped the baby wouldn't have to see the doctor for a while. Even though Jim's insurance paid 80 percent, the remaining 20 percent was horrendous. A routine visit to the pediatrician, who was known for the reasonableness of his fees, now cost $175. She wondered what people without insurance did.

But she was much more concerned about Jim and Marie Adams—they were number one. It was a good thing there were people like Bob Hartley around to help her get the things she needed to keep them happy.

Shelby Kelsey sped along the New Jersey Turnpike and listened to what the radio announcer was saying: "Republican members of the House Judiciary Committee plan to introduce a resolution calling for an impeachment inquiry to begin as soon as Congress reconvenes. Congressional experts give it little chance of adoption, but the Republican leaders say they will press nonetheless."

He tried to piece together what had happened in New York before he left two hours earlier. But all the images had blurred together in his mind: the tall buildings, the beggars, the diamonds, the acne-scarred faces, the blood on the sidewalk.

He pushed the accelerator almost to the floor, passing one Howard Johnson's after another in rapid succession. He couldn't get away fast enough. New York City was a nightmare come to life.

It could have been avoided if he had gone ahead and bought the engagement ring in Maryland. But Kelsey had seen *The New Yorker* at Ridgeley and the fancy jewelers advertised there, and he wanted to buy Alexandra's engagement ring in New York City. So on a bone-chilling Saturday in January he had driven along a deserted New Jersey Turnpike to New York City.

He knew the city was in bad shape, but nothing had prepared him for what he saw. The sidewalks of Fifth Avenue were filled with beggars. It wasn't right, Shelby thought, to see that many beggars on the streets of a city where so many rich people lived. Maybe it did make sense though. Beggars would be pretty stupid to do their begging where people were poor. He also accepted a pamphlet from a sweet-faced, short-haired blond girl in coveralls. The pamphlet was about making America safe for Christianity and featured a long quote from William Whitelaw.

Harry Winston occupied an imposing fortresslike building at 56th Street and Fifth. Mr. Rothman, the salesman, was waiting for him, as he had said he would be. As Mr. Rothman led Kelsey back to a small cubicle on the first floor, Kelsey felt in his pockets to make sure he had brought everything. In his jacket pocket were the two envelopes. Each held $25,-000 in cash. No one took credit cards or checks any more, but that was all right. Kelsey had plenty of cash. The .38 revolver was snug in his pants pocket. New York was a dangerous place and Kelsey had to protect himself. Carrying a gun was illegal, but so was mugging.

Mr. Rothman, a short, prosperous-looking man, brought out a tray of glittering diamonds resting on a background of black velvet. "I think you will find something here that meets with your approval, Mr. Kelso," Mr. Rothman said.

"Kelsey," Kelsey corrected him.

"I'm terribly sorry."

Kelsey looked at the gems. He had never bought jewelry before.

"Actually," Kelsey said, after a minute of trying to locate just the right ring, "these aren't exactly what I had in mind. I was thinking of something bigger, in more of an oval shape."

Mr. Rothman flushed slightly. "Of course. Let me

show you something else." He disappeared to return with another trayful of diamonds.

These were more elaborate. Shelby studied them carefully and found the one he was looking for. It had many facets and shone brilliantly in the flattering light of the showroom. "I'd like that one," Kelsey said.

Mr. Rothman disappeared once again and returned with the single stone on a smaller bed of black velvet. "This ring is twenty-seven thousand five hundred dollars," he said, "with gold or platinum setting."

"Gold," said Kelsey.

"It will take about an hour. Perhaps you could return at four?"

Kelsey had walked down Fifth Avenue toward Rockefeller Center to pass the time. As he headed for the ice-skating rink two sallow teen-agers with acne followed him. They hung back about half a block behind him, and when he stopped they stopped.

His attention was diverted at the skating rink by the whirling, leaping girls in white skating outfits with short skirts. As he leaned on the railing above, a woman wearing a short, tight skirt and a lot of makeup approached him.

"Lonely, cowboy?" she asked. Her teeth were framed by beet-red lipstick. "Wanna go someplace and have a good time?"

Kelsey stared at her. Under the makeup her face was splotchy and wrinkled. She was certainly no kid. She wouldn't have turned him on even if she had been.

"No," Kelsey said, and walked away.

"OK, sport. Let me know if you change your mind."

When Kelsey turned around to look, she was gone. So were the two teen-age boys. He bought a hot dog from a vendor for $6.50 and started back up to Harry Winston.

The ring was even more magnificent than he remembered. Maybe it had been polished. It lay there, dazzling his eyes, in the little box whose silk lining bore the name Harry Winston.

"I'm sure the young lady will be happy," Mr. Rothman said with a little bow.

"I hope so," said Kelsey. "Thank you."

"That will be thirty thousand, two hundred and fifty dollars, including the ten percent New York sales tax," Rothman said.

Kelsey counted out the money, handed it to Mr. Rothman, and walked out the door with the ring in his pocket. As he headed toward the lot where he'd left his car, it was dark. Kelsey started to daydream. If someone had told him two years ago that he would be proposing marriage to the likes of Alexandra Hanrahan, with an excellent chance of being accepted, he would have called the person insane. And if someone had told him two years ago that a New York syndicate would be offering him $10,000,000 for a farm that he had bought with a $1,500 option, he would have called that person equally crazy. But that's what had happened last week. Kelsey had to face the incredible fact that he was rich, and growing richer. He liked it.

"OK, man, give us everything you've got!"

A sallow teen-ager—one of the pair from Rockefeller Center—stood in front of him with a knife. The other kid stood behind him, holding a knife against his back.

"We don't want no trouble," said the kid in front. "Just hand it over and nobody gets hurt."

There were a few passersby. One man who saw what was happening turned his head and hurried on. Kelsey had not seen a cop since he had reached Manhattan.

Kelsey took one rapid step forward and kicked the kid in the groin with his booted foot. It was a violent blow, and the kid slumped to the sidewalk in pain, his knife falling to the ground. Then, as the other kid lunged, Kelsey stepped out of the way. His hand came up with the .38 pointed straight at the kid's chest.

Maybe the kid didn't see the gun, or maybe he was just crazy to start with. He screamed, "You fuckin' bastard," and he might have said more, but as he lunged a second time, Kelsey fired. The bullet shattered the kid's chest and threw him against a building. Kelsey fired again, also toward the chest, and the kid crumpled over on the sidewalk, heaving. Blood poured out of his mouth.

The first kid was still writhing. Kelsey did not want to shoot him. He ran all the way to the parking lot. Incredibly, no one followed him. He paid the attendant, got into his Buick and drove away.

So far, there had been nothing on his radio about a dead teen-ager on West 56th Street.

There was a lot about what Patti Matson, the President's press secretary, had said about the threatened impeachment—that it was just politics as usual, instead of trying to cooperate with the President's plan to redistribute wealth in a growing economy, for one thing.

The radio also had a lot to say about Harry Ratner's explanation that December's extraordinary half percentage point rise in unemployment was a fluke and was not expected to be the start of a trend.

Kelsey thought of the kid's chest and the hole his gun had made in it. If he weren't rich, if those kids hadn't seen him walking out of Harry Winston, the whole thing might not have happened. Those kids had probably never had jobs, never earned any money. What happened to kids? What happened to people who couldn't stay ahead of inflation? Who paid for Shelby Kelsey's $400 wheat and his beef at $10 a pound on the hoof?

Was anybody helping those others? What was happening to the people who were making Shelby Kelsey rich?

And where was that kid he had shot? Probably lying on a slab somewhere, with no one to care. Except for the man who shot him. Kelsey shivered. Come to think of it, he didn't give that much of a damn himself.

## 7

GODDAMMIT!" said Les Levine. "They made me get out of my car and then they searched me like a fuckin' nigger."

"Where did it happen, Les?" Hal Burton asked.

"In front of the roadblock at Sunset and Beverly Drive. Goddammit to hell. I thought they knew me by now. I said I was on my way to your house. But they've got a new crew working there, and I swear to God, they came damn near to shooting me."

Burton leaned back in his living-room chair. "That's too bad, Les. But you have to expect some shit. I got searched on Stone Canyon Road last week. I mean, after what's been happening, you've got to expect a little trouble."

"I guess so," Levine said, feeling a bit calmer. "But, goddammit, I don't look like a nigger."

"The people who burned Dean Martin's home to the ground with him in it were white, Les. So were the people who kidnapped those girls at West Lake School. That's the way it is," Burton said. "It's not a question of black and white. It's a question of who's got and who doesn't got."

"I guess so," Levine said again. "I guess you're right."

"You know I'm right," Burton said. "The whole fucking town is going bananas. I mean, it's like a war here."

He walked across the room. He reached into the closet and pulled out a shotgun, carried it back to his chair and laid it across his knees. "I've got three of these babies," he said. "Remington twelve gauge.

147

They're good as riot guns. I keep one here, one in my car and one at the office. And I'll use 'em too. How long have the cops been on strike now?"

"A fuckin' month," said Levine.

"Yeah, I'll use 'em all right. I've been practicing. It's not hard to hit somebody with one of these."

"I wish to Christ the guards at Paramount had used 'em. That place is a total wreck. Burned to the ground. KTTV and KTLA too," said Levine.

"It's time to go," Burton said. He walked back to the closet with his shotgun. He laid it gently on a shelf, then turned around and pulled back the front of his jacket. The butt of a revolver showed just above the belt. "This is a Colt three fifty-seven Magnum, brand-new model. It stops anything that moves."

Levine got up. "I still think we should postpone the picture, Hal. It's ridiculous trying to meet schedules while all this shit is coming down."

Burton glowered. "No, goddammit. This picture is damn important to me. Nobody's gonna keep me from making it. And I mean no one."

Levine retreated. "OK, Hal. OK. But the place we're going to is not the safest spot in town. I just want you to know that. I mean it's West L.A. and not Bel Air."

"If that's where the coke man is, then that's where we're going. If the crew wants to get paid in coke, I'll pay 'em in coke," Burton said.

A few minutes later, Burton's gleaming Jaguar sedan glided down Coldwater and turned right onto Beverly Drive. When the car reached the six-way intersection at Sunset Boulevard. Burton and Levine could see a newly erected barrier and men with rifles on their shoulders carrying powerful flashlights. Burton stopped the car. An elderly white-haired man walked over to them.

"Hi, Norman," said Burton.

"Everything OK up where you live?" the white-haired guard asked.

"So far, so good," Burton said.

"Do I know that fellow with you?" The guard flashed his light on Levine's swarthy face.

"I don't know if you do or not, Norman. But he's already been searched once tonight, and I'm not a bit happy about it," Burton said testily. "And please get that light out of his eyes."

"OK, Hal," the man said. "OK. Just trying to do my job. We gotta be careful. You know that Carroll O'Connor got it?"

"No, Christ," Burton said, genuinely shocked. "I didn't."

"Yeah. Walking into the Beverly Wilshire. Carful of spades drove by and blew him to pieces. They've got roadblocks up on Wilshire and Rodeo and Cañon now, but Christ."

"Yeah, Christ," Burton said.

"Well, you be careful." He waved them through.

They headed for Wilshire Boulevard, looking carefully around them.

"I don't know why the hell the government doesn't just give the niggers food and then keep them quarantined in their part of town," Levine said. "I don't care if they can't buy bread. I'd pay for their bread if that would keep them from going berserk."

"It's not only that." The car was approaching Rodeo and Wilshire. Burton signaled for a right-hand turn. "Joan Bellamy explained it to me. The people here are coming unglued. Back East they've got customs and traditions. Here there's nothing. And when something like this inflation comes along, the people who're getting burned worst want to strike back at society. To them, we're society. That's why I've got this." Burton reached over behind his bucket seat and came up with a sawed-off shotgun.

"Jesus," Levine said. "They got Carroll O'Connor. I feel like leaving the fucking country."

"You think things are better somewhere else? Joan says it's gonna happen everywhere. Look on TV, Les. People are getting kidnapped and blown up and hijacked and maimed all over the world. It's fucking scary, all right. But Carroll O'Connor. Christ.

When they got to Century City, where Santa Monica Boulevard and Avenue of the Stars intersected, an immense roadblock of concrete, cinderblocks and barbed wire had been set up. Mounted searchlights swept every car that turned south onto Avenue of the Stars. Burton slowed down the Jaguar and pulled up to a checkpoint.

A man wearing a Pinkerton uniform walked up to the car, a revolver in his hand, and said, "Where you people going?"

Levine gave him an address in West L.A.

"This your car?" the guard asked.

"Yes," Burton said. "Want to see the registration?"

"That and your driver's license."

Burton fished around in his glove compartment, took out his wallet and produced the two documents. The guard took them, quickly handed them back and gave a smart salute.

"I'm sorry, Mr. Burton. I didn't recognize your face." He waved the car on.

Les Levine laughed. "Oh, the rewards of being rich and famous."

As they pulled away from the roadblock, a battered Chevrolet roared up to the roadblock from the opposite direction, tires squealing. Someone inside threw two objects toward the roadblock. Explosions shot up in the barricades, and at the same time the car was punctured repeatedly by double-ought buckshot fired at close range. The Chevrolet spun crazily out of control into the cinderblock barrier, crumpling up like a paper toy.

The two bombs that had been thrown from the car had exploded into balls of fire, which the guards were trying to extinguish. Then the smashed car, inside of which no one moved, went up in a huge ball of flame. Gasoline fumes filled the air.

"Let's get the hell out of here," Levine said.

Burton accelerated the Jaguar rapidly down the Avenue of the Stars. He saw the car burning in his rearview mirror. Then he went over a rise in the road just before it hit Olympic, and he no longer saw the flames.

Levine gave him clear directions, and soon Burton was moving along Pico toward a half industrial, half residential section of town. After a few right and left turns on streets Burton didn't know, they reached a street of two-story stucco houses. At the third one on the right, Levine told Burton to stop.

The transaction was not difficult. Burton and Levine took seats in a seedy living room with one bare light bulb hanging from the ceiling by a wire. The glow of a prehistoric black-and-white TV further illumined their faces. Two expressionless young men with beards sat opposite them. The young men spread out rows of cocaine from different plastic bags, and Levine lightly touched each one with liquid from an eye dropper. Then he looked to see what color the cocaine turned. Not one single sentence was spoken.

After fifteen minutes, all the bags had been tested. Levine leaned over to Burton. "As advertised," he said.

"Good," said Burton. He picked up a bound sheaf of pages behind him—very slowly so the young men would not think he was going for a gun. Burton put the pages on the table. The young men watched with interest. Burton deliberately opened the sheaf. Attached to each page was a thousand-dollar bill. One of the two young men started counting the pages. He counted extremely fast. There were a total of two hundred pages and two hundred bills, each bill for one thousand dollars.

"It's cool, man," the fast counter said. Levine raked thirty-two one-ounce bags of cocaine into a briefcase. Without another word, he and Burton got up and walked out.

Not until the silver Jaguar moved along Pico by the gutted warehouses and factories did Burton breathe easily.

"I thought sure one of those dudes was going to come up with a gun," he said.

"They don't dig violence," Levine said. "Any more than we do. It's tough on them, too, these days."

"Yeah," said Burton. "Tough." He looked thoughtfully ahead of him. They were approaching the roadblock on Avenue of the Stars. The car that had carried the Molotov cocktails was still smoldering. The shift of guards had changed, but by a stroke of luck the guard who stopped them recognized Burton. "I've seen *Seven Soft Sonatas* five times, Mr. Burton," he said as he waved them through. The guard was a young man who probably worked as a lifeguard during the day. He was carrying an AR-15—a gas-operated semiautomatic rifle.

"Did you see that gun?" Burton asked Levine. "It fires a shell that tumbles when it hits something. If it hits you in the shoulder, it'll tear your arm off. I'm gonna get one."

The car sailed along Santa Monica back to Beverly Hills and up Coldwater Canyon to Burton's house.

Later, Burton and Levine sat out in Burton's back yard watching the lights of the city below. They could see the fires burning in Watts and Compton, and toward the west in Venice and Santa Monica.

"The fires are getting closer and closer," said Burton. "It's fucking scary."

"Definitely," Levine said. "For sure."

"If they get to Malibu, we'll see a horror show. What a movie that would make! The whole place is made out of wood."

Neither man spoke for a while. Then Burton said, "I think we've got Audrey Hepburn signed for the wife. Long as she doesn't have to come to L.A."

"She really likes the script?" asked Levine.

"Yes, she does. I talked to her in Rome. She loves it. She says she hardly ever goes out. Half her friends in Europe have been kidnapped," Burton said, as a huge beacon of fire flared off to the west, north of Santa Monica.

Burton whistled. "That was scary. Tell you what," he said. "Let's have a taste of that coke."

They went inside. Burton took out his coke spoon. Levine opened one of the bags and Burton dipped his spoon in. Then he took two hits in each nostril. Levine did the same.

"It's strong stuff," Burton said, sniffing, as they walked back outside.

"Definitely good stuff," said Levine. "But I think it's cut with speed."

Burton knew that Levine was right. He started to

feel that slight sense of panic which amphetamines always gave him. He could hear his heart laboring.

"Jesus. We saw some scary stuff tonight over at Century City," Burton said, and suddenly he felt very scared. Even the butt of the .357 Magnum he could feel against his gut didn't make him feel safe. He looked out over the twinkling lights of the city. Maybe the whole place was coming apart, like Joan Bellamy said. Maybe he should just take his marbles and go home, go up north somewhere. But there was the movie. There was the explicit story of his life. If he left now, maybe the movie would never get made. As he looked out over the lights and the fires of the city, he thought that the lights of the city were moving apart. The city looked like it was disintegrating in front of his eyes. Jesus, he thought, as soon as I'm starting to find out what it's all about, it's coming apart.

The ambassador looked grave. Wassily Sobolevsky looked somber under the best of circumstances, thought Peter Hanrahan. To see him at a moment of special strain was something quite striking. Ambassador Sobolevsky resembled an elderly patriarch from an old movie about Russia. Well up in his sixties, overweight, gray-faced, with bushy eyebrows and a beard, he wore a suit that would have been out of fashion in 1955. In 1982, it was a joke.

Sobolevsky was completely fluent in English. Hanrahan theorized that he had probably been trained as a spy; but instead the Soviets had made him, at least on the surface, a diplomat. Thus he could serve a double function.

They had been friends since before Peter entered government. The Hanrahan steelworks had built an immense factory for the Soviets in Siberia. Peter took a lot of kidding from his friends for that. They called him the capitalist who sold the Communists the rope to hang him with.

Hanrahan knew that Sobolevsky was in his office because he wanted something in the trade line. From the expression on his face, he wanted it badly. Peter thought he knew what it was. For the last couple of weeks, since the President had persuaded him to stay on, Peter had been besieged by foreign officials wanting to barter for food. Inflation had placed American wheat at an impossibly high price for money or gold. At the same time, there was a severe worldwide shortage of wheat. These countries had to try to buy their wheat somewhere. The U.S. and Canada were the only countries with a lot more than they needed, so the two North American countries were being bombarded with trade offers—tin for wheat, manganese for wheat, chromium for wheat, virtually anything in the world for wheat.

But the officials who made the trade offers had usually gone away empty-handed—at least so far. The United States and Canada, as governments, no longer stockpiled wheat for trade. Most of the trades were made in the open market, and it was a very tricky matter to find someone to handle a trade of one commodity for another. Prices were constantly shifting, and the number of middlemen involved in such deals was immense. Farmers wanted their payment in dollars—lots of them—or gold—not in tin, manganese, or whatever. And those who wanted tin or manganese preferred to buy it outright rather than enter the grain market to pay for it.

"How are you today, my dear Peter?" Sobolevsky said. It was apparent that he was prepared to be his most accommodating.

"Very well, Mr. Ambassador. And how may I ask, are you?"

"Personally I am well. But there are bad things happening all over the world. You know that." Sobolevsky was obviously beginning a speech he had rehearsed.

"But always, when we have inflation, it is good for some and bad for others." Peter was handing out the administration line, as the President had asked him to.

"No," said the ambassador. He smiled. "We think it is bad for most and good for the privileged few. Like everything else in your system." Why was it, thought Peter, that Russian officials—high or low—always wound up sounding doctrinaire and wooden?

"I would be surprised to hear you say otherwise," Peter said. He smiled in turn.

"In the Soviet Union," said Sobolevsky, "we have had extremely bad weather. As you know, this has had an adverse effect on our grain crops."

Peter murmured the appropriate words of regret.

"We must buy some of your grain. That, in short, is why I am here." Sobolevsky at last had put his opening cards on the table.

"We wouldn't think of stopping you," said Hanrahan, "though you must know that we no longer control the exporting of food."

"Untrue," said Sobolevsky. "You stop us by making your wheat too expensive for us to buy. It is too expensive for your own people to buy. Naturally it is therefore too expensive for us to buy. We are still a developing country."

"Are you applying for foreign aid?" Peter asked with a straight face.

His irony was lost on Sobolevsky. "In a manner of speaking," he said, "yes, we are. We want to buy the wheat but we must work out some kind of a deal for it. Perhaps we could barter, or agree on some adjustment in the price."

Peter looked his friend in the eye. "Wassily," he said, "you and I have been friends a long time. I know that the Russian people are human too. They must eat, like the rest of us. But your government has failed to understand something fundamental for a very long time.

"You cannot have the best of both worlds. You cannot kick us around in Africa and Europe and expect us to love you in return. We may not be able to summon enough power to stop you in South Africa or Yugoslavia," Peter said, referring to the two most recent examples of Soviet interventionism, "but we are no longer going to pay you to do it by feeding your people at cut-rate prices."

Sobolevsky looked stricken. "We help our ideological comrades as we expect you to help yours."

"True enough, Wassily. But the Soviet Union is not our ideological comrade. Not by a damn long shot." Hanrahan knew he could talk straight to Sobolevsky —sometimes.

"We know that, of course, my dear Peter. But we look upon it in less mercenary ways, Peter. First, we are not asking that you *give* us the wheat. We will pay for it, though we cannot pay gold as we have in the past. We have been selling our gold for too long, and there is too little of it left. I tell you this as a friend, and it is not to be widely publicized, although I shouldn't expect you to keep it a secret. Indeed we will pay, and our barter will help your farmers. We merely wish to work out terms—like a young couple buying their first car." The ambassador was pleased with his metaphor.

"Our situation is honestly not good. If you don't know it, the CIA does. Our people have become used to a stable price level and to a few more pounds of meat each year. We have had to raise our prices too. We have less meat in our stores. People are restive. That puts pressure on certain circles that would like to divert attention with power plays abroad. Of course, those circles are not in power, but things can change suddenly. Indeed, that sometimes happens in your own government, I believe."

Peter Hanrahan looked hard at Sobolevsky. Then he looked around his office. It was a large, extremely well-furnished office, with modern furniture that Peter had chosen himself. Eight years earlier it had been occupied by Peter Flanigan, one of President Nixon's staunchest supporters. Hanrahan had recently reminisced about those days with Flanigan, who was a distant relative of the Hanrahans from generations back in Ireland. Yes, indeed. Peter Hanrahan knew about sudden shifts of power. He knew a great deal. He looked across West Executive Avenue to the White House.

It was late in January. The sky was clear and the air outdoors was bitingly cold. Something in the ambassador's tone sounded ominous. Is this how nuclear blackmail begins? Hanrahan wondered, as he looked at the beautifully landscaped view from his windows.

He picked up a paperweight. It had been a gift from Lyndon Johnson. "Wassily," he said, his voice steady, "are you threatening us?"

Ambassador Sobolevsky also gazed into the distance. "I make no threats, Peter. Quite the reverse. We need your help. We need it badly. We are not threatening anyone. I tell you only that I think it would be best for all parties if you sold us the grain—it would be best by far."

Peter Hanrahan replaced the paperweight on the table. "I'll certainly relay what you've told me to the President, Mr. Ambassador. I'm not enthusiastic, but we'll see what he has to say."

"I would be grateful," Sobolevsky said.

Then, after the usual courtesies, the ambassador took his leave.

Hanrahan wondered how the Soviet Union would react if the people of America were going hungry and threatening the government. On his dictating machine, he made as accurate a recollection as he could of his conversation with Sobolevsky.

He had tried to handle Cathy Graham with the same dispatch. After several evenings of discussion, he had at last convinced her, he hoped, that there was no future for them as lovers. He cited many reasons: Cathy was too young; he himself was too old. Cathy had her whole life before her; his was half over. Cathy had no interest in government; government was his life. Cathy liked to play; his playing days were over. Et cetera, ad infinitum, all to sever a relationship he should never have encouraged in the first place.

After her initial shock, Cathy had appeared to recover and finally even to agree. She was very caught up in the first New York show of her artist friend, and she admitted that they had more in common than she and Peter had. All in all she had taken it well. And when he had put her into a taxi on the very last night, Peter had heaved a sigh of relief, grateful to have that chapter of his life over at last.

He felt like a heel, but Cathy was young, and there was nothing else he could do. Claire Beaton was the woman he loved. Each time he saw her served to convince him anew that she was the woman for him.

And yet, and yet. There was that firm, wonderful young flesh and those eager, innocent eyes. There was that quality of excitement each time they were together.

Before he left his office, he looked at his teletype. From Abu Dhabi, a new report about the amount of shut-in capacity in the Persian Gulf. Such bulletins were getting to be a regular thing. At the new OPEC price of $400 a barrel for light Arabian crude, demand had fallen dramtically. Nevertheless the Saudis, true to their word, were keeping production down in order to keep prices up. It was estimated today that an additional 10 percent of Saudi capacity was being closed down.

And South America was having its share of trouble. Riots in São Paulo, Brazil, over shortages of food and other things were everyday occurrences. Nothing the poorer countries could sell had kept up with food prices. And the U.S. government could no longer afford to buy grain and ship it to those countries. It was a kind of miserable justice, Peter thought. They had been kicking the United States around for so long, and now when they were in trouble, they looked to Uncle Sam to bail them out, and he wasn't doing it. The shit that the Third World countries had been dishing out for years to the United States had given the President the perfect excuse for not doing something he couldn't afford to do anyway.

Twelve thousand people were on their feet, whistling, stamping, shouting, waving their hands in the air. The man with the finely chiseled features stepped up to the podium. His eyes were lowered, as though modestly affixed by the force of gravity. He gripped the sides of the rostrum so hard that his knuckles showed white, as though, by the strength of his purpose, he would lift it from the stage, and the stage from the auditorium, and the auditorium and all the people in it from the earth.

He kept his head down as the crowd clapped rhythmically and shouted, "One with God, One with God," over and over again. He kept his head down as the wrinkled old woman in the first row climbed up on her seat and shouted, "Yes, Lord, I have seen the light!" and he lifted his head slightly only when a young man shouted, "We need you, Governor. We need you now."

And because he kept his head down he could not see the banners that read "This Is Whitelaw Country" surrounding the top tier of the Capitol Centre. And he could not see the wholesome, clean-cut young people in denim coveralls, thousands of them, shouting in a frenzy of worship and anger.

Finally, as if he were heaving up some elemental force, William Whitelaw lifted his head and held his hands up high. The crowd screamed louder than ever. The Capitol Centre shook. Then William Whitelaw looked straight at the hypnotized crowd and the cries of "One with God" subsided to a whisper.

"They think they are so smart," Whitelaw began. "They think they are so smart they can steal an entire country from its people." Then in a voice to do Him justice: "They think they are so smart that they can run this great country and turn it away from God. They think they are so smart that they can bleed us dry and lifeless while they grow fat in their evil."

The crowd was hushed now, listening to the Whitelaw magic. The kids in denim sat and smiled. There was an air of expectation. Whitelaw had given no warm-up remarks. He had dived right in. The crowd could feel the power. It was coming.

"Who do they think they are that they can do this to us? Have you in your lives ever imagined the arrogance of the people who run this country, and run it into the ground and think they can get away with it?" He paused to cock his head at an angle, that fine, large head. "Can you believe that? They call it giving the little man a new start, and they think we'll just follow along like hogs to the slaughter. Can you believe that?"

The crowd was on its feet again, hot-eyed and angry, shouting "No!"

Whitelaw lowered his head to look at the podium. Gradually the crowd became quiet.

"They try to run this country without any regard for the things that made it great. They forgot God and they forgot man. And, God willing, some day we're going to forget *them*." The crowd screamed again.

"But we can't forget *them* just yet," Whitelaw continued. "We can't forget them because they've come damn close to ruining this country. We can't forget *them* because they've made retired people so poor they're eating dog food—when they can get it. We can't forget *them* because they took away your savings and made them worthless.

"And we can't forget *them* because they make fine young boys and girls drop out of school because they can't afford to go any more. They took people who used to hold their heads high and made them into beggars on the government dole. We can't forget that. We can't forget *them* for that. Or can we?"

"No!" the audience roared.

"And we can't forget *them* because some of our cities are burning now and fine men and women are dead because others don't have enough to eat.

"No, we can't forget *them*. We can't forget our neighbors in Washington who ride in shiny black limousines while we can't afford the gas for our cars.

"And we can't forget *them* because they took away your self-respect and my self-respect, and can no longer stand up in front of our God as decent men and women."

Whitelaw thrust his massive head forward above the podium. "We've got to get back our self-respect. And the only way we can get it back is by getting rid of the people in the White House who took it from us by getting rid of *them*. They called that robbery 'Giving the little man a chance.' A chance for what? To be poor? To be hungry? To be afraid?

"They took our country. But we'll get it back. We'll get it back and we'll break the people who took it away. With God's help we'll break them into a million pieces. We know them. We know who they are. And soon they'll know who we are."

The woman who had climbed up on her seat earlier shouted, "Go get 'em, Governor! Get the hell after them!"

A young man wearing a Whitelaw T-shirt screamed, "We're one with God." And the crowd picked up the chant. "One with God, One with God." The denim coveralls were carrying the cadence. They looked as if they wanted to kill someone.

The Capitol Centre, which was just outside Washington in Landover, Maryland, shook to its foundations with the rhythmic shouts.

Whitelaw lowered his head and stared down once again at the podium. Then he raised his arms and the crowd grew silent. The clean-cut girls and boys smiled again.

"In your hearts is my strength," he said. The crowd whistled and stomped.

"In your suffering is my justice."

More screaming.

"In your needs are my commands."

The crowd would not be still. They jumped up and down and shouted, over and over again, "One with God."

Whitelaw watched them steadily. He looked out over the crowd that was shouting and screaming and raving, and waved his arms once more. His large head dominated the enormous arena.

"We'll make an America safe for Christians."

The crowd barely heard him because it was still thundering with shouts and clapping and chants. The kids in denim coveralls were the loudest of all. Whitelaw looked out over the crowd and felt pleased. Here he was, on the doorstep of the enemy stronghold, and the people were going wild. Whitelaw was so occupied with looking at the banners and hearing the screaming adulation that he didn't see an ascetic-looking man, past middle age, with piercing, deep-set eyes, get up from his seat in the third row, accompanied by a much younger man.

The two men walked rapidly from the arena and out to the parking lot. They quickly spotted their sleek black Chrysler. The driver was waiting for them.

As soon as he entered the car, George McConger picked up the telephone in the back seat. "Get me Milt Greenberg."

After some static, a tired voice said, "Greenberg."

"Milt, this is George McConger. I've just come from the Whitelaw rally here. This man is dangerous. We can't have people talking treason like that. We've got to do something about him."

"What do you want us to do?"

"Make a law putting limits on this kind of incitement. I want to see the President first thing tomorrow. Arrange it and call me back with a time." McConger hung up the phone.

At the White House, a weary Milt Greenberg turned to face the President. They were in Greenberg's office two down from the Oval Office.

"McConger wants a new law to shut up Whitelaw."

"What?" The President was furious. "Is he crazy? I can't do that and he knows it. What the hell is wrong with him?"

"I don't know," Greenberg said resignedly. "He wants to see you about it."

"Oh, for Christ's sake. For Christ's sweet fucking sake. He really is out of his mind. I've got a bunch of goddamn lunatic assholes telling me what to do," the President said and walked from the room.

Back at the Capitol Centre, the crowd was still screaming.

## 8

A T six A.M. the alarm clock rang. Hanrahan reached over and turned it off. Next to him, Claire Beaton groaned and pulled the covers over her head. Peter smiled. Some things still worked the way they were supposed to. His alarm clock did what it usually did, and Claire responded in kind.

He walked into the bathroom and turned on the light. Mercifully, it, like the clock, was working. There had been so many blitz work stoppages at the Potomac Electric Power Company lately that Peter considered the day off to a good start if the electricity was working. The utility workers were angry. Even with supposedly full cost-of-living raises, they weren't keeping up with inflation. They couldn't go on strike, because missing a whole week's pay would put them in debt for years. But hit-and-run strikes for a few hours had been spreading all over the country.

Hanrahan turned on the radio. Dallas Townsend said that the previous day's rate of inflation worked out to a weekly rate of 250 percent, a new high. Soon, Hanrahan knew, it would be over 1,000 percent per week.

The newscaster also reported the rumor of a massive uprising in the Ukraine over shortages of bread and meat. Soviet troops had allegedly fired into the angry crowd, killing over fifty persons. In a more desultory way he also reported riots in Jakarta and Addis Ababa.

But his final item was a blockbuster: A report out of Minneapolis stated that the British royal family was negotiating with a large American grain-exporting firm to trade certain of the crown jewels for large quantities of American wheat.

Hanrahan finished shaving and went into the bedroom. Claire was still asleep. He gently pulled the covers down below her mouth so she wouldn't suffocate. She claimed it was impossible to actually suffocate that way, but he wasn't so sure. He dressed and picked up the telephone to the White House garage. It took over a minute to get a dial tone. That surprised Hanrahan. He knew that sabotage by workers at the Chesapeake and Potomac Telephone Company had made it hard to get a line in the middle of the day, but this was 6:30 A.M. When he finally got the garage, he told them to send a car to take him to the airport. And if the newspapers had come, Hanrahan wanted them sent along with the car.

It wasn't easy getting the papers. Publishing personnel too were staging quick strikes, and although the papers usually got out, they often hit the streets at noon. Hanrahan hoped to be lucky and get the day's *Wall Street Journal*. It would be helpful at his New York meeting.

He was not looking forward to the meeting, not one bit. A group of investment bankers had asked for someone from the government to come and explain what the hell was going on. What, precisely, did the Better Deal mean? Harry Ratner usually did that kind of dirty work, but today Harry was speaking to a Shriners' convention in Santa Fe, so Milt Greenberg had called on Hanrahan.

He didn't know anything he could tell them that they didn't already know. In the month of February, just ending, the rate of inflation had reached two and a half times the rate of late January. And there was no prospect of reversing it soon. McConger had gotten them all into a box.

Government expenditures were mushrooming, and the government wasn't receiving enough money to pay its bills. The rate of borrowing by the government of the United States was approaching infinity. There was no end in sight. The only institution capable of buying all that government debt was the Federal Reserve Board. As it bought the debt, the Federal Reserve paid with money that it essentially printed. Its printing presses were going faster than ever.

This, with appropriate sugarcoating, was the basis of the Better Deal.

Hanrahan began to scribble a note to Claire. How had he ever gotten along without her?

"Are you leaving already?" Claire's voice was groggy.

"Yes. I'm sorry I woke you up."

"You didn't. I just woke up. I hope they send you back in one piece," Claire said.

"They will. I promise."

Hanrahan brushed her lightly on the lips, running his hand over her body as he did so.

"Well, I guess you're a soldier," Claire said.

"Right now I feel like a deserter."

"So do I. Let's run off to a place where they never heard of inflation."

"Find it, and we'll go there—when I get back from New York City."

The phone rang. It was the doorman to say that the car was in front.

"See you tonight. I'll call from New York if the phones are working." He waved goodbye and went out the door.

Claire began to organize her day. Her problems were mushrooming too. She still worried about the wage-price-control disaster of two weeks earlier. It had been her idea. Legislation was already on the books allowing the President to impose comprehensive wage-price controls at the retail level. She persuaded Donnelly, Hanrahan and Ratner to approach the President with the idea of putting on controls suddenly. It would have a great psychological effect, they told him. It would signal to the nation that the government really meant to do something about the situation.

To the surprise of everyone except Donnelly, who had hinted the idea to the President before and gotten encouragement, the President was extremely receptive. He liked dramatic initiatives. Besides, he was worried about McConger. The Federal Reserve Chairman had come to him a few days before with a cockamamie idea about suspending the First Amendment. McConger was exercised about a speech by William Whitelaw; he wanted the man stopped. The President told McConger he would think about it, but he never considered it. If there were one sure way of going the way of Richard M. Nixon, McConger had put his finger on it.

In great secrecy, Claire Beaton wrote the first draft of the controls speech. It went through seven drafts, and McConger got a copy only fifteen minutes before the President went on the air—a sign of the President's anger and fear of him. The President had announced a 90-day freeze on all wages and prices at the retail level.

It was an unmixed disaster. The morning after the President's announcement, there was chaos on the nation's commodity markets. Prices of food at the wholesale level skyrocketed. Grocery stores simply shut down. They were losing money on every loaf of bread. The nation was hit by a series of paralyzing wildcat strikes. Workers claimed that they weren't being allowed to catch up with the inflation that had already occurred.

Within three days of the announcement there were the bloodiest riots yet in front of shuttered grocery stores. A black market sprang up that made the old prices of the week before look good. What the people of the United States faced was essentially fixed wages and nonexistent products or products at soaring prices. By the end of the week, the President had abandoned the wage-price controls. Claire had submitted her resignation, but the President refused to accept it.

"If I don't fire McConger," he said, "how can I possibly let you quit?"

From that point on, Claire realized something that made her shiver whenever she thought about it. The whole country was now riding the tiger. There could be no easy way to dismount and live.

The Monday after the President had taken off the wage and price controls, the Bureau of Labor Statistics announced the largest monthly increase in unemployment since it had started keeping records—two full percentage points in a single month. Later in the week the Federal Reserve reluctantly reported industrial production had dropped by the largest amount in a month since 1937.

That kind of economic slowdown was supposed to stop inflation, according to theory. But the theories did not work, Claire knew, when the government was printing money full tilt. What Claire did not know, and what she desperately wanted to know, was whether there was any way out for the nation now at all.

As she was turning these and other grim facts over in her mind, Peter Hanrahan pulled up in front of National Airport in Virginia, just across the river from Washington. It was 6:45, and if he was lucky he would make the 7 A.M. shuttle. He wondered how much it would cost. The airlines were no longer accepting credit cards or government vouchers, so Hanrahan was carrying what he hoped would be enough for any eventuality—almost $100,000.

He also had with him something he had never thought he'd need to carry in America. He had bought them for a trip years ago to South America, where paper money, even in the late 1970s, was regarded as worthless. They were four gold wafers. Each one weighed two ounces. At current prices, they were worth more than $600,000.

The terminal was emptier than Peter had ever seen it. He went down to Gate 22, where the Eastern shuttle boarded. There was the electric sign with numbers showing the fares for that day. The Civil Aeronautics Board had given the airlines permission to revise their fares on a daily basis in accordance with their changing costs and a complicated formula. The one-way price for today was $8,010. Even though Hanrahan was not paying with his own money, he gave a low whistle when he saw the figure. How in God's name could people conduct any sort of business at that level of prices? The whole goddamned world was coming unglued, and here he was going up to

New York City to tell people it was all right if you called it the Better Deal.

A few airline clerks were selling tickets to the dozen or so passengers waiting for the first shuttle. Hanrahan peeled off seventeen thousand-dollar bills and bought a round-trip ticket. The harassed agent told him he was lucky to be making his trip today.

"This is the last day we're selling round-trip tickets," he said. "Tomorrow, we're back to selling only one way at a time."

"That's right," said a black agent. "We're going to adjust the price at the beginning of the day and at two P.M."

Hanrahan didn't reply. He wondered if it was worthwhile to take the trouble to put the one-dollar bills that were part of his change back into his wallet. He was tempted to throw them in the trash can conveniently at hand. He wondered how much longer the Bureau of Printing and Engraving was going to bother printing one-dollar bills. Maybe they had stopped already. He would have to check on it when he got back.

Except for specimen coins in the Smithsonian and elsewhere, pennies, nickels, dimes and larger coins were used only by Parker Brothers for Monopoly sets. Boardwalk, in the newest sets, sold for $750,000, at the ratio of one cent per thousand dollars. Some classrooms used Monopoly to teach arithmetic. Each set weighed thirty pounds.

Where the hell had all the gold gone? Hanrahan speculated that private hoarders must have bought it, because it was not showing up in any country's reports on gold transfers to central banks. Of course he didn't have reports on the Communist countries, but Hanrahan thought that if the Russians had the gold, they would surely be selling it now to pay for the wheat they needed so desperately. It must be in private vaults, Hanrahan decided.

The flight was uneventful and Hanrahan was inside the terminal at La Guardia by 8 A.M. He looked around for a newspaper; the New York papers weren't yet on the stands. But he heard the man at the news-stand say that there was a subway strike today.

That would make it rough. When Hanrahan went outside to the taxi stand, where only a few weeks earlier there had been dozens of taxis lined up, there were none at all. Only one other person, a man in his late twenties, was waiting for a taxi with him. Hanrahan asked the young man where he was going.

"To Wall Street," the young man said.

"Me too. We could share a taxi," Hanrahan said. "If we're lucky enough to get one."

"Great. My boss won't mind a bit if I save a few thousand dollars on cab fare." The young man studied Hanrahan's face for a moment. "Aren't you a big wheel in the government?" he said. "I have a feeling I've seen your picture somewhere."

Hanrahan hated remarks like that. How was he supposed to respond? "I'm Peter Hanrahan. I work in trade for the government."

"Of course," the young man said. "Now I remember. You must have your hands full. I'm Larry Hyde. I'm very pleased to meet you, Pete."

Hyde may be gauche, Hanrahan thought, but at least he's not hostile. In fact, the young man started telling Hanrahan what a great job the government was doing. Larry Hyde said that his business had never been better.

"What business is that?" Hanrahan asked.

"Gold bullion," Larry Hyde said with a touch of self-importance. "We're dealers."

"Well," said Hanrahan, "I'm glad to meet you. Perhaps you can tell me who the hell's been buying all the gold?"

Hyde laughed. "We keep our transactions confidential. But just between you and me, I don't know myself. It goes through a very private bank. But whoever's it is has sure made a bundle."

"To say the very least," Hanrahan said.

A battered Checker taxi pulled up in front of them. The driver looked as if he had just led a charge at Gettysburg. "Where you guys goin'?" he asked, as he rolled down the window.

"Wall Street."

"That's a tough one. Traffic is hell today, with the subway strike. It'll cost you a flat six grand."

Both men accepted immediately and got inside the cab. Hanrahan felt as if he were living in a fantasy world. A man used to consider himself lucky to get six thousand dollars for a year's work. Today it would hardly buy the cabbie a good meal.

The sense of departing from reality grew when Hanrahan saw Grand Central Parkway. It was filled with slowly creeping cars as far as he could see. And he had never seen such beat-up cars. At regular intervals, cars that had given up the ghost lay on the shoulders, stripped of anything of value.

The cabbie would drive a few hundred slow feet, then stop dead for five minutes. "Crazy people take their junk heaps out of the garage and drive them to work," said the driver. "And I ain't making any promises about the one you're ridin' in. It's a fleet cab, and it ain't maintained that well."

The cabbie's remarks set Larry Hyde off on a long speech about his own car. Just last week he had bought a used Mercedes 750SL, "the kind like the movie stars have," and now he was afraid to take it out of the garage because the streets were so filled with potholes and there were so many bad drivers in unsafe cars on the road. Not only that, but with the police on strike half the time, "the damn thing might get stolen at any minute," Hyde said.

Hanrahan had taken the ride in from La Guardia to Manhattan perhaps a hundred times. He was familiar with the route. The changes in the last six weeks were amazing. Whole blocks of Queens were abandoned. Hanrahan saw small apartment houses with smashed windows and dangling TV antennas. The City of New York had forbidden landlords to raise their rents, even though the costs of fuel and maintenance had risen to a hundred times what they had been when the leases were signed. The landlords had simply abandoned the buildings. The utilities had stopped supplying heat and electricity, and the buildings became uninhabitable. The tenants who had originally asked to be protected from higher rents found that their buildings became heatless, lightless, powerless havens for youth gangs and rats. Soon even the last of the tenants left, to live in areas where there was still heat and electricity.

On the blocks of small row houses, on the other hand, things didn't look too bad. Those houses were often owned by people with small businesses or by union men. They had been able to keep up with inflation well enough to keep their houses and pay the astronomical utility costs. Some of them, if they had a single good week, had been able to pay off their mortgages.

Twenty-first Street, a major thoroughfare in Queens, looked like an armed camp. Every single store had heavy iron or steel bars in front of the windows. Most of the windows were shattered. In front of the grocery stores, knots of people waited to be allowed in. Truckers' strikes in the New York area had made food supplies shorter than they were elsewhere, and stores had imposed their own rationing systems on the public. Only a certain number of people were allowed into the stores at any one time; they were asked to wait in line both outside and in. The stores were taking no more chances with excitable, hungry people.

Larry Hyde told Hanrahan that he was planning to buy a co-op in Manhattan *and* a house on Long Island. "It's fabulous, man. The money keeps pouring in. I shouldn't be saying this, but my firm is making out like crazy with this inflation. We hope it never stops."

Hanrahan smiled at him. "Oh, it'll stop. You can be sure of that."

"What's gonna make it?" Larry Hyde asked. "Is the President gonna put the economy through the wringer? I don't see him doing that."

The taxi driver joined the conversation. "I'd like the answer to that one too. I can't see those bastards down in Washington stopping it. Their attitude is 'Fuck you, Jack. I'm doin' OK.' When they start to suffer, there may be a change."

Hanrahan didn't know what to say. In his heart he

agreed. "The President's got a lot of smart people working on the problem."

"Bullshit," the taxi driver said. "They're the same people got us into this mess in the first place."

It was too complicated to even try to explain. Hanrahan was beginning to regret that he hadn't hired a helicopter. He'd never get there on time at this rate. It was taking forever to reach the Queensborough Bridge.

Finally, the cab reached Manhattan and Second Avenue. Hanrahan was taken aback. Even on the East Side, apartment buildings which had recently been elegant were completely abandoned. In the smashed windows of some he could see Puerto Rican teen-agers staring out at the cars. Buildings that used to have handsome exteriors sported spray-painted slogans in Day-Glo colors: "Raymond—Bold as Love," "Royal Kings of 125th Street," "Fuck you."

But some buildings, thank God, were still in good shape. Hanrahan decided they must be co-ops whose owners willingly paid the higher utility costs to maintain the buildings decently. Hanrahan wondered where all the people who had lived in those rental buildings had gone. Perhaps a lot of them had moved out to the trailer parks that were growing up all over the country.

Trailers or mobile homes on tiny parcels of land had become one of inflation's great growth industries. People could live in them and pretend that they had a hedge against inflation. Normal brick-and-mortar houses had become prohibitively expensive even for those who were doing unusually well.

As the taxicab threaded its way down Second Avenue, Peter Hanrahan saw another of the big growth-inflation industries. Though it was a cold and cloudy day, the girls were everywhere. In short skirts and platform heels they lounged against the sides of the buildings. On one block, Hanrahan counted sixteen. As the taxi pulled over near the curb to stop for a light, two of them strolled up to the taxicab window.

The girls smiled at Peter and Larry. The redhead said, "Want me to give you some head? Come on, be a sport. I'm good. It's only ten grand."

Jesus, thought Hanrahan. Ten thousand dollars for a blow job.

Her companion, a blonde, tried to open the door of the taxi. "We can do it in the cab. I'll give you a package deal: both of you for fifteen grand."

Peter Hanrahan studied the girls' faces. He shook his head, No. Larry laughed nervously. The blonde might have been fifteen years old, the redhead not much older. When the light changed and the taxi took off, the girls walked back to the building. Why, thought Hanrahan, do they all look so clumsy? It must be the shoes.

The whole area around 14th Street and Second Avenue was one large sexual bazaar. Cars with New Jersey and Connecticut license plates slowly cruised the scene. Women came up to the cars, talked a few seconds with the men, then disappeared in the cars. Sometimes the men in the cars gestured instead to boys on the sidewalk, and the boys, dressed in leather jackets, with chains and rings of keys hanging down from their studded belts, hustled the cars.

"You know, it's shocking how big this has become," said Larry Hyde.

"I thought sex was always pretty big," said Hanrahan.

"But nothing like what it is now. I stay away from those girls. They're too dangerous for me."

The taxi moved through the East Village and into Chinatown. The streets reminded Hanrahan of the pictures he had seen of Berlin after World War Two— one gutted building after another. Whole blocks had been abandoned, the stores looted and set on fire.

When they got to Wall Street, there was at least an appearance of order. Though vacancy signs were up, the buildings were well maintained, and the people on the street looked prosperous.

The cab stopped at Broadway and Wall Street. The two men split the fare of $6,000 and each kicked in a $500 tip. The trip from the airport had taken over two and a half hours. Hanrahan said goodbye to Larry Hyde, who told Hanrahan what a pleasure it had been to meet him and then walked briskly down Wall Street.

Peter turned at Broad Street, one block down, and headed for the Recess Club at 60 Broad Street. He got there a few minutes early. It was not quite eleven, and the meeting was scheduled for 11:30.

Hanrahan walked inside and took the elevator to the top floor. He was almost overcome when he saw the club. He had never been a member, since he had worked uptown when he lived in New York, but he had been there often before he joined the administration, and the club always exuded a distinguished, reassuring calm. It was a refuge for those of the well-to-do who might be battered around by Wall Street battles or any of life's poundings—which had been especially severe of late, thanks to Peter Hanrahan's colleagues.

It was the same as it always had been. There were the same fabric-covered walls and polished wooden furniture. The servants were elderly and respectful. There were the same magazines. The men who sat in the armchairs perusing *Fortune* and *The Wall Street Journal* looked well fed, as usual. Hanrahan got a good feeling inside to know that there was still someplace where the hysteria of inflation had not taken the upper hand. The Recess Club might have been situated on another planet. It no longer belonged to New York City.

A waiter asked Hanrahan if he wanted a drink. He ordered a glass of white wine. While he was waiting, he browsed among the magazines. Inflation, that week at least, had been pushed off the covers. Both *Time* and *Newsweek* had cover stories dealing with New York's controversial proposal to legalize and tax prostitution. Peter didn't need to read them. His own theory was that if prostitution were taxed, it would decline rapidly. It was in great part because prostitution offered tax-free earnings that it was so attractive —to prostitutes and their pimps, anyway.

Wine glass in hand, Hanrahan walked toward the windows. He noticed a prominent black-bordered bulletin board, with many formally engraved announcements attached—probably a list of members who had died within the year.

He studied the names. There were some fifteen of them. Then Hanrahan noticed something strange. All of them had died since Christmas—a span of only a few months, coinciding almost exactly with the time that inflation had gone out of control. The causes of death were not given, but the birth dates were, and Hanrahan noticed that most of those who had died were in their forties or fifties.

"It's no accident, you know. They didn't all die from the onset of winter."

Hanrahan looked around and saw a short, balding man with a European manner looking him over. The man looked vaguely familiar and extremely old. He continued. "You might think they were all suicides, but they weren't. At least not clearly."

Now Hanrahan remembered. It was Dr. Kurt Block, a German economist-consultant from a large investment bank. Hanrahan had met him years before when his own investment bank was putting together some financing for the Hanrahan family steelworks. Hanrahan put on his best smile and extended his hand.

"I'm Peter Hanrahan, Dr. Block. I met you a number of years ago during a steel-financing deal."

"I remember you well, Mr. Hanrahan, and I also know what you're doing these days."

"How have you been, Dr. Block? You look very well."

"You also look well, Mr. Hanrahan. But that doesn't mean that you *are* well."

This conversation is taking a strange turn, Hanrahan thought.

"I am well, Dr. Block. Things are hectic around the White House, but I am quite well," Hanrahan said, beginning to hope Dr. Block would go away.

"Examine those obituaries," Dr. Block said. "Half of them were out-and-out suicides. They couldn't take the strain of being rich one day and wiped out the next." Dr. Block pointed at the list with a crooked finger. "They went home and blew their brains out. That's the best use for a gun, yes? To protect yourself against adversity? The others—heart attacks mainly. A few automobile accidents.

"All were victims of inflation. Every one of them. Normally, in two months, we might have two die. But this, this is from inflation. You think that people get sick from viruses alone, Mr. Hanrahan? I assure you it is not so. When the economy is incurably ill, people get sick from that too. I have seen it before with my own eyes."

"Yes, Dr. Block. I'm sure you're correct. The club looks so good, one would—"

"Before lunch it looks fine." Dr. Block fixed Peter Hanrahan with his melancholy eyes. "We don't put the corpses on display. The people who come here are all still alive.

"But this morning you don't see the ones who stay here all day, drinking, drinking. You don't see the others who leave here drunk, and go to their offices and drink some more. But I see them all, day in and day out. And I'll tell you something, Mr. Hanrahan. I've seen it before."

Hanrahan wished that his host from the investment bankers' group would appear to rescue him from Dr. Block.

"How old do I look, Mr. Hanrahan?" Dr. Block asked.

"I'm sorry, Dr. Block. I'm not very good at guessing ages. You'll excuse me. I must find the people I'm talking to here."

"I just want to tell you something first. I know what you people in Washington are doing. I've seen it before."

The old man's German accent had become more and more pronounced.

"I saw it in Germany before you were born. I saw it in 1923, when the mark went from four point two to the dollar to four point two trillion to the dollar. That's right. Four point two trillion to the dollar. Do you know what that did to our country? Do you think we would ever have turned to so warped a man as Hitler if our backbones hadn't been broken by inflation?"

Hanrahan had given up trying to escape.

"I was a young man, but I saw it. I watched shop-girls saving up for their weddings see their money become worthless. They became whores. I saw bright young men ruined. I saw them become Nazis. I saw the whole middle class of Germany turn upside down."

Hanrahan had to protest. "I understand what you're suggesting, Doctor. But Germany was psychologically prepared for a dictatorship. Germany had hardly been a republic at all. And Germany's inflation was far, far worse than ours."

"Completely true, Mr. Hanrahan. Back in 1923, the rest of the world was stable. There was some underpinning for returning one country to a stable price level. But today the whole world is gripped by inflation. Where is it going to stop?"

Hanrahan said, "It'll stop when the government puts on the monetary brakes."

"Ah, Mr. Hanrahan. It's too late for that. You know it yourself. You can't stop it now. You have to keep printing money to pay for the government, for the unemployment insurance, for the welfare, for the Social Security, for everything. Your Chairman McConger has got you in a stranglehold.

"One final thing, Mr. Hanrahan. Our inflation led to a dictator, who would seize power and protect the middle classes. It didn't happen right away. Hitler took a while to harvest what inflation had planted. Tell me, how are you going to avoid the same fate?"

It was cool in the club, but Hanrahan was sweating slightly. Dr. Block was making him very nervous. "We have a long democratic tradition. We don't need a dictator to solve our problems." Even as he said it, Hanrahan wondered if he was convincing anyone. He certainly wasn't convincing himself, but it was the best he could do.

Now Dr. Block seemed offended. He executed an old-fashioned courtly bow. "It would be nice to think so," he said, and walked away.

Hanrahan decided he had just experienced one of

those moments people dread, when something terrible and inevitable is foretold. He shivered.

It was a relief when Eric Cooper of Goldman Sachs came up to him and gave him a friendly smile and handshake. Cooper took him into a private dining room overlooking the harbor, where fifteen men were assembled.

After lunch—a lunch Hanrahan barely noticed because of his concern about what Dr. Block had said —he presented the standard talk about the Better Deal.

Inflation was bad, he said. It had gotten worse than the government had anticipated. But nonetheless the economy was holding up quite well. The rises in unemployment and the declines in industrial production were expected, although they were of a greater magnitude than anticipated. The President was aware that the bond market had been pretty much destroyed by inflation, but there was no point in crying over spilled milk. The main things were to adjust the economy to the inflation by being as flexible as possible and to cooperate when the government finally decided to put the squeeze on. And, above all, to trust the American government.

The reactions of the investment bankers were fairly mild. Hanrahan barely heard them. He was considering what Dr. Block had said. How in God's name *were* they going to stop it? Even as Hanrahan talked about a gradual slowdown in the rate of inflation because of gradually reduced government borrowing, he had in the back of his mind the images of the German inflation of 1923, of the storm troopers gathering support, and the prostitutes clogging the streets—a scene already reproduced in cities across the United States.

And what about William Whitelaw? Who was to say what the final chapter of his book would be?

A young man wanted to ask a question. "Mr. Hanrahan, couldn't we stop inflation cold simply by returning to the gold standard? Why don't we have money that is redeemable in gold?"

Hanrahan thought about that for a moment. "Well, there are a few answers to that. The important one, at this point, is that we don't have enough gold to be able to make more than a token underpinning of the paper money. You know, I'm sure, that most of the government gold supply was auctioned off, along with other commodities, in the late 1970s.

"Another reason is that if we did allow people to redeem their paper money for gold, there wouldn't be any gold at all. With the kind of psychology that we have now, very few people would hold paper money if they were allowed to use gold.

"And finally, for those who do want gold, there is still an active bullion market. In fact, I rode in from the airport with a fellow who works in the bullion business, and he says that they're thriving. So if people want to hold gold, they can buy it."

The young man had listened carefully. "But what about a system where people had a good assurance that there was gold backing for their money, even if they couldn't convert directly? Wouldn't that give them some kind of psychological boost? I mean, if they thought their money was connected with something as solid as gold even in an indirect way."

"I'm afraid," Hanrahan said, "that the problem would be the same. People know that there isn't much gold left in the country's stockpiles. We can't convince them that there is, and that even in some tangential way it's standing behind their money. If we still had a lot of gold, it would be a damn good idea."

The questions went on for a good hour, but all Peter Hanrahan could think about was Dr. Block and the list of deceased club members. He wondered how long the list would be in a year if inflation kept up.

At about 3 P.M. Eric Cooper called the luncheon to a close. As the group slowly went out, Hanrahan wondered which of these solid, substantial men would not be able to take it much longer. How many of them would be on the obituary list by the end of the year?

Luckily, when Cooper learned about Peter Hanrahan's experience coming in from the airport, he offered a car from Goldman Sachs to take Hanrahan to the airport. It was a long and shiny Cadillac limousine.

The driver was expert. He chose a roundabout but quick and comparatively safe route.

In Greenwich Village, posters advertised an appearance by William Whitelaw at New York University. Hanrahan was surprised. So Whitelaw's influence had reached even into big city universities. He was getting to be a force all right, no doubt about it.

He saw the famous lights on the Allied Chemical tower. As a public service, *The New York Times* flashed daily food prices to passersby, within an anticipated $500 fluctuation range for the day. He watched them. Rice, per pound: $235–$735; eggs, $619–$1,119 per dozen; Coca-Cola, $850–$1,350 per six-pack.

The Cadillac was stuck for a while when a broken-down car blocked traffic on 58th Street. A group of black youths, not yet in their teens, came swaggering down the street. One of them caught sight of the shiny Cadillac and immediately the group started throwing stones, bottles, beer cans. "Don't worry," the driver said. "This happens all the time. We have shatter-proof glass." The driver was not the slightest bit perturbed. Hanrahan thought, It's amazing what people can learn to live with.

And once we get used to a distorted way of life, Hanrahan wondered, what will it take to restore us? If hostile groups are that mad and that brazen, how can we maintain a healthy, functioning society? How can we prevail? We do need a strong man, he thought. How easy it would be to be seduced by a despot.

He thought about a wonderful hypothetical society in which things ran smoothly. No telephone strikes, no electricity strikes, no garbage strikes—the garbage on the streets of New York on this trip had been stupefying. In the society Hanrahan envisioned, government would be the source of order, not of chaos, as it was now.

As he got out of the car, Hanrahan realized that what he had so deliciously fantasized was exactly what Dr. Block had predicted would happen—a strong man, a man on horseback, who would lead the country back to order. Hanrahan had been happily dreaming about a dictatorship. God, Hanrahan thought, I'm starting to crack up.

No, he thought, it isn't cracking up. We're in this so goddamn deep now that the only way out may be just what Dr. Block predicted. And as the plane soared above New York on its way back to Washington, Hanrahan had a sober thought. If he longed for a man who would forcibly restore order, how many other people were longing for such a leader, too? How long would it take before storm troopers marched up Fifth Avenue?

William Hanrahan looked out his living-room window. It was the first of April, and his fields of grass that sloped down to the Choptank River were turning green again from their winter brown. The river itself was moving more quickly, shaking off the lethargy of winter.

He refolded the piece of paper he held in his hand. It was a letter from the Trust Company of Manhattan informing him that the transactions he had entered into on that horrible Friday before Christmas for buying into the land trust were null and void. The Securities and Exchange Commission had ruled that a period of ten business days must elapse between the time such a plan was set up and the time it could offer its shares to the public. The Trust Company of Manhattan had not complied with the requirement. Therefore the plan had been invalidated.

That was all fairly complicated. What it boiled down to, in plain language, was that William Hanrahan, who six months earlier had been one of the richest men in Maryland, was virtually wiped out. His bonds would some day pay off in full, and he would realize $50 million for them. At present, they were simply unsalable. No one wanted a bond that paid 6 or 8 percent a year when inflation was running at 1,000 percent per week. The yield of $3.5 million a year he got from his bond trust was the equivalent of about $10,-000 a year only twelve months ago. And you couldn't do much on $10,000 a year. In another week, it would be worth only a few hundred dollars a year—at the old value.

He still had Ridgeley and the land around it, and they were worth a great deal, several hundred million at today's prices. But if he sold Ridgeley, where would he live? In a trailer park? And what was he going to use to keep Ridgeley up?

His son-in-law, Shelby Kelsey, had been telling him that he shouldn't rely on any complicated deals where he just owned a piece of something. He should put his money into a nice working farm, which Kelsey would find for him. But William Hanrahan had believed that the Trust Company of Manhattan would assure his future through thick and thin. What a fool he had been.

Kelsey had insisted on a small wedding. Even though he was a rich man, and even though his in-laws—everyone thought—were also rich, so many others were suffering that he and Alex had decided it would be ostentatious and cruel to have a lavish wedding. So, following a private ceremony at the local Episcopal church a few weeks ago, about fifty people had come to a buffet dinner at Ridgeley. Hanrahan's brother, Peter, had driven over from Washington with his new love affair, a famous economist, who was charming and warm.

William Hanrahan reflected on his life. He had been born rich; he had had a wonderful wife; he had a lovely daughter and now a fine son-in-law. Life had been good to him in many ways. But even as he considered those things, he decided that perhaps his luck had run out. He was very, very tired. The letter from the Trust Company of Manhattan felt as if it weighed a hundred pounds.

He missed his wife terribly. As he looked out now at the Choptank, he didn't see the river. He saw himself and Norma dancing at their favorite clubs in New York, lying in each other's arms, planning the future of their daughter.

His whole world had changed when she died. In many ways he hadn't really been alive since. He wanted so much to see her again. Now his daughter was in Europe on her honeymoon. Almost every day he got a postcard or letter telling him how people were suffering from inflation. She had been in Paris when a coup took place, putting a right-wing military government in power. That was sad, but his daughter was still young enough to adjust to such changes.

He wasn't. He felt sure that if Shelby Kelsey had gotten a letter saying he was ruined, he would go out and start again. But William Hanrahan was not Shelby Kelsey. He was not tough enough to survive at all costs. He was not prepared; he was not equipped to live in this kind of world.

He decided that it would be best if he didn't even leave a note. Then he thought better of it; he had best leave something for Alexandra. He went upstairs to his bedroom and got out some stationery. With a fountain pen, he wrote:

DEAREST ALEXANDRA,
I am going to join your mother. I am leaving you with someone who loves you and will take good care of you. I know you and Shelby will be happy. You will have Ridgeley free and clear and I hope you and Shelby will make it your home.
Please pray for me and your mother, and know that we love you very much.
DADDY.

It would not be necessary to date it.

He went to the safe he kept hidden behind his ties in the closet. He dialed the combination and swung open the door. From behind a sheaf of papers he took the pistol—a Walther .32 automatic. He had bought it years before at Abercrombie and Fitch to use against intruders. As he put a shell into the chamber, he remembered that his wife had been with him when he bought it.

The gun was smooth and bluish-black. It felt cold and efficient in his hand. For a moment he wondered if he should be leaving Alexandra after all. Then he remembered the letter from the Trust Company of

Manhattan. He sat down on the edge of his bed. He put the gun in his mouth with the barrel pointing up and toward the back of his head. Silently, he said a prayer to God asking for mercy and a reunion with Norma. Then, with his right thumb, he pulled back the hammer of the automatic and pulled the trigger. The bullet blew out the back of his head.

## 9

HAL Burton slowed down his Jaguar as he approached Sunset and La Cienega. On one of his rare trips outside the West Side of Los Angeles, Burton had gone to visit Les Levine in Hollywood. It was the least he could do. For Levine had been shot while on business for Burton. As traffic inched along Sunset, Burton tried to piece together exactly what had happened.

Two weeks earlier, in the middle of March, Burton had decided that he wanted William Wylie's advice on *The Wonderchildren*. The veteran director had extremely good judgment, and even though Burton planned to direct the picture himself, he wanted Wylie's suggestions.

"You're nuts to go all the way out there," Levine said when Burton put the idea to him.

"No, I'm not. He's a great director and I want his reaction on a couple of ideas."

"It's ridiculous to schlep all the way out to Malibu with gangs roaming the hills. I don't think Wylie's reactions are worth getting killed for," Levine said.

"Nobody's gonna get killed. Don't forget that I have this," Burton said, hefting his new AR-15, "and besides, there are roadblocks all over Malibu."

"Yeah? Well how did they get Tippi Hedren and cut her head off?" Levine asked. "Those crazy bastards on motorcycles pop up everywhere."

"I'm going," Burton said.

"Well, I'm not gonna let you go alone," said Levine. They had been working together for twenty years.

By the time they set out, Burton's Jaguar looked like a small battleship. Both Burton and Levine cradled shotguns in their arms, poking out on each side. Burton's AR-15 lay on the back seat, where he could grab it in a hurry.

The men at the roadblock at Sunset and Beverly waved them to a stop.

"Hi, Hal," said the guard. "Where you going?"

"Why?" Burton asked.

"It's not a good day. We've been getting bad reports all morning. I'd stay home."

"Can't do that," Burton said. "I've got business in Malibu."

"Jesus, not Malibu," the flak-jacketed man said. "That's the worst place. They're in bad shape there. Three small fires and one big one last night. I'd stay the hell away."

"We'll take our chances," Burton said.

"Whatever you say. Good luck."

Burton turned right. They drove past the gutted pink facade of the Beverly Hills Hotel. Fairly early on, shortly after the New Year, the gangs had first started their cruising around Beverly Hills. When the police went permanently on strike—mostly to take higher-paying jobs as private security guards—the gangs grew more daring. Their first big burn had been the Beverly Hills Hotel. The fire department was also on strike, and the hotel's interior was gutted within hours. For some strange reason the heat had not affected the pink exterior very much. From a distance, the hotel looked slightly singed.

"I don't know why you're in such a goddamn hurry to get killed," Levine said as they passed Beverly Hills and entered Bel Air. They slowed for another roadblock at Stone Canyon Road. "You can't make the picture if you're dead."

The guard who stopped them at Stone Canyon Road looked a lot like Ryan O'Neal. "I wouldn't go to Malibu, Mr. Burton. There's been a lot of trouble there. The highway patrol won't let them put up a roadblock on the Coastal Highway, so it's rough."

"Thanks for the advice," Burton said. "But we'll be careful."

The Jaguar passed other roadblocks in Brentwood and Pacific Palisades. Then, as they approached a huge curve in the road, they saw the ocean sparkling below them.

The cottages and more substantial homes of Malibu lay strung along the beach. "It looks safe enough," said Burton, as they sped up the highway toward the prize gem in the Malibu tiara, the Malibu Beach Colony. At its entrance, where once there had been a guardhouse, appeared the familiar sight of concrete blocks, concertina wire and hard-eyed men with shotguns.

Burton pulled up and held out his driver's license and registration. "Mr. Wylie's expecting me," he said.

The guard, cradling an Ithaca 12-gauge shotgun, walked into the guardhouse and checked his list. Then he came out and passed them through.

At Wylie's house, Burton parked in front; they walked the few yards to the front door. Both men left their weapons in the car. But the stoop-shouldered, elderly Wylie greeted them at the door with a sawed-off shotgun pointed at their chests.

He smiled when he saw who they were and lowered the gun.

"How are you, Hal? Les? Sometimes people sneak in past the roadblock."

"I'd do the same thing as you," said Hal.

The three men sat out overlooking the beach and talked scripts and tone and pacing. Wylie analyzed the two scenes Burton was worried about. The sky and sea were both a dull gray. The lapping of the waves drowned out all but the noisiest traffic on the Coastal Highway.

The whole scene was so soothing, in fact, that Burton didn't hear the noise at first.

"What's that sound?" asked Levine.

Wylie sat bolt upright in his chair. "Oh, my God. They're back!"

"Who?" asked Burton.

"The bikers. Get your guns."

Burton and Levine ran to the Jaguar and took out both shotguns and the AR-15. Then they went with Wylie to the second floor of his house. Through the trees between the house and the highway they saw a frightening sight. One mile away down the highway, a double line of motorcycles was heading straight for the Malibu Beach Colony. Behind the line of bikers and to the right, flames were shooting from cottages along the shore. Thick black smoke reached up to the gray sky and blended into it.

"Jesus Christ," Burton said. "All of Malibu is on fire."

The bikers roared up to the roadblock at the entrance to the Beach Colony. A few riders were blown off their machines by blasts from the guards' shotguns, but there were too many bikers for the outnumbered guards. Within a minute the motorcycles were roaring into the Beach Colony. Burton could see the skulls and crossbones on their fuel tanks. Groups of two or three dismounted, took Molotov cocktails from their pouches, lit them and threw them at the elegant houses. The gasoline-fed flames licked at the chrome-and-leather furniture and heavy carpeting of Wylie's house.

Wylie was already firing his sawed-off shotgun. It was devastating at close range, but only one side-burned, leather-jacketed man rode close enough for Wylie's shots to blow his face apart. Levine was firing too, and a steady hail of gunfire was coming from the houses in front of which the motorcyclists raged.

Burton saw a cyclist about a hundred feet away take aim at them with a hunting rifle. But Burton was fast. He squeezed off three shots from his AR-15 before the bearded biker could fire. The second shot caught him in the abdomen and spun him around before he fell to the ground and bled to death.

The steady fire from within the Beach Colony was

having a good effect. The bikers slowly fell back. With the houses burning, they apparently considered their work done. Those who could roared out the entrance-way, past the bodies of ten guards and onto the Pacific Coast Highway, heading north. It was a victory.

Flames began to rise inside the Wylie home, and no fire engines were in sight. Burton, Wylie and Levine ran out of the house past the flames. Fortunately Burton's car was hardly damaged at all. Only the rear window was shattered.

Looking back at his burning house and at the other people fleeing the burning development, Wylie cursed. "Goddammit," he said. "Goddammit to hell! What did they have against us?"

Suddenly, a small rear guard of motorcyclists roared by and fired directly at the car. Levine screamed in agony and fell to the ground, his chest covered with blood. Burton and Wylie lifted Levine into the car and Burton whipped into high gear, speeding toward the nearest hospital.

The emergency room at UCLA Medical Center in Westwood was mobbed with casualties of the day's fighting all over the West Side, but Burton was persuasive, and he got Levine tended to quickly. The wounds were fairly minor, but an operation was necessary to remove the pellets. Burton left Levine and took Wylie to Wylie's wife's home in Bel Air.

The Ryan O'Neal look-alike at the Bel Air road-block greeted them. "See?" he said. "I knew there'd be trouble."

"Shut the fuck up," Wylie said to the guard, who did. When Wylie got out of the car, he thanked Burton and said, "I just don't get it. What do they have against me?"

Les Levine mended quickly, and soon he was convalescing in his own house on a side street in Hollywood. Burton had hired around-the-clock guards for him. And today Levine was in pretty good spirits.

"I still don't understand why, after all this time, people here have become so violent. There've always been rich people and poor people, here and everywhere else," Levine said.

"It's the inflation, according to Joan," Burton said. "They just can't stand not ever having enough money. They get their expectations raised by earning such enormous sums of money and then it doesn't buy anything. I don't blame them. I'd be violent too."

But Hal Burton didn't want to upset Les Levine further, so he told him about plans for his party. As he drove home, he went over them again.

He had plenty of time, because he had to detour around Sunset Strip. The Strip had become virtually impassable at any hour because of the throngs of young people who were more-or-less permanently camped out there. Where they came from, no one knew. They came like a devouring army to the Strip. They had put the shops and restaurants out of business and now they camped in the buildings. To attempt to pass them was to play Russian roulette with three bullets in the cylinder. It was not a smart thing to do.

So Hal Burton went far out of his way up into the Hollywood hills and through many side streets until he came to Sunset Boulevard beyond the Strip and to relative safety.

Laurie Adams lay in bed. She was watching her husband get dressed.

"Goddamn them," Jim said. A lock of this thick hair fell over his forehead and his muscular arms bulged as he put on his T-shirt. "Goddamn those bastards in Washington. Goddamn those fuckheads at the gas company. I don't believe they cut off our gas because we didn't pay the bill on time. We've paid them like clockwork for ten years. Then, when we're late one time, they're willing to let us freeze."

"The heat will be on this morning." Laurie tried to calm him. It upset her to see him so angry.

"Over one hundred and fifty thousand dollars for one goddamn month," Jim said. The bedroom was chilly, warmed only by a small electric heater. "We are not being mistreated," Jim went on. "We are being royally fucked over."

"Maybe the union can help," Laurie said. She snuggled deeper under the blankets to keep warm.

"If we've got to strike, then we'll strike. Everybody else is doing it. The fucking gas workers do it."

"Well, maybe the union will vote for a strike," Laurie said.

"Then how the hell are we going to pay the bills?" asked Jim. "We don't stop eating when we go on strike."

"I don't know what else you can do," Laurie said. She was exhausted with worry about money. She felt as poor as she had as a child.

"Did I tell you that one of the teachers saw girls from his French class turning tricks at a bar in the Loop?" asked Jim. "And the boys are doing it too—Steve Mayhew told me at assembly yesterday. They're hustling all over downtown Chicago. I wonder how he knew. I'll have to ask him. Jesus," he said, on his way to the door, "high-school kids turning tricks. Whitelaw is right. What are we coming to?"

After Jim left, Laurie picked up the remote-control switch of her Zenith Super Chromacolor V set and turned on the *Today Show*. The announcer said that they were about to go live to London. An astonishing thing was happening there because of the inflation.

A man stood in front of a bank in the City of London. Tom Pettit, reporting from Threadneedle Street, described one of the strangest transactions ever made.

"This morning, inflation was brought home to the British people in a heartbreaking way. The Queen of England, with the consent of the House of Commons, has sold the greater part of the crown jewels of Britain to Cargill, Incorporated, an American grain dealer. Their sale is for an unspecified but reportedly very large shipment of wheat and soybeans."

The camera panned around the room at the Tower of London, where the crown jewels had been kept.

The Queen stood in all her majesty and spoke. "The British government, with my full approval and endorsement, has agreed to sell a large number of the crown jewels to buy the wheat and other grain we need so desperately in order to survive. Like every

Briton, my heart is heavy to see them leave their home. But this shows how serious the situation is, and what serious measures we must all take to meet it.

"Some day, God willing, we will have these national treasures back. We are a great people. We can recover from even the worst of adversity. History has shown us that."

The camera picked up Tom Pettit in front of the bank. "This morning, an armored car surrounded by British army troops took the crown jewels to the Bank of England, where they were delivered to the American buyers here. The American buyers in turn took the jewels to another armored car, surrounded by private security guards, and the stones were then taken to London's Heathrow Airport, where they were put on board a specially chartered plane bound for Minneapolis."

Tom Pettit looked grave: "Forty-three years ago, Britain underwent another dark hour. Then the speeches of Winston Churchill rallied them against the Nazi menace. But what can be done today to save England from the ravages of this worldwide inflation is not known. Will England survive? Will mankind survive? Perhaps someone will show us the way. Tom Pettit, Threadneedle Street, London."

In the shock of the news, the idea came to Laurie like a flash. Of course. Why hadn't she thought of it sooner? Survival—that was the real issue. No sacrifice was too great when you thought of it that way.

Was she still pretty enough? Quickly she got up, went to the mirror, took off her nightgown and looked at herself. Her face was still fresh, her body still good. She thanked God she had kept up with her exercises; many of her married friends had just let themselves go.

She smiled in what she hoped was a seductive way. Suddenly, she remembered the dream, the nightmare. Several years ago she dreamed that Jim had died and she had fallen in love with another man. He had made her do things in bed Jim never wanted to do, and then she had discovered that he was a pimp.

Was that the next step? How far should she let herself go?

The whole world was going to pieces. She wished that William Whitelaw would take charge and get things back to rights again. She and Jim had heard Whitelaw at a rally in Comiskey Park several weeks before, and he had made a lot of sense to them. Some of the people in the crowd, who were talking about shooting a few speculators to make a point, had scared her then. Now she understood what they were talking about. Tough times called for tough actions.

She made herself a cup of coffee. Then she applied her makeup, using about twice the usual amount. Finally she dressed, choosing the shortest dress she owned. Her legs had always been good. Then she looked in the full-length mirror again. If she did say so herself, she looked terrific.

But she didn't feel terrific. She was scared stiff. She woke up Marie, then fed and washed her. Afterward she took Marie to the day care center. It was not yet nine, and she had time to get there quickly. She might as well start with him.

Bob Hartley had been beating around the bush for all these weeks. Yesterday he had told her he couldn't keep giving her extra meat. He was getting very little meat in, and some ladies were offering him twice what he was charging her. Not only that—there was the $210,000 she already owed him. He was sorry to nag, but she had to pay him.

Laurie was bewildered. Jim was so upset about money. If he found out that she owed $210,000, plus the fact that she was not going to be able to get much meat any more, she didn't know what would happen. She didn't want him getting upset. He came home from school sometimes so mad and frustrated he couldn't sit still. Other times he was so tense when he went over their monthly bills that sweat broke out on his forehead.

Bob Hartley had made a suggestion. "Mrs. Adams, I find you very attractive. I think about you a lot. If you and I could be good friends, really good and close friends, if we could get to know each other better, I think we could forget about all these little problems. I'd treat you good. I'd treat you as if you had five million dollars in your pocketbook."

"What do you mean?" Laurie had asked.

"Well, I live alone in a house less than a mile away. Why don't you come over and visit me and we could get to know each other real well?" His small face wore an imitation smile. Before she left, Laurie had made an appointment, figuring she could always change her mind. It was for 9:30 that morning. And Laurie was on her way to keep it. As she drove along, she cried softly to herself. She had to do it. There was no other way. She was doing it for Jim and Marie.

When she got to the door of his house, Bob Hartley was still in his pajamas. He offered her a cup of coffee. She sat down in his living room full of Naugahyde furniture and tried to look seductive. Instead, she looked forlorn.

"You don't have to feel this way," said Hartley. "It's this inflation. Money has got everybody doing nutty things. Anyway, I'll make you like it. I'll do it so you have a good time. I'm not a bad guy."

One hour later, Laurie got dressed and washed off her makeup. Bob Hartley was right. He wasn't a bad guy. He hadn't been rough. In fact, he had been very gentle. In fact, she felt confident she'd be coming again. She didn't really mind. It was this inflation. These nutty times.

Later, at the lab, Laurie didn't talk to anyone all day. When she got home, she had two fine rib steaks for Jim, and the next morning she gave him six lean slices of bacon. He told her what a great shopper she must be to be able to get such good meat on his salary.

"Most of the guys at school have forgotten what bacon tastes like," he said.

When Jim left, Laurie went back to the mirror to see what she looked like. It was funny. She didn't look any different. She thought about it for a minute and decided she didn't really feel any different either.

Aram Khashoggi did not look good. He did not feel

good either. "Perhaps it is a mistake to have this meeting at all," he said to no one in particular as he stared out the window of his suite on the twenty-first floor of the Sherry-Netherland Hotel.

He was not conversing with himself. In one chair sat the short, squat body of Ismail Stanfi, who was thoughtfully stroking his chin. In another sat General Porto, his posture stiff and upright.

"I've never seen New York City like this," General Porto said. "It looks as if a civil war is going on. And I know how that looks."

Khashoggi did not acknowledge the statement of his friend. "I don't know why OPEC even bothers to stay together. It's meaningless. Six months ago we were the most successful cartel in history. Now we're a shell enclosing nothing."

The silence was heavy for a moment. The three uneasy foreigners sat like fugitives in a city that had become strange even to the natives.

"I don't see any other way out," said Stanfi.

"Nor do I," said Khashoggi. "To all intents and purposes, the United States no longer imports oil, because of the inflation and the Better Deal. Europe and Japan have cut back severely on their oil purchases. And," he added with a meaningful glance at Stanfi, "any price we set can be undercut by you or by Abu Dhabi or Kuwait."

"That's the way it has to be," Stanfi said. "In reality there is no more OPEC. We sell what we can, each in his way. If we can sell for less than you, we do. But please, my friend, do not pretend that we break an agreement. You understand that OPEC is dead."

"If it's of any possible consolation," said General Porto, nodding toward Khashoggi, "OPEC wasn't killed by you. The Russians killed OPEC."

"True," said Khashoggi. "That is undoubtedly true. The Russians do not have a lot of surplus oil to sell, but they sold enough to break the cartel, at first secretly, at ten dollars less than the OPEC price. Then, as they needed more money, they did it openly, at up to a third less."

Then General Porto said, "But you began the whole

process. Both of you. You thought you could play with matches around gunpowder forever without getting burned." The olive-skinned Ecuadorian was angry, but he was accustomed to keeping his emotions in check. "I warned you in Hawaii—I warned you sincerely. Today people in my country are starving. That's right, starving. Because we can't trade our oil for food. We can't even trade it to Argentina, because whatever price we offer to sell it for, Saudi Arabia undercuts us."

General Porto paused to blow his nose. "I want you to understand that. People are starving in my country as a direct consequence of your delusions of grandeur, your greed."

Khashoggi laughed softly. "Do you think, General, that we are happy about what has happened? Do you think that we have prospered? People are starving in Iran too. The country is restive. The whole city of Teheran is like a skeleton. The Shah's model projects have come to a dead stop. The Shah didn't squander that income—he put it into weaponry and developing industry. Now the money has slowed to a trickle. Meantime, the country can't eat airplanes and unfinished buildings."

General Porto smiled. "Perhaps you would like to remain in New York and seek political asylum here?"

Khashoggi was not amused. "The idea of raising the price so high came from the Shah of Shahs. When he learns that this mission too is a failure, that the Americans will not or cannot trade food for oil, he will be most disappointed in me. And on the other hand, our people will be very disappointed in him." Khashoggi stood in front of the mirror, the better to appreciate his moustache. He had recently had it shaped in the style of Clark Gable, whose movies he much admired. "My countrymen do not do things halfway." He tested its appearance with various facial expressions. When he smiled it accentuated his perfect white teeth.

Satisfied, he continued: "Libya was selling its oil this morning for eight hundred thousand dollars a barrel. That's almost two hundred thousand below the posted price and sixty thousand less than you're selling it for." He gestured toward Stanfi. "We just can't compete. You can't compete. Neither of us can produce it that cheaply."

"Was Hanrahan at all encouraging?" asked Porto.

"No," said Khashoggi.

General Porto was glum. "So now we are reduced to an insignificant group of squalling, pitiful countries, just as we were fifty years ago. What marvelous progress! And you touched off the whole thing. Before God, you bear a heavy burden." General Porto looked at each man in turn as he spoke.

But Aram Khashoggi was not thinking of his responsibility before God. He was remembering how the Shah had told him that this mission was absolutely crucial—that the whole future of the Pahlevi dynasty depended on it. Khashoggi did not want to be the one to tell the Shah of Shahs that his own brilliant idea to raise the price of oil was going to put an end to the Shah's dynasty.

He looked thoughtful.

Peter Hanrahan was surprised to discover that the minister at his brother's funeral was black. He had thought of the Eastern shore as particularly Southern —not an area where a black man would be presiding at the funeral of a white man. Apparently things were changing, even on the Eastern shore.

The funeral home appeared to date from the Civil War. The cortege of Cadillacs carried the casket and the mourners away from the funeral home southeast to the Episcopal church with its small graveyard. There were no more than fifty mourners. Peter Hanrahan noticed no one from New York City except their distant relative, Peter Flanigan, who looked as if he might have discovered the secret of perpetual youth.

The casket was lowered into the black earth. The minister said, "For those of us who knew him, William Hanrahan will be a shining light. He thought only of the happiness and comfort of those around him." As he droned on, it occurred to Hanrahan that this bleak Maryland countryside, on this gray and threatening day, was a perfect place for burial. It had a timeless, reassuring quality that transcended whatever drivel the minister, who obviously had never known William Hanrahan, had to say. Beyond the church grounds stretched a newly plowed field, perhaps already planted, although this time of year was a little early. And beyond the field stood a grove of trees. The elements of the landscape blended perfectly. It was not the wild, majestic beauty of the California coast or the Alaskan mountains, but a place where the labors of man had blended perfectly into God's handiwork.

". . . Ashes to ashes and dust to dust." The casket was covered with Astroturf, for the hole would be filled in later by machine.

"Your father was a wonderful man." Hanrahan was talking to his niece, Alexandra Kelsey, as they left. Alexandra was quiet and pensive. Her auburn hair was done up in a bun. Her face looked remote and strained. Even Kelsey, normally robust, looked somewhat haggard.

"Yes, he was. And kind. Too kind for these times," Alexandra said. Her voice was tired, her manner listless.

"If only he had let me know he needed money," said Kelsey, "I would have been glad to help."

"It seems so pointless," said Alex.

"Yes," said Hanrahan. "It does."

"He wasn't really poor," said Kelsey. "He still had Ridgeley, and that's worth a lot. It wasn't the money. I think he felt that his world didn't exist any more."

The funeral group broke up. Alex and Shelby went back to Ridgeley, where they were going to live. Hanrahan got into his Chrysler and headed back to Washington.

As his car pulled into West Executive Avenue, he heard a loud chop-chopping and looked out the back window. Marine One, the Presidential helicopter, was descending onto the South Lawn. That meant that the President was taking off again for Camp David.

The President spent less and less time at the White House. Hardly a day passed without a key political figure's calling for his resignation. Whitelaw's powerful voice had joined in and now led the chorus. Even the Democrats were loudly critical, although the Congressional liaison people at the White House advised the President that there were not yet nearly enough Democrats in Congress ready to depose one of their own for the President to feel alarm.

Yet whenever Hanrahan saw the President, he saw a changed person. Underneath his perpetual tan the President looked haggard. Hanrahan hated to converse with him now because the experience had become so painful. The President's mind wandered. He talked of his childhood; he talked of destiny; he talked of real estate; he talked of the roof caving in, and he didn't know why. He listened to the most harebrained ideas on saving the economy.

To outside groups who came to see him, the President appeared hearty and full of confidence. It amazed Hanrahan that the President could still put on these shows. But underneath, Hanrahan knew, the President was clutching a lion cub to his stomach and that cub was tearing out his guts.

That cub was the certain knowledge that he, the President, had lost control of the situation; that the murderous inflation fed on itself as the Federal Reserve printed more money to pay for more expensive welfare and food stamps, and back and forth, higher and higher; the certainty that he, the President, had pushed his country over the brink for what were, at this point, grave political consequences; the belief that he, the President, had fundamentally nowhere to turn, no place to go except a far worse place than the one he was in now.

In his office, Hanrahan heard the chop-chop-chop start again and saw the helicopter lift itself up with a strong heave and take off to the north. As he watched the helicopter disappear, his buzzer rang.

"Yes, Eliza?"

"Mr. Ratner is here."

"Send him in."

Ratner walked into the office, looking tired and in-creasingly overweight. He seemed to gain five pounds each week. His double chin quivered.

"I'm very sorry about your brother, Pete," Ratner said. "You missed a big morning."

"Thanks, Harry. What happened?"

"Nothing—yet. But Greenberg told me, off the record, that the President is planning big things."

"What kind of things?" asked Hanrahan, above the final throbs of Marine One.

"He wants a law declaring a state of emergency so he can use the army to impose wage and price controls and have the government regulate commodities sales." Ratner paused to let that register. "He means to put the country on a virtual war footing. A civil war footing." Ratner was watching Hanrahan's face. "But as terrible as that sounds, at least he's not suggesting shooting anyone; shooting is what I hear from the Whitelaw people."

"Is he doing this mainly to get something going before May Day?" Hanrahan asked.

"Possibly. I think so. Whitelaw says he'll have a million people in Washington by May Day, and I don't doubt that he will. A million Whitelaw people in touch at the same time could persuade a lot of Congressional minds to abandon the President and put him out of office. And don't believe what those Congressional liaison shmucks say. They were telling Nixon that things were going great until the roof fell in. Whitelaw wouldn't be putting on this kind of a show if he didn't think he could pull off something big."

"How can the President hope to get Congress behind him if he's so weak that they may impeach him?" asked Hanrahan.

"It depends on who can pick up the ball and get some momentum going. At this point, the ball is definitely up for grabs. And," Ratner added, "a lot of people think the Whitelaw movement is taking an ugly turn. Remember that ten people were killed after his last big rally in New Orleans."

The buzzer interrupted. "Yes, Eliza?"

"I've got to go," said Ratner and left.

"It's Miss Graham. She says it's urgent."

"All right," said Hanrahan.

"Peter?" Cathy said, her voice muffled. "Peter?"

"Yes, Cathy. How are you?"

"I want to see you. I've got to talk to you."

Cathy's voice was shrill, tearful.

"Where are you?"

"The Watergate. Please come quickly." There was a click and then the dial tone.

Hanrahan was quick. He was out the door and on the street with only a brief stop to tell Eliza that he needed a White House car in a hurry. The car was there when he reached West Executive Avenue.

"The Watergate. It's an emergency," Hanrahan told the driver.

The black Chrysler took off like a rocket. Once, when they were behind a slow-moving car on F Street, the driver reached under the dashboard and touched a button. A loud siren sounded from the Chrysler and the car in front pulled over to let the Chrysler by. At the door he asked the driver to wait.

Hanrahan was at the Watergate elevator within ten minutes of the call. When he opened the door to his apartment, Cathy Graham was curled up, nude, in an armchair. He knew by her appearance that she was drugged.

"What did you take, Cathy?" he said.

Cathy, her face listless, opened and closed her mouth.

Hanrahan ran over and shook her. "Jesus, Cathy, what did you take?"

"Everything I could get my hands on," Cathy said and smiled. Her eyelids fluttered and she dropped her head on her chest. She was asleep.

Hanrahan grabbed her bag. The bottles were on top: Seconal, Doriden and Quaaludes. He looked at her again. She was sound asleep. He slapped her across the face. Cathy opened a bleary eye.

"Why? For God's sake, why?" Hanrahan asked.

"What have I got to live for?" she said groggily. Then she smiled and went back to sleep.

"How many did you take?" Hanrahan asked.

There was no answer. He shook her and got no response. For a second he thought she might already be dead. He took her pulse; it was surprisingly strong.

He picked her up and wrapped her in one of his wool bathrobes. Then he carried her out the door and down the hall to the elevator. By a stroke of good luck, an elevator was waiting, and no one was in it. He took it to the ground floor, then past the startled desk clerk and the doorman and to his waiting car.

"The G.W. Hospital," he said. "The emergency room."

The driver looked discreetly at the crumpled form in the bathrobe and hit the siren. They were at the emergency room in less than a minute. Hanrahan and the driver took Cathy Graham into the hospital and up to the desk with a sign that read "Emergencies Register Here." The woman behind the desk was filing her nails. She did not look up.

"This girl has taken an overdose of sleeping pills," said Hanrahan.

"What?" asked the woman without looking up.

Hanrahan reached out and grabbed the woman's smock. "Goddammit. I said this girl has taken an overdose of sleeping pills. She needs help. Right now, goddammit." The woman pressed a button on her desk. He released her smock. Two orderlies brought out a stretcher. Hanrahan and the driver put Cathy Graham on the stretcher and the orderlies took her away, down a long hallway and into a room.

The woman behind the desk suddenly became very lively. She asked Hanrahan to sit down. She asked him what kinds of pills Cathy had taken and how old she was. Then she went down the hall to the room where Cathy had been taken.

When she returned, she told him, "I'll need some more information. Are you the young lady's father?"

Hanrahan felt as if he'd been punched in the gut by Muhammad Ali. He fought the nausea that welled up inside him and said, "No. I'm a family friend."

The woman asked some more questions and then told Hanrahan to wait in a nearby room. Hanrahan and the driver, who had not asked a single question, sat in a room painted yellow with green tile flooring.

For about an hour Hanrahan tried to read an old copy of *Forbes*. Then the admitting woman appeared in the waiting room and said, "Mr. Hanrahan, could I see you for a minute?"

She led him into a small cubicle. A younger woman wearing street clothes was waiting in the cubicle. She was a psychiatrist, she said, and she would have to talk to Cathy when she revived.

"Does that mean she's going to make it?" Hanrahan asked.

"Yes, she's going to be fine. She's on IV now, but she'll be all right by tomorrow morning."

Jesus, why hadn't they told him? He was furious at the callousness of people in hospitals.

"Just what is your relationship with the patient, Mr. Hanrahan?" the psychiatrist asked with a smile.

"I'm a friend of the family," Hanrahan said.

"Why was she with you when she took the sleeping pills?" the psychiatrist asked.

"She wasn't. She took them before I got there." Hanrahan paused. "But I'm not going to answer any more of your questions. You can ask Cathy anything you want."

"All right, Mr. Hanrahan. You can see Cathy in the morning."

An hour later, Peter Hanrahan was back at his desk in the EOB. He felt weak with guilt, remorse. First his brother, then Cathy Graham. He had no experience with suicides but he respected the successful ones. If they wanted that much to die, surely the choice should be theirs. It was the unsuccessful ones who disturbed him—the Cathys of the world.

He had to face it, had to face the kind of man he had been. The things he had done in his bedroom were catching up with him. The consequences of his actions could not be escaped.

When visiting hours began, he went back to see Cathy. She was in a room by herself, which Hanrahan had requested. Tubes and nozzles surrounded her. At first Hanrahan thought she was asleep. Then he realized she was awake with her eyes closed.

"Hi, Cathy," he said.

"Could you get me some water?" Her voice was weak and hoarse with tension.

Hanrahan poured water from the plastic pitcher into the plastic glass and held it while Cathy drank. Her hands were cold and moist.

She looked at him with sky-blue eyes. "Pete," she said, "will you do me another favor?"

"Of course," he said.

"Next time don't take me to the hospital."

It was unusual to have a cast party before shooting, but this was a special movie. Burton wanted everyone to know how important it was. Sally was in New York City visiting her sister as usual, so Burton could have a party with all the stops out.

The first thing he did was put out a bowl of cocaine in the living room, a number of coke spoons next to it. He also had two young plainclothes security guards to make sure no one walked off with the bowl. Burton had had one room entirely remodeled for the party by Larry Wilson, the famous Hollywood party designer.

It was called the "Environment Room." Completely dark, its walls and floors were covered with micro-thin plastic coating. On the floor were enormous water-filled plastic pillows. The floor and the pillows were covered with a mixture of K-Y Jelly, warm water and mineral oil. No one was to be allowed in the room with clothes on.

But Burton was really proud of what he had done with the swimming pool. There was always a lot of talk around Hollywood about this producer or that producer being short of money. In some cases, it was more than just talk. Three major studios had stopped production because of inflation. Even though revenues had gone into the trillions, costs were rising just as fast.

Burton's swimming pool was designed to show that he was not facing a money problem. He had taken $100,000 in hundred-dollar bills from the bank that morning. A few minutes before the guests were due to arrive, he took them out of their neat packages and spread them over the surface of his pool. When he

finished, there were still a few bare patches, but to all
intents and purposes the entire surface of the pool was
a 900-square-foot blanket of floating, bobbing, floodlit
hundred-dollar bills. Hal Burton didn't know whether
his guests would be impressed, but *he* certainly was.

The first guests to arrive were Larry Wilson and his
co-designer, Elisha Shapiro. They were both swarthy,
bearded men of medium height.

A few of the stagehands arrived next. They nervously talked to Burton about the movie. To them
Burton was the big enchilada. They had to be nice to
him. If they were very nice to him, good things would
ensue: extra pay, extra cocaine—all kinds of things
that could be useful in a rapidly inflating economy. A
few minutes later two script girls arrived, then a few
of the actors and actresses in some of the smaller roles.
They began to drift from the foyer into the living
room, and Burton could see their heads bobbing up
and down over the bowl of cocaine.

More and more people arrived. Many of them had
brought their own joints, which they smoked after tok-
ing up on cocaine. Soon it was dark both inside and
outside, since Burton had the rheostat turned down to
a dim gray. The uninvited guests started to arrive—
the perennial Hollywood gate-crashers. Burton knew
it was hopeless to try to keep them out; he didn't even
try.

He was waiting impatiently for Joan Bellamy. She
had never been to a party like this, he was sure, and
he wanted to impress her with the free spirit of his
friends. It was after 10 P.M. and she was late.

Burton heard giggling down the hall from the living
room. He could barely make out a few young men and
women taking off their clothes and going into the Environment Room. Larry Wilson had charged a small
fortune for his talents as a party designer. Burton
hoped that his guests were starting to make use of Wilson's creation. And he wasn't disappointed. Gradually,
more and more people were discovering it.

Large puffs of marijuana smoke wafted out of the
room. For his part, he planned to stay completely sober. No matter how many parties he gave, he was al-

ways nervous about them. So many things could go wrong.

By now, many of his guests—tall, short, beautiful, lithe, clumsy, young and otherwise—were jumping naked into the pool. They'd dive in and bob up with hundred-dollar bills clinging to their hair, their faces, their bodies.

It was a thrilling sight to him—all those glamorous, vulnerable bodies swimming around in his money. Scrooge McDuck, Donald Duck's rich uncle, had a swimming pool filled with money in which he would dive and cavort. This, too, was a scene out of a movie. He hoped some of them were screwing in the water. That would be extra special.

There it was—sex and money, all brought together by power. And it was his power—Hal Burton's power— that put it all there. He could turn it on, and he could turn it off.

"Hello!"

Hal turned. Joan Bellamy was standing beside him, an amused smile on her face.

"Hello! I've been waiting for you," he said.

"It's a very Hollywood party."

"It is that. You know, I never realized so much why Hollywood is the creator of the American dream. I mean, here it all is—the beautiful girls, the swimming pool, the money, the glamorous, carefree life. It's great!" Burton looked for approval to Joan Bellamy.

She didn't respond. Instead, even in the semidarkness her face looked sad. She looked like a bird poised for flight.

"Am I wrong again, Joan? Isn't this what it's all about?"

Joan spoke gently, carefully choosing her words. "May I tell you something, Hal? Something you might not like?"

"Sure," he said. "I've got enough yes-men. I'm tough. I can take it."

"Hal, if the life were so great, you wouldn't invite a hundred people. You'd just do it with a few close friends. You wouldn't have to advertise if it were so wonderful. Everything that you say is here is here. But other things are too. Confused, frightened, unhappy people. Is that your dream?"

"They're having fun," said Burton. "They're enjoying themselves."

Her face looked a little sadder. "Excuse me while I get a drink."

Now Burton worried. He looked again at the faces of the swimmers. Lights played on the glistening wet bodies diving in and out of the water. Was the laughter forced, even hysterical? Did the faces of the young men and women have a crazed look about them? Was Joan Bellamy right?

As he studied them, they acknowledged his interest with smiles, bright, eager, seductive. But when no one was looking, did their faces looked pinched and anxious?

Burton walked back inside the house. He had to find Joan Bellamy. She was in the den, alone, watching television. It was a Bruce Lee Kung-Fu movie. Joan was eating an apple as she watched.

"Jesus, you sure know how to ruin a guy's party."

She took his hand as he sat down next to her. "I'm sorry, Hal. I didn't mean to do that. But I think it's good to see things plainly. I want you to see what's going on around you for what it is. How can we film the story of your life if you're not prepared to face it?"

"For Christ's sake, Joan, I thought that was the story of my life—the very fact that I don't understand what's going on. Isn't that the point of *The Wonderchildren?*"

Joan Bellamy smiled, a warm, thoughtful smile. "I've been criticizing you, Hal, and I apologize. You understand a lot if you understand that. You're going to make a great picture."

Burton felt angry. Not only was Joan Bellamy not so smart as he had thought she was, she was also rude. She was condescending to *him*. He felt short-changed and insulted at the same time.

"Enjoy yourself, Joan. Have a good time. Don't worry about me or the picture. Your work is finished. You've been paid." Burton got up and patted her on the back. "I'm going to have a good time anyway. That's the least I can do at my own party."

The hell with her, he thought. He walked to the living room where the coke was and took three good toots. Even before the third one grabbed him, he was sailing. Patty Shoreham, an actress with whom he had had an early affair in *The Wonderchildren*, walked by wearing a large towel. She was sucking on a joint. "I want some of that," Burton said.

"Be my guest. It's very primo dope. Maui wowee." The redheaded girl handed the joint to Burton. He took a few hits.

Pat threw her head back and laughed, lips red and vibrant, her teeth perfectly capped. "I never thought I'd see you stoned," she said slowly, having to organize each word.

"You just haven't seen me often enough," Burton said. "Let's go in the room. I paid for it and I haven't even used it yet."

"Whatever . . . you . . . say . . . boss." She took his hand and led him down the hallway of his own house to his own Environment Room. Burton took off his clothes, his shoes, his socks, his underwear. He kept on only his watch. Pat took off her towel. She had small, pointed breasts. Burton suddenly realized that she couldn't be much more than eighteen, if that. She probably also weighed half as much as he did.

They walked into the absolutely dark room. Burton fell down almost immediately. It didn't hurt, though, because the room was thoroughly padded by the water-filled pillows and the plastic covering and the rugs underneath. Pat was still holding his hand, and she fell down with him. They rolled around together, over and under and beside each other in the wet, slippery room. Burton had the fleeting thought that Larry Wilson might be a genius. The room made him feel completely cut off from everything in the outside world. The only dimension here was pleasure.

He felt Pat's long, firm leg. Then he realized that Pat was shorter than that. He was feeling someone else's leg. Whoever's leg it was, she giggled and started touching him. It was so dark that all Burton could be sure of was that the incredibly voluptuous creature he was embracing was a woman with long legs and medium-sized breasts and a very wet vagina.

He pulled the girl closer to him, teased her until he couldn't stand it any longer, and entered her. As he fucked, he had the sensation that this was the only reality. He was screwing a total stranger, and that was the way he wanted it.

He came. He knew it was as good a thing as had ever happened to him. He lay a moment in growing relaxation and then he said, "Whoever you are, that was one of the great moments of history."

"That's okay. Enjoy yourself," Joan Bellamy said.

Claire Beaton was eating breakfast in the White House mess with Harry Ratner. It was early. They were the only people in the room. Entirely for Ratner's pleasure the President had ordered the mess to stock bagels, cream cheese and lox. The President had undoubtedly forgotten his thoughtful act long since, but Ratner was happy to remember it almost every morning.

"The President has stopped seeing McConger," said Ratner. "Now he won't let him in the door."

Claire snorted. "It's about time."

"I think the President figures he's in so goddamn deep now that McConger plus a miracle wouldn't get him out," Ratner said. "Also, the same people McConger said he'd deliver are lining up with Whitelaw. McConger has just been an unqualified catastrophe for the President, and I guess he's finally figured it out."

"When I talked to him yesterday he asked me if I thought it would help his cause if he had McConger publicly executed," Claire said as she daintily buttered her toast.

She looked terrific. Ratner had to admit it. Not that he minded. She was wearing a tailored navy pants suit with a yellow blouse and a small cockatoo pin in her lapel.

"Harry," she said, "I have a new theory about where all the gold has gone."

"Where? What's your theory?"

"I think someone has been trying to get a corner on

the market with borrowed Eurodollars," Claire said. "It may sound farfetched, but that's my theory for today."

"Who?"

"I don't know. Somebody big. Like Saudi Arabia."

Ratner frowned. "It's a brilliant idea, but it doesn't work. We tried to trace the Eurodollar borrowings. They couldn't be traced. The Zurich bankers wouldn't tell a thing. If the Saudis had done it, we'd know from our people in Riyadh. They even tell us when King Fahd farts, if you'll pardon my crudeness. And for a whole government to do it, well it would surely have to be listed in records of their transactions. Unless it's some far-out country like Chad or someplace—and they couldn't get the money together to buy that much gold. No one would lend them the Eurodollars."

"What about a wealthy individual or a corporation?" asked Claire.

"No private entity could borrow that much," Ratner said.

Claire ate silently for a moment, then said, "Well, I still think it's worth pursuing. If we could get some gold back, we could start a new monetary system people might have some confidence in."

"It's certainly worth pursuing," Ratner agreed. "But how the hell do you pursue it?"

Claire didn't know. But the gold had not vanished into thin air. Somebody had that gold.

"Did you hear that the Treasury's going to stop printing anything smaller than a thousand-dollar bill?" Ratner asked. "Line up to convert your money. And the President's creating a new bill. He's calling it a megabuck."

"Jesus," said Claire. "A megabuck! For how much?"

"One zero zero zero zero zero zero. And the President has a message to go with it. Want to know what it is?"

"I can't wait," said Claire, her hand stalled in midair on its way to her mouth.

"Every man a millionaire. All you need is one bill."

William Whitelaw loved birds. They were beautiful

in flight and they were never lazy. They had to be constantly alert to survive. Yet they traveled in flocks and helped each other find food. It was the end of April, and in Washington the birds were coming back. From his office in Georgetown Whitelaw could see the birds alighting on trees that lined the streets, then flying off again in search of food.

He turned his chair back to face the man in his office. The man was named Reilly, and he looked Irish if he looked anything. He also looked beefy-faced and cunning. He was Deputy Chief of Police for the District of Columbia, and he had come to Whitelaw's office to discuss the upcoming Whitelaw May Day demonstration.

His message was coming across strangely to Whitelaw, and that made the Nebraskan careful. At first Reilly seemed to be saying that the police would not stand for any violence, and that if the crowd got out of hand, Whitelaw could expect mass arrests like the ones in May of 1971.

Then Reilly did something startling. He asked Whitelaw for an autographed picture. Whitelaw politely told him that he would be glad to autograph something for him, but that as a matter of policy the organization did not distribute autographed photos of Whitelaw. That was meant to show that it was the movement, and not the man, that counted.

He scribbled his name on a letterheaded sheet and gave it to the deputy.

Reilly told Whitelaw that Mrs. Reilly was a great admirer of his. "Yeah, she'll be glad to have this autograph. She thinks you've got all the answers. She's listened to you on the radio a hundred times."

"Well, I'm not sure I've been on that many times," said Whitelaw. This was more like it. This was the kind of talk he was used to. "But that's very nice of you to tell me."

"I'll tell you something else. A lot of the cops on the force that I've heard from would just as soon take off on May Day and join your demonstration."

"That's very thoughtful of you to tell me so," Whitelaw said. "How do you yourself feel about the movement?"

"Me, well, I'll tell you. Just between me, you and the lamppost, and not to be repeated under any circumstances, sometimes the chief and I talk about it. And if we could snap our fingers and have this whole crowd that's in charge go up in smoke, here and now, and then have somebody like you take charge, well, it might not be such a bad idea. But that's strictly between you and me, you know what I mean?"

Whitelaw had been intrigued. That was when he turned around to look at the birds. As he swiveled back, he asked, "Do you ever talk about how it might be possible for our present leaders to go up in smoke?"

"Well, that's the tough part. I don't really know. But I do know, just off the record and unofficially, that if you could somehow do it, you'd have a lot of good people behind you." Reilly winked at Whitelaw.

Whitelaw gave him back a big smile and said, "Well, I'll certainly keep what you told me under my hat."

Reilly smiled too. "For the record, though, this demonstration's got to be peaceful. That's orders from the President himself."

"Of course. It will be. Thanks for coming by, and please thank your wife for her support."

When Reilly walked out, Whitelaw buzzed his secretary. "Send in Jimmie and Marvin, please," he said.

His two aides had come into the movement as speechwriters, but they had been given many additional duties since then. Like so many of his followers, they were always smiling.

"Sit down, Jimmie, Marvin. How you two doing on the march?"

"Pretty well," Jimmie said. At first Whitelaw had been uncomfortable when his people kept smiling the whole time they talked, but he became used to it—as long as he wasn't expected to smile in return. "But we've still got a lot of people coming on buses who're going to have to leave the demonstration early so they can get home. There's no place for them to stay. We've beat the bushes for beds for fifty miles around, but there's gonna be too many people."

"Jimmie," Whitelaw said, "there can never be too many people. It would be good if we had every person in America marching."

"Of course, I know that," Jimmie said. "I just meant too many people for staying the night."

"You know, boys," Whitelaw said, "I just had a visit from our city's Deputy Chief of Police."

Whitelaw told the two younger men about Reilly's words and his puzzling reference to the government's going up in smoke. All three men were thinking very hard.

Whitelaw broke the silence. "I believe he's telling us something. I believe he's telling us something very important." As he waited for his aides to respond, he turned his chair once to look at the birds. The attendant at the gast station below him was posting the new prices. Unleaded regular was $900,000 a gallon. There were few cars pulling in and out of the station. Someone had smashed the front windows, which were now covered with plywood boards. On the boards were "One with God" posters.

"Well, maybe now's the time," Jimmie said.

"Could be," Marvin said. "It definitely could be."

The three men reviewed the several visits they had had in the last couple of weeks from Congressmen and Senators wishing them well. Could that mean that the time was ripe for making America safe for Christians? Was the moment upon them at last?

The governor's phone rang. "Yes?" he said.

"It's General Steinbrenner, Governor. You're expecting him."

"Of course. Send him in," said Whitelaw. "Jimmie, Marvin, you'll excuse us. The general probably doesn't want witnesses."

Jimmie and Marvin passed General Steinbrenner on their way out. The general was a surprisingly short man. His jowly face was fretful. He did not look pleased to encounter Jimmie and Marvin.

"It's a pleasure to meet you, General," Whitelaw said, flashing a radiant smile and squeezing the soldier's hand. "Please sit down." The general sat.

"You're the military commander of the District of Washington, I understand."

"Indeed," said General Steinbrenner. "I am indeed. I should like to talk to you about plans for your demonstration."

"Of course," Governor Whitelaw said. "Would you like some coffee?"

"No, thank you," the general said. He looked carefully around the room. Then he looked directly at Whitelaw. "Is this conversation being recorded?"

"Certainly not," Whitelaw said, making a show of being offended. "Why would I want to record our conversation?"

"Sometimes people do foolish things," the general said, smiling effusively. "I hope you won't mind if I set this thing up while we talk." The general reached into his briefcase and took from it a tube. About one inch wide and one foot long, it was attached by wires to a small black box. There was a button on top, which General Steinbrenner carefully pressed. The device made a humming sound.

"It's nothing more than a strong magnet," Steinbrenner said. "It erases all tapes nearby. I hope you don't have any tapes in storage here?"

'No," said Whitelaw, "I don't. But you might have warned me in advance."

"I'm sorry, but it's a somewhat delicate maneuver," Steinbrenner said. "What I have to say is for your ears only. Would you please pull the curtains, by the way? You understand me?"

"Yes, I do," Whitelaw said.

"I am charged with maintaining order in the Capital area at all times. However—" and the general paused to open the door to the only closet in the room. It was empty. "—However, a lot of different interpretations can be applied to how. You understand me?"

"Of course," Whitelaw said. This was promising.

"I could, for instance, move the troops in to break up your little rally pretty near as soon as you started speaking. I could do that. And I could then arrest you. The President would back me up, I assure you."

"I hope you won't," said Whitelaw, keeping the smile on his face.

"I don't plan to." The general was still apprehensive. "Would you mind closing the curtains?" he asked. "There may be telescopes or people outside who can read lips."

Whitelaw got up and closed the curtains. He knew a lot more about how seriously the government was taking him than he had known before the general's arrival.

When Whitelaw sat down again, the general said, "There are many of us who see a lot wrong with this country. I think I can tell you now, completely off the record, that if we could just press a button, so to speak, and see the crowd that's now in charge go up in smoke, we might just do it." Whitelaw's mind was whirring madly. "Yes," Steinbrenner continued, watching Whitelaw's facial expression carefully, "we might just do it."

"How might it be done?" Whitelaw asked. "Have you given any thought to that?"

"Not by violence," said the general, a note of sanctimony in his voice. "At least not completely. That can't be tolerated. But if the President were to feel that his continuance in office was harming the national—" the general paused to search for the perfect word—"*essence*, we wouldn't stand in his way. You understand?"

"Yes," Whitelaw said, "I do."

"And if the Vice President were to resign—which wouldn't be that surprising, considering how sick he is —then a new man could step in. You understand me?" Steinbrenner asked.

"Yes, I certainly do," Whitelaw said. "Indeed. I certainly do."

"You can open the curtains now," the general said. When Whitelaw did so, the general said, very clearly, "There must be no violence. I will not stand for it."

"I quite understand," said Whitelaw. "It was very kind of you to take the time and trouble to visit me."

The general rose, shook the governor's hand, and took his leave.

Whitelaw summoned Jimmie and Marvin back into

his office. He closed the curtains and told them about the visit.

"Does he know about the calls we've had from Capitol Hill?" asked Jimmie.

"I don't know," said Whitelaw thoughtfully. "Maybe he does. It's obvious that I'm getting some kind of signal. But exactly what kind? And is it a trap to make me move too soon?"

"Maybe it could be," Marvin said. "It might be better to wait until you get an open call to office."

"I think so too," Whitelaw said. "I definitely do."

"We don't want any coups," Jimmie said. "We want to come in because the people want us in."

Whitelaw pondered. "Exactly. That leads us back to the movement. I have to show that I'm responsible, but the movement, the people are impatient. They're *forcing* me to do it."

"Righto," said Marvin.

"That could mean that a few people get roughed up and a few things get broken. I'm not saying I *want* that, but it could happen, you know what I mean, Jimmie?"

Jimmie smiled. "The easy thing is to get it started. The hard thing is to get it stopped. People get to really like breaking things up."

"That's why I hire good men like you—for doing the difficult jobs."

When they left, Whitelaw returned to his speech. He was trying to write the best speech of his campaign. There would be a lot of TV coverage, and this was the time to send the Whitelaw message across America in one big swoop.

Then the governor did something he rarely allowed himself to do. He thought about what he would do when he became President. He thought that it would be soon now. He knew he could stop inflation, if only by using the army to enforce wage and price controls and by extremely harsh punishment of offenders. He saw, as he was sure the American people saw, that the death penalty was justified for many crimes.

Perhaps his most important consideration was whether the death penalty would be the right thing for members of the old administration—the President, McConger, Donnelly, that rich bastard Hanrahan and the others. It would mark a drastic departure from the past, but perhaps that was precisely what was needed. If a few of the right people were shot for doing such outrageous things against the nation and against God, that might be the very thing to make true Americans sit up and take notice of the fact that a new order was necessary, where discipline was the rule, and people were held to account for their sins.

Yes, thought Whitelaw. It might be a very good idea to shoot a few people—the right people, of course. Sometimes violence was necessary to cleanse a nation. Some people were going to have to pay with their lives for what they had done. And on their graves a better America would grow.

The Russian Ambassador perspired heavily, although it was exactly 70 degrees in Peter Hanrahan's office. Hanrahan wondered if Sobolevsky was on the verge of an attack of some kind. If so, he was in the right place. The White House complex had at least three doctors on hand at all times. One of them was a cardiac specialist.

But Sobolevsky went right on talking, without keeling over or passing out. "The situation is critical, Peter. Extremely. I am not sure that I can overstate how serious it is."

Hanrahan looked attentive.

"We are having difficulty keeping order in our country. Our people have grown used to a stable economic system. It isn't like here, where people are accustomed to a roller-coaster ride of boom or bust." The ambassador, pleased with the fluency of the English translation of his Crimean thoughts, allowed himself the luxury of a smile.

Hanrahan was patient. He inclined his head.

"Of course, you know about the floods," the ambassador continued. "We have had many floods this spring. We were already short of grain before the floods. This means that now we're going to be in an even worse situation. You, on the other hand, based on your own Department of Agriculture predictions, are going to have ideal planting conditions this spring. We also happen to know for a fact that you have a lot of grain on hand."

"Wassily, we've discussed this before. Why don't you buy some of that grain? It's for sale—it's not in a museum," Hanrahan said.

"As if you didn't know," the ambassador said, "we cannot afford to pay three million dollars a bushel for ordinary wheat. No one can."

"Gold would buy it for less," Hanrahan said. "Why won't you part with your gold to feed your citizens?" Another shot in the dark.

"Peter, I've told you repeatedly, we have little gold left. We paid through the nose for your wheat and your computers with gold for years. We started off this year with gold, but it's wiping us out, to use your expression. We have no more gold to pay. If we still had a lot of gold, we would use it." Sobolevsky looked exasperated.

"Perhaps you could trade us ballistic missiles," Hanrahan said.

Sobolevsky grimaced. "Very funny, my dear Peter. Very humorous."

Hanrahan became serious. "Listen, Wassily. Why don't you stop spending so goddamn much on your army and spend more on feeding your people? We're not going to bail you out at the present price of wheat after the way your government has treated us. I've told you that before."

Sobolevsky sighed. "Peter, our country is very different from your country. Our people don't expect to get rich quick, like your people. But they do expect a better life, slowly but surely. Now they're not getting it and they're mad. We've had disturbances. I won't go into their exact nature, but we've had difficulties. So we have to clamp down. And we don't want to clamp down too hard, because that makes it harder to produce things."

Hanrahan wondered what point Wassily was making. That was the trouble with diplomacy—the room for doubt, the margin for error. Sobolevsky was not the most accomplished of the breed.

Sobolevsky narrowed his eyes. "Our people are capable of unlimited sacrifices if they are properly motivated. I think I need only mention Stalingrad and Leningrad to make myself clear."

"Wassily, no one doubts that the Russians are tough. But how about your platinum? Sell that. Then take the money and buy wheat." Hanrahan hoped to head Sobolevsky off.

"There is not much of a market for platinum, as you should know, for the simple reason that platinum is mostly used for catalytic converters in automobile mufflers, and your country is not selling many new cars to anybody," said Sobolevsky. The Russian sighed. "And we have already sold almost the entire collection of Impressionist paintings from the Hermitage in Leningrad to an American grain exporter. We do not enjoy such trades."

Hanrahan was tired of the whining. His robber-baron genes took control and he flashed his Irish teeth at the ambassador. "Could you tell me precisely what you're driving at, Wassily?"

"We could justify the sacrifices our people must make in only one way. That would be if we had a foreign adventure—if we were at war, if you like. They realize that things cannot be the same if we're at war," Sobolevsky said. His shirt was moist with sweat.

"I think this is a conversation you had better have with the President and the Secretary of State, Mr. Ambassador," Hanrahan said with great formality and severity.

Sobolevsky was exasperated again. "Peter, I don't want it to go that far. We are not threatening you. It would do us no good to have a nuclear exchange with you. Other, closer nations have provoked us, and hostilities could break out at any moment. Who knows where that would lead? I want our agreement to be settled long before. We need the grain. We want you to sell it to us." The Russian's face was red with effort.

Hanrahan's voice was steady. "You know, Wassily, we had a similar conversation a few months ago. The only thing that's new today is that your threats are more explicit."

Hanrahan waited for Sobolevsky to say that he wasn't making any threats. But Wassily Sobolevsky, Ambassador Extraordinary and Plenipotentiary, no longer denied it.

"I have found it almost impossible to see your President and talk seriously with him. The same for your Secretary of State. I hope you will pass along my conversation." The old Russian looked deeply troubled and moved. Still, Hanrahan thought, I wouldn't trust him as far as I could throw a chimney by its smoke.

Sobolevsky rose to go and Hanrahan saw him to the door.

"Goodbye, my dear Peter. I hope you can help us with this problem."

Hanrahan was noncommittal. "Goodbye, Wassily."

Hanrahan closed his door and went to his dictaphone. He recorded the exact substance of his conversation with Sobolevsky. "It is my impression," Hanrahan said into the machine, "that Sobolevsky was talking about some kind of armed adventure into a neighboring state—perhaps Turkey, perhaps Iran, perhaps even China."

Hanrahan added that he believed that the Russian was giving "an authentic and serious warning," and that a meeting of the Cabinet, the National Security Council and the Congressional leadership was warranted. Hanrahan stopped dictating. He remembered that he had had an almost identical conversation with Sobolevsky months ago. What had changed in the interim? Why was this conversation so much more ominous? He asked Eliza to bring him his notes of that meeting.

After reading them, he realized what the key difference was. Earlier, Sobolevsky had talked about "certain circles" who wanted to "divert attention." Now Sobolevsky was drawing no distinction between the Soviet government and those circles. That would indicate that those circles were now in the driver's seat. Earlier, Sobolevsky had clearly placed himself, as the representative of his government, in opposition to the people who wanted to embark on a "foreign adventure." Now, Sobolevsky would seem to be saying that an *even worse* situation might require a foreign adventure.

A foreign adventure! Jesus, the old Crimean certainly had a way with words.

The more he thought about the two conversations, the surer he was. Today's performance was not the delivery of a shopworn statement by the Russian Ambassador. The threat was real and immediate.

Hanrahan punched the button that read "W.H." He asked to speak to the President. The operator said that the President was sleeping and was not to be disturbed except for emergencies. Hanrahan asked how long the President would be sleeping. About an hour. Hanrahan made his decision.

"All right," he said. "When he wakes up, please ask him to call me as soon as possible."

Then Hanrahan called Sobolevsky at the Soviet Embassy, the new one on Wisconsin Avenue. He reached him just as he came in the door.

"I just want you to know that I will be talking to the President today," Hanrahan said. "You can tell your people that we're dealing with it as a top-priority item."

"Thank you, my good friend Peter. I hope you will make the right decision."

Hanrahan said he hoped so too and hung up. Then he called Claire and asked her to come to his office immediately. No, he couldn't tell her why.

When Claire arrived, Hanrahan told her of the two conversations. "I know defense and foreign policy aren't your fields, Claire. They're not mine, either. But see if you find the same things in the second conversation that I do."

Claire read Hanrahan's notes of the conversation. Then she listened.

"Absolutely," she said. "Have you told the President?"

"He's taking a nap," Hanrahan said in a voice that sounded more sarcastic than it actually was. "I'll tell him when he wakes up. I didn't want to scare him to death with something I might just be imagining."

"You aren't imagining it."

Hanrahan's buzzer sounded. Eliza told him that the President was on the line.

"Mr. President," said Hanrahan. "I hope I'm not disturbing you."

"Christ," the President said, "today has been the day I carry around fifty pounds of shit in a twenty-five-pound bag, and a lot of it is falling out all around me. What's your contribution to the pile?"

Hanrahan spoke carefully. "I had a rather disturbing conversation with Ambassador Sobolevsky about an hour ago. I need to talk to you about it."

"Well, hell. Who else if not me?" the President said. "Come right on over. I want to tell you a few things too."

The solarium on the third floor of the White House faced south, and it was sunny almost all day. Today, on a late afternoon in spring, it was a magnificent setting. The room was in happy contrast to the subject under discussion.

"Before you begin about Sobolevsky," the President said, "here's a sample of the shit that's going on here. I just want you to know what we're facing." The President's eyes looked puffy and red, and he spoke rapidly, out of excitement and tension.

"You know this big rally Whitelaw's having on May Day? You also know there're some people on the Hill who want my ass out of here?"

"Of course," Hanrahan said.

"Get this," the President said. "Those assholes are so goddamned dumb that they've been parading in and out of Whitelaw's office all day. We put a few people around Whitelaw's office taking pictures, and you see some mighty familiar faces. Are those guys so dumb they don't think we'd be watching?" It was a rhetorical question. "Either that or they figure I'm so far gone it doesn't matter."

The President sat forward. It was a clumsy movement. His voice grew raspy. "But it does matter, by Christ. I'm not going to have some piss ants get together with a lunatic to topple the President of the United States."

Hanrahan was pleased. The President had shaken off his torpor. He was ready for a fight, and he was ready to fight dirty.

"Now this part is almost funny," the President said. "We've got this tin-star fuckhead General Steinbrenner in charge of the Military District of Washington, which means he is the fallback guy in case of trouble during Whitelaw's rally. Well, we heard some stuff about him that wasn't good, so the FBI gave him this tape recorder inside a tube, and a box, and they told him it was a device for *jamming* tape recorders."

The President was shrewd enough to locate the almost imperceptible look of astonishment on the face of his friend.

"You think the taping stopped with Nixon? Not a chance. That was when people learned how valuable it was. Now it's just done a lot more carefully. A lot. Our guy in the general's office took the tape out yesterday—he knew that Steinbrenner had been to see Whitelaw—and that asshole Steinbrenner is talking on the tape about helping Whitelaw take over the fucking country. But Whitelaw's clever. He didn't say a single incriminating thing."

"That is amazing," Hanrahan said. He wondered if his office was bugged.

"We'll have Steinbrenner's ass out of command tomorrow—and talking to people about a plea bargain the next day. I mean, he's going up for incitement to riot and conspiracy unless he tells us everything." The President shook his head. "I may be in trouble, but I'm not gonna let that kind of shit go on." The President laughed. "I'm lucky. I've got enemies who're even stupider than I am."

"This is outrageous," Hanrahan said. "It's nothing short of treason." But he still wondered what the President knew about Peter Hanrahan.

"It's serious, all right," the President said. "You predicted a fucking catastrophe, Pete, and that's just what we've got. Now what kind of shit can you add to the day?"

"Sobolevsky desperately wants our wheat. He's talking about going to war over it."

"With us?"

"I think with the Chinese or someone who's closer geographically to the Russians. They want to divert the people's attention from their troubles."

"Why did this come to you instead of to me?" The President was in a suspicious mood.

"Probably because Sobolevsky and I have known each other a long time," Hanrahan said carefully.

"You think that's the reason?" the President asked.

"I don't. It's because those guys at State are such assholes. He knows they wouldn't get a clear message if someone put it up on a billboard. They're like whores. I mean, they're professional because they get paid for what they do. But that doesn't mean they're any better at it than people who aren't getting paid. I never met a whore who was as good as some college girls I knew. And some of them were cheerleaders."

Hanrahan could see the streetwise, savvy politician in the President coming out.

"Anyway," said the President, "what the hell should we do?"

"We've got to buy time."

"Definitely," the President said. "It's a buy-time thing. We'll have to get some decent people from CIA and Defense in on this." The President sighed. "Jesus Christ. The whole fucking ball of wax is coming apart."

"Suppose I call Sobolevsky back and tell him we're considering some way to get grain to them that won't be politically impossible," Hanrahan suggested.

"Oh, definitely," the President said. "Definitely. But Christ, it's coming at a bad time."

The phone next to the President chimed and he picked it up. "Steve, I told you I didn't want to be disturbed," the President said. Then he listened for a minute, looking pained. "Oh, for Christ's sake. He just fucks up everything. Well, hell. Thanks for letting me know. Better have somebody from the speechwriting department get something ready."

The President hung up the phone. "McConger's

had a stroke. He's at Georgetown University Hospital. It doesn't look like he'll pull through."

"I'm sorry," Hanrahan said with mixed emotions.

"Well, it's probably the best thing. That means I won't have to get into a fight with him too. Screw him anyway. He got me into this goddamned mess with those promises about all his supporters. And now they're out marching for Whitelaw. —Where were we?"

"We were talking about what to tell Sobolevsky," Hanrahan said.

"Don't promise a goddamn thing," the President said. "Just hint a lot." He shook his head. "Can you imagine the nerve of that asshole Steinbrenner? I ought to pin his balls on the wall of the E-ring at the Pentagon, just to show who's the Commander in Chief."

"I think I should go call Sobolevsky," Hanrahan said.

"Christ, and now McConger's out of the picture," the President went on, as if he hadn't heard. "Listen," he said. And just at that moment the door to the solarium was pushed open and Freda leaped into the room and onto the love seat with the President. "Listen," the President said as he pushed Freda's wet face away from his, "I'm also going to do something about the inflation, and damn soon, too. McConger's stroke makes it easier. But what I'm going to do will jolt a lot of people. The circle is growing smaller. I want to be sure I can count on you, no matter what."

"You can," Hanrahan said. "Of course you can."

"And, Peter, when this thing is over, I'll make you the head of the Office of Education, and you can inspect all the girls' boarding schools." The President smiled broadly.

Hanrahan was stunned. The President had probably known about Cathy Graham all along. He probably also knew about Claire Beaton. But Hanrahan had heard what the President said about tape recorders. He didn't say a word.

"We may have to really crack down for a while," the President said, serious again. "I mean, we can't have people tying us up in knots in the courts when we put on regulations. There'll be a lot of whining about the Bill of Rights. Don't worry about that. If I don't do something, and something tough, there won't even be a Constitution any more."

Hanrahan took a deep breath. "Mr. President, I'm with you. But I can't go for setting up a dictatorship in this country. I can't support that."

"It wouldn't be a fucking dictatorship, Peter. Things are rough. We need strong measures. Christ, I've got my generals going around talking treason. I've got to take the gloves off. I got myself into this mess, and it's got to be me that gets us out. If it's Whitelaw, then you'll see some real blood." The President paused to pet Freda. "You know that you're on a list of possible executions if he takes over? Did you know that? I haven't got any lists like that. So think about it."

## 10

SHELBY Kelsey couldn't get over the change in Denton. The whole town looked like one large Cadillac showroom. It seemed as if every man, woman and child in Denton had been issued a brand-new Cadillac. Even people who didn't own land were making money. A whole new shopping center was going up on Route 50, just east of town. It would have luxury shops, jewelers, furriers, the kinds of stores Kelsey never imagined would someday come to Denton.

This is how it must be in a place like Kuwait, he thought. It's as though we were manufacturing money here. Construction was booming in other ways too. New security warehouses and grain elevators were going up all over the county. Shelby Kelsey had seen it coming, and he had cashed in on the boom. He had, with an old friend, started a firm that built storage facilities for crops and for poultry, and he had begun another firm to provide guard service for the buildings.

The guards had been busy, too. More attempted thefts of animals and crops were reported every day. Manpower in the sheriff's office had quintupled since the fall. And people who came into town with out-of-state license plates were more or less routinely stopped to see if they had legitimate business—or if they were casing some farm for a theft. Stealing from farms and farmers had become big business, too.

It didn't surprise Kelsey a bit. Everybody was playing hardball these days. The farmers were trying to get the last million they could out of every sale. That meant that people in the cities were going crazy trying to get the ordinary things they needed for life. A lot of the farmers, like Kelsey, were keeping most of their produce off the market, and waiting for even higher prices. They were getting them too. Already Shelby had turned down an offer for all the wheat he could deliver at $5,000,000 a bushel. He knew that he wouldn't have a full crop until fall, and by then $5,000,000 would be a drop in the bucket.

Kelsey had just done something he had wanted to do for a long time. He had bought a plane of his own. It was only a small Grumman corporate jet, and it was a used one, but still and all Shelby had bought it. And he had just acquired the services of a pilot, recently laid off by Eastern Airlines, who would be at his beck and call. That meant that he and Alexandra could just pick up and go any time they wanted.

He hoped the airplane would cheer Alexandra up. Her mood had not been good since her father had died and they had moved into Ridgeley. Kelsey had tried to persuade her that it wasn't a good idea to move back there after the terrible thing that had happened, but Alexandra was adamant. Her father had wanted them to live there; therefore they would live there. She could handle the problem of memories.

Shelby Kelsey had remained skeptical, but he had agreed. He had promised Alexandra when he proposed to her that she could have anything she wanted. But was this what she really wanted? During the last two weeks she had become gloomier every day. She hardly ever left the house; she just stood at the window, looking at the river. Shelby was worried. He had seen a psychiatrist in Baltimore about it—a cool $45,000,000 for a fifty-minute hour—and the doctor had diagnosed it "impacted grief"—the lingering effects of her father's suicide. She had at first suppressed her feelings, but now they were coming out.

Kelsey was worried about her. Sometimes she seemed to walk around in a daze, like a child in strange surroundings. It broke his heart to see her grieve not just for her father but for the world.

A trip would be good for her, the doctor had said, a change of scene. Even though they had just come back from a trip, Kelsey thought a vacation in the Virgin Islands would be nice. As he headed along the riverside to Ridgeley, he hoped he would find Alexandra in a better mood and interested in going somewhere. His new pilot was to begin work tomorrow. Too bad it wasn't tonight.

When Shelby got to the house, Alexandra's Datsun was exactly where it had been when he left that morning. She hadn't gone anywhere. She was upstairs in bed, but she wasn't asleep

She was watching a special report about a mass uprising in Dacca.

"How you feeling, sweetheart?" Shelby asked.

"I don't know, Shelby. I really don't know." She said it as though she had to persuade him. "I don't know what's the matter. I don't understand what's going on."

"What do you mean?" Shelby asked.

"All those people starving and rioting and dying. I mean I just don't understand it. If it's happening everywhere else, why isn't it happening to us?"

Shelby sighed. "Well, sweetheart, that's the way things work. Supply and demand is one way of looking at it. I've got a lot of what some people need, so they pay me a lot for it."

"Oh," Alexandra said. "Food, right?"

"Of course," Shelby said. "Of course. And of course I don't want anyone to starve, but I've got to try to charge as much as I can for it. If I don't, why then, after a while you and I will be the ones who don't have enough."

"That must be right," said Alexandra.

"You bet your ass that's right," Kelsey said, suddenly exasperated. "Listen: I lifted myself up out of the mud to be somebody. And I'm not giving that away. That's for sure. It's yours and mine and we're keeping it." Then he relaxed again.

"Listen, honey," Shelby said, moving over and sitting on the bed next to his wife, "I bought something today that'll make things brighter for you."

Alexandra didn't reply. She had never looked so pale—even when she had learned of her father's death. She had also lost weight. She had never been fat, but she was beginning to look emaciated.

"I've bought a plane and hired a pilot so that we can go on trips. I thought it would make you feel better. Maybe we could go somewhere this weekend. I was thinking that maybe we could go to the Virgin Islands. It's a lot warmer there than it is here and we could get a little cottage for the weekend, and then we wouldn't have to watch the news or anything. It would just be you and me, like it was in Europe." Shelby looked at her expectantly.

"That's thoughtful of you, Shelby," Alexandra said. She lifted herself up and kissed him on the cheek. "But it doesn't seem right to leave when such terrible things are happening."

"What are you talking about, Alexandra?" Shelby asked. "We aren't responsible for all the bad things that are happening. We didn't make this inflation. We didn't push the price of bread so high. The riots in Dacca are not our fault. God has been kind to us and I don't think we should reject His bounty. That's all. I wasn't always rich. It means something to me to be rich, to get away from poor people now. I know it isn't right for people to be starving, but that's the way things are. Nobody gave a damn for me when I was a kid and didn't have all I wanted to eat. The world has changed since then, and things are better for me. If they're worse for some other people, well, that is just the way things work out."

She was so goddamn isolated.

"Jesus Christ, Alex. Do you want me to feel guilty because we're not starving? What in hell do you want?"

"I don't know, Shelby. That's the trouble. Sometimes I feel guilty to be alive at all. Can't you understand that?"

The psychiatrist had suggested that she would wonder why, out of all her family, she was left alive.

"Yes, sweetheart, I can. I don't think it's right, but I can understand it."

"Am I supposed to celebrate because I'm still alive? Am I supposed to feel overjoyed because we're swimming in megabucks while people are starving in Dacca, wherever that is?"

"Honey," Shelby said, "there isn't anything wrong with having money. Try not having some for a while, and tell me how you like it. Tell me how much pity you feel for other poor people when you're poor too. Listen, try just getting out of bed."

"I'll be glad to do that," Alexandra said, after a long pause. "I know I've been a terrible drag. Especially when you're doing so well. Will you hand me my jewelry case?" If only he were interested in something besides money.

Sometimes, Shelby thought, her fabulous jewels might just as well have been colored glass, for all she thought of their value. Rather, she loved to play with them. It was another childish thing about her; she seemed attracted, distracted even, by their color. They seemed to bring her to life.

But Shelby felt a great surge of relief. Alexandra was making a real effort to shake off her depression. He handed her the black leather box, which she opened and spilled the contents on the bed. The jewels were dazzling. Emeralds, diamonds, garnets, rubies, zircons, pearls—some had been presents from Shelby, others had been in the family for generations.

Alexandra rummaged through the stones and found

a thin diamond necklace. She got up, went to the mirror and put the necklace around her neck.

"Beautiful," Shelby said. "You'll be the prettiest girl at the party. You always are." He meant every word.

In the reflection of the mirror, Alexandra could see her face, the glittering diamonds, and the grotesque, lifeless colors on the television screen. The announcer said, "State Department experts believe that mass starvation in India on a scale never believed possible is a virtual certainty." The announcer also reported that those firemen not on strike in St. Louis were fighting a major blaze in the downtown area that had broken out when a crowd tried to loot a large department store.

What had happened? Alexandra wondered. The world had taken off on a strange new course and left her without direction.

Shelby didn't see the look on her face. He was running his fingers over the jewelry, still spread out on the bed, and saying, "The prettiest girl at the party."

"It can't be that bad," Hal Burton said.

"It can be and it is," Les Levine replied. "I'm telling you, Hal, you've got to just plain forget it. That's all. At least until things get better."

They were sitting in Burton's back yard, next to the pool, shotguns on their laps.

"We can't even move the equipment," Levine said. "You can hardly drive around town. Even where it's safe, and that ain't very much, there's torn-up pavement because of the tanks. You should see it on Vine. It's amazing. You can hardly drive around there any more."

Burton slumped in his chair. It was still daylight, but already, down toward Watts and Compton, he could see fires starting to leap upward and funnels of flame.

"Look at that," he said to Levine. "I wonder what the hell is left to burn."

"Oh, Christ," Levine said, "they go around and

steal cars and when they're through with them they set them on fire."

"Well, there must be something we can do to make some progress. I mean, I don't like to mark time," Burton said. He looked worn out. He had put on weight from sitting around without much to do, and his face sagged more than it should have.

"Look," Levine said. "I got shot. You've got a heart condition. We're not starving. Let's just wait it out. It can't go on like this forever. When things calm down, we'll do something."

"You know what really bugs me?" asked Burton. "What really hits me where I live?"

"I know. Doey."

"That's right. I just can't get over it. I mean I really can't. How the hell could she drop out of Stanford to work for Whitelaw? To make America safe for Christians? She knows she isn't a Christian. What the hell is with her? It's killing Sally. You know that, don't you? It's killing Sally."

Levine said, "I know it."

They both sat quietly and watched the fires getting higher. Fire-watching had become one of the inflation's major spectator sports in L.A. From their locations in the hills, the wealthier parts of the city could watch the poorer ones burn. Only occasionally did a fire reach a place on the West Side, and then it was usually put out quickly. The citizens of the West Side had their own fire companies. And since the National Guard had taken up positions around town, blocking most movement from the poorer areas to the richer ones, fewer and fewer marauders reached Beverly Hills and Bel Air.

Still, everyone had a gun, and there was a lot of shooting. Ammunition was another one of the inflation's growth industries.

"I don't even know where Doey is now," Burton said. "She's our baby. And she's going around putting her life on the line for that lunatic Whitelaw. What a criminal waste! A Whitelaw kid got beat to death on the Strip last week. He was sweeping up trash, and one of those bikers came along and beat him to death."

"It's definitely bad," said Levine.

A sudden sound came from the direction of the house. They whirled around, leveling their shotguns toward the rear door. Through the picture window, Burton could see a body moving inside. He aimed at it, but it moved out of sight. Both men tensed, their fingers tightly around the triggers. When a shadow appeared at the rear door, Burton cut loose with two blasts from his Remington 12 gauge. Glass shattered somewhere and chips of brick shot into the air.

Then a woman screamed. "Jesus, Hal, it's Joan," shrieked Joan Bellamy.

Burton ran quickly up to the house. "Are you all right, Joan?" he asked.

"Well," she said shakily, "I think so. But it's just blind luck that one of those shots didn't blow my head off." She picked up a shard of glass six inches long.

"It's dangerous as hell to creep up on somebody, Joan," said Levine. "Don't you know that?"

"No kidding," Joan said. "I would have called, but the phones are out again. So I just drove over. Something big is happening on the Strip. I heard on the radio that tanks and troops are coming in from all over the country."

"That makes it a great place not to go," Levine said.

"I'm not suggesting we go," said Joan. "But maybe we could get closer than this, just to see it."

"Forget it," Levine said.

"Maybe Doey's down there," said Burton. "Let's go."

Fifteen minutes and a lot of arguing later, Burton, Levine and Joan were driving in Burton's Jaguar down to Sunset Boulevard. They stopped at the roadblock next to the gutted Beverly Hills Hotel. The gray-haired man who headed the roadblock waved at them as he walked over to the car.

"Sad," said Burton. "He used to be a big TV comedy producer."

"Hi, Hal," said the guard. "Where are you going?"

"Over toward the Strip," said Burton.

"The Strip? Don't you know what's going on over there?"

"No," Burton said. "What the hell is going on there?"

"Well, the Hell's Angels from all over the state are coming there today. They had some guy, Sonny, or something like that, on the radio, saying that they were going to take over the town. And the National Guard is waiting for 'em. Jesus, they've got tanks and even helicopters."

"Hal, let's get the hell out of here," Levine said. "This is strictly crazy. Really."

Burton turned to him. "If the National Guard is there in force, no one'll start shooting."

"That's bullshit, Hal. Those bikers are crazy," Levine said.

"I think it's an event we shouldn't miss," Joan Bellamy said.

"Then we're on our way." Burton turned to the gray-haired man. "Well, I think we'll go down and have a look, Norman."

"Your funeral," Norman said. "But if they come here, we'll blow them to pieces. Look at this," he said, and pointed to a twin-mounted 20 mm. aircraft cannon set on the back of a truck. "This is what they used to use in Lebanon back in the seventies. Very good for crowd control." The gray-haired man laughed.

The road was chewed up. Tanks had obviously preceded them. As they approached Trousdale, just before the Strip, there was, instead of traffic, a line of tanks blocking all eight lanes of Sunset Boulevard. A block farther east stood a line of armored personnel carriers.

Burton parked the car. They got out and walked up to the line of tanks. A young man with a scowl manned the .50-caliber machine gun on the turret of the closest tank.

"What's going on?" Burton asked.

"An exercise," the gunner said.

They cut off to the left, up the hill, to where they could see down the road.

A mass of human bodies were walking at a leisurely

but purposeful pace toward the tanks and APCs. It was the teen-agers from the Strip. Behind them roared the motorcycles. The Hell's Angels were advancing on the National Guard; the teen-agers were their shield.

Even from where he stood, several hundred yards from the marchers, Burton could make out among them the "One with God" salute of the Whitelaw volunteers. He could see their blue denim coveralls. He felt a sudden chill.

An amplified male voice blasted from a loudspeaker. They could barely make out its message: "Stop where you are. You are in violation of the law. Stop or we'll fire. Halt!"

But the advancing crowd kept moving. Following a few snaps, like the popping of corn, clouds of tear gas exploded in front of and in the midst of the marchers. The marchers faltered but kept on going, much faster now.

They began to shout. At first their words were lost in the general ominous sound of their voices. Then one phrase, repeated time and again like a broken record, became clear: "One with God."

The great mass pressed forward; the megaphone repeated its warning. Then, out of a large truck jumped fifteen men with snarling Doberman pinschers straining at their leashes. The dogs had picked up the scent of the tear gas. They formed a line in front of the APCs and advanced.

The marchers, already confused by the tear gas, slowed as the dogs approached. The men halted the dogs some ten yards in front of the marchers, and at that point the mass of bodies stopped altogether.

Suddenly three of the men holding dogs were thrown backward. Dots of red blood appeared on their uniforms and grew larger. There was a sharp exchange of rifle fire. Then the bikers sped forward to confront the dogs directly. There were dozens of them, some riding two on a bike, with the one in the back carrying a rifle.

In the confusion, marchers ran in every direction, screaming, scrambling for safety. Some of them made it. Others were mowed down and mangled. One boy's pants leg got hooked on the back of a bike. He was dragged on the ground through the crowd until he was jarred loose. He didn't move after that.

There was a deafening roar, as though thousands of rifles were firing at once when the machine guns opened up. Bikers were blown off their machines as they spun crazily around. In the melee, bullets were flying everywhere, and the troops were now firing directly into the crowd. Bodies were lifted into the air, twisted and bloody, from the force of the heavy machine guns.

Smoke and noise filled the air. The ground in front of the APCs was now a mass of writhing, bloody bodies and roaring upended motorcycles. The cyclists who hadn't been shot turned their machines around and roared away. Then suddenly, just as abruptly as it had begun, the firing ceased, and the only sound in the air was the screams of the wounded on Sunset Strip, bleeding and dying. There were hundreds of them. The firing had lasted less than five minutes.

Medevac helicopters were landing. The sky was full of them.

"Let's go, Hal," Levine said gently. "You don't want to know if Doey's there."

"You're right," Burton said. "I don't want to know. At least not now."

They walked back to the Jaguar and got in. They were at the roadblock again. The gray-haired man said with a smile, "I heard there was a hell of a turkey shoot down there."

"Oh, for Christ's sake, Norman. Those were young kids," Burton said.

But he didn't want to argue. He drove up to his house and just sat in the living room looking out over the city. It was getting near dusk and a fire from the direction of Long Beach was sending huge balls of flame and black billowing smoke high into the twilight sky.

The phone rang. "I guess the phones are working again," Burton said, and picked up the receiver. The line was dead. "Well, at least it works a little bit," Burton said.

Joan Bellamy spoke, breaking the brooding silence she had been in since the massacre. "This is it, you know. The whole society is coming apart. You know that, don't you? It's just like Weimar Germany before Hitler. The society is being torn apart so bad that we'll never be able to put it back together again. Not after things like what happened today."

"This kind of thing has been happening every day," Levine said, "in different parts of the country."

It was impossible to relax. Later, sitting on Burton's terrace, all of them were still visibly shaken. Burton was especially tense. Occasionally his hand would tremble involuntarily so that the ice in his glass rattled.

"The society is crying out for peace and order. They want a strong man to make sure this doesn't happen again," said Joan. "That's what happened in Germany when it took a wheelbarrow full of money to buy groceries. People wanted someone who would make sure it never happened again. That's why they turned to Hitler. He promised them strength and order. And that's what's happening here."

"You're talking about Whitelaw, right?" Burton asked.

"I think so," Joan said.

The phone rang again. Burton picked it up. He could hear the sound of a long-distance call. The operator said, "I have a long-distance collect call from Doey Burton to anyone."

"Yes, I'll take it," Burton said. He felt dizzy.

"Hi, Daddy," Doey said. "How are you and Mom?"

"We're going crazy worrying about you, that's how. Where the hell are you?"

"I'm all right. I'm in West Virginia. We're assembling to march on Washington for Governor Whitelaw."

"Jesus, Doey. I saw some Whitelaw kids marching today. I saw them get mowed down. It'll be worse in Washington."

"No, Daddy. It'll be safe," Doey's little-girl voice said. "It's completely nonviolent."

"Look, fly home. I'll send you money. Don't do this

thing to me—to your mother and me." Burton was pleading.

"I've got to do it. It's the only thing left."

"But you could get killed," Burton argued.

"If you're ready to kill, you've got to be ready to die," she said, and hung up.

A shooting pain, sharp as a needle, traveled down his arm and back to his chest. The pain grew until he felt as if someone were driving a thin stake through his heart.

Jim Adams was crying. He had been crying uncontrollably for at least fifteen minutes. Laurie was timing him, though she did not look at her watch. First he had screamed. Then he was silent, his face in his hands. Finally he started crying.

He had found out. Laurie wasn't exactly sure how he had found out, but someone must have seen her and known what she was doing. Whoever it was had apparently known Jim fairly well and called him at work. "For his own good," no doubt. He had confronted her, disbelieving but fearful. Laurie had admitted nothing, but Jim had believed his friend. Watching him, listening to his moans and groans—unmanly sounds to be coming from an athlete—Laurie felt sorry for him in a vague, housewifely way. Because the truth was, what she had done hadn't made the slightest bit of difference in the way she felt about him. He was still her husband, and when she was with him she still felt like a wife, a mother. After the first time it had been easy, though she had never enjoyed it, not for a second.

Laurie had been at home cooking dinner—a dinner which, despite everything she had done for Bob Hartley and with him, contained no meat. It was ironical. She was glad, though, that the gas bill had been paid and the gas turned back on, so she could cook without having to use the fireplace. The electricity was also back, so she had been listening to SAM all-news radio: "Give us your ear, and we'll give you America." It was Laurie's favorite station.

The announcer was talking about how the Whitelaw Volunteers to America were assembling around Washington. "Tens of thousands are camping on the Mall," the announcer said. "Initial speculation that the police would move to evict them was not correct. Police sources say that as long as the Volunteers are peaceful, they can remain on the Mall. Meanwhile, Virginia police stopped a van in Rosslyn and found two shotguns and a quantity of Whitelaw literature. The occupants have been arrested."

The announcer continued, "Park police say that estimates of a million Whitelaw Volunteers in town to pray and hear Governor Whitelaw speak may prove to be too low. Some estimates say that up to two million people will mass here to call for an America that is safe for Christians, as Governor Whitelaw says."

Laurie had been visualizing the excitement when the kitchen door opened. She realized as soon as she saw Jim's face that he knew. Now she waited for the initial effects of the shock to wear off, feeling much as she had when she took her first bath following . . .

Jim smashed his fist on the table with a resounding thud. The crying stopped, but his bloodshot eyes were closed with anger and frustration, his face wet with tears.

"I see how it was. I wasn't a decent provider." Now he was trying to understand. "I made impossible demands in an impossible time." Then he was silent again.

At that point, Marie, the baby, started crying. Laurie went to the baby's room, to discover that she hadn't been burped. When she came back, Jim was huddled on the kitchen floor again, crying softly to himself. He didn't make the slightest response when she talked to him. She might as well have been in Timbuctoo.

Is it all gone now, Laurie wondered, all over? Everything she had tried to do to make a decent and respectable life for her family? Those years in high school, making herself neat and clean because her mother was a slob—gone? All that restraint in college, remaining a virgin until she met Jim, and even then for a while—gone? All the scrimping and saving so that

Jim could have what he wanted to eat—gone? All for nothing?

"It's not your fault, Laurie. I would have done the same thing." Jim was wiping the tears from his face.

Then Laurie started to cry. It was such a relief to see him trying to understand her, to realize why she had done it.

"I do. I understand," he continued, looking more and more like the old Jim, the Jim she knew and loved. "I'll tell you. We are through with being kicked around and humiliated."

"What should we do?" asked Laurie.

"I'll tell you what we should do," he said. "First, we're going to cash in on what the government is throwing around so freely. If they're so generous with welfare and food stamps, we'll get ours too. We're through being too proud to take what everybody else is taking."

His eyes were puffy but dry. "And I'll tell you something else, Laurie. The only man making any sense at all to me is William Whitelaw. And when he marches in Washington, I'm going to be marching with him."

"You can't go to Washington. Where will you get the money?"

"I'll go with Steve Mayhew. He's been talking about it for weeks. If he won't go, I'll hitchhike. I'll sell my camera."

Marie and that camera were his pride and joy. It had cost a fortune. "But school, Jim. You can't leave school!"

"I'll take my sick leave. Yeah. Because that's what I am—sick of being kicked around. Sick of working my ass off for nothing while those rich bastards live off the fat of the land!"

"I don't know what good it'll do, honey. Why don't we just lower our expectations?"

"The hell with that. We're going to get ours. And if anybody tries to stand in my way, they better watch out for James McDonald Adams. I'm through being the fall guy." His face was fierce with frustration.

Laurie smiled. He looked so cute.

"I'm not kidding," Jim continued. "Let some speculator or some rich sonofabitch get in my way, and he'll learn to move. Nobody's gonna stand in my way any more. I'm marching."

Jim had pulled himself up to his full height. He went to the closet and rummaged inside it. Laurie wondered what he was doing. He turned around with a revolver in his hand. Laurie hadn't even known it was there. When had he bought it? Now he looked almost like a cowboy.

She watched him practice a quick draw, using his belt for a holster. She was safe and secure once more.

## 11

THE smooth power of his Mercedes 750SL was like a drug. Larry Hyde sped along Old Georgetown Road toward the Madeira School. He turned the radio dial to change the station. All he could get was news about the Whitelaw rally. He didn't give a shit about that. He was thinking of Cathy Graham.

Two weeks earlier, he hadn't known such a girl existed, except in his dreams. That was before the morning he had gone to the offices of Graham Engineering in New York to discuss with Richard Graham the possibility of selling him some options on tin. It was a very boring meeting until the most beautiful girl Larry Hyde had ever seen walked into the office. She was tall and blond with blue eyes and the carriage of a movie star. She was a knockout.

"Sorry, Daddy," she said. "Didn't know you had company."

"Well, hello! Don't leave. I want you to meet Mr.

Hyde. This is my daughter, Cathy. You can entertain him while I speak with Etheridge."

Graham excused himself. Larry Hyde wanted to put his best foot forward. He was afraid to use his old line—the one he used at singles bars. This girl, he knew, was different. He was glad he was wearing his new Gucci loafers.

"Do you live in New York?" Hyde asked. It sounded dumb, but he needed the information.

"Only during the summer. I go to school in Virginia." Now he knew who she reminded him of. It was that French actress, the sexy, high-toned, suggestive one. What was her name . . . the blonde?

"The University of Virginia?" asked Hyde.

"No," she said. "Madeira. It's a boarding school near Washington."

Hyde had never heard of Madeira, but he smiled and asked her if she was taking a long weekend.

"No. I'm recovering from a case of pneumonia," Cathy said. It was the lie she had practiced, and it was almost true. She had been very sick.

"Do you like New York?" Hyde asked.

"I love New York," Cathy said, "but it's falling to pieces. It breaks your heart to see it. So I don't go out too much. And I'm getting bored at home."

Hyde figured the time was ripe. "Maybe, if it's all right with your father, I could take you out some time."

Cathy Graham looked demure. "That would be nice," she said.

That was how he got his first date with her. Before picking her up he made sure he looked good. He wore his purple-tinted glasses and the best of everything else. He knew Cathy would be impressed with his Mercedes. And apparently she was, because after a quiet dinner at Lutèce, while drinking at a private club called East 56, she didn't object a bit when he kissed her. She didn't object, either, to going back to his apartment with him.

She cried a little in bed, but she was very affectionate and loving. The only thing that set him back a little was her calling him "Peter" when she came. But as he

kept telling himself, that could have happened to anyone.

She left for school a few days later.

That was why he was driving so carefully toward
Madeira in his Mercedes and trying not to get lost.
He looked at the road map again. With so much at
stake, he couldn't afford a wrong turn now. Not in
this day and age. No telling where he'd wind up.

The road was plastered with Whitelaw signs—even
the superhighway. He didn't know what the hell everyone was so excited about. Far as he could tell, those
Whitelaw guys were a bunch of bums who couldn't
get together the smarts to make some money out
of the inflation, like he had. He was doing better
than ever. The orders for gold bullion were getting
smaller and smaller because there were no longer many
sellers—but he was getting along fine. Although volume
was low, prices were astronomical. And even better,
Larry Hyde had scraped together enough megabucks to buy a little gold for his own account. Its
worth, too, was astronomical. He could hardly believe
it was possible. Last night in New York gold had closed
at $180,000,000 an ounce. No doubt about it—Larry
Hyde was doing fine.

And he knew Cathy would be impressed by his plans
for the evening. First, dinner at La Grande Scène, the
French restaurant atop Kennedy Center. Then they
were going to see the Stuttgart Ballet dance *Eugene
Onegin* at the Concert Hall. That was class, a whole
night of it. That should be enough to get her to come
back with him to his room at the Watergate Hotel,
maybe even spend the night.

He saw the sign for the Madeira School and pulled
in. The place looked snazzy as hell. There were rolling
green fields and fences that horses jumped over. As
he drove down the driveway, he saw some young girls
in the distance on horseback, with jodhpurs, and little
caps and everything. Wow! This place was class with
a capital C.

When he reached the gatehouse, he told the guard
that he had come to pick up Cathy Graham. The
guard went inside his shed and made a call. When he

came back out he told Larry Hyde to go to the new building, Keyser Memorial Hall, to park. It was just beyond the swimming pool.

This was definitely a classy place. Larry passed ivy-covered buildings and rich-looking girls walking around. It might have been a wonderful little island that the magical powers of money and good family prevented the disturbing outside world from entering. It was exactly the kind of place where he wanted his daughters to go.

He couldn't be positive, but Larry Hyde believed that several of the girls were giving his car an approving once-over. That was what he had bought it for. Too bad they couldn't see his shoes.

At a parking space in front of Keyser Hall, Larry Hyde parked and got out. Inside the dormitory a girl with light-brown hair in braids sat at a reception desk. He asked her to tell Cathy Graham that Larry Hyde was there. The girl pressed a button, picked up a telephone, waited and said, "Cathy, there's a Harry Hyde to see you."

Larry gestured awkwardly. "That's Larry Hyde."

The girl giggled. "Cathy? It's Larry Hyde."

Larry and the girl at the reception desk smiled. He walked away when she told him that Cathy would be right down. He could tell she was looking at him. It was probably because of his snappy suede jacket. One hundred and seventy-five million dollars at Barney's. He knew it had been smart to buy it.

A moment later, Cathy Graham came down the stairs. She was dressed completely in white and looked fabulous. Another girl was with her, a shorter, more bosomy girl with reddish hair. "Hi, Barry, this is Nan," Cathy said.

Larry smiled. "Hi, Nan. It's Larry, uh, Hyde. Larry."

"Sorry," said Cathy.

"We've got reservations at La Grande Scène," Larry said. "We'd better be going."

"Yeah, I'll see you later, Nan," Cathy said.

Larry Hyde hoped that Nan would have a chance to see his car. She turned around and went back upstairs, turning once to wave. Perhaps she would watch them from her window.

They walked to the car. Cathy stood by her door and waited for him to open it. He watched her long, sinuous legs as she got in the car, then went around to his side and got in too. He leaned over to kiss her and she offered him her cheek. "Jesus," she said in a languid voice, with just a trace of French in it—it was sexy as hell—"have I got a headache."

That was a blow. Of all times for Cathy to get a headache.

Somewhat distracted, Larry tried to get a station that would show off his great stereo, but all that came on was news of the Whitelaw rally.

"Turn that goddamn thing off," she said. "I told you I had a headache!"

He turned it off. Larry Hyde was bewildered. He didn't know what to say. Maybe the ballet would chase her headache away. Jesus, she was so beautiful. What did you say when someone like that had a headache?

"Gee," he said, "I'm sorry you have a headache."

"Yeah, well, me too," she said. "By the way. I have to meet someone at ten. He's from New York, too."

Larry Hyde was floored. What did she mean, having him drive all the way from New York for a few hours of her company? Christ! Was this the way the rich girls behaved?

He knew it was the worst thing in the world to say but he couldn't help himself. "Who is he?"

"An artist. A really good one. He's been compared to Red Grooms."

Who the hell was Red Grooms? Larry Hyde was growing more and more uneasy about his plans for the evening, not to mention his more distant plans for Cathy Graham.

"Well," he said, "I guess we can skip the end of the ballet. Where do you have to meet your friend?"

"The airport. He's coming in on the Eastern shuttle."

"Are you serious about him?" His voice was beginning to quaver.

"I'm serious about all of you. I've changed my field.

I'm majoring in men." And as of yesterday, thanks to Nan, she was minoring in women. That should leave little time for boredom. And it also broadened the field. Now there was no one she couldn't seduce

Larry Hyde was more relieved than not. Hell, it just amounted to a little competition. He knew how to deal with competition. A good cocksman like him could outsmart an artist. An *artist?* A pushover.

"And Ba—Larry," said Cathy, "next time you come I'll make sure we have the whole night to ourselves."

See? A pushover. His charisma was already taking effect.

Cathy reached in her bag, took out her last Demerol, and popped it. She could afford to. A two-week supply was coming in on the ten o'clock plane.

# 12

THE time had come.

Governor William Whitelaw rose. The mantle of destiny lay on his shoulders. He looked out over more people than had ever assembled in one place in America before. He was proud. It was early evening, and as far as the eye could see, red, white and blue banners proclaimed the new law: AMERICA IS WHITE-LAW COUNTRY.

The crowd extended down the Mall as far as the Capitol. They overflowed onto 18th Street and around the reflecting pool and around the Lincoln Memorial. They spread out behind the White House and lined the wrought-iron fence behind it. They flowed behind him to the Jefferson Memorial. It was a rolling sea of humanity.

Whitelaw gripped the podium and struck a Presidential pose. Humbly he lowered his large, handsome head. The crowd swayed back and forth in the last of the sunshine, waiting for the words from his lips, the holy words, the words that would be their salvation.

Slowly, proudly, Whitelaw lifted up his head so that he could see the people closest to the platform, closest to the Washington Monument, tens of thousands of smiling, clean-faced young men and women in coveralls. Whitelaw did not smile back.

"We are not afraid to stand up for what we know is right," he began. "We are not ashamed of the truth. We are not afraid to volunteer for America."

And with a colossal, deafening roar that echoed throughout the city, they shouted, "One with God!"

"Over two hundred years ago, men of principle stood up to the whole world and created the first American Revolution. They knew, and they wrote it into the Declaration of Independence, that when a government becomes intolerable, the people have the right to abolish and overthrow it. They had that right. They sought God's help, and so do we. The time has come for the new American Revolution." He paused for the thunderous cheers. "With God's help." Once again came the deafening roar: "One with God."

Whitelaw looked out at the crowd. To his hungry eyes, it seemed to go on forever. A young man in denim coveralls shouted, loud enough for Whitelaw to hear, "We are not afraid. Kill them, Governor, kill them!"

The sound of the crowd's roar reverberated off the Federal office buildings, through the labyrinth of the city-scape, along the Potomac River and into the surrounding countryside.

"Why is it time for the new American Revolution? The answer is all around you. Our country is run by big lies and big liars. Our country is run by men with no respect for the people they govern, no respect for law, for principle, and, worst of all, no place in their hearts for God.

"I see an America great and proud, living by the laws of God and man, standing tall and strong at the head of all nations. I see an America safe for Christians. Can the men who are running this country see God? What do you think?"

"No!"

A wave of boos and catcalls spread around the speaker, rolled away for half a mile in every direction and came crashing back at the man with the large, finely shaped head. A middle-aged woman pushed her way to the front and screamed, "Get them out, Bill! Kick 'em the hell out."

The clean-cut-looking kids in the front rows got on their feet and started to shake their fingers, their right index fingers, and shout, "One with God!"

It took five minutes for the crowd to quiet down enough for the man with the movie actor's profile, the man with the grip on the lectern as if he would rip it off the stand, for that man to speak.

"They have unleashed a monster in this land, the monster of inflation. It has taken away our savings, taken away our jobs, taken the food off our tables while the storehouses are bursting, taken the clothing off our backs, and worst of all, stolen our peace of mind and our self-respect.

"They will try to take me away from you. They have already taken away our friends in the armed forces of this country because those people refused to destroy us with arms. They will try to take me, too. *Do not let them!*"

The crowd roared like a furious, frustrated, caged animal. Boos and screams came together to form a torrent of hatred from the two million for the people who might take Whitelaw away from them.

Less than half a mile away, troops surrounded the Executive Office Building. Inside, Claire, Hanrahan and Harry Ratner somberly watched the threatening crowd below and listened to the voice of William Whitelaw over the television set.

"Where the hell are the troops and tanks?" asked Ratner. "We got Steinbrenner out of the picture, but what happened to the troops that were supposed to insure peace?"

"It wasn't just Steinbrenner," said Hanrahan. "Disloyalty within his command went so deep the President ordered them all confined to barracks. Now he's relying on the police."

"Then where the hell are the cops?" exploded Ratner.

Claire explained, "At the last minute he found out he couldn't trust most of the police either, although there are some there. So a battalion of paratroopers was flown in to guard the White House and the Capitol, and that's the nucleus of the security there is. Whitelaw could take over Washington in fifteen minutes. But maybe, just maybe, he doesn't know how easy it would be."

"If Whitelaw doesn't, the rest of the world does. The people on the Hill who are wondering whether to kick out the President can see it. The rest of the country can see it. The Russians can see it," said Hanrahan. The President was probably in Camp David because he simply was not safe in Washington. Other people must be guessing that, too. "If the President doesn't make a move soon, the whole country is going to Whitelaw."

"I think he's going to move soon," Ratner said. "He may be waiting for Whitelaw to look bad on television."

Claire waved toward the window. "Listen. Whitelaw's not looking bad to those people out there."

The oratory raced on: "I have walked the streets of this city. I have seen the men who made you ragged swaggering rich in their tuxedos. I have seen the men who took away your gasoline gloating rich in their limousines. I have seen the men who took your food gorging themselves in rich, fancy restaurants.

"When a country is run for a few while the many are starving, we have the right to fight. Because we are through with that kind of government.

"We will not listen, Gene Donnelly. We will not starve, George McConger. We will not obey, Mr. President. Our obedience is to God!"

One continuous roar came from the crowd. Young men and women in blue denim coveralls shouted

"One with God" in counterpoint, their faces now contorted with rage.

Standing in the crowd near the Lincoln Memorial, the man felt white-hot fury building within him. He and William Whitelaw knew what to do.

The roars of the crowd crashed around him like waves. Whitelaw was solemn. He was the island stronghold. He would lead them.

"We are going to win. We are going to take this country back for the people, Mr. President. Don't try to stop us!"

Again the roars and screams, the AMERICA IS WHITELAW COUNTRY banners lifted high and higher still. Whitelaw raised his arms for silence as if giving a benediction, and when the silence came at last he said:

"In your hearts is my strength."

And the crowd screamed and stomped their feet.

"In your suffering is my justice."

And two million people shouted and whistled.

"In your need is my command."

And a sea of voices cried out, "One with God."

And as William Whitelaw raised his arms for the crowd to be still, he bowed his head and said quietly, "In your prayers is an America safe for Christians."

A country singer named Johnny Winter began to sing "God Bless America." And two million people's voices joined in.

Whitelaw raised his head and looked at them. The time had come. Now, there would be no stopping him. He smiled inwardly. A better America would come from the rage of these two million people.

When the song had ended, there was a moment of absolute, terrifying silence. Then he blessed them, gave the final benediction with his hands, and slowly stepped down from the platform.

Marvin was waiting for him. "Jimmie's got them headed toward Kennedy Center," he said.

"Good. But Jimmie better be smart enough to move his ass if the police get rough."

The man in the crowd fingered his gun. Though he had slept only an hour on the bus coming in the night before, he felt no fatigue. Each nerve was taut, ready.

This was the night, but it was early. He decided to move with the crowd.

Parts of it dispersed. But the solid core, as if by instinct, stayed together, thousands of people walking slowly around the Lincoln Memorial and down 23rd Street toward the State Department.

The noise of the crowd was muffled. The great mass of bodies expanded and contracted, like a giant accordion adjusting to the pace of its leaders.

As the mob passed by the west entrance of the State Department, the man near the edge of the crowd saw glass shatter and doors smash as people threw rocks and bottles against the building. The few policemen on guard retreated inside the lobby.

That gave the crowd courage, momentum. Moving past the State Department, they came to a site where a new building for George Washington University had been under construction until the Better Deal made it impossible to continue. Many in the crowd stopped to pick up bricks and whatever else they could lift in their hands.

Then they continued walking.

The crowd was stopped dead on 23rd Street by a solid wall of motorcycle policemen carrying tear-gas rifles. When a few people started to throw rocks, the leader of the crowd, a bullhorn at his mouth, shouted, "Leave them alone. The police are our friends. Do not harm the police. Repeat. Do not harm the police."

The mob was obedient. Slowly, patiently, each line waiting its turn to advance, the crowd marched left down Virginia Avenue. The balconied curvilinear facade of the Watergate appeared, shrouded in dusk, shrouded in history, like a myth. The mood of the crowd went from docile to savage in moments. Bottles and bricks were thrown at the building. Some men, their bottles filled with gasoline, lighted the rags at the tops and threw them into the broken windows and the lobby. Almost immediately flames spread inside. More gasoline bombs were thrown in, and the flames rose higher. People started to run out of the building in a panic and the crowd pelted them with stones and bottles and bricks. Some fell to the ground, their faces bloody.

At a top-floor window of the Watergate, the figure of an elderly woman appeared. As she looked down at the crowd, she raised a shotgun, aimed, then opened fire. She was only one woman, and she fired only three shots, but their effect on the mob was instantaneous; the crowd ran in all directions, part of it dispersing, leaving the Watergate to smolder and burn. Sirens could be heard in the distance.

The crowd was louder now, smaller but more intense. The streets of Washington had grown dark. But as the crowd made its way up New Hampshire Avenue toward the Kennedy Center, their faces reflected a special glow.

When he saw it, Jim Adams knew at once that this was the target, the perfect place. Men and women in expensive clothes were emerging from limousines, their faces smug with comfort and wealth, the men in tuxedos, the women covered with jewels. Jim moved to the front of the crowd.

Shelby Kelsey held out his arm for his wife as she stepped from the car, his other hand holding the tickets. He had been lucky to get them—two cancellations at six. His driver had picked up the tickets. Alexandra looked lovely, her face a mask of composure. She was wearing the emerald necklace, the brilliant green of the stones highlighting her auburn hair. He looked at her tenderly, reassuringly.

"Shelby, there's Cathy Graham. I haven't seen her in months. We must speak to her."

Alex and Shelby walked toward the spectacular blonde, who had also sighted Alex. As they drew abreast, Alex dropped her bag. Bending to pick it up, both Alex and Shelby heard two successive gunshots.

When they stood upright again, they saw blood oozing from holes in Cathy's neck and the forehead of the man who was with her, just before both bodies slumped to the pavement.

Turning, Shelby only had time to see the gun, flashing black in the brilliant outdoor lighting, and the maddened face of the man who had apparently shot it, before Alex, he, and the two dead bodies, were enclosed by a tightening knot of first curious, then incredulous people intent on viewing the carnage.

I've got to get her out of here, thought Shelby, deathly calm. That crazy fool must have been aiming at us.

But it was going to be difficult. Because by then all hell had broken loose.

An hour later, after fifteen policemen had broken up the mob with tear gas, Kennedy Center was shattered. Not a single unbroken pane of glass remained. Bodies lay everywhere, some still living, most of them dead.

The fire department had gone from the Watergate Hotel to Kennedy Center, adding to the confusion but keeping the fires inside the buildings that made up the complex to a minimum.

The man who had fired the first shots had escaped in the melee.

As the youngest of the ambulance drivers picked up the inert body of the teen-age girl—the last to be gathered off the sidewalk—she watched him with glazed eyes.

"They . . . said . . . it would be . . . nonviolent."

Then the fingers of her hand went slack and the ticket she was clutching fell to the floor.

The orderly was puzzled by the message on her T-shirt: *Doey*. She carried no identification.

## 13

ALL morning, ever since daybreak, helicopters had been landing on the pad next to the skeet-shooting range at Camp David. Cabinet members jumped out of the helicopters and boarded golf carts for the trip to Laurel Lodge, where breakfast was being served. Two gleaming new helicopters arrived with the Joint Chiefs of Staff and their aides.

At Laurel the men ate at small tables and watched TV sets on which a continuous stream of news about the Whitelaw rally from the day before was unwinding. Thirty yards away, in Sycamore, a much smaller cabin, Harry Ratner, Claire Beaton and Peter Hanrahan watched the *Today Show,* on which Jim Hartz was reporting in front of Kennedy Center, cordoned off and ghostly against the morning sky.

"Police have now confirmed," said Hartz, "that at least thirty bodies have been taken from the wreckage of Kennedy Center. Senators Bob Clarke and Thomas Long were among the dead. Last night there were calls from members of Congress for speedy passage of a bill of impeachment to remove the President from office for a variety of high crimes and misdemeanors."

A photograph of Representative Lewis O'Neal, majority whip, appeared behind Hartz. "Congressman O'Neal said that the violence yesterday left no room for doubt that a new administration led by William Whitelaw, a man whom the people could trust, was an urgent necessity."

"God almighty," Hanrahan said. "Even O'Neal is climbing aboard the bandwagon."

He had not slept all night. Alex Kelsey, knowing he was a friend of the Graham family, had called at 11:45 to tell him that Cathy and her companion—some young man from New York—had been fatally shot. The Kelseys were unhurt, though Alex was very upset and heavily sedated.

The news hit Hanrahan in the gut. Cathy dead—not a suicide, but dead nonetheless. He was grateful to be alone. For the remainder of the night he paced his apartment trying to come to terms with his role in her life.

At five in the morning, just before he had left for Camp David, he was able to learn that the funeral would be the following day in New York. Of course, he would have to go.

"The rats are leaving the sinking ship," said Ratner. "You seem distracted, Peter. Anything wrong? Anything more than we know about, that is?"

Hanrahan grimaced.

The telephone rang. Hanrahan picked it up.

"Mr. Hanrahan? Ambassador Hsing is calling."

Hanrahan was puzzled. "Put him on."

After a pause and a click, an Oriental voice said, "Good morning, Mr. Hanrahan, this is Ambassador Hsing. How are you?"

Hanrahan, red-eyed and weary, said, "All things considered, not bad. How are you?"

"I must talk to you urgently. This is undoubtedly a bad time for you, but I must speak to you soon." The voice of the Ambassador from the People's Republic of China was oily but tense.

"May I know about what?"

"We want to buy wheat." There was a pause. "A great deal of wheat."

"I mean no disrespect, Mr. Ambassador," Hanrahan said, "but so does everyone else."

"We will make an offer you cannot refuse," Hsing said with a slight laugh.

Hanrahan was surprised. "Well, that can probably be arranged."

"The earthquakes have slowed down our rate of progress. Also, our rice crops have not been as productive as we had antici— Would you be so kind as to hold one moment?"

"Of course."

Hanrahan put his hand over the mouthpiece and told Claire and Ratner that Ambassador Hsing was interested in buying wheat for the Chinese people. "A deal we can't refuse. That's what he said. Their rice crops haven't come up to expectations."

"We knew that," said Ratner. "But we thought they had enormous stockpiles."

A series of loud, screeching clicks through the earpiece forced Hanrahan to move the telephone away from his ear. Even Claire and Ratner could hear the noise.

Hanrahan frowned. "This is most peculiar," he said. He tried the earpiece again. All was calm. He settled it at his ear and looked at his watch. The meeting was scheduled for ten, and it was now eleven minutes to. He hoped it would be an easy one. He was exhausted.

At eight minutes to ten Ambassador Hsing had still not responded. Hanrahan considered hanging up. Ratner was pacing the floor and Claire was working with figures on a pad. He sighed and was on the point of replacing the receiver when another series of screeches heralded the voice of Ambassador Hsing.

"Mr. Hanrahan?"

"Yes, Mr. Ambassador. I'm still here."

"Mr. Hanrahan, I'm afraid I'll have to call you back."

"Very well. I'll be—"

But there was a final click and the line went dead.

Shaking his head at the puzzling Chinese, Hanrahan replaced the receiver. The phone rang again. He picked it up.

"Hanrahan," he said, and listened. "OK." He cradled the phone. "The President is on his way to Laurel. The meeting's about to start. Isn't it just like the Chinese to begin a conversation they can't finish? He said he'd call back."

The three advisers walked out into the clear Catoctin Mountain air. On the way to Laurel, Hanrahan and Ratner discussed the violence at Kennedy Center. Claire seemed preoccupied.

As they entered the cabin, they saw every member of the Cabinet, plus the Joint Chiefs, filing into the long, narrow room. The military men talked quietly among themselves.

Then the President walked in. Hanrahan gasped when he saw him. He no longer reflected even a semblance of health. His face was wan and pale. His bloodshot eyes were ringed with red, his cheeks puffy from lack of sleep. The fine toothsome smile had disappeared. He walked quickly to his seat and sat down.

"All right," he said in a gravelly voice, without further introduction, "let's begin. I don't know any way to sum up the situation better than to say that things couldn't be much worse." The President slammed the table with his open hand.

"I don't know where to begin. We've got a fucking insurrection in the military. That's right," he said, glaring at the generals across the table. "We have a base in Georgia that has stopped accepting outside calls. The commander says his men are going to take Atlanta for Whitelaw. We already know that the Military District of Washington is a hotbed of traitors. I don't know who the hell to trust. The police can't be trusted in any city in the country." The President's face was growing flushed.

"I think it'll take one or two weeks, maybe less, for the Congress to impeach and convict me *and* the Vice President. They think they can get me to swear Whitelaw in. Jesus Christ. They think I'd turn this country over to that lunatic murderer. I'd rather turn it over to Charlie Manson."

Everyone in the room was sweating although the air was cool and dry.

"And now we've got this Russian-Chinese thing. I don't know what in the hell to do about that. We're hardly a unified state at this point. I don't know what in the hell to do if the Russians move into Chinese territory."

The door opened and an aide walked swiftly to the President and handed him a note. The Chief Executive read it quickly and put his left hand over his eyes. "Oh, for God's sake," the President said with disgust. "McConger has just died. A heart attack. I don't know whether to laugh or cry. What he did, what he and *I* did—this goddamn inflation—is the root of our troubles. And inflation continues whether George McConger is dead or alive."

"Mr. President?" It was Claire.

The President shook his head. "Not now," he said with finality, and then resumed:

"I want to tell you something. You may, some of you, think that perhaps you should get on the Whitelaw bandwagon. Maybe, you think, it's time to bail out. Well, too fucking bad. Whitelaw has a list of people to shoot after he takes over, and every person in this room is on that list." There was a collective gasp from his listeners. "Even you, boys," he said, pointing at the Joint Chiefs. "That's right. So you better stick with me, because I'm all you've got."

The reality of power could hardly have been better dramatized.

"The truth is, and I know it as well as you do, that I've just let the country sink deeper and deeper into the shit. I know I did it. I know there are people at this table who told me not to do it, and I didn't listen to them. I'm sorry, but that doesn't do us any good right now.

"We're all in the fucking mess together—those who were right and those who were wrong. All of us. Even those who didn't have a damn thing to do with it." He shot a quick look at the Secretaries of Commerce and Labor, who had been babes in the woods about everything and who now looked bewildered and frightened.

"Mr. President," Claire said, but the President again cut her off.

"We'll hear from you later, Claire. What I have to say now is urgent. After it's done, you can write all the memoirs and all the books you want to about how bad it was. But now we've got to do it.

"We've got to do several things at once. We've got to stop the fucking inflation cold, and reverse it. We've

got to cut off Whitelaw. And then we've got to deal
with the Russians. And I'm gonna tell you right up
front that it's going to take some very big steps, and
some of them may make the more delicate among you
queasy. I can't help that. I'm going to try to save a
civilization.

"If I'm doing the wrong thing, the burden falls on
me, not you. No one's going to remember who my Director for International Economic Policy was," he said,
glaring at Hanrahan. "And no one's gonna remember
who my Chairman of the Cost of Living Council was,"
he said with an equal glare for Claire. "And later you
can all go out and get a big advance and write books
about how wrong I was and how you stood up to me
but lost.

"But for now," he said, his eyes downcast, looking
at the table, "for now, we've got to save the country."

To Hanrahan, the President looked ravaged. This
is how Lincoln must have looked when he decided to
fight to save the Union.

"Now this may sound like rhetorical bullshit, and
maybe it is, but what it boils down to is this: I will not
surrender the country to mob rule. In most states I
am calling up the National Guard. They'll take over
for the police where cops won't work. I'm sending
the FBI to arrest all military commanders who refuse
to obey my orders. General Ordway here—" and
he pointed at the Air Force general on his right,
resplendent in full uniform—"will guarantee that Rob-
bins Air Force Base in Georgia will be rendered unimportant if it continues to refuse to receive my orders."

Claire and others wondered what the President
meant by "rendered unimportant."

"I will also use whatever units of the Army, the
Navy and the Marine Corps I can trust to keep order.
That means no more Whitelaw rallies, no more of this
shit in Los Angeles, New Orleans or anywhere. No
more nothing, except peace and quiet." He smiled
slightly. "And the ACLU and all those little shits can
sue until they turn green, and the courts can find me
in contempt if they want to. We're gonna have law
and order. And we're not going to execute anyone.

"Now I've already got legislation authorizing me to fix prices and wages and to compel any economic entity to sell at the designated price. There's a lot more to it, but you don't have to know all the details, at least right now."

The President noticed Claire writing furiously on a piece of paper. "I don't want anyone taking notes of this meeting."

Claire looked up at the President with her light-blue eyes. "I'm not taking notes, Mr. President. I'm calculating something." Hanrahan looked at her. Claire was amazing. In a room with the President of the United States, while he proposed making America into a dictatorship, she was working on a mathematical problem.

"I'm glad to see you take this so calmly," the President said, and continued: "New legislation will also empower me to compel economic units to hire numbers of people at wage rates which I will designate.

"Now, some of you may wonder why you weren't consulted on this," the President said evenly. "It was because I knew you would be against it. Gene Donnelly's lawyers at Treasury drew it up You can register your objections in your memoirs."

Harry Ratner had never seen the President so curt and rancorous.

"I fully intend to eventually go back to a free market, but not for a goddamn long time. New legislation also ends the independence of the Federal Reserve Board and places the chairman directly under me. We will have no more fucking McCongers."

The President paused. Hanrahan decided that this was a buildup for a historic speech on television.

"Now that will take care of the domestic problem. It will hurt, but right now the whole goddamn thing is killing us. There's no way out without hurting. I know that this isn't what any of us would like to do. But it's what we've got to do. It comes from pissing away all our advantages until all we have are desperate measures. Sorry, folks, but that's how it is."

The President swiveled his chair and looked down at the military men at the other end of the table.

"Now some of you already know about the foreign problem. Basically it's this. The goddamn Russians are starving. They want our wheat and they can't pay for it. They claim their people will only tolerate this kind of hardship if there's a war going on. We think they mean to start a war with China. I'd just as soon let them kill each other, but it's not that easy, as you know.

"A war between Russia and China is a very big proposition, and we could get drawn in. Even the fallout will hurt. If China goes under, we'll look bad. I think if we give the Russians the wheat, we not only look bad, but it means that the Russians are calling our domestic shots. We can't have them do that, and that's for sure.

"So we've got to stop the Russians. Accordingly," he said with a heavy sigh, "I plan to hint to the Soviets that if they attack China with nuclear weapons, we will not stand idly by. Nothing firm. I further intend to tell them, however, that once the economic situation is stabilized here, we will resume normal sales to them at prices that bear some relation to sanity. It's the stick and the carrot, and I think it'll work. We can always trade them wheat for oil or something. But it mustn't be at the point of a gun, and it must be when we want and not when they want."

Hanrahan looked around the room. Everyone else was staring straight at the President. Ebersole, Flynn, Trout, Colonel Edwards, Donnelly—they were all looking at the apocalypse, some ten months after they had first gathered for Ding-Dong School. Everyone was sweating heavily. Claire worked furiously on her pad of paper. Hanrahan had to admit that what the President was proposing, while probably fatal to the American way of life, was nonetheless necessary.

The President resumed. "Peter, I want you to transmit to Ambassador Sobolevsky that we are serious about wanting to help, but that we are also serious about not letting China be obliterated and about not being dictated to. Let them think we're in trouble, but that we're also a little crazy. Let them sweat a while."

"I'll do that, Mr. President," Peter said.

"Secretary Marshal and Admiral Burns have assured me that the military will move with us. That's terribly important, of course. Also, they'd better, or I'll have their asses, and when I'm through, then Whitelaw will make a better world without them," the President said angrily.

Claire Beaton raised her hand. The President nodded. "Mr. President," said Claire, "what you're suggesting may be necessary, however terrible. But I believe we're about to learn of new circumstances that will make it unnecessary."

"What in hell are you talking about, Claire?" the President snapped. "This is no time for academic theorizing."

"Well," said Claire, trying to keep her voice firm, "if we could have a new currency in this country, backed by gold, trusted by the people, we could return to a stable price level without compulsion."

"That's a splendid idea, Claire," said Secretary Donnelly drily. "Where do we get that much gold? Have you figured out how to manufacture it from lead?"

"Mr. President," said Claire, "I think I know where the gold is."

"Oh, shit, Claire. No goddamn academic thumb-sucking, OK? If you've got a plan, let's get our asses on the table and get down to it," the President said.

Claire leaned forward. "Let me start about three years ago, when you made George McConger Chairman of the Federal Reserve Board. He started revving up the money-making machine. We all know that. At the same time, the volume of Eurodollar borrowings rose dramatically," Claire said.

"For Christ's sake, Claire," the President snapped, "that's exactly the kind of academic gobbledygook we don't need. Don't you realize that the country is on the brink of World War Three? I don't give a shit about Eurodollar borrowing."

"Mr. President—" It was Hanrahan. "Claire should be allowed to finish. I believe she knows what she's talking about. If she takes a few minutes of our precious time to save the republic as a democracy, it's worth the fucking time." Hanrahan could hardly believe he had spoken so sharply to the President. But he had. And he meant it.

The President sighed. "OK, Claire. But hurry the hell up."

Claire cleared her throat. "At the same time Eurodollar borrowings were rising so rapidly, gold began to be sucked out of this country, out of Europe and out of Japan at a rapid rate. That process has continued up to present. All the gold seems to have been dropped into a hole somewhere, and no one knows where it is. Until today."

The room became still. Claire had the shaky feeling that this was not only the most important thing she had ever said, but that it might also be a turning point in history.

"I don't think the Arabs have it, because they usually put their money into development projects. Also, why would they need to borrow Eurodollars to buy gold? And the Eurodollar borrowings are almost certainly connected with the gold movements because the two rose and fell simultaneously.

"There is yet another theory—that private individuals have it—but I don't think that theory holds water. Private individuals simply could not arrange for gold purchases on that scale."

"OK, Claire," Donnelly said, "we've gone through all that. Now who the hell's got it?"

The President added, "Come on, Claire. Get moving. Now who the hell's got it?"

"The Chinese!"

With the exception of Peter Hanrahan, the face of every male in the room registered shock.

"The Chinese have pulled off the greatest speculation in the history of the world," said Claire. "They saw the inflation coming, and through Swiss intermediaries they borrowed Eurodollars to buy gold. They collateralized the gold, borrowed more Eurodollars, bought more gold, and now they've virtually got a corner on it."

The President still looked astonished. "How the hell do you know?"

"I don't know for sure," Claire said, "but theo—"

The President cut her off in a snarling fury. "You mean you're jerking us off over a theory? Something you imagine? Are you out of your female fucking mind?"

Claire kept her feelings in complete control. In a calm, firm voice she said, "I'm sure enough of that theory to suggest that you take fifteen minutes to find out if I'm right or not before you turn this country into a police state."

Hanrahan backed her up. "She's right, Mr. President. She has to be. It's the only logical explanation. If she isn't, you haven't lost a damn thing. And if she is, just for starters, she'll have saved the ass of everybody in this room." Hanrahan was at his most persuasive. "One hundred thousand people have died in this inflation from riots and burnings. Do you know how many more will die if you put the army on the streets? For the love of God, give Claire's idea a chance to be proven or not. Why can't you take good advice for just once in your life?"

The President looked speculatively at Hanrahan. Then he looked at Donnelly. "What do you think, Gene?"

"I don't know, Mr. President," the wily Texan said slowly. "It might be worth fifteen minutes to find out if the Chinese have the gold. And if we're going to somehow get it back."

"All right, Claire. Continue. Tell me a little more," he said, "but make it snappy."

"Ambassador Hsing called Peter this morning and asked to buy wheat, lots of wheat—I think it will be for gold. Nobody else has made us that kind of offer," Claire said.

The President bowed his head. His neck looked small and vulnerable. Then he raised his weary red eyes and said, "All right. Get Hsing up here right away."

At that precise moment the telephone rang. The President picked it up.

"Yes?" he growled, drumming his fist on the table. *"Who?"*

It was an exclamation, not a question. An incredulous, disbelieving exclamation.

The name was repeated. The President's face went white. Then, with a visible effort at composure, he said, "Put him on."

He covered the mouthpiece with his hand. "It's Chairman Pak Su-chang. Of the People's Republic of China," he added unnecessarily.

"Does he speak English?" asked Ratner.

"He better," said the President, "because I sure as hell don't speak Chinese. Pick up the extension, Peter. I don't know what in the name of God he wants."

Peter picked up the extension. The whole room heard the gruff bass, unmistakably Chinese voice say in fluent English, "Hello, Mr. President."

"Hello, Chairman Pak," said the President.

"I am speaking to you from Peking."

"Yes, Chairman Pak. I am speaking to you from Camp David, near Washington."

"I know where Camp David is. I should like to visit you there at Camp David."

"You would like to visit me? Well, of course, that would be a great honor and pleasure. We should be happy to welcome you any time. All you have to do is let us know when."

Beads of sweat were flowing down the President's forehead. The temperature in the room seemed to have risen to ninety.

"What? Yes, it would be a historic occasion and we would like to repay you for the wonderful hospitality you showed President Nixon when he visited the People's Republic of China. Have you thought about setting a date, Chairman Pak? Do you perhaps have a definite month in mind? Would you like to come to our country this year? At Christmas time, maybe?"

There was a blast of static. Both the President and Hanrahan jammed the earpieces to their ears to better understand Chairman Pak's reply.

They looked at each other aghast.

"The day after tomorrow, Chairman? Is that what you said?"

"Yes. At exactly two o'clock P.M. on July twenty-third I should like to land in Washington. Do not stand on protocol. I will come straight to Camp David. I believe the Chinese people have something your country needs."

There was a pause in the dialogue. The President had no immediate reply.

He cleared his throat. "Per—perhaps that is what you would like to discuss?" Now the suggestion of a quaver had entered the President's voice.

"Yes. You and I should have a discussion, Mr. President. That is what we will do at Camp David. We will discuss what you can do for us. And we will discuss what we can do for you. Agreed?"

"Hadn't you rather wait until we can have sufficient time to prepare for your visit? We can't do a helluva lot in two—"

"No. This is not a trip for pleasure. Pleasure will have to await another opportunity. We will be a party of seven, plus our crew of eight, Mr. President, and we do not plan a prolonged stay. Depending, of course, on the outcome of our discussion."

"Of course."

"Ambassador Hsing will be in touch with your State Department. If you would be so good as to tell them of our talk?"

"Of course, we—"

"I look forward to our visit, Mr. President. Thank you for your kind invitation."

"So do I," said the President. "The American peo—"

But the Chairman of the People's Republic of China was no longer listening. He had hung up on the President of the United States.

A loud hubbub followed. Everyone wanted to talk at once. Everyone had a dozen questions, all of them on the same subject.

What they boiled down to was, How much wheat did the Chinese need, and how much gold would they be willing to pay for it?

Donnelly was pessimistic. "They've got us over a barrel, Mr. President."

Claire was hopeful. "The speed with which Pak is acting suggests that they're in worse trouble than we are. Forty-eight—what is it, fifty-one hours' notice for the first visit by a Chinese Chairman in modern history? That is unheard of."

"Past tense, Claire. *Was* unheard of. We've got to get moving. Peter, get Rockefeller at State, tell him to keep plans simple. Spell it for him. S–I–M–P–L–E. The Chinese are down-to-earth people. I'll announce the news to the press at four o'clock. We'll go to the White House as a group. Until then, nobody leaves and no phone calls go out of here. Don't even *try* to make phone calls. It would embarrass you."

The President spoke with his usual authority, but his face was a wreck. A nervous tic had developed on his upper lip. He had affected a lip-clenched grimace to keep it from showing.

The newspapers had a field day. With only one guaranteed on-the-stands edition before the Chairman's impromptu visit, reporters dug up everything they could find on the man who had survived the struggle for power following the earthquakes and the death of Mao. There wasn't all that much.

Unusually tall for a Chinese (six feet one), athletic (he was an expert at Kung-Fu), Chairman Pak Su-chang was descended from the Mongols. He was believed to have split with the pro-Mao faction (though he had maintained close ties with two of its leaders) and to advocate somewhat more progressive, though far from liberal, social and political policies.

There was no previous record that he had ever in his life stepped foot off the Chinese mainland. His visit to Camp David was alleged to be the most important test he had faced since assuming the chairmanship.

His most distinguished facial characteristic was a scar that began on the upper left side of his forehead, touched briefly on the bridge of his nose, and continued across his right cheek, ending at his jawbone, acquired—no one knew how—before he entered public life at the age of twenty-six. No attempt was ever made to disguise the scar, either in photographs or in life.

His favorite food was raw, marinated eel.

He was an expert at smashing bricks with his hands. He was, in fact, an enthusiastic advocate of all athletics, sports and feats of strength, and was rumored to be training teams in acrobatics and the decathlon for the 1984 summer Olympics.

He was married and the father of two teen-agers, Yukio and Anna. Anna was the spitting image of her father.

He had the highest IQ measurable in China.

The purpose of his visit was the subject of long and fulsome editorial speculation. Some conservative papers suspected the worst: Was Pak seeking foreign aid? Was his visit the beginning of a new infiltration into the U.S. government by the Communist underground? Was it a showdown? Could capitalism, such as it was at this point, survive?

Many of the more liberal papers were hardly less inflammatory. One Texas daily, widely circulated, saw Pak's visit as the diversionary bridgehead for a Chinese invasion of Hawaii and urged Honolulu to be on the lookout for hostile aircraft and submarines.

The President got the most intense briefing of his career. Facts were shoved at him, between massages, whirlpool baths and mild calisthenics. And after the facts came the theories. On the night before the Chairman's visit, he managed to get a good eight hours' sleep with the help of an injection. When he awakened in the morning, his tic had finally disappeared.

At 10 A.M., Intelligence informed the President that the Russians were massing large numbers of troops near Sinkiang Province at the Chinese border. This was obviously crucial news. Had the Chinese known of the Russian plans to threaten their territory? Was that a factor in the timing of the Chairman's visit?

Meanwhile the Gallup Poll indicated that on the whole the American people, perhaps remembering the hospitality rendered the Americans by the Chinese, were prepared to be cordial. A relatively small percentage were not; 3 percent were undecided.

Congress was horrified.

At 1:53 P.M. the Chinese plane landed at Dulles International Airport. Inside the tightest security the damaged city of Washington could provide, Chairman Pak and his party were officially met and transferred to a helicopter. All three TV networks carried the shift of aircraft live.

Twenty-three minutes later, the Chairman and his party stepped onto the landing pad at Camp David. Six reporters, representing a political cross-section of the American press, and Tom Chartley, the official White House photographer, were present. No television coverage was permitted.

Chairman Pak was ushered to Aspen Lodge. The President, now a picture of health, was waiting there to greet him. The two men shook hands vigorously and spoke briefly on the circumstances of the Chairman's pleasant trip and safe arrival. Reporters were interested to note that Chairman Pak's once perfect smile now displayed a gold tooth. An upper.

The two men, followed by the Chairman's party, walked into Aspen Lodge. The President's representatives were waiting inside. Then the door to the lodge was closed. The time was 2:41.

For the rest of that afternoon, television programs were interrupted every fifteen minutes to report on the status of the door to Aspen Lodge. It remained closed.

WTOP in Washington devoted the afternoon to a panel discussion on the topic "The Fate of the Western World: Can Capitalism and the American Way of Life Survive?" Moderated by William F. Buckley, it was carried by independent stations across the country and registered the largest Neilsen in the history of the ratings system. WNEW in New York alone garnered a staggering 57 percent of the viewers in the greater metropolitan area. On that program, Senator Heniford of North Carolina, a long-time critic of the President, referred to Aspen Lodge as the President's "last bunker, or, in other words, his Waterloo."

Four and a half hours after the President and Chairman Pak had disappeared into the lodge, the door was seen to move. Slowly at first, and then quickly, until it was thrown wide open to reveal a perspiring Harry Ratner, mopping his forehead with a handkerchief already wet. He walked outdoors, to be followed by the Chairman's entourage, who were followed by Claire Beaton, Peter Hanrahan, Gene Donnelly, Ambassador Hsing, two gentlemen and a lady from State, and the rest of the President's advisers. All of them were plainly exhausted.

Tom Chartley kept his camera focused on the door. Three more minutes went by. Chartley waited, camera poised. Finally, the towering figure of the Chairman could be seen, first in the shadows, the outline of his form barely recognizable, then more clearly as he neared the door and stepped outside, followed by the President, blinking rapidly at the sudden outdoor light.

Both men were smiling.

The two leaders stood side by side, posing. It would have been impossible to say which smile was the more inscrutable. As they faced the west, Chairman Pak reached out and placed his left arm across the President's shoulders. The setting sun shone directly on the Chairman's handsome gold tooth, causing the brilliant reflection that was so remarkable in the photograph taken by Tom Chartley, later reproduced poster-size and sold in countless numbers in the United States and China for a dollar or its equivalent in their respective currencies.

There was a hastily improvised state supper in the White House that night, with a first course of marinated eel. At the conclusion of the meal, Chairman Pak proposed a toast to the President and Claire Beaton, following which he kissed her on both cheeks in the Continental manner.

When asked where he'd like to proceed from Washington, the Chairman replied, "To New York City. I should like to observe your United Nations. Then, if she would so honor me on my way back to China, I should like to have the pleasure of meeting, in person, in the flesh, Miss Barbra Streisand."

Later, in privacy Harry Ratner and Claire Beaton discussed how the Chinese had managed to acquire the gold.

"I think they started about two years ago," said Claire. "Borrowing small amounts of Eurodollars to buy gold. As the price of gold went up, they used some of the gold as collateral for larger loans—with which they bought still more gold. They made it a condition of the transactions that the customer and borrower always be kept secret. They probably did it through Zurich, with private dealers who think secrecy is a wonderful reason for living.

"Finally they had so much gold, they realized they were able to buy their way to safety against the Russians, who had been selling them gold all along without knowing it."

Ratner was impressed. He had no option but to agree.

The rough basic outline of the Chinese-American agreement set sales of the next day's newspapers at another record high. For China, twenty million tons of wheat per year. Also for China, a clear United States announcement that it would consider an attack on China an attack on the United States.

For the United States, the immediate transfer of 75 percent of China's gold, presently stored in Zurich, to the United States in full payment for the wheat.

At lunch the next day, the President sat with Claire, Hanrahan and Ratner in his living room. "I'll go on television tonight and announce the new currency based on gold, plus the freezing of all prices for sixty days at their levels in the new currency. We'll still have some problems—but people believe in gold. We've broken the back of the problem."

"I think we have," said Ratner. "What problems remain, we can handle. Once people know there's gold behind the money, they'll settle down."

"There'll be no more incentive to hoard, and supplies of everything will come pouring out. The rest of the world will cool down as we do, because they can peg their currencies to ours, plus with stabilized prices, we can sell to the Russians and cool them off," Hanrahan said.

The door opened. Freda came running in and jumped up on the President.

"Kiss her, Freda," the President said, pointing to Claire. "She saved my ass."

# Epilogue

AUGUST 15, 1982

A LEXANDRA Kelsey drove along Route 50 in the shimmering late-summer heat. The windows of her Chevy Nova were rolled up, and with the air-conditioning the heat wasn't bad. She had just turned off at the unfinished, deserted shopping center. It was to have been filled with luxury shops, but the price stabilization had changed all that. It was just as well, Alexandra thought. There was no point in bringing the pretentiousness of Fifth Avenue to people who were fundamentally fairly straightforward.

People were still doing well in Caroline County, Alexandra knew, but there was nothing like the gold-rush atmosphere of the last days of the inflation. Most of the farmers and townspeople who had bought Cadillacs still had them, but they weren't buying any more. The stores in Denton generally were quieter. The situation was settling back to what it had been like before the inflation.

That was a disappointment to a lot of farmers who had thought that they were going to be Rockefellers, but it was all right with her. Shelby was still one of the biggest landowners in the county, and now he was expanding his grain-storage construction business. With the sales to the Chinese and the rumored deal with the Russians, there was still good money to be made in farming.

They had returned from a one-week stay in the Vir-

272

gin Islands right after May Day to find a much subdued atmosphere in Denton. There was no more talk about revolution. People weren't posting armed guards around their crops either. And very quickly those horrible pictures on TV of poor people rioting at grocery stores were gone too. The people from the city who had come to prowl around Denton stopped coming, and most of the traffic now was from people from Washington headed through town on their way to Rehoboth Beach. Life was definitely settling down, not only in Denton, but all over the country.

There were still lots of shows on TV with talk about the economy and gold deals and swaps and OPEC price pledges, but people didn't seem to want to talk much about it on the street.

Alexandra didn't know that much about mental illness, but she knew, as she headed east toward Easton and Cambridge, that she had been in a deep depression for a while last spring. She really wasn't exactly sure why it came, although it certainly had something to do with her father's death—she still shook when she thought of it—and her seeing other people starving when she had so much money. Just as she didn't know exactly why it came, she also didn't know exactly why it lifted—but it certainly was gone.

She had taken up a new hobby during the early summer—photography. Her black-and-whites of the Maryland wetlands were so good that she had sent a few of them back to some photographers she knew in New York City. Almost by return mail, she had gotten an offer to sign a contract for a book about the Eastern shore—with lots of black-and-white and color photographs. It was a thrill, and she had taken the publisher up on it. Now she was planning to drive along the stretch of bayline between Easton and Cambridge to get some good shots of snowy egrets in the marsh.

She and Shelby didn't have the plane any more. They might have been able to afford to keep it, but the pilot had been called back by Eastern Airlines, and she didn't want Shelby flying it. It was too dangerous, and it was a reminder of days when nothing seemed fair, and that was something they didn't need.

Life was better now. There weren't the ups and downs that had marked the year before. When she thought about those times, it was a mishmash of jewelry spilling on a bed and horrible long-distance phone calls and cemeteries and scenes on the television that made her never want to get out of bed. She loved putting on hip boots and walking up creeks and into marshes to snap pictures with her Nikon Z. She was the only person there, and she was in a place where everything seemed to be in harmony, everything in equilibrium, neither too much nor too little. It was definitely what she wanted.

As the car headed up the highway she could see clouds gathering toward the east. That was all right. She didn't mind these warm summer rains. She had what she wanted, Shelby and a quiet life, and the rain didn't bother her. She knew that no matter how hard it rained, it would stop.

Harry Ratner lay in the hammock between the oak trees in his back yard listening to the baseball game. He had taken the afternoon off. He had gone to work that morning and realized that he hadn't had an afternoon off in over a year. So he told his secretary that if the President called, he'd be at home. But he didn't want to take any other calls except from Peter and Claire.

Even though the announcer was talking about the Washington Capitols, that incredibly bad National League expansion team, Harry Ratner was thinking how fast things had mended. The people of America had been looking for a savior, and in this case at least, their savior was the golden calf. Prices had tumbled, even in the new dollars, as hoarders released their goods. For a while the real price level was actually lower than it had been before the September 1981 OPEC price rise. And, in fact, OPEC had rolled back the oil price to twenty-five dollars a barrel, amidst signs that the Iranian-Saudi Arabian Friendship and Nonaggression Treaty was no more.

What an incredible time it had been. He had been

riding in the front seat of the roller coaster and it had been a frightening trip. But at least in retrospect, it was a good trip to have taken. He would be leaving Washington soon to return to his teaching duties at the University of Chicago. He chuckled to himself, remembering the worst. It had been horrible, but it had been exciting, the biggest challenge of his life.

George McConger had died, appropriately enough, on May Day. He had never regained consciousness after his stroke. Harry Ratner still did not know, could not decide, whether McConger was actually insane or whether he was just unusually ideologically ignorant. Perhaps at some point the insanity and ignorance had blended. Probably no man had ever done more to hurt the American people than George McConger had —and all in the name of giving the little man a fresh start, Harry Ratner thought. Well, that was the way it always was. The people who wanted to make all men brothers were the ones who brought out the guillotines and the death camps.

Harry Ratner would miss Washington. His life would be fulfilling back at the University, and he had already been offered some consulting deals that would make him better off than he ever thought he would be. But still, he would miss those days of Ding-Dong School and the feeling that he was sitting at the very center of things. He knew it was a bad set of values that was making him nostalgic, but he wondered whether it was better to be happy with a bad set of values or sad with a good set of values. He was pretty sure he knew the answer.

General Porto's olive complexion blended with those of the Italians eating outdoors at the restaurant on Via Veneto. He and Ismail Stanfi made an unusual pair. Goya might have done them justice. The Roman air was balmy.

"A tragedy about our poor friend Khashoggi," offered Stanfi, speaking in English.

"Yes," agreed General Porto, wiping his chin with his napkin. "It is hard to believe that the Shah was convinced that Khashoggi was plotting against him. He was shot only because he had done what the Shah told him to do. He was only obeying orders. The Shah could not very well shoot himself, so he shot Khashoggi instead. One takes risks, and sometimes one loses. Khashoggi was warned."

"Indeed, yes. By you. Tell me, are you enjoying life in Rome?" asked Stanfi.

"I like it well enough. I miss Ecuador, but I had rather be alive here than in an unmarked grave in Quito. But I often wish I might have been more eloquent in Hawaii. Was it only a year ago? Disaster lay so clearly ahead. You simply cannot throw a bomb and expect not to hurt the people it falls on. We were playing with a very large bomb."

He watched two slender Italian women pass by in transparent cotton dresses. "I prefer Ecuadorian women," he said. "The stylish ladies here are too thin. But I was lucky to get out alive. They were attributing things to me, all kinds of unsavory things."

"They blamed things on me, too," said Stanfi. "But the King is my brother, and that still means something, fortunately for me."

General Porto looked sadly at the shops across the street, still charred and boarded up, remnants of the worst of the inflation violence that had gripped the ancient city.

"The final chapter has not been written," General Porto philosophized. "The world cannot go through a convulsion like this and return to normal. Especially in the United States. That country is not used to such terror. The people will always be warped by it, and that will help warp the world."

Stanfi smiled. "You're pessimistic, my friend. The world is recovering nicely. We'll have OPEC back on its feet in no time."

"Will you then try to squeeze the world dry?" asked Porto. "As you squeeze the oil from the ground?"

"I don't know. I will counsel against it. But people do not always learn from experience. Sad," Stanfi said, "but true."

"Or they learn the wrong things," said Porto. "It will come back to haunt us. We cannot go through something like this without becoming twisted. But for God's sake, don't let it start with OPEC. Because the next time, they will take away your oil, or destroy it, rather than pay you for it." General Porto paused. "The world is a fragile net. You cannot squeeze it too hard. We know that. You can learn that. I hope you will."

"Perhaps," said Stanfi, but it was plain to see that Ismail Staufi preferred to keep an open mind.

Hal Burton, pale and thin, sat with Joan Bellamy at the new outdoor wing of La Scala in Beverly Hills.

"What does the doctor say?" Joan asked.

"He says I should have moderate exercise, no tobacco, no excitement and no drugs. Eventually, he says, I'll be right up to speed." From outward appearances, Burton would never be up to speed. His sallow skin hung limply on the bones of his face.

"I won't try to sell *The Wonderchildren* anywhere else," said Joan.

"On my account?" asked Burton.

"Well, maybe. After all, I wrote it for you. It's your story, and since you aren't going to make it, maybe no one should." Joan was not hungry. She picked at her fettucine.

"I don't feel like making any more movies. I don't feel like doing anything much," said Burton. "I visit Doey every day. I feel like doing that."

"Does she know you're in the room?" asked Joan.

"The doctors say she doesn't, but I think she does. We had a hell of a time getting her back to L.A. It happened the same day I had my heart attack. She wasn't even carrying an ID."

"Does she have any chance at all?" Joan asked quietly.

"Well, the doctors say she doesn't. They want to turn off the respirator. But I said no. Hell, no. Some day they may want to operate on her brain. They can't do that if she's been dead six months. I'll just keep her in there. They say she doesn't have any dreams, but I don't believe them. Maybe not dreams, but feelings, at least. Even a plant turns toward the sun."

Hal Burton looked as if he had seen the face of God, and it was not kind.

Across little Santa Monica, he watched two clean-cut, smiling blue-denimed young men passing out flyers. He glared at them.

"Don't get excited," said Joan Bellamy. "Remember what the doctor said."

Burton continued to glare. Then, in an obvious effort, he snapped himself out of it and asked, "What are you working on now?"

"I'm doing a piece on the Better Deal for *Esquire*. If it turns out interesting, I'll make it into a book."

"Do people want to read about that?" asked Burton.

"If they don't, they should. We just barely missed total destruction. Something's happened to us, and I want to discover what it is, explain it," Joan Bellamy said. But Hal Burton was no longer listening. He just stared with empty eyes at the smiling kids in blue denim coveralls.


"We wanted you to be the first to know," Peter Hanrahan told the President.

"Let me kiss the bride," said the President. "Hanrahan, you're a lucky man." The President leaned forward and kissed Claire Beaton on the cheek.

They stood in the solarium of the White House on a scorching hot day, though inside it was cool.

"I believe this will be the first inter-Cabinet wedding in history," the President said. "Will it be a big event?"

"No," said Hanrahan. "Small. But you'll be invited."

"How do you like it over at Treasury, Claire?" the President asked.

"Well, a few offices still have Donnelly's picture up and not mine, but they're adjusting to having a woman Secretary of the Treasury pretty well," Claire replied.

"You know," the President said, "when I think of last May, I still get the shivers. You saved my ass. You saved the whole country. I won't ever forget that."

"We'll need to talk to you about that, Mr. President," said Claire. "On the surface, things are picking up wonderfully. But we must work very hard to make sure it never happens again."

"Too many people will never be the same," said Hanrahan, "and they won't forget what happened. They won't forget that they saw a demagogue start a movement to save them from their own government. Whitelaw looked good to them at the time, and he can again, or another one like him."

The President looked sober.

"We are the survivors," said Claire, "standing on top of a hundred thousand corpses and millions of ruined lives. The streets of America still have shards of broken glass in them, and the people of America carry wounds in their hearts. They—we must do everything we can to keep it from happening again."

"What can I do myself?" asked the President.

"The best you can," replied Claire. "That's all any of us can do. We're still on shaky ground and we will be for a long time. A new OPEC increase or a big recession or a bad harvest could touch it off again."

"Things look pretty good now," Hanrahan said. "But we're mortgaged to the Chinese for ten years. If we should have a bad harvest, then prices will start going up again, and people may not stand for it. Next time, the demagogue—whoever he is—may win."

The President looked grimly out the window. "I know what you're saying," he said. "Perhaps nothing I do can repair what I've done to the American people. I'm not sure I can ever make it up to them. I probably can't. I'll sure as hell try, but I'm not sure I can."

He turned around to face Claire and Hanrahan again. "And all along, I thought I was doing the right thing, not just for me, but for the country. I didn't set out to hurt anyone."

How many of us do? thought Hanrahan. In the whole of Washington, in all of America, in the whole world, how many of us ever do?

Claire thought she saw the President's eyes grow moist, and there had certainly been a catch in his voice. He turned his back to them for a moment and then faced them again. His face was smiling and flushed. "Anyway," he said, "I'll dance at your wedding, and that's something."

Yes, thought Claire, that's something, but it's not enough. And what was more, she did not know what was enough. America was now a civilization doing pirouettes and leaps on a sheet of ice under which there was a grinning death's head. A large, handsome, movie actor's profile of a death's head.

The birds outside the Volunteers to America headquarters—bluejays primarily—were in for a treat. William Whitelaw opened his window and threw out his torn-up toast. He himself was on a diet. He watched the birds scramble for the crumbs. Then he turned around to face the three young men in his office. He knew two of them well. They were his speechwriters primarily, Jimmie and Marvin. Sometimes they did other things, too.

The new recruit looked good. He had come on board the Whitelaw bandwagon as other people were leaving in droves after the inflation stopped. That was a sign of conviction that Whitelaw liked. The recruit worked long hours and would do anything. That's why he was working with Jimmie and Marvin.

Jimmie said to Whitelaw, "Sir, I think membership has about touched bottom. I don't think it'll go down any more. I know that the ratings for your radio show are up slightly."

"That's good, Jimmie. It's good to have the facts at your fingertips. Jim Adams, it's also good to be brave and to risk things for what you believe in. You married, Jim?"

"No," Jim Adams said. "My wife died right after May Day in an accident involving a gun I kept at home." He said it very calmly, as if he had said it many times before.

"A great tragedy. Still, Americans must have the right to bear arms. You agree with that?"

"Yes, sir," Jim Adams said.

"That's good. I'm glad you're going to be working

here at headquarters. We've got a lot to do. It may take years, but the American people came damn close to seeing the light, and they can see it again. Things will get rough again, and they'll remember who they can turn to.

"We've just got to cut out this Mr. Nice Guy stuff. We've got to emphasize not only God's love, but also his justice for those who offend him. We've got to learn to recognize our enemies better. But we'll keep working at it; we'll never give up, and we'll work harder than ever. Any questions?"

There were no questions.

## We know you don't read just one kind of book. | That's why we've got all kinds of bestsellers.